SMOKE

DARCY WOODS

CROWN
NEW YORK

Text copyright © 2021 by Darcy Woods
Jacket art copyright © 2021 by Agustina Gastaldi
Interior art credits: p. 1 mikeledray/Shutterstock.com, p. 173 Jan Havlicek/
Shutterstock.com, p. 227 Boyan Dimitrov/Shutterstock.com, p. 317 PopFoto/
Shutterstock.com, p. 357 mikeledray/Shutterstock.com

Visit us on the Web! GetUnderlined.com

Educators and librarians, for a variety of teaching tools,
visit us at RHTeachersLibrarians.com

Library of Congress Cataloging-in-Publication Data
Names: Woods, Darcy, author.
Title: Smoke / Darcy Woods.
Description: First edition. | New York : Crown Books for Young Readers, [2021] |
Audience: Ages 14 & up. | Audience: Grades 10–12. |
Summary: Sixteen-year-old Honor Augustine is determined to save
her family's greenhouse and keep her veteran father afloat,
even if it means breaking the rules—and a few laws.
Identifiers: LCCN 2020046321 (print) | LCCN 2020046322 (ebook) |
ISBN 978-0-593-30590-4 (hardcover) | ISBN 978-0-593-30591-1 (library binding) |
ISBN 978-0-593-30592-8 (ebook)
Subjects: CYAC: Fathers and daughters—Fiction. | Brothers and sisters—Fiction. |
Dating (Social customs)—Fiction. | Post-traumatic stress disorder—Fiction. |
Marijuana—Fiction.
Classification: LCC PZ7.1.W66 Smo 2021 (print) |
LCC PZ7.1.W66 (ebook) | DDC [Fic]—dc23

The text of this book is set in 11.25-point Apollo MT Pro.
Interior design by Jen Valero

Printed in the United States of America
10 9 8 7 6 5 4 3 2 1
First Edition

For my father, who taught me the meaning
of strength and sacrifice

And to my brothers and sisters in the armed forces,
who remind me of these lessons every day

PART I

The Seed

April 18 — May 18

1

Sometimes you feel the whisper of a storm before it hits. Smell the tang of ozone as it punctuates the air. Watch the once-lifeless hair on your arms rise like the dead. The energy, the charge, it becomes a real and palpable thing.

But other times, like tonight, you sense nothing.

No whisper.

No warning.

And it's of little consequence to the storm whether or not you're prepared. Because, either way, it's coming.

Lightning carves jagged marks across the sky. My attic bedroom explodes with brightness. I squeeze my eyes tight, willing the storm to pass. *Praying* for it to pass. But the foreboding zigzag pattern that lingers behind my eyelids kills those fragile hopes. My pulse gains speed.

One Mississippi. Two Mississippi. Three Mississippi . . .

I get all the way to *seven Mississippi* before the deafening crash. Thunder punches like a fist through the atmosphere, pounding against the earth. The powerful echo carries inside my body, reverberating through every limb.

By my count the storm's about a mile away and closing in.

Dread sinks into my skin, takes residence in my bones. My fingernails, barely long enough to scratch an itch, dig hard into my palms. Because I know what comes next. And it's a force as unstoppable as the storm.

This is going to be bad.

I fling back the covers, my feet hitting the rug as the sloped walls flare again with light. Seconds later the boom of thunder hits.

And a scream follows. Just like I knew it would. I feel the cry like it's borne from my own throat.

I race down the narrow staircase to the second floor, where Geronimo paces. He whines, scratching at the bedroom door as the sky breaks open to release its sadness. Tears tick against the hall window like tiny pebbles.

"I know, Geronimo. I wish I could make it stop, too."

Our beloved boxador—boxer-Lab mix—knows I'm not talking about the rain.

"Stay back," I say into his good ear, giving his frayed collar a tug. "You can't help him this time."

Geronimo whines again in response, blinking his helpless onyx eyes before reluctantly backing away.

I open the door to where my father lies, painted in shadows, imprisoned by a past that stays all too present.

His breath erupts in sputtering gasps. "Foxtrot niner two seven . . . Bravo Company under attack. Repeat, Bravo—" His chest hitches before unleashing another bloodcurdling cry. "*Noooo!*"

"Dad!" I lunge to his side, where he's tangled in sheets. "Dad, wake up!"

He doesn't hear me. I grip his arms in hopes of tethering him back to reality. To *this* reality. But he's too strong; the muscles the military trained into him never left. And his skin is too slippery with sweat to keep hold of him anyway. My father's face contorts in agony as he thrashes away, knocking a picture frame from the nightstand. It clatters to the floor.

"Dad, it's Honor. Listen to my voice. Whatever you're seeing isn't real. Not anymore. Wake up. *Please,* you have to snap out of it!"

His sparse bedroom is illuminated with pulses of light, glancing off the brass latches of the footlocker at the end of his bed. Ancient windowpanes tremble with the battle cry of thunder. A battle cry that transforms an ordinary storm into the terrifying sounds of warfare. Atmospheric cracks become the pop of rifles, while thunder detonates like bombs.

My father's eyes are open now, but they don't see me. They see the Iraq War. Tears slip from the outer corners of his eyes, held captive by silvering sideburns. "His leg . . . I found his leg."

My heart throbs with a dull, all-consuming ache. I *hate* this. Hate seeing him lost in the dark place I can't reach him. The room empties of air. When I go to swallow, a fist feels lodged in my throat. *Hold it together. You cannot fall apart.*

So I take a slow, deliberate breath. Try once more. "You're safe now, Dad. You're *home.* Far away from the—"

"You're gonna get yourself hurt again, Honor," Knox grogily mutters, clicking on the lamp on the dresser. But even with the light, the shadows in the room are smothering. "I got Dad. You roll." My brother staggers across the room, still in yesterday's jeans and T-shirt, and flops beside me on the bed.

"Go on," he says, before turning toward our father, who's now curled away from us, whimpering like a wounded animal.

If I could claw the sound from my ears, I would. Focus on something. Anything else. "You reek of cheap beer," I tell Knox.

"Yeah? You reek of sad. Trust me, cheap-beer smell's an improvement."

"Whatever, Knock Knox." Not sure why I choose this moment to call my brother by the nickname I haven't used since I woke up crying from my own nightmares, but here we are. Only this time, my brother can't chase away these monsters with terrible jokes.

Knox jerks his chin toward the dresser, then resumes coaxing our father back from the abyss.

Opening the top drawer, the drawer that used to be Mom's, I remove the old cigar box and plastic baggie inside it. I shake out what's left of the dried bud, breaking off tiny nuggets of leaves, plucking away the stems. This is the only thing I know to do that helps in the aftermath of these episodes. Which is why I've gotten so good at it.

Somehow the ritual calms me, quelling my hyperactive heart, soothing my fraught nerves. Ironic I should find the same relief in the simple act of rolling a joint that my father will have in smoking it. But there's comfort in the way my fingers know what to do without being told. Following one step with blissful surety into the next. Knowing that the outcome will be the same even as the sky falls around me.

"Honor?" Dad rasps, sitting upright. He rubs his eyes and sees me, for real this time.

And it doesn't matter that my brother's buzzed. He is, and

will forever be, the PTSD Whisperer when it comes to our father.

"I'm here, Dad," I reply, filling the crease of the rolling paper with bits of pungent green. And with painstaking care, I roll the most perfect joint imaginable. Tight. Fat. No holes for smoke to escape.

My father cradles his head, running his hands along his shorn hair as his breath steadies. "Did I hurt you?" He looks up. Worry deepens the faint grooves in his forehead. "I couldn't handle it if I hurt you or—"

Knox squeezes Dad's shoulder, putting a tourniquet on his words. He has our father's hands, large with pronounced knuckles. Although my brother's hands don't have calluses and scars from years of manual labor like our father's. "She's fine, Dad. We're both fine. That was the nightmare talking."

"I'm fine," I repeat firmly. For my own sake as much as his.

His color slowly returns—shifting from chalk white to deep tan, the result of countless hours of construction work. "Thank God," he murmurs. "I'm . . . I'm sorry you had to see that. Again."

"Dad . . ." A sharp twist of pain prevents me from saying all the things I wish I could say. But he's not—might never be—in a place to hear them. To hear it's not his fault. That he didn't choose to be sent to some war-torn desert thousands of miles from home. That his struggles don't make him weak. Quite the opposite. My father's one of the strongest people I know.

But in the end, all I can manage is a quiet "Please, don't."

Last year, right after he and Mom split, Dad suffered one of his worst night terrors. Which is how I wound up with a hellacious black eye. He didn't remember a thing. So Knox and I concocted a fantastical tale involving my face and a wayward baseball. Plausible given my complete lack of athletic ability. Then I wore sunglasses the size of satellite dishes until the bruise turned sunshine yellow.

"Need to use the head?" Knox asks in his easy way, giving our father's back a gentle clap.

Dad wipes his face and nods. Squinting at the clock, he says, "It's after one in the morning. Don't you two have school tomorrow? You should be in bed. Go on now. Your old man can take care of himself." He trembles as he rises, checking to see if we notice.

We feign oblivion.

Dad ruffles Knox's hair like he's five, repeating the gesture as he passes me. The action's meant to convey everything is fine.

But it isn't.

Geronimo's tail thumps the wall like an enthusiastic battering ram as Dad steps into the hall. That dog would surgically attach himself to my father if he could.

I wait until I hear the bathroom door close. "I feel like he's getting worse." I sink down beside Knox on Dad's bed of bricks.

"Yep." My brother catches a burp in his fist and stretches out his long legs. His big toe peeps out of the hole in his sock like a fleshy periscope.

"You think there's something else going on? Besides the storm." With PTSD, the trigger could be anything—sights, sounds, smells . . . even feelings that associate with a trauma.

Knox sways a little as he ponders. "Dunno. He's been a little quieter. Spending more time in the barn than usual."

Something I noticed, too. I anxiously twist the ends of the

joint. "What am I going to do when you leave for college this fall? I mean, how will I handle Dad?"

"I hear scientists are making major headway with clones. Imagine a world with *two* of me." His dark brows bounce up and down. "Utopia, right?"

I jab him with my elbow. "This is important. Can you at least *try* to be serious?"

"Is this a trick question?" He snorts at my stony expression. "I swear to God you were born like eighty years old." Knox curls his hands into fists, rubbing his eyes like a sleepy toddler. "Look, it's just community college, Hon. I'll be living half an hour from home. Not like I'm headed off to some far-away, fancy Ivy League school with gold-plated urinals."

The water pipes let out a soft moan, the sound overlapped by the scrape of the shower curtain along its rod.

Guilt stabs me in the belly. While my brother's never had the academic prowess for the Ivy League, it's the mention of "faraway" that's piercing. Because Knox traded his dream, re-flected in every snowcapped mountain poster on his bedroom wall, to stay here in northern Michigan.

You could still end up in Colorado, I want to say. *Working at a resort and snowboarding your heart out.* But the reality is my brother doesn't postpone. He either does things or he doesn't. And that's not a character trait I can reverse tonight.

"But you won't be *here,*" I add. "So you have to tell me ex-actly what you say to Dad. I must be doing something wrong, because he never comes out of it when I try."

God, school is so much easier—study, apply yourself, get an A. The path is direct and linear. But real life doesn't work that way. Real life resembles the messy root systems of plants, with tangled, squirrely paths branching out in dozens of directions. How can anyone ever be sure they choose right?

"How do I bring him back?" My brother does one of his patented full-body shrugs. "I just . . . talk to him, I guess. Remind him to breathe and where he is. Then once he starts to come around I talk about dumb stuff, like how much I hate algebra. I mean, what kind of flaming asshole dreams up math with letters?"

I shake my head. Because I honestly don't know the flaming asshole who dreamed up algebra.

He sniffs. "Really, it's the same thing you do with the plants at the greenhouse. Sort of, I don't know, remind 'em what they're there to do."

For once my brother doesn't mock me for talking to the plants. Or for how much I love the feel of dirt in my hands and the intoxicating scent of things that grow.

Knox plucks the J and lighter from my hand. "This is a masterpiece," he says, inspecting my handiwork. "How'd you get so good at this, anyway? You don't even smoke."

I lift a shoulder. "Practice makes perfect."

"See, that's where you're wrong. Perfection's an illusion, sis." His words are muffled by the joint bobbing between his frowning lips. "Nothing but smoke and mirrors. Every person on the planet is messed up. 'Perfect' people are just better at hiding it. But me? Won't do it. I'm not into the bullshit game. What you see is what you get."

I snatch the joint from his mouth when he goes to light it. "Last I checked, the name on the medical marijuana card was *John* Augustine. Besides, Dad catches you and he'll make you drop and do push-ups till your arms fall off."

"Truth," he concedes with a sigh, resting back on his elbows. "And being armless would definitely cramp my style with the ladies."

Push-ups were often Dad's preferred method of punishment when he wasn't doling out extra chores. Our father never raised a hand to us. Probably because he's seen enough violence to last a lifetime.

Now it's my turn to frown as I dissect Knox's comment. "So, what, you're calling me an illusion? Because of my grades? Because I try? Sorry we all can't embrace mediocrity with your level of enthusiasm."

"My perfect, *perfect* sister. You are Houdini!" His declaration is followed by a theatrical flourish of his hand. "The great and powerful!"

I roll my eyes. "That's Oz, you nitwit." Cocking my head, I study my brother—now flopped back on the bed, his eyes closed, grinning like a fool at the ceiling. *What you see is what you get, all right.*

"Whatever." His mouth opens in a cavernous yawn.

Besides inheriting Dad's knuckles, Knox also got his nose, cleft chin, and soulful eyes. Girls think he looks like James Dean. I think they must be smoking more than weed.

As for me, I look nothing like my father. Sure, I have his introverted tendencies and strong work ethic, but otherwise there's no physical evidence of his genes. Instead, I'm the spitting image of my auburn-haired mother (although I was robbed a good two inches in the height department). I even have her abysmal lack of hand-eye coordination.

But there is one major difference between Mom and me. I don't give up on the people I love.

Which is why I'm still here.

On this bed of bricks.

While the storm rages on.

Minutes pass as I count the widening gaps between thunderclaps. The rumbles grow more distant.

Leaning over, I grab the picture from the floor and return it to the nightstand. My dad's handsome, boyish face grins back. He's wearing desert fatigues, his arm hooked around the neck of another uniformed soldier—his battle buddy, Sergeant AJ Knox. Sergeant Knox never made it home to US soil. But his name did, and it lives on with my brother.

Abandoning Knox as he drifts in and out of consciousness, I return to the dresser to put away the remains of Dad's stash. A fat envelope slides to the front of the drawer. I pick it up.

Divorce papers—nothing new there. The ink's been dry since last August. But my eyes still catch on the lawyer's name, printed in bold, executive font.

Scott Jorgenson, Attorney-at-Law

AKA: my mother's fiancé. Talk about two birds with one stone, Mom. I push away the image of the nuclear family that is now Mom, Scott, and his twin seven-year-old daughters.

Tucked under the divorce papers, there's a much slimmer envelope from the Department of Veterans Affairs. The word *URGENT* is stamped across the front. It's postmarked from a couple of weeks ago. My fingers graze the papery fringe along the top where it's been torn open. What if this envelope holds the key to Dad's recent setbacks? My heart bangs hopefully at the thought.

Glancing to my passed-out brother, I ignore my screaming conscience and ease out the letter, quickly scanning it. And in a matter of seconds, my heart goes from banging to sinking like a boulder. *"No,"* I murmur. Buried within all the military jargon, articles, and codes, I decipher an alarming message.

My father is losing a significant amount of financial benefits. Benefits we've come to rely on to make ends meet.

I frown, struggling to understand the specifics. Something to do with deep program cuts and changes to his eligibility status. The squeak of the shower as it shuts off causes me to jump. My eyes flit to the door.

Dad has a neurosurgeon's precision when it comes to his placement of things. He'll notice a letter like this missing. Quickly tucking the paper back inside the envelope, I return it *exactly* as I found it in the drawer.

"Knox!" I whisper-shout.

"Huh," he grunts.

"Come on. Dad needs his bed."

He grunts again as I tug his arm, using my body weight to leverage him up to a seated position. Knox is intentionally being useless and flops forward like a boneless chicken.

"Hey. Ever notice how the wood looks like super jacked-up teeth? You, sir, need an orthodontist," he informs the floorboards with a bobbing finger.

"Knox." At this point my patience is more worn than the hardwood.

"Gimme a hand, would ya?" He waves his arm around as if

landing a plane. I catch his hand, helping him the rest of the way to his feet.

Once my brother face-plants in bed, I head upstairs to my own.

The storm is finally passing, but for the rest of the night I lie awake. Staring at the attic rafters and counting the knots in the wood like sheep. Wondering about the other storms on the horizon.

The kind I can't see.

2

Click-click. Click-click.

The sound persists, annoying like the constant buzz of a trapped fly. I crack open the eye not submerged in my pillow. *Click-click.* "What are you doing?" I croak.

Knox lowers his cell phone. "Photographically documenting a miraculous event. *Duh.*"

As my sleep fog lifts, I note his damp hair. He's also wearing different clothes from last night. Then realization hits like a sledgehammer.

I bolt upright. "Shit! Oh, shhh—! What time is it?"

"Give you a hint." His diabolical grin makes him look like a cartoon villain. Minus the twirly mustache. "Dad already left for work. So unless you wanna hump the thirteen miles to school, you've got exactly seven minutes." Consulting his phone, he adds, "Starting . . . *now.*" Knox takes another picture of my disoriented morning face and tsunami of hair.

"Get out!" I throw a pillow at him.

My brother ducks, though he shouldn't bother. The pillow

sails three feet to the right of him, narrowly missing my vase of curly bamboo before hitting the wall with a fluffy thump.

"Tick-tock, Honor Roll. I'll be in the truck praying you don't tarnish my good name with a tardy. Because unlike *some* people, I'm a responsible, mature adult."

Sure. Maybe on planet Backward.

"Out!" I repeat, catapulting from bed.

OhGodOhGodOhGod . . . How did I sleep through my alarm? This is a first. I can't *believe* I did this.

Anxiety floods me as I race about the attic. My closet door has swollen shut with April's humidity, and it takes all my strength to pry the damn thing open. But I do, so at least I won't go to school naked.

But instead of my panic subsiding, it rises. Even the air's changed states of matter, going from a gas to a thick and viscous liquid. I tell myself to stop freaking out and breathe—in through my nose, out through my mouth. Knox is late all the time, and there's been no systematic collapse of humanity. Logically, I know this.

Except, *I* have never been late to school. Never had a detention. Never gotten less than a 92 percent on a test. My list of nevers could fill a book that rivals the page count of *War and Peace*.

It's just . . . coloring inside the lines is the only thing bringing order to the chaos of life. So even if it's all an illusion, even if *I* am an illusion, like Knox said, following rules gives me a sense of control. Everything feels safer, the outcome more certain.

So being late? Not an option.

I thunder to the downstairs bathroom, where I set the land

speed record for Fastest Hygiene Ever Performed. Then seven minutes and zero seconds later, I'm out the front door, blindly jamming an arm into my sweater. The screen door triple bangs in my wake. Clumps of tulips and daffodils lining the front of the farmhouse pass in a smear of dazzling color.

Knox lays on the horn, startling the nearby flock of chickens. Feathers fly as they squawk, leaping as high as their wings will carry their plump bodies. "C'mon, let's go!" He revs the engine of his pickup as I dart past the shining grille. Next to his snowboard, the truck is easily his most prized possession.

"Not a word," I warn Knox, heaving myself onto the passenger seat.

His gloating smile rises like the sun at our backs. "Well, good morning, Crabby Appleton. Are you as eager as I am for a day of higher learning?" He jams the truck in gear, churning up the wet gravel. "Ha! I'll take that *eat shit and die* look as a yes."

Once we turn off our long, pothole-riddled driveway, I flip down the visor. My hair's a disaster, poking out like a weather vane in all cardinal directions. I scrape it into a messy bun and slick on some old lip gloss I find in the bottom of my bag. The shockingly vibrant gloss was a stocking stuffer from Mom several Christmases ago, but desperate times and whatnot.

Knox rolls through a stop sign, rows of newly sprouted spinach waving us on with infant leaves. I bite my tongue as he breaks his eighth traffic law in as many minutes. Because, really, who am I to lecture anyone this morning?

"Since when do you wear lipstick?" he asks.

"Since the bags under my eyes got large enough to hold loose change." I hate the color's brightness, but the red does shift attention from the puffed, bloodshot orbs posing as my eyes.

"That coffee might actually help your cause if you drank it." My brother nods to the travel mugs in the console.

Eyeing the second battered mug, I'm reminded of why—despite being seemingly forged of different DNA—I love Knox. Topping the list: thoughtful when you least expect it.

"Wow. That's really . . . thanks," I finish softly, taking the coffee and hoping the scorching liquid will melt away the sudden lump in my throat. I check the time. We won't be late. My shoulders drop a good two inches with relief.

I look over at Knox gently drumming his man hands on the steering wheel. Everything about him is loud, even when he's silent. It's in his nature to stand out, be seen. Obvious from the mocking way he's redrawn the lacrosse sticks on his Ravenswood High T-shirt to resemble hot dogs . . . that I guess are supposed to be giant penises? Art has never been his strong suit.

Still. If I look at him more closely, with softer eyes, I see the brother who can always fix Dad. The brother who chose this family over Mom's new one. The brother who stood up for me when that creep Xander Salzburg was dragging my name through the mud.

If only Knox had been more stealthy in his retaliation. Then the school wouldn't have found the cache of empty Easy Cheese cans in his truck. And put two and two together when Xander's locker was mysteriously oozing with neon-orange cheese.

But Knox is nothing if not loyal. So maybe I should level with him about the VA letter I found in Dad's drawer last night, and how I couldn't sleep because of it.

"Hey," he says brightly. "Did I tell you Jason Stiles ended up in the ER the other night?"

"Oh God. What bone did he break this time?" Being the town daredevil makes Jason a regular at the emergency room. I'm surprised the hospital hasn't dedicated a wing to him yet.

"Mostly his pride. So get this, somebody dared him to set his fart on fire. Except Jason held the lighter too close and ended up with an ass full of flames!" He laughs hysterically and pounds the dash. "Oh man! Take my money now! Seriously, I'd sell all my earthly possessions to see that."

He nudges my arm, egging me to join in.

A reluctant smile pulls at my lips. Not because I find the idea of flatulence arson or first-degree butt burns as hilarious as Knox. But because of the genuine way he shares his happiness—freely, like it'll never run out.

Like Mom, my brother's greatest gift has always been his ability to outshine the sun.

And as I sit in the passenger seat, basking in his brightness, the thought of snuffing it out (again) with my endless worrying feels wrong. So for now, I'll carry the cloud of this secret.

According to Dante, there are nine circles of hell, but I've discovered a tenth.

I'm currently within inches of Van Gogh–ing both ears as Mr. Durand's monotone voice manages to do the impossible— suck the soul out of Robert Frost. It's criminal. And it's only second period.

Good God, this day will never end.

Whoever thought sticking me in a junior-level class as a sophomore (in lieu of an *actual* AP Lit class) would somehow bridge my educational gap was sorely mistaken. But eventually Bland Durand finishes the last stanza of "Stopping by Woods on a Snowy Evening"—may it rest in peace—and carries on with the lecture.

My mechanical pencil scratches with 0.5 mm precision against my paper.

FROST ALWAYS DRANK A DAIQUIRI BEFORE EACH MEAL AT HIS FAVORITE RESTAURANT (WAYBURY INN, VT)

Since Mr. Durand favors obscure facts over anything with informational substance, I'm forced to take annoyingly detailed notes. My hand cramps, curling in like a bird foot by the time he concludes the twenty-five-minute monologue.

Mr. Durand then stretches his neck high, mimicking the sandhill cranes that canvass the adjacent field for bugs. "I think now is an excellent time to assess your knowledge retention with a pop quiz."

A chorus of groans fills the classroom.

"Unless you prefer a series of essay questions?"

The groans stop, replaced with fear-stricken silence. Not a soul moves. Not an eye blinks.

"All right then, it's unanimous. Mr. Salzburg, would you kindly do the honors?"

Xander Salzburg, cocaptain of the lacrosse team and lowest common denominator of douche, rises and saunters to the teacher's desk. Entitlement rolls off him in nauseating waves, toxic as his body spray. He takes the stack of papers from Mr. Durand, giving him a mock salute before leisurely working his way down the columns of desks.

A number of girls suddenly become bright-eyed and alert at Xander's approach. Hair is twirled and eyelashes are batted, ensuring his ego will be well fed for the remainder of class.

Shrinking in my seat as Xander nears, I make myself as compact as possible, fixating on the uniform lines of the fake wood grain on my desk. He pauses in front of me. The gelled tips of his blond hair cast a porcupine-like shadow.

Nothing to see here but an uninteresting collection of tiny molecules.

A soft chuckle rolls in his throat. "Nice lipstick, Hummer," Xander sneers, low enough for his voice to get lost in the noise of shuffling papers. Lost on everyone but me.

The muscles in my body seize. My eyes betray me by flicking up in horror. His smile is as calculated and malicious as his choice of words. He slides the quiz in front of me with a wink, knowing I'm powerless to reply.

Because Xander has ambushed me. Cruelly dusting off the nickname that's lain dormant since my earliest weeks at this school.

My gaze drops to the quiz as I drag the back of my hand across my mouth. Shame colors my face and knits my organs in a web of knots. A shame I should not own but do.

Multiple-choice questions blur as my eyes sheet with tears that I refuse, *refuse* to let fall. The ball of hurt pulses in my chest. I push it down, but it keeps bobbing up like an ever-expanding black balloon.

Focus. I command my hand to grip the pencil. Command the graphite to connect with paper. Command my brain to supply the answers.

This is when I miss the anonymity of larger schools, like the one I left in Detroit. But disappearing is a foreign concept at Ravenswood High. A place where your every mistake is immortalized. Tattooed in the minds of the student body. Till . . . pretty much the end of time.

But I can't hop in a time machine and go back to last summer. Can't undo that I willingly went into that closet with Cole for a stupid game of seven minutes in heaven.

All I wanted was to escape my own skin for a night. Become somebody else. A carefree girl who giggled and flirted and drank shitty beer from a plastic cup. That lapse in judgment cost me everything. The one time I deliberately colored outside the lines, and look where it got me. Labeled a slut. A whore. Before school had even started.

Sure. Even *I* can admit how damning the scene was when the closet door opened, but that didn't make it true. Since then I've learned most people aren't interested in the truth. Luckily, Zareen Kapoor isn't most people. If not for Zee, I'd be completely friendless here.

Xander returns to his seat behind me, whispering to Ravenswood's lacrosse legend and cocaptain—Cole Buchannon. Yes, the very same Cole who's the reason for my social fall from grace. They quietly laugh at my expense.

I squeeze my pencil tighter while staring at Mr. Durand, willing him to notice. But he's far too busy harvesting lint balls from his sweater vest. Their whispers continue like rapid-fire arrows at my back. And then I hear it again. The nickname.

Hummer.

My resolve to hold it together snaps like the tip of my pencil.

"Shut up! Just shut up!" My voice shatters the silence in the room. The boys stare up at me, bug-eyed.

Up. They are staring *up* because somehow I'm looming above them. *When did I stand?* Curious heads pop up around the classroom. This is the opposite of disappearing—and so not me! It's like I've accidentally channeled Knox. Difference is, he doesn't sweat in the spotlight.

"Miss Augustine?" Mr. Durand's tone is as befuddled as his expression. He pushes up his glasses like a reset button. Like that will help him understand why his star pupil is causing a scene. "What's this about?"

My mouth soundlessly opens and closes like a guppy. Humiliation gives my face its own heartbeat.

Mr. Durand frowns, looking to the guys for clarification. "Mr. Buchannon? Mr. Salzburg? What's going on here?"

"I—I . . ." Cole stammers in an attempt to master his vowels. Then his mouth hinges shut, his full lips flattening in a tight line. And beneath his residual spring break tan—his face blossoms, red as our tulips.

Xander steps in with eerie composure. "Mr. Durand"—he tucks his pencil behind his ear, leaning forward with a false earnestness that turns my stomach—"I think I can speak for both of us when I say we have no idea what Miss Augustine's outburst is about. We were just sitting here concentrating on our quizzes when she started screaming at us."

And I have no defense. None. Unless I want to share with the class what they called me. No. No, I'd sooner die. Or worse, get an F. The victorious glint in Xander's eye tells me he knows this.

Mr. Durand's expectant gaze swings back to me.

But I've got nothing. No reasonable explanation to offer for my behavior. The second hand on the clock ticks off the last thirty seconds of class. Grabbing my bag, I speed-walk to the front, dumping off my quiz and mumbling an apology to my slack-jawed teacher. Twentysomething pairs of eyes follow my every action.

The bell rings as I exit, scrubbing my hand over my mouth once more. Then I break into a run. Fast enough to be out of their sight, to outrun my humiliation.

My shoes chirp against the waxed floors. *Outside.* I just need to be outside, where there are no walls pressing in. No ceiling dropping on my head. Students begin to swarm the hallway, but in ten more feet, I'll be free of them.

Shoving open the door, I burst into the sunlight. Soak the warmth into my skin. Breathe the cool spring air. It smells like a promise—new beginnings beyond this two-story brick-and-mortar hellhole.

I race past the tennis courts and groomed soccer field, heading to the north edge of campus where my favorite tree waits. The grandiose weeping willow beckons me with her long, slender branches. I part the curtain of green buds and collapse underneath.

My jeans might get a little damp, but who cares. I gather my legs up to my chest, a turtle retreating to its shell. Then I shut my eyes, absorb the strength of the tree at my back, and let my lungs fill with the blue of the sky.

And for a while, that's all that exists.

A few minutes later a twig snaps, followed by a hushed parting of branches. I have company, and there's only one person it can be.

My fingers graze a patch of velvety moss at my side. *Nature's carpet,* as Grandma Augustine was fond of calling it.

"Word's already traveled about my spectacular meltdown, huh?" I mutter.

Zareen purses her lips. "What'd you expect? You of all people know the primary currency at this school is gossip." She spreads her jacket on the ground before taking a seat beside me. There's a moment of stretching silence. She nudges me with her hand, forever smudged with ink from rigorous note-taking.

"Thanks," I murmur, accepting the candied ginger she holds out and popping it in my mouth. The intense spice tingles, a welcome distraction from my thoughts.

"So," Zee begins, the candy clicking against her teeth, "I already told Mrs. Henderson you might not make it for independent study. Said you were in the bathroom with severe nausea and stomach cramps. Most likely from exposure to enteritidis—that's the bacterial strain most commonly associated with food poisoning. Should buy you a pass home from the school nurse, if you want it. No question." She flicks her hair over her shoulder; it cascades like a black river down her back.

Leave it to my brilliant friend to recall the exact name of a bacterial strain. Zareen once told me as long as you speak with authority and use big, official-sounding words, adults are as malleable as clay.

"You're a genius, Zee. But I have to pick up some extra shifts at the greenhouse, so unfortunately, I need the study time."

She nods once, tugging down the sleeve of her favorite

Harvard cardigan. The crimson-colored one she always wears for luck on debate days. Not that Zee needs any luck, since she habitually mops the floor with her opponents.

Her intense brown eyes blaze with concern. "Honor—"

"I'll be *fine*. I just need a minute." I chew the rest of the candied ginger, which burns like her stare. "And stop looking at me like Aditi."

Aditi is Zee's younger sister and the sibling most likely to give their parents a myocardial infarction. Unlike Zareen, who's known from the womb she wants to be an attorney, Aditi would rather go where the wind blows her. And this week, the wind insists she become an international pop sensation who wears more glitter than clothing. I hear Mrs. Kapoor required smelling salts.

"Want to talk about it?" she asks, folding a leg up to her chest.

By way of an answer, I drop my head to the crook of my arm.

But Zee won't let me hide inside myself. "I'm a top prosecutor at the US Attorney's Office in New York," she begins, crunching the remains of her candy. This is a game we invented called "ten years later," where we fantasize about our lives a decade from now. "Criminals fear me because I wield justice like the grim reaper's scythe. And I have never lost a case. *Ever*. Your turn."

I consider telling her what Xander said. For a moment, I even feel myself bend and sway like the canopy around us. But I can't. Reminding her of the nickname I've tried so hard to forget would only reopen a barely stitched-together wound.

So I lift up my head and dutifully play along. "I'm a master gardener who's transformed Augustine Greens into the most coveted greenhouse in all the world. The beauty of my calla lilies has been known to make grown men weep. Naturally we're both absurdly rich and want for nothing."

"Naturally," she says with an infectious grin. Her eyes suddenly narrow as her nose wrinkles. "*Ew!* Gross, do you smell that?" Fanning a hand in front of her face, she parts the branches to investigate.

But I don't need to look. I already know what she'll see.

"Burners," she mutters in disgust. "Always out there smoking weed between classes. And you just *know* every single one of them will wind up living in their parents' basements. Eating Funyuns and going nowhere in life. What a waste. . . ."

Her voice grows more distant as I sink deeper into my thoughts.

This is why I've never confided in Zee about my father's issues. Not the PTSD. And certainly not about the pot he uses when things get bad. Because it's one thing for her to judge the kids at school, but I couldn't bear it if she did that to my father. It would spell the end of our friendship. And I can't chance losing my only friend here.

"Hey, you look all sad again," she says, turning back around. "What's wrong?"

"Mm? Nothing." I stand up. "Come on, we should head back inside," I say, and hug my secrets tighter.

3

I brush at the dark smudges on my coveralls, and the stubborn marks fade but don't go away. Great, another stain. Like the humiliating scene yesterday in lit class. At least *that* stain doesn't show on the outside.

I dump more soil and fertilizer mix in the terra-cotta pot, stabbing it with a garden trowel to break up the black lumps. But my time at the greenhouse isn't delivering the usual escape.

Aunt Maeve slides a flat of purple-and-white pansies onto the opposite side of the potting station, tunelessly humming as she joins me. The antennae on her bumblebee pin quiver with her movements. She pauses, eyeing me curiously from beneath the brim of her straw hat. "Care to tell me who you wish was on the receiving end of that trowel? Or was the dirt just extra uppity today?"

Biologically speaking, the seventy-two-year-old gardener and bee aficionado is not my great-aunt. But she's been a member of our family since around the time the foundation to Augustine Greens was poured, so she's my great-aunt in all the ways that matter.

"Oh, nobody." I try to make my actions less homicidally stabby, but the older woman's gaze is unrelenting. A minute, maybe more passes, and Aunt Maeve still hasn't blinked. In fact, her stare remains as stubbornly fixed as the legions of freckles that dust her skin.

I buckle. "Okay, all right." The trowel clatters against the metal surface when I set it down. "It's school, and I hate it, and I'd rather swan-dive into the compost pile than go back."

The crow's-feet gather at the corners of her eyes. "Well, that is a vivid picture." Aunt Maeve works the roots of the pansy between her fingers, gently massaging them apart, cradling the plants like precious babies she's about to tuck in. "But you always said you loved school, Pip."

Pip being short for pipsqueak. A nickname originally bestowed by my tall-as-an-oak granddad. Being the shortest, at a meager five foot three, I am a hobbit among elves. And Aunt Maeve's the only person who can get away with calling me that anymore.

"No. I love *learning*. Two different things." I slide the prepped container across to her so she can add the flowers and greenery.

Aunt Maeve's silent a few beats as she nestles the pansies in the dirt. "You know what you need?" she declares suddenly with a wag of her trowel.

I raise my brows. "To be homeschooled?"

"Ginseng, lemon balm, and peppermint," she replies, unflapped by my sarcasm. Maeve Hannigan holds the same faith in home-brewed teas that some hold in religion. Her special blends have been known to treat everything from sour moods to sour stomachs, and a whole lot in between.

Dumping soil into another pot, I tell her, "I don't think tea will help in this particular case, Aunt Maeve."

"Nonsense, tea always helps. Nothing chases away the gloomy grumps like a spot of tea."

I don't hold the same certainty but grin and nod anyway.

Knox hollers something about leprechauns from the front of the greenhouse. Aunt Maeve's face scrunches in confusion. "Did he say *leprechauns,* or do I need new batteries in my hearing aids?"

"Your batteries are fine." I brush off my hands. "I'll go check on him." Before leaving, I ask, "Oh, have you seen my hand rake? The one with the squishy, comfort-grip handle? I just used it last week and now I can't find it anywhere."

Aunt Maeve shakes her head apologetically. "I'm sure it'll turn up, though. Lost things have a way of returning to us eventually."

Heading through the main building, I pass tables packed with green, some bursting with color, some a budding prelude of the flowers to come.

When I reach the front checkout area, Knox thumbs to the wagon behind him. An army of red-hatted, bubble-cheeked garden gnomes stare goofily back. "Since when do we sell leprechauns?"

"Gnomes," I correct.

Knox waves a hand like he can't possibly be bothered to know the difference. "Whatever. Do you know where they go? Delivery guy swore up and down it wasn't a mistake."

"Let me see." I fire up the ancient computer. The monitor, yellowed by time and christened with dirt, blinks to life. My fingers peck at the smudged and gritty keyboard. "Ah, here it is. Looks like they're a special order for Mrs. Amelia Rotterdack, 1193 Huron Way."

"Fifty bucks says Mrs. Amelia Rotterdack has a cat calendar on the fridge and one of those knitted cozies for her extra toilet paper."

I roll my eyes. "Please, like you have fifty bucks." After printing out the invoice, I pass it to him.

"Let's bounce, creepy dwarfs," he mutters to the eternally happy statues. "Oh, hey." He snaps his fingers. "Almost forgot. Party at the Hole tonight, mostly juniors and seniors. But you should come, you know, do human-y stuff."

The Hole is a large pond on the back forty of my family's property. Secluded enough for teenage debauchery without consequence of law. And frankly, I'd rather roll naked down a hill of stinging nettles than join them.

Because the Hole used to be a sacred place. A jewel known only to Knox and me, founded eight summers ago when our grandparents were still alive. We claimed it with flags. Mine painted with images of the water lilies that huddled at the pond's edge. My brother's painted with misshapen gourds meant to be human skulls.

"I claim this land in the name of Honor Elizabeth Augustine!" I shouted, then pierced the embankment with my stake and crowed like a wild thing at the sky.

Not to be outdone, my brother scrambled to a higher embankment, slipping on mud and leaves along the way. Once he reached the top, where the tree with our rope swing clung desperately to the earth, his cry rang from above, "And *I* claim this land in the name of Knox Henry Augustine! The Forever King!"

Dissatisfied with my relegated title of queen, I challenged Knox to a duel with sticks. Queens wore dresses. Rode sidesaddle. Drank tea from dainty cups. I did none of that. So I thrust and parried, taking more hits than I delivered, falling down, only to get up again. Until finally, sweaty and mudstreaked, Knox declared us both the Forever King.

Together we ruled this magical place. A place for catching dragonflies and dreams. Our heaven on earth.

And it belonged to *us*.

Then my brother turned fifteen and took it. Something that was innocent and ours. No longer a secret. No longer revered. My kingdom had been lost to boys and girls discovering booze and each other's bodies.

I was not the Forever King after all. Knox was. And is still.

"Sounds great." The words come out flat as pennies and taste like them.

He rests a hand on one of the gnome heads, frowning. "I don't get it. You used to love going to the Hole."

"I did. But that was before."

"Before what?"

How can he be so clueless? "*Before* someone soaked our flags with Bacardi 151 and used them as kindling!"

"Oh, *come on*, Honor. Who cares about some dumbass flags we made as kids a million years ago?"

"I do," I reply, angry at how my voice betrays my hurt. A hurt that makes me feel childish and small for lugging around years later.

"Well, that's your problem right there. You care too much,

Hon, about friggin' everything. Always have. You gotta learn to lighten up."

Lighten up? Knox is so light he's practically 90 percent helium. I should be tying a precautionary string to his toe.

"You done?" I ask, scraping the dirt from under my nails with a bent paper clip.

"Hey, don't get all defensive. I'm only looking out for you. Believe it or not, there're some decent kids at this school if you gave them a chance. Maybe try to be a little friendlier. Honey. Flies. Insert obvious cliché here," he concludes, using air quotes.

With the nails of my right hand soil-free, I move to the left.

"So nothing, huh?" My brother cocks his head. "God, would it *kill* you to cut loose and have some fun?"

"Why?" I toss the paper clip; it skates across the counter. "You seem to be having enough fun for everyone. Or maybe you haven't noticed how Dad's struggling and now he's"— I catch myself shy of blurting about the lost benefits—"not . . . really sleeping," I finish with a huff.

The muscle in Knox's jaw twitches. "Yeah, I noticed. But guess what? It's not my job to fix everyone." He leans over the counter and stares me hard in the face. "And it's not *your* job, either." Turning around, he snatches the cart's handle, the gnomes/leprechauns/dwarfs clinking together as he whisks them away.

"Don't forget to Bubble Wrap those!" I call after him in frustration.

But my brother's out of earshot. Or simply stopped listening.

As I near the farmhouse, the determined pound of my father's ax cleaving the fallen wild cherry grows louder. The half-mile walk home usually clears my head. But not today. None of my resets seem to be working.

Geronimo whizzes like a black-and-white bullet from around the back of the house to greet me. It's impossible not to smile as he spits his slobbery prize at my feet and barks.

"Hard at work helping Dad, I see."

His tail wags hard enough to fracture shins. I give his ears a scratch before picking up the soggy tennis ball and throwing it.

Geronimo thunders off, clawing up the ground with his scramble. I circle to the back.

My father pauses to catch his breath before swinging the ax high above his head, then slamming it down. *Ker-rack!* The chunk of wood splits, becoming two.

"Hey, Dad. Need anything?" I ask, even though it's a fruitless question.

"I'm good." His muscles coil as he winds up for another swing, his T-shirt soaked with sweat.

"How about a break?" I root around my bag and pull out a water bottle, giving it a shake. He's less inclined to say no if it's there in his face.

"S'pose I could use a short one." He waves me closer before rolling over one of the larger wood segments. It thuds to the ground, cut side up. "Have a seat, daughter."

"Sir, yes, sir," I say with a grin. My standard reply to any *daughter* command.

Geronimo joins us, dropping his ball and backside to the

ground. He pants, his tongue lolling out the side of his mouth like a pink wind sock on a windless day.

We sit on the hardwood as I pass my dad the water.

He guzzles half and wipes his mouth. "So, I've been thinking."

When he doesn't elaborate I ask, "About anything in particular or just synapsing in general?"

With a noncommittal smirk, he settles his gaze on an orange-bellied robin wrestling worms from the ground and takes another drink. My father's true language has always been the space between words. So I listen close to what's not being said.

"I've got some"—his pause drags out long enough for me to count eight growth rings on the wood beneath me—"concerns."

Based on the measured stretches of speech, I'd say this goes above and beyond simple concern. I tense, racking my brain for what I could've done. *Does he know I snooped and saw the VA letter?* It *was* missing when I went back to find it. Drawing in a breath of piney air, I brace myself.

Dad rubs his chapped hands slowly, pulling in his own breath of pine. "Honor, are you happy?"

"Er . . . *what?*" Maybe I don't speak his language as fluently as I believed. An unsettling thought. "Am I happy?" I test the words, finding them as confusing and foreign the second time.

He wipes his neck with the handkerchief from his back pocket. "I realize the past year has been tough on everyone. We're all still . . . adjusting. But I'm wondering if the move to Ravenswood was the best thing for *you*."

Alarms sound in my head. I don't like this conversational detour. "Dad, I—"

"Listen, Honor, what I did, maybe it was selfish. Wanting for you to choose a life way up here over the life you had in Detroit. I don't know. Maybe you'd be better off with your mom and your old friends—Shannon and Hux, was it?"

"*Shayla* and Hux," I correct, listlessly watching the crabgrass I've plucked rain green over my shoes.

The texts and calls with my friends started off strong following my move to the great north—five, almost six hours away. But month by month, time began to stretch like the distance. Until having any communication felt more awkward and strained than having none at all. Because apparently we'd lost the one thing that united us.

Geography.

But I belong here, in Ravenswood. As sure as the apple blossoms that'll give way to fruit on the trees. I've known it ever since I was old enough to hold a memory. From the moment I stepped foot in the greenhouse I knew—I was home.

Which is why before my grandparents died, Aunt Maeve promised them she'd care for the greenhouse. Keep the business afloat, until one day, I was ready to run it myself.

So bottom line: There *is* no going back. Because I'm already home.

"Thing is," Dad continues, after another long pause and twist of his handkerchief, "you haven't really made much in the way of friends here."

"But I have Zareen! And . . . and my grades and progress reports are off the charts. Really, Dad. Talk to any of my teachers."

His brown eyes soften. "Grades have never been an issue, honey. For Knox, sure, but not you. You've always been ten steps ahead. The kid who messes up the curve."

Sickness looms in my belly. "Then I don't understand what this is about."

Dad picks up Geronimo's gooey ball and throws it, sending the dog off on another joyous chase. "There's more to life than working hard and doing good in school. You should be going out with friends. Having fun. Raising a *modest* amount of hell, and—"

"I don't believe this." I shake my head, but the nagging sense of betrayal doesn't cast off so easily. "You've been talking to Knox, haven't you? About me."

He frowns. "No. Honor, your brother has nothing to do with this."

"So then, you're punishing me for not being more of a . . . delinquent? What kind of a parent are you?" The question comes out sharper than I intend. But *Dad's* the one in crisis here! Would he rather I get knocked up? Binge-drink till my liver turns the size of a watermelon? Shoot heroine into my eyeballs? Maybe then my father would get off my back and place his worry where it's needed—on himself.

"I am the kind of parent"—he stops to take my hand, sticky with newly sprung sweat and grass—"who wants what's best for his child. And so far, I'm not convinced that's here."

I swallow hard, choking back the queasiness. *Think of something. Anything that will put his mind at ease. Anything that will demonstrate I'm just an average teenager who—*

"But I have plans tonight!" I blurt.

Dad's eyes widen in shock.

"Yeah." I nod to myself, the momentum of my idea building. "I'm meeting up with some kids from school. Knox will be there, too. Should be a good time. Fun. The modest hell-raising kind." Before he has any room for doubt I add, "And I'm also going to the next lacrosse home game. With Zee." This will be news to her, but hey, I'll lacrosse that bridge when I have to.

"Well, that's . . . huh." The lines on his face lose some of the hardness, dissolving years from his features. "That's great, Honor. I'm glad. Real glad." He gives my hand a squeeze before letting go. "Guess your old man's not as in touch with your social life as he thought, eh?"

"Wouldn't be the first parent."

Dad processes the news of his daughter's budding social life he didn't know existed. That makes two of us. The corners of his mouth slowly ascend in a grin. "Okay. So you're happy, then?"

"I'm happy, Dad." And the bigness of my smile consumes my whole face, threatening to split it in two. "So, uh, I should probably get cleaned up."

"Wait. Before you go," Dad says, leaning to the side and digging in the pocket of his jeans, "I forgot to give you this. Found it up in Laramey at a work site. Thought you might like it for that jar of yours."

The stone he places in my palm isn't much larger than a quarter. It's the color of firehouse brick, with bands of white and onyx girdling the middle. The colors are dull now, un-remarkable. It makes me wonder how many eyes dismissed this ordinary stone, not knowing its potential to be extraordinary.

"Thanks. It's beautiful, even prettier once it's polished up. Looks like quartz, maybe?"

But this isn't a rock for my jar. My father doesn't under-stand those are special because they are my memories. Every stone in my mason jar tells a story. Some happy, some sad, but each one has made me the person I am. So, I figure, they're worth remembering.

I lean in to hug him. Not part of the act or because he sees beauty in the unremarkable, but because I need one. I need reassurance he won't send me away. And I need him to know that I belong here the way I do.

He recoils a little. "Ah, might not want to do that with me wearing the stink of the day, daughter."

"Sir, yes, sir." Then I wrap my arms around him anyway and squeeze. Hard. Infusing all that goes unspoken into the embrace.

4

With the sun snuffed out on the horizon hours ago, I continue at a brisk pace. My cell pings with a text from Zee, who's bitter about being on parental lockdown tonight. As if the Kapoors would ever get behind an unsupervised, middle-of-the-woods party. Meanwhile Dad practically threw a damn parade (complete with pantomimed confetti tossing) as I stepped out the door. So, really, I have no choice but to soldier on.

My mini flashlight pans over the tall grasses, illuminating the matted trail leading up to the woods that surround the Hole. Not much farther.

My breath erupts in puffs of white. I tug the zipper of my fleece hoodie until I feel the cold metal rest at my chin. The damp grass squeaks under the soles of my duck boots. And I'm close enough now to smell the smoke of their fire. Feel the vibrating *thump thump thump* of their music. Hear the sounds of their shouts and laughter.

All reminders of my kingdom lost.

My boots suddenly feel immersed in quicksand, because every step requires quadruple the effort than the one before.

Knox just has to see me. Bear witness I came. This buoys me as I make my way through the woods, dodging low-hanging branches and taking care not to stumble on the tree roots that run like veins along the forest floor.

The orangey glow of the fire highlights the opening at the tree line, although my inner compass could probably find it in the dark. Emerging from the woods, I sidestep some crushed beer cans at its edge.

"Waste of time," I mutter to the trees I'd rather be hiding in.

As I click off the mini flashlight, my eyes follow the gentle slope of land to the water that marks its end. The bonfire's reflection transforms the pond into a mesmerizing pool of burning ink.

Knox is the first person I see, standing tall and kingly on a stump near the reedy shoreline. He raises a can high in the air, addressing his rowdy subjects.

"And here's to all my BFFs!" he shouts over the music. "Beer friends forever!" They laugh. "May your lives be full but your cans never empty. Ravenswood senior class, I salute you!"

Everyone whistles and cheers. God, he makes it look so easy. Being adored. With everyone hanging on his every—

"Hey." A male voice drifts from the shadows.

I yelp and spin around. As my eyes adjust, I spot one of the last people I'd voluntarily choose to share atomic space with—Cole Buchannon. He's slouched against a tree about ten feet away, a half-empty bottle of liquor in his hand. Most surprising of all, he's alone.

"What are you doing here?" he asks.

My hand falls away from my chest, but my heart continues its erratic rhythm. I pull the strings of my hoodie tighter, seeking refuge in the fleece, wishing it could swallow me completely. "This is my family's property. Technically I have more right to be here than anyone." And really, I could throw his question back at him. Why is Cole hanging here, on the fringe of the party, when he's normally at the center of it?

"I didn't mean"—he hiccups—"you aren't welcome or whatever. I've just never seen you at one of these parties before. Didn't think it was your thing."

"It isn't." The implication hangs uncomfortably, like the damp chill in the air. My hands burrow into the depths of my pockets, ferreting out the warmth. I take a step away from Cole and toward the party, which suddenly holds a lot more appeal than it did five minutes ago.

"So yesterday at"—he hiccups again and I stop—"school. You seemed pretty upset in class."

I blink several times before whirling around to face him. "Are you for real?"

"Well, I might be a little drunk." Cole rubs his forehead, causing the knit beanie to slide farther back on his head. "But, yeah, as far as I know I'm real." He pinches himself and winces. *"Ouch."*

Anger breaches the dam of words I hold back. "You think this is funny, Cole? Like I'm supposed to laugh off what happened? How can you be so cruel? It was bad enough when Xander said it, but then you had to join in? When I heard you call me—"

I bite my lip, halting the flood. The wound in my voice is too pronounced. And I'd sooner tear open my skin with my teeth than let him see the wreckage underneath.

"Whoa, whoa!" He makes a crooked *T* with his hands as

he holds the bottle. "Time-out. Honor, what are you talking about? Xander was just telling me about how he got caught pulling some dumbass stunt and might be grounded. All I said was 'bummer,' and next thing I know you jumped up and—" Cole stops like my breath. He rubs his head again, piecing together the puzzle I've already solved. "You thought I called you . . ."

I turn away, unable to look at him. Wishing more than anything yesterday's incident would decompose like the rotting leaves under my feet. So I created a scene for nothing. Played right into Xander's manipulative little mind game. And now Cole has a premium seat at my parade of humiliation. For the second day in a row.

At least he spares giving voice to the nickname. I'm not sure it matters, since we both think it.

There's a clumsy thump and rustle as he stuffs the bottle in his back pocket and climbs to his feet. "Honor."

God, why does he have to say my name with the same kind of gentleness Aunt Maeve used handling those pansies?

"Hey. Would you look at me?" he pleads.

Hugging myself tighter, I watch the distant flames lash furiously at the night. "Just"—I shake my head—"leave me alone, Cole."

"Not until we get something straight." He zigzags over, bringing with him the scent of campfire and pine, spiked with alcohol. He jams his hands in the pockets of his down jacket. "I would *never* call you that, Honor. I swear," Cole says with alarming sincerity.

Okay, fine. Maybe not in this instance, but what about before? When the rumors were blazing fierce as the bonfire. I lick my lips; the chilly air feeds off the moisture. "Why should I believe you?" I brave a look up at him.

He sniffs, the tip of his nose pink with cold like his cheeks. "Because it's the truth. But if you really think I'd talk shit about you, disrespect you that way, then . . ." He pauses, his Adam's apple rises and falls. "I guess I finally get why you hate me. Why you refused to talk to me all these months. Hell, I wouldn't have talked to me, either, if I thought that."

"I don't *hate* you." What I feel for Cole is infinitely more complicated. I kick loose a pine cone wedged in the ground. "And I want to believe you. It's just, how can you be friends with someone like Xander?"

"We have history, Xander and me."

I want to tell him if history's all they have, he's better off without him. The pine cone under my boot makes a satisfying crunch. "Xander's an ass barnacle."

In addition to also being a sorry, soulless excuse for a human being. And while I lack the courage to say this to Xander's face, telling his closest confidant feels like a decent consolation prize.

"Ass barnacle?" he repeats with an amused snort. "Look, I get it. He can be a real dick sometimes. But if you knew what he—"

The icy laugh tumbles from my mouth, surprising us both.

"What?" he asks.

My eyes slide to his. His baffled expression emboldens me. "Come on, you can't possibly think his dickishness is a rarity."

Not when Xander enlisted a small army of girls to speak in hushed whispers and spread lies. Got them to write awful things about me on the bathroom walls for everyone to see.

"No," Cole replies slowly. "I think it's more of a symptom. Ever met his dad?" His question is punctuated with a humorless laugh. "Vic Salzburg makes my dad seem like Father of the Year, and *that's* saying something."

My toes curl, forming tiny fists in my boots. No. Xander doesn't get my sympathy, not with yesterday still feeling tender as a bruise. But the revelation does make me consider something.

What if Cole—blinded by compassion for his friend—doesn't see the ugly side of Xander? Doesn't know the depth of it? Is it possible all this time he never knew his best friend lit the fuse that would detonate my reputation?

Maybe. Which would mean Cole was never complicit in the way I thought him to be. I watch my breath spiral up to the stars, longing for the same weightlessness.

Cole makes a noise of disgust, pulling me away from the sky. "This night keeps getting better and better." Removing the bottle from the back pocket of his jeans, he plops down onto a fallen tree trunk.

I follow his gaze to a couple below. The girl has long blond hair, curled and perfectly tousled. The sort of girl who probably smells like vanilla, wears lip gloss with sparkles, and sings off-key in a way that makes her endearing.

She giggles as she topples back onto the guy's lap. He pulls aside her hair, breathing in her skin before kissing her neck. She smiles, turning so her lips find his.

Something isn't right. The girl seems familiar, except it's hard to see clearly with the distance. And then it clicks. I frown. "Wait. Is that—"

"My girlfriend, Chelsea?" He unscrews the cap and takes a generous gulp. "Yup."

"Cole, I . . ." My mouth hangs open. If it were blackfly season I'd be catching them. I don't know what to say, but I know he doesn't deserve that. Sympathy pushes me to close the space between us. Finding a spot on the log where the fungus hasn't taken over, I sit down and lower my hood.

"The irony is I wasn't even gonna come tonight. But then she asked me, like, three times if I was going, and I got suspicious. Looks like I had reason to be, huh? God, if there's one thing I can't stand, it's liars. Especially the cheating ones." He holds out the bottle to me. "Drink?" The clear liquid glimmers with the light of the fire and full moon.

But I remember too well what happened the last time I drank with Cole. "No thanks."

Retracting his arm, he goes back to watching the scene. "Shouldn't be surprised, I guess. Neither of us has been happy for a while. Just didn't know we were officially over." He gestures with the bottle as his now-ex mauls another guy. "Till now."

It doesn't get more official than that. Or more heartless. "I'm sorry."

"I'm not." His gaze cuts to mine and moves quickly away. "I mean, it was never gonna work. Didn't need a whole six months to figure that out."

"Then why did you stay together?" I cringe at the way the question torpedoes from my mouth. This is why Mom has always called me the black coffee to Knox's cream and sugar. "I . . . Forget I asked. It's not my business."

"No, it isn't." Cole hunches forward, leaving me to percolate in my bitter grounds. But then to my surprise, he continues, "It's not like I didn't see her flaws from the start. But Chelsea could also be sweet and fun, thoughtful even. You know she never missed a single lacrosse game? Not one. So I focused on that stuff—the good. Until the good got too hard to see."

I'm beginning to see a pattern here. First Xander, now Chelsea . . .

"Maybe you give people more credit than they deserve," I say softly.

A few heartbeats pass. "And maybe you don't give people enough."

I frown. How can he even say that with his ex making a gross, face-sucking spectacle below? It defies logic.

"Anyway," Cole says, flapping a dismissive hand at them, "she kinda did us both a favor pulling the plug. Least now I don't have to get a tux for prom."

But I recognize false bravado when I hear it—the way the syllables insist and try too hard.

Now I understand why Cole's sequestered himself in the lonely, shadowed spot on the hill. He was confirming what he already knew. And pretending to be okay with it. Which is a lot easier to do without an audience.

I search for the right words to say and come up short. So I do the one thing that doesn't require me to say anything . . .

I hold out my hand.

Cole rocks away. "Wait, is this a pity drink? Because really, I'm *fine*. You don't have to—"

"Just give me the damn bottle, Buchannon." One drink won't kill me.

The glass feels cold in my hand and glacial on my lips. Then the vodka fills my mouth. Gulping it down feels like swallowing a colony of pissed-off bees. I immediately cough as the liquid sears my esophagus, not stopping until the inferno erupts in a full-belly blaze.

He laughs, gently slapping my back. "Yeah. Not exactly quality vodka on the bottom shelf, but it's all my cousin had."

I wheeze, letting loose a final rattling cough. "*God*. How can you even drink that?" My face scrunches. "Tastes like lighter fluid and turpentine had a baby." I wipe my mouth in disgust.

Cole chuckles again. "Honor, I can pretty much guarantee nobody here is drinking for the taste. They're drinking for the feel or . . . the numb. Gets a little less terrible by the second or third try." As he takes the bottle from my hand, his fingers brush over mine, making the rest of me burn like my stomach.

I jerk away, cramming my hands back in my pockets. If he noticed our touch, he doesn't show it. Someone turns up the music. The bass pulses through me, bringing a warm, lulling sensation with it.

After a few minutes of staring at the ground, Cole turns his gaze on me. "Can I ask you something?"

I nod, despising the way my heart knocks harder.

"It was girl's pick at that party last summer. You could've asked any guy to go in the closet. So I've always wondered, why'd you pick me?"

His question possesses the kind of magic that bends space and time.

And suddenly, I'm back . . .

Back to that night in August, when summer blushed like my skin and the cicadas held a steady serenade. I was wearing a red sundress that tied at the shoulders. One my mother bought me, shoved deep in my closet and resurrected for a single night. Boys back home never looked at me. At least not the way these boys did, wearing this girlish dress that didn't hide how my body had changed. Didn't bury my femininity.

Cole approached me through a sea of faces that looked as fuzzy as I felt. His eyes were pale, like the barren blue of a late-October sky, and kind—unlike the suggestive stares of some of the others. He told me his name and asked mine. When I told him, he repeated it; the sound of my name became a song on his lips.

Of course I noticed he was gorgeous. Charming. But that wasn't what drew me to him. It was his eyes. Not the pretty color, but the surprising loneliness in them. This beautiful boy surrounded by so many people all vying for his attention. Yet somehow in his gaze, I saw the same loneliness I felt.

And in that moment, I saw a kindred spirit. Someone whose outsides didn't quite match their insides. Someone who understood.

"Your dress," Cole said simply. I looked down and saw one of the ties had come loose. Whether my doing or someone else's, I wasn't sure. "Can I?" Fix it. He wanted permission to fix it because I was too tipsy to realize how close I was to Mardi Gras flashing everyone at the party.

I nodded. And with bleary eyes watched as his nimble fingers made bunny ears, looped them around each other, then secured the tie. A perfect bow perched like a bird on my shoulder. After double-knotting it, he reinforced the other side and smiled. "All good, Honor Augustine," he said, letting the song of my name play once more.

And for the first time in more months than I could remember, it was. *All good.*

"Bunny ears," I mumble, still swept up in summer. The most dangerous season of the year.

"Bunny ears?" Cole repeats in confusion. "Are you saying I have big ears?" He self-consciously pulls down his hat to cover them.

"No! That's not what I . . ." But I can't explain. Because for whatever reason, explaining will make me feel more exposed than if the sundress had completely shed my body that night.

"You were . . . you were nice to me, okay?" I snap.

His brows ascend to the moon. "And that was a good thing? Because you make it sound like I'm guilty of crimes against humanity or something."

I do. I know I do. Once again, my words and tone are inept, provoking instead of comforting. If this were an exam I'd be failing. "I didn't mean—" But my reply is cut short by the odd sound echoing from the depths of the woods.

"Owwooo! Ow! Ow! Owwoooooo!"

Cole glances over his shoulder and sniffs. "Lacrosse team. I'd know those dogs anywhere."

The boys parading as wolves continue yipping and baying at the moon. One wolf howls louder and longer than the others—the alpha. Instinctively, I know it's Xander.

"I—I gotta go," I say, scrambling to my feet and flipping up my hood. A chill slices through me as the predators draw nearer. "When you see my brother tell him I was here, okay?"

"Wait, you're leaving?"

"Just promise you'll tell him," I repeat more forcefully.

"Yeah. Sure. But we were finally talking and—" Cole tries to get up from the log too quickly, and gravity drags him ruthlessly back to earth. *"Son of a—"* He struggles to sit back up.

"Honor," he says, slightly out of breath, "it doesn't have to be this way. Stay. Just for a little while. Please?" His eyes implore like his tone.

I hover at the edge of the woods where the trees stand shoulder to shoulder. There are more brambles this way. More prickers. More things that will want to pierce and claw at my skin.

Still. They're less fearsome than the wolves on the main trail. Namely, the alpha.

"I can't, Cole."

He still doesn't get it. How the whole situation would get spun if we were seen together again, alone in the dark. So I dive, fighting my way into the tangle of forest. Branches part with reluctance and scratch in protest.

Once I break through the worst of the thickets, darkness settles like a blanket over my shoulders. Cole calls for me again. But in my mind, his voice has grown as far away as last summer.

Then I turn on my flashlight and let the beam of light guide me home.

5

How did my life become irreversibly altered in the span of twelve hours? All because I turned right instead of left. Had I taken the trail that veered left, I would've gone straight home.

Which meant I wouldn't have discovered the catastrophic secret I now carry. In fact, I might never have discovered it.

Until it was too late.

It happened in the wake of last night's party that wasn't. After I wandered the woods like a reclusive sasquatch, texting Zee about the "epic time" I was having at the Hole. I'm not sure why I lied. I guess I felt ashamed, like I'd failed us both with my inability to raise even a modest amount of hell. Maybe Knox was right and I really was born eighty.

Anyway, a half hour into my forest meandering, my toes had gone numb and my shivers bordered on convulsions, so I decided to thaw at the greenhouse, since I couldn't go home. Showing up two and a half hours *before* curfew wasn't exactly going to sell Dad on this whole normal-teen facade.

Little did I know that trip would change everything. Because once you've pressed a button, you can't *un*press it.

I figured the blinking light on the office answering machine would be the mulch guy with a delivery date. It wasn't. Maybe I should've known better. Because does anything good ever come from a flashing red light?

So I played and replayed the message, my heart sinking lower with each repetition. Until eventually, my rib cage felt hollowed out and empty, and the message had imprinted on my brain in a way no button could erase.

Even now, slumped against the wall Sunday morning while Knox hogs all the hot water with his marathon shower, I can recall every word. Every breath. Every loaded pause . . .

"Good afternoon, Ms. Hannigan. This is Lydia Katchurski at Ravenswood Community Bank," the woman stated crisply. "This is my third attempt to reach you in regard to your delinquent business loan. Please contact me *immediately* to discuss arrangements on this account to avoid the legal action and penalties outlined in our previous notices." She rattled off her availability and phone number, ending with a curt goodbye.

And I sat there, shell-shocked and unblinking, struggling to comprehend just how dire our situation was. Sure, business had taken a hit with the big-box stores opening, but it couldn't be that bad, could it? Besides, Aunt Maeve hadn't given *any* indication we were in a financial suckhole. Why would she intentionally hide something so huge?

Maybe she was in denial. Or maybe she was keeping our money troubles under wraps for the same reason I was hiding out in the greenhouse—to protect Dad. To shelter him from the kind of stress that could trigger another episode. To make him believe everything was okay.

It wasn't until I tore apart the office that I found out what *legal action and penalties* truly meant. And it was worse than I could've imagined.

The bathroom door suddenly swings open, and Knox shuffles out, steam billowing in his trail. His hair drips like the showerhead, towel slung at his hips. He stops to sniff the air before staring at me as intensely as his bloodshot eyes allow. "I think you might be taking your tree hugging too literally, Hon."

My thoughts are still swarming with secrets and how I'm going to face Aunt Maeve and Dad, so his comment doesn't register. "Huh?"

He gestures to my head with a smirk. "Your hair."

"My hair?" I repeat in confusion and push from the wall. Anything that can garner the amused attention of a hungover Knox can't be good. I race into the foggy bathroom, rubbing the steam from the mirror. *"What the hell?!"* I squawk, inspecting the shiny-looking glob. It's super thick and tacky and— "Oh no, it's sap!"

"Explains why you smell like Christmas." My brother leans in the doorway while I assess the damage, his devilish grin widening by the second. "Buchannon said you showed at the Hole last night. Didn't believe him until now. Puffy red eyes, accidental sapping . . ." His face erupts in full glee. *"You* imbibed, didn't you?"

"No! It must've happened last night when I tripped in the woods."

"Classic," he chuckles. "Stumbling drunk in the dark—we really *are* related."

I pin back the nonsticky sections to see what I'm dealing

with. "Shit," I moan. "It's right at the front in the middle of my hair! How am I going to get this out before brunch?"

Knox bursts into laughter. "Sorry. I was just remembering the time Dylan Caldwell passed out after a night of partying and woke up with his gum in his pubes."

I shoot him a dirty look as he doubles over, clutching his stomach.

"Swear to God!" he cries, lifting a hand. "He had to use ice to get it out. Except, well, then he ended up freezing his nutsa—"

I kick the door shut and focus back on my fraught reflection.

"Hey! Dude, I just told you how to fix it," Knox calls from the other side.

When I don't respond he adds, "What, you're just gonna ignore your wizened elder?"

That is precisely what I intend to do. Also, everything about that statement is wrong.

My brother sniffs. "Fine, have it your way. Enjoy your bald spot!" he shouts into the keyhole.

But there won't be a bald spot, because I've already figured out how to fix my hair. It's everything else, the stuff that matters most, that I have no clue how to fix.

Because the legal action and penalties Ms. Katchurski threatened in that message all boil down to this bleak reality: we have until August to come up with $25,897 to pay off the delinquent loan or the bank will seize the greenhouse *and* the farmhouse.

Four months to come up with the cash or . . .

We lose everything.

Thirty-five minutes later, I descend the stairs and into the maelstrom of monthly brunch. Aunt Maeve cackles at something Knox has said as she pulls her famous egg casserole from the oven to check the temperature.

I watch them from the hallway. Every one of them hiding something in between their easy banter. Even Knox. True, his secret isn't money-related, but I know for a fact he said he was going to hang with Jason Stiles the other day and didn't. I know because Jason called our landline four hours into their "hang" when he couldn't reach him by cell.

So where was Knox all that time? Beats me. And frankly, I'm fine not knowing. My headspace is already at maximum capacity, standing room only.

Aunt Maeve takes several gulps of her special stress-busting tea. It makes sense why she's been downing the infusion like whiskey shots lately. Now that I've seen all those damning emails and hidden bank notices, it casts everything in a new light.

And that's the thing about revelations—nothing ever looks the same after them.

"Come on, Aunt Maeve," Dad goads over the hissing strips of meat on the griddle, "spill the tea. Did you go and get yourself a fella? Is that why you're all gussied up?"

"Oh, please," she replies, tightening the apron over her linen dress. "As if any man around here could keep up with me. They're either married or fuddy-duddies with no sense of adventure and a surplus of ear hair. No, I'm hosting book club later this afternoon. Which I've learned is actually just an excuse for a bunch of old ladies to get together and get snockered."

Dad and Knox laugh.

"I'm serious! They talk book for five minutes, then it's all gimlets and dirty martinis for the other two hours and fifty-five—" She cuts off when she sees me. "Hey! Morning, Pip," she says brightly.

"Ah, the creature lives!" my father declares, giving the bacon slices a flip. Geronimo licks his chops, willing gravity to deliver a morsel of meat his way. "Thought we were going to have to send up a search party for you. How's my social butterfly this morning?"

My brother snorts.

Before I can answer or respond to Aunt Maeve's cheerful greeting, Dad does a double take, pointing at me with the tongs. "Something's different about you."

"Um . . ." My eyes self-consciously jump to Knox. He smothers his smile and clears his throat, then resumes slicing the tops off the strawberries. "I wanted to try a new look," I fib.

"Bangs!" Aunt Maeve gestures to my forehead, her hand covered by the rooster oven mitt. "She got bangs!"

"Yeah," I mumble, beelining for the fridge to get juice. The bangs ended up shorter than expected, too. But really, that's the least of my concerns this morning. Hair grows. Money doesn't.

"Well," Aunt Maeve continues, pulling the foil from the casserole, "I think the bangs make your hazels absolutely pop. You look *très* sophisticated."

"*Très très* sophisticated," my brother obnoxiously parrots, setting the bowl of berries on the table with a smug expression. Then he hums "O Christmas Tree."

Shut up, I mouth to Knox, and grab a stack of plates from

the cupboard. The dishes rattle in my unsteady hands, but nobody seems to notice.

Dad's grouching over yet *another* burner that's gone out on the stove as Aunt Maeve commiserates over the poor manufacturing of appliances today. For the record, that stove is twice as old as me.

With breakfast ready, we gather at the oak table while Geronimo helicopters around it. Conversation swells, food is passed, and silverware scrapes over chipped heirloom porcelain.

But my stomach has gone sour with acid. I don't know how I'm going to make it through this breakfast, much less eat it. What should be an ordinary moment now feels like a brutal reminder of what's at stake.

"Something wrong with the bacon?" Dad asks, nodding toward the crispy strip inches from my mouth.

Not something, everything. *And the wrongness has nothing to do with bacon.* But I shake my head and take a bite. Because that's what we do.

We are a family of well-meaning pretenders.

So I play my part. Like always. Dutifully sitting in my place at the table. I force food into my mouth and down my throat while I pretend this is just another Sunday. Pretend I don't notice the tightness of Aunt Maeve's too-quick smile, or the worried set of my father's jaw when he thinks no one is looking. Pretend everything we hold dear isn't slipping away.

Dad cannot know about the bank loan. And Aunt Maeve's been taking steps to conceal the gravity of our financial situation, so I have every reason to believe she'll continue living on her island of denial. I could talk to Knox, but . . . well, his skill set doesn't really lend itself to a problem of this magnitude. Besides, he's far better at spending money than sourcing it.

Which leaves me. So I have to find a solution so my family doesn't end up homeless. Or worse.

And I have roughly 120 days to do it.

6

With a heavy sigh, I flop down on the bench outside the school's media center, where I stayed after to study with Zee. Nine days of brainstorming, and I *still* have no viable solution to show for it.

Usually, I'm great at solving puzzles. My mind latches onto them with the same ferocity as Geronimo's jaws on his rope toy. But never have I come up against a puzzle like this. One where the fate of my family's future hangs so precariously on my ability to solve it.

My ears perk at the sound of an aging muffler. Dad angles the work truck up to the curb. The brakes release a pitiful whine.

"Sorry I'm late," he calls over the *blub-blub-blub* of the exhaust. "Picked up another job at the Hollands'. They're looking to put on a new deck, so I stopped to give them an estimate."

I hop off the bench, hefting my messenger bag to my shoulder. "No worries. Zee and I just finished in the library." Tossing my bag to the floor, I slide into the cab, fragrant with sawdust and metal. *No worries,* I think. If worries were currency,

I'd be filthy rich and our money problems would be a distant memory.

"I recognize that kid from the paper. What's the Buchannon boy doing hovering?" Dad asks, motioning with his chin toward the bench I just left.

Sure enough, Cole hovers several feet away, a bulging equipment bag weighing down one shoulder. He quickly looks away and busies himself with his phone.

Was he there the whole time? My insides contort like a prize gymnast.

"I don't know," I reply, answering both our questions. "Practice must've gotten out. Waiting for a ride, I guess?"

Cole and I haven't spoken since that frigid night at the Hole. Unless I count my mumbled *thanks* and his equally mumbled *no problem* when he handed me a pencil that rolled off my desk.

Even Xander's returned to treating me with the kind of interest reserved for dentist office wallpaper. Status quo. Exactly what I want when everything outside of school feels anything but.

"Mm." Dad glances over to me before pulling away. "You be careful with that one, Hon."

"Meaning?" I nonchalantly check my side mirror. But Cole's already disappeared. Odd. I could've sworn I saw him appear then disappear near my locker last week, too.

"Meaning when it comes to jocks, playing isn't always just on the field," he replies, turning onto the main road.

My brows lift. "Wow, Dad. So now you're throwing stereotypical shade? Wait." I eye him with suspicion. "Didn't *you* play sports?"

"Yeah. That's how I know." He chuckles at my horrified expression. "Oh, settle down. I wasn't referring to myself."

"Can we be done with this conversation, please?" Under none scenarios do I want to think about my dad or any of his high school buddies hooking up with abandon. *None.* I fix my gaze back on the town as it slides by the passenger window. "Anyway," I add, "Cole and I aren't exactly friends, so it's kind of a nonissue."

Sure, I felt bad for Cole and the crappy, public way his ex ended things. And yeah, I believed his explanation that led to my mortifying misunderstanding, but those two things don't amount to full trust.

Besides, I have much bigger issues than Cole Buchannon. Like manifesting about $26,000 into existence.

"Is it safe to ask if you—Oh." Dad breaks off with an enormous yawn. "Did you have a good day at school?" I *thought* I heard him pacing sometime around three this morning. The visor of his Crawford Construction ball cap shades his eyes, but I'd wager there are dark circles beneath them.

"Uh-huh," I reply, studying him with a frown.

Sleeplessness is never a good sign. It hasn't even been two weeks since his last episode. Obviously there's a lot on his mind he's not sharing. This was always a sticking point with Mom, who'd complain that Dad was "about as transparent as a brick wall."

My mother's kinda right, though. Because Dad still hasn't said boo about the VA benefits he lost, which must be the reason for picking up these side jobs. And while I can't read my father's mind, I can put it at ease when it comes to me. So I go all out.

"It was actually a great day," I chirp more effusively. Then I throw in a bunch of details so he knows how wonderfully well-adjusted and happy I am. Little parental gems like how I aced my chemistry test, got excused from taking the final exam in government, and plan to go to the lacrosse game tomorrow with Zee.

I *almost* convince myself of my own normalcy.

Dad's mouth crooks into a fragile grin as he listens, the faint dimple appearing at his left cheek. When we reach the main intersection in town, he turns on the blinker in the opposite direction of home.

"Where are we going?" I ask.

"Northern Lights." The marijuana dispensary. "Should be quick. I know Aunt Maeve could probably use some extra hands at the greenhouse tonight to get ready for the weekend spring sale."

Ah yes. Now that I'm aware our business is in the financial gutter, I'm starting to see all the ways Aunt Maeve is scrambling to get us out of it. Including the decision to have a booth at the farmer's market this year. But I'm a realist. Seasonal sales and quaint markets aren't going to be enough.

We pull into a parking spot outside the unassuming building, which leans a little to the left like it's architecturally exhausted. The storefront window is decorated with a large seven-pronged leaf, with a stem curling into letters that read:

NORTHERN LIGHTS
Licensed Medical Marijuana Dispensary

Dad pauses, his hand at the ignition. "You all right?" His face has defaulted to its usual angles and hard planes.

"Yeah." But I can't produce a reassuring grin. That asks too much of my mouth. "Mother lode of homework," I fib, nudging my bag with my foot.

He nods. "I'll be back as quick as I can, okay? Their stock's been a little slim lately." Hopping from the cab, he takes a moment to brush the workday from his Carhartts before stepping into the dispensary.

As soon as I'm left alone in the truck, I wish I wasn't. Because all I can think about is our mountain of debt and whether Dad's worse off than he's letting on.

Desperate for distraction, I reach for my lit folder. At least *this* is something within my control. A sharp pain pierces my hip bone. *"Ow."* I wince, shifting to remove the object from my pocket.

The small granite stone—mottled with pinks, grays, and whites—rests in my palm. Its splotches of color look as chaotic as I feel, a perfect reflection of the messiness climbing the walls inside me. Which is why it'll have a home in my mason jar, rough and unpolished, the way nature made it.

But I've placed a promise on this rock. That somehow, I'll figure out a way to source the money we need. And until I do, I will carry the stone with me like the secret it holds.

Placing the rock on the dash, I force my attention back to the folder in my lap, flipping to Mr. Durand's latest assignment: select a favorite Frost quote and write a five-hundred-word essay explaining why.

I've already highlighted some strong contenders. But as the minutes tick by, thoughts of my father and our looming bankruptcy elbow the poetry from my head.

With a frustrated sigh, my eyes wander back to Dad as he talks to the budtender behind the counter. The guy's beard has taken over the lower half of his face, while his man bun reaches for the sky and—

Has NOTHING to do with my assignment!

I steel my gaze back to the notebook and one of the curated Frost quotes. It's the opening line of "Nothing Gold Can Stay." My handwriting has perfect posture, the letters all lined up like good little soldiers.

NATURE'S FIRST GREEN IS GOLD

I read the phrase aloud, feeling its weight and texture on my tongue. Hoping the sound will inspire something to shake loose and spill onto the page.

As I rapidly click and unclick my pen, I stare back to the window of Northern Lights, where the giant pot leaf halos my father's head. And something . . . strange starts to happen. My scalp prickles, the tingling sensation heightens with each repetition.

Nature's first green is gold.

Nature's first green is gold.

Nature's first green is gold.

I've read this quote a thousand times. Why does it feel like I'm reading it for the first? And why does it feel like I'm missing the most important message wrapped inside it?

Think, Honor. Think!

The words cram together with urgency as my subconscious taps a relentless Morse code my conscious mind struggles to decipher.

The stone on the dash, the quote, Dad beneath a leaf of green—my eyes move quickly between the trio of images. It's not a coincidence. There is meaning here. There has to be—

Then a flashbulb, luminous as the sun, goes off in my head. The blinding light blots out the world around me. Until there's nothing but the brightness of this idea. This potentially *life-saving* idea.

Sucking in a breath, I stare at the unassuming stone on the dashboard.

"Oh my God," I murmur.

Suddenly . . . I know how to save my family.

7

I'm carrying another secret. Even bigger than the one before it. So huge I'm afraid it will outgrow my body. Sprout legs so it can crawl from my mouth and into Zareen's ear as we sit, sardined on the bleachers at Tuesday's lacrosse game. A game that I could give precisely one point five shits about.

Because the seed of my spectacularly insane idea has already taken root in my brain. No matter how many times I tell myself it's . . .

Crazy.

Impossible.

Dangerous.

The idea continues to germinate. Not even the cold metal of the bleachers biting through my jeans can kill it.

Zee squints out at the field. "Uh, does this game strike you as being unnecessarily violent?" The question is barely out of her mouth when someone from the opposing team sweeps a stick under the legs of one of our players. He crashes hard to the ground.

Boos erupt around us.

"It's no badminton," I concede. My body tenses with every hit like I'm on the receiving end. I've now added lacrosse to the long list of sports I find physically painful to watch.

"Remind me again why we're here?" she asks. "*Please* tell me it's for extra credit."

"Because the Chiefs are undefeated?" I hedge.

My eyes glom on to number nine as he sprints across the field, muscles firing like pistons. I know nothing about lacrosse, but I know this player's movements are calculated and decisive. I know the opposing team fears him, hanging back when they should charge.

But most of all, I know number nine was born to win.

Because Cole Buchannon's father will accept nothing less.

His dad has been helicoptering his arms and screaming nonstop from the sidelines. I don't know how he hasn't blown a vocal cord or rotator cuff yet. Guess his career as a cop has made him accomplished in the art of yelling and arm flapping.

"Undefeated, huh?" Zee repeats skeptically, leaning her head close to mine. "Honor, you can't be serious. *Cole?!* You told me nothing happened at the Hole!"

"Shh! It *was* nothing!" I nudge her away, peering around us.

Her eyes glitter with interest. It's the same look she gets whenever she's rushing to solve a *Law & Order* case before they reveal the criminal. "'The lady doth protest too much, methinks.'"

"Quote *Hamlet* all you want, but us coming here has zero to do with Cole, and you know it." I steal some popcorn from the bag in her lap.

"Yeah, yeah," she replies in a bored tone. "Your dad's concerned about your lack of participation in school events and this is supposed to offer some kind of parental peace of mind. Snore dee dore."

"Most importantly," I add, "it keeps me from getting shipped back to Detroit."

"At least Detroit has diversity," Zee points out, her eyes scanning the overwhelmingly white crowd. "Living in Ravenswood is like going from a cultural melting pot to a cultural teaspoon."

"That must be so hard," I acknowledge. And while I do miss Detroit's diversity, I know I can never experience the impact of its void in the way my friend does.

She crams a handful of popcorn in her mouth, cheeks puffed like a chipmunk. "God, I'd give my right kidney for some authentic dhokla. But I think I also just *miss* the city, you know? The lights, the sounds, the . . . absence of manure in the air."

Like me, Zareen's a transplant to Ravenswood—via the DC area. It happened three years ago, when her dad's phone rang with a generous offer from the nearby Charlevoix Hospital. And the rest is history.

But *unlike* me, Zee deeply misses urban life. For me, living in the city always felt like wearing clothes that were four sizes too small. It made it hard to breathe. There was never enough air. Never enough sky. The people and buildings had gobbled them all up.

A horn sounds to end the quarter. The crowd explodes into a choreographed stomp. Shoes rhythmically pound the aluminum bleachers until my bones rattle with the vibrations.

Voices overlap as they chant, *"Chiefs! Chiefs! Chiefs!"* Between the chants I hear someone shout, *"Handker!"*

"Is that Knox adding the 'Handker' to the Chiefs?" she asks, brows arched.

"Probably. He was wearing about a dozen of them when we left the house." I wait for the noise to subside to a dull roar. "Hey, Zee."

"Yeah?"

My stomach hitches. "So, *hypothetically,* if your family was in trouble, how far would you go to help them?"

She gives me a puzzled look. "Why? Honor, is something going on with you? Or Knox? Oh no, did he finally carry out that moronic plan to fill the pool with inflated glow-in-the-dark condoms?" Zee glances around, panicky, like a glowing prophylactic might float by any second.

I shake my head, sensing the acute weight of the speckled stone in my pocket. "Not yet, no. Like I said, this is entirely hypothetical."

"Okaaayyy," she says, stretching the last syllable like bubble gum. "Ugh. Hold that thought." Taking out her cell, she reads the screen, then rapidly taps a response. "My omnipresent mother. Who now requires a blood oath that I'll remind Dad to pick up milk on the way home."

As Zee sorts out the Kapoors' dairy situation, my eyes nervously drift back to the field, where the teams huddle. Cole removes his helmet, his face an intense scowl. He drags his arm across his sweat-covered forehead. When he glances up to the stands he does a double take, tracking back to where I sit.

Our eyes meet.

It's not exactly a smile, but something soft touches his mouth. I should look away. *Why can't I look away? Jeez, what is wrong with me?*

"Get your head in the game, son! You will not lose to this second-rate team! Do you hear me? You will *not* lose!" Mr. Buchannon's voice booms from the front row. Cole's scowl immediately returns as he offers a stiff nod to his dad, pulling back on his helmet.

Zee pockets her phone, turning her attention back on me. "Crisis averted. Unless I forget the milk. Then I'll have to assume a new identity and live in the shadows. You were saying?"

I swallow. "Um, yeah. So if your family was genuinely in trouble, would you—I don't know—commit a misdemeanor? Or . . . wait. A felony. Would you commit a felony if your family's future depended on it?"

"Curious question from someone who claims they're not in trouble. Did you douse this popcorn with intrigue instead of butter?" She peers into the bag and shakes the contents.

"No." I scramble for something that will normalize our conversation. "It's . . . I'm working on this paper for AP Bio. About the, uh . . . psychology of social bonding."

Zee grins and rolls her eyes. "Why didn't you say so? *Sheesh.* Here I was thinking you were planning to *Ocean's Eleven* the Kewadin Casinos."

I chuckle. "Don't be ridiculous."

It's worse. I'm contemplating becoming a minor drug lord by growing and selling a giant bumper crop of weed.

Potato, potahto.

A whistle blows on the field. I flinch, cursing my jumpiness.

Zee's expression grows more serious. I squirm with guilt as she purses her lips. "All right," she finally says. "Then I have some questions."

Yeah, so do I. A metric ton of them that banged like pots

and pans around my head until the wee hours of the morning. I let out the captive breath in my lungs, grateful she's putting real thought into my proposed "hypothetical."

"Sure. Fire away," I reply.

The crowd goes ballistic, rocketing to their feet. In keeping with appearances (and to escape the wall of asses now inches from our faces) we stand and half-heartedly clap.

The Chiefs scored, surging ahead of the rival Hornets.

Zee shouts over the crescendo of cheers, "Okay, first question: Would it involve assault or murder?"

I pretend to mull this over between the whistles and claps. "No. Let's say it wouldn't involve physically harming anyone."

"But you're saying the future of my family depends on my committing this felony, right? So it's life or death?"

"Not exactly." I try to massage the scenario so it better fits mine. "But the impact on your family, on the life that you know, would be catastrophic. No Harvard," I say, delivering the metaphorically fatal blow.

"No Harvard?" Zee echoes, eyes wide. "But that's my biggest dream! Ever since I can remember, that's all I've wanted!"

It's true. She boasts more Harvard paraphernalia than most card-carrying students. Hats, mousepads, pennants—her bedroom is an homage to the institution.

I solemnly nod. "Your dreams, your family's dreams—*poof!* Gone."

We sit back down. Mainly because Zareen's gone weak in the knees. "Well, would I get caught? Become someone's prison bitch?" Anxiety bumps her voice an octave higher. "Honor, I'd make a *terrible* prison bitch. You know how much I hate people bossing me around."

Now it isn't just my knees—my entire skeletal system buckles under the implication of her question about getting caught. The very *realness* of it. My heart slams viciously at my rib cage. "That would depend"—I search her dark eyes—"entirely on you."

She stares down at her crimson Ivy League scarf, her fingers twisting the tassels together. The fabric twirls and joins until the individual threads are one. One small, fibrous family.

I'm not sure when I scooted to the edge of my seat, but there I hang. And it has nothing to do with the dwindling minutes of this tight game.

Zee lets go of her scarf, but the fringe stays bound together. "Then that's easy, Honor. I wouldn't get caught. Period."

I blink. Multiple times. "But . . . how can you be so sure? About not getting caught?"

Her fierce gaze turns on me. "Because I would have to be. For the sake of all our futures. I mean, half the time I want to put a muzzle on Aditi. And let's be honest, I've seen titanium softer and more bendable than my parents. But I would still do anything to protect them. So failure, getting caught"—she shrugs—"I would make it an impossibility. Or as close to impossible as any human can get. What about you? Would you commit a felony?"

A question I've obsessively pondered the last twenty-four hours.

Because I am the girl who's always taken refuge in rules. Coloring inside the lines. But for the sake of family, some lines must be crossed.

So would I commit a major felony? Would I risk jeopardizing

my own future in hopes of preserving my father's, Aunt Maeve's, and Knox's?

The answer crystallizes in a way that deep down I always knew to be the truth.

"Yes," I answer aloud. "Yes, I would."

8

Critical Mass. Blue Dream. Bubba Kush. Skywalker. Liberty Haze.

The list of names fills the screen. I scroll down.

Down.

Down.

Good God. I'm going to wind up with carpal tunnel at this rate. The list just . . . doesn't end. So. Many. Names. So many names, and all of them shouting the same thing.

MARIJUANA.

Of every imaginable name and strain.

I have lost my ever-loving mind.

My eyes sweep over the Ravenswood public library—the school's library being too conspicuous and high-risk. At least here the likelihood of running into classmates is low. And so far, the place is about as empty as you'd expect on a Wednesday afternoon. Especially with the senior center's book club ending after a very heated debate over whether George Washington's dentures were made of horse teeth. (They were. Among other animals and metal alloys. *Gross.*)

So I should feel at ease with the relative emptiness here. Instead, it feels like my research is broadcasted like a flashing pot leaf above my head. As I peer over the top of the monitor, my leg anxiously bobs.

Laura Salzburg—the head librarian, according to the nameplate—sits at the circular information desk in the center of the room. Shelves jut out around her like spokes on a literary wheel. Her head tips down in concentration as she writes, a tiny cross slipping out from her pretty wrap dress, which is the color of marigolds. The cross dangles above her words.

Blessing them.

Damning me.

Mrs. Salzburg's writing hand suddenly goes still. I notice her free hand, wrapped in a beige bandage, slide slowly from the desk and into her lap before her wary eyes lift to mine. And I swear she can read every thought in my head like the books that surround her.

My lips twitch and arrange themselves into a panicked smile. But my nerves make the smile too big and wide for the occasion. For any occasion, really.

"Research for a biology assignment," I call across the room, pointing my pencil to the monitor only my eyes can see. "Photosynthesis! Wow, I mean, there is nothing those chloroplasts can't do."

Dear Lord. I'm singing the gospel of *chloroplasts* now? I slouch lower in my seat. She knows. Knows the illegal, desperate deed I'm plotting. She's going to call me out. I feel it coming the way Aunt Maeve senses impending rain in her arthritic knee.

Then the librarian's ruby lips stretch into a sweet smile. Not maniacal like mine. And it reminds me so much of Mom's—radiant, dipped with the sparkle of a thousand stars.

The exact smile Mom wore to soften the blow before delivering bad news. "Sweetheart"—dazzling smile—"I realize this may come as a shock, but your father and I are separating." And before she reached the end of that sentence, her smile blinked out. Left me in total darkness. "We both love you more than anything, but this is for the best."

For who? That's what I wanted to scream in my mother's face but didn't. Because I already knew the answer. So I stoically nodded, sat like a lump of granite as she hugged me, and then searched our tiny yard for a stone as black and jagged as my feelings. And in the mason jar it went. That's why well-meaning smiles are wasted on me. Rather than being a source of reassurance, my muscles instantly tie into sailor's knots.

The librarian's smile ominously hangs there as the wall clock announces the passing seconds. *Tick. Tick. Tick.* Just as I prepare to throw myself at her feet and confess everything, Mrs. Salzburg replies, "Well, it's nice to see someone so enthusiastic about research. Let me know if you need help finding anything, okay?"

Yeah. Imagine how well *that* would go. *Hey, Mrs. Salzburg, can you please point me in the direction of the criming books?*

"I will. Thanks," I say, going limp with relief and hunkering deeper in my corner cubicle. "Get a grip," I mutter to myself. Forty-five minutes into my criminal foray, and I'm already folding like a damn lawn chair. Doesn't inspire a whole lot of confidence.

Closing my eyes, I try to channel Zee's immovable resolve and how she'd make getting caught an impossibility. But where do I start when this entire venture feels impossible?

I click off the site featuring endless strains of cannabis and narrow my search on the basics of growing: Temperature. Photoperiod. Humidity.

Now *this,* I get. A hum of excitement buzzes through me. Because peel back the illegality, and we're talking basic foundations of horticulture here. I can do that!

My mind begins whirring with the wheres and hows of implementation. Augustine Greens being the most obvious choice for a grow room. Except, how am I going to hide $26,000 worth of plants? And all the equipment required for growing?

There *is* the greenhouse basement. I've never actually gone down there, since according to Aunt Maeve, it's unusable space. Apparently the spring thaw invites all kinds of leaks and water damage, making it unfit even for storage. But it's space. Forgotten and potentially *large* space. And we're well past the spring thaw . . .

I make a note to recon the basement the next time nobody's around.

But my premature enthusiasm starts to fizzle out as I take in my expanding list of questions. In particular, the ones related to constructing a grow room and the electrical requirements necessary to run it—the area I feel the least qualified to tackle. And it's not like I have time to master these topics. Not when I'm looking at a full nine or ten weeks to go from flowering time to harvest, landing me dangerously close to the bank deadline.

There's no way around it: I need an expert to fast-track this.

An expert who can offer guidance in grow-room setup. Who's willing to share what they know . . . with a sixteen-year-old. A minor. I tap the mechanical pencil against my lips. That's a tall order.

My fingers fly over the keys as I try a new direction with my search.

medical marijuana dispensaries Ravenswood, MI

The screen blips, and a list magically appears—it's short. So short that Northern Lights is the only dispensary on it. Even if I came up with a killer cover story, stepping into a place where Dad's a regular customer is begging to be caught. Or at the very least, would invite a deluge of unanswerable questions.

New approach. *Someone at school?* Names and faces flip through my mind like the rapid shuffle of a card deck. I pause on one name in particular. A name only whispered in hallways, beneath bleachers, and in bathrooms. Interesting. Maybe I could try—

"Penny for your thoughts," comes a voice at my ear.

"Xander!" I yelp, too loud for the quiet space. But Mrs. Salzburg appears to have abandoned her post to shelve some books. "What are you doing here?"

Then I remember the incriminating monitor. I flick off the screen faster than you can say *cannabis indica*.

He chuckles, pulling out the chair from the cubicle next to mine, flipping it around to straddle it. His muscular arms drape along the seat back. "Came to pick up my mom, but she's not ready yet. Thought we could pass the time together."

How did I miss that his *mom* works here? They share the same last name, so it doesn't exactly require Sherlockian skills in a town this size.

I lean over to gather the notebook that had gone flying. "You thought wrong."

"*Ouch*. Well, that was stone-cold." He tilts his head to the side, studying me with detached interest. Like I'm a creature to be dissected and placed in a jar of formaldehyde.

How anyone at school finds him appealing is a mystery to me. Maybe (and it's a *big* maybe) in an alternate universe I might find Xander attractive. That is, if he grew a heart, hermetically sealed his mouth, and decreased his hair gel usage by a factor of ten. But even then I'd probably prefer the company of poison oak.

"Leave me alone. I'm studying." I flip open to my chemistry notes, hoping he doesn't notice the slight tremor in my hands.

"Heard you were at the Hole the other weekend." He tips forward on the legs of his chair, moving closer. "Cole had a lot of questions about you and me."

My murderous gaze snaps to his. "There *is* no you and me."

"But there could be." His lecherous smile makes me want to vacate my own skin.

He's baiting me. I see it in his dead blue eyes. Wants me to speak so he can twist my words, shape them into weapons of torture. I bite my tongue, forcing my attention back on my notes.

"Can I tell you a secret?" Xander tips close enough for me to feel his hot breath. "I kinda have a thing for you," he whispers.

Anger-fueled heat surges to my face.

He chuckles softly. "Aww. You're blushing. C'mon, you had to know, Honor. Why else would I tease you the way I do?"

Because you're a damn sociopath. My pulse quickens. The edge of my paper curls with the perspiration from my palm. I search for Xander's mom, spotting the top of her head deep in the shelves of the Renaissance section.

"It's *because* I like you," he continues. The legs of his chair thump back to the carpet. "But I had a feeling you might not believe me. So then I thought, what could I do to prove I'm really into you? And you know what I came up with?"

My heart hammers out an SOS distress signal in the seconds it takes for Xander to answer his own question.

"*Sebastian's.*"

The single word shatters my will to keep quiet. "*Sebastian's?!* You can't be . . ."

No. All of this, this whole setup, has to be another sick joke. And I have no interest in being the sexual punch line. Because not only is the high-end restaurant known for being the most romantic (with some guys crudely calling it the Panty Melter), but it also has a secluded lookout, synonymous with the back seat romps that often follow.

Xander capitalizes on my mute horror. "Look, I feel like we got off on the wrong foot when you started here, but I—"

"No! God, why on earth would I go *anywhere* with you? Least of all *Sebastian's?*" My voice ratchets higher. "You trashed my reputation. You go out of your way to humiliate me every chance you get!"

He holds his hands up in a placating way. "Hey, don't get all hysterical and blow things out of proportion, okay? Sure. I made a few harmless jokes, but that doesn't mean *I'm* the one responsible for trashing you at school. I mean, why would I do that?"

The million-dollar question. But simply because his motives are unclear doesn't make him innocent.

Xander nudges me with his elbow. "Come on, let's leave all that in the past. Sebastian's can be our clean slate. And whatever happens after dinner"—the disgusting grin returns—"will be up to us. What do you say?"

Rage pulses hot and molten through my veins. And even if his offer *had* been well-intentioned, how could he so flippantly dismiss the damage he's already done?

The entire first week of school I ate in the girls' restroom, the bread of my peanut butter and jelly sandwich soaked with my tears. Surrounded by nothing but the metal walls of the bathroom stall, still bearing the faint, ghostly image of my name and the names they called me. It couldn't be scrubbed clean.

Now the painful memory of those early weeks levels me. The harassment. The whispers. The laughter. My sandwich tears return.

"Fuck you, Xander," I whisper.

He rears back, revealing the most genuine emotion he's shown since sitting down.

Shock.

"*What?* What the hell kind of response is that? Christ, you're a real head case, you know that? Just like your demented dad. I heard he has to hide in the basement every Fourth of July because he's too mental to know the difference between a firecracker and a goddamn grenade."

My anger boils over. "How *dare* you talk about my dad, you lowlife piece of—"

But Xander ignores me, my rebuke falling like empty shell casings to the floor. "Do you know how many girls would've creamed themselves at my offer? Fuck me," he disgustedly echoes, standing and shoving the chair so it bangs against the desk. "You think you're so much better than everyone, don't you? I knew it from the second I saw you. But the truth is, you're pathetic."

I lift my chin high. Feel the quiver of my nostrils as I strain to keep from falling apart again. Not in front of him. I can't let him see how deep his cuts go.

He bends so his face is inches from mine. "Cole might not see you for what you are, but by the time I'm finished, he'll realize what I already know." His cruel eyes drop to my lips and back up to my watery gaze. "That mouth of yours is only good for one thing."

And I see *red*. The impulse so sudden, so quick, it overrides all rational thought.

But Xander's quick, too. He catches my wrist before my palm collides with the side of his face. "You're gonna regret that, too. I promise."

I wrench my arm away from his strangled grip and massage my wrist.

"See you at school, Hummer," he sneers, and walks away.

9

I must've checked the note slipped inside my locker Monday a dozen times. This is where I'm supposed to be. *This is progress.* So why does progress feel so vomit-inducing?

Jess Rennert shoves an open bag in front of my face. "Frito?" The scent of stale feet assaults my nose. A hundred times more offensive than the intense, herbaceous smell baked into her car's upholstery.

And if anyone told me a week ago I'd be sitting in the vehicle of one of the most notorious drug dealers at Ravenswood High, much less having her offer me smelly-foot corn chips, I would've laughed my ass off.

But here I sit in the passenger seat, ass notably intact.

"Uh, no thanks." I gently nudge the bag away, glancing for the fiftieth time out the cracked windshield of her battered GMC Jimmy. So much for the myth that drug dealers have flashy cars.

"More for me," Jess says with a shrug, plunging her hand back into the bag. "What was your name again?" Her heavily lined eyes go squinty because she's stoned out of her gourd.

"Discretion is sort of the objective here, isn't it?" The steadiness of my voice is one part lie, three parts miracle. I quickly fold my arms so she doesn't see the way my hands shake.

Jess snorts, brushing the yellow crumbs from her hand onto her plaid pleated skirt. Any schoolgirl innocence is obliterated by her combat boots. And the fact that her tights look chewed rather than cleaned by a washing machine.

"Tough talk for a girl wearing a Science Olympiad Championship T-shirt. But have it your way. Discretion's my middle name."

"Cool," I reply. Another lie. Cool is out of reach for me on a good day.

A freshman stumbles by, lugging an instrument case larger than he is. I slouch lower in my seat. Luckily most of the student lot has cleared out since today was early release. Well, it's probably less about luck and more of a tactical move on her part. I imagine in Jess's line of work, the fewer witnesses the better.

"So," she says, pushing the red bangs from her forehead. The piercing in her eyebrow looks angry with infection. "What's your endgame? Looking to score uppers? Downers?" She taps a cigarette out from the pack, sandwiching it between her dark purple lips. "Cerebrals usually want uppers—gives 'em more study power. Stamina. Better focus and shit."

"No. I mean, neither. I'm actually . . . I'm looking for information." It takes everything to resist the urge to grab one of the fast-food paper bags near my feet and breathe into it.

She smiles, revealing bits of corn chips stuck in her teeth. "Well, Jane Doe, that's gonna cost you, too. Depending." She lights her cigarette and takes a long drag.

"On?"

"*On* what you want to know. Let's start there, then I'll put a price tag on it."

"But"—I frown—"I'm just asking for information, not . . . *product*. It doesn't cost you anything."

Snorting like I've said something hilarious, she asks, "You had econ yet?"

I shake my head, thrown by the jump in conversational track. "Next year."

Jess slumps back in her seat with a blissful grin, rolling the cigarette between her fingers. "Well, Mr. Lander's a perv, so don't sit in the front row. Always 'accidentally' knocking stuff off his desk. Gives him an excuse to sneak a peek up the skirts."

"Um, okay. Thanks for the tip."

"Okay." She nods, blowing a hazy stream from the side of her mouth. "So now I'm gonna educate you on one of the fundamental concepts of economics." Her head lolls in my direction. "Supply"—she jabs her thumb to her chest—"and demand." Her index finger then points to me, forming a gun. She pulls the pretend trigger. "The way I see it, you want something I have. Doesn't matter if it's blow or info." Jess smirks. "Listen to me, I'm like goddamn Thoreau. Minus the dick and beard, obviously."

Her smirk disappears as she ashes in a Styrofoam cup. "And for the record, this *is* costing me. It's costing me time." The dealer casts her narrow eyes back on me. "So either tell me what you're looking for, or get the fuck out of my car."

Gulping down my fear, I keep my gaze level, staring back at her. I remind myself why I'm doing this. *Who* I'm doing this for. It gives me the adrenaline boost I need to push out the words.

"I'm looking for a grower. Marijuana. Someone who will talk to me about"—I falter, wishing I'd rehearsed this better— "about the logistics of growing."

Then Jess starts . . . *laughing.* Cackling, more like. Mouth open like she has a flip-top head; her laughter threatens to blow a hole in the roof. She flicks her cigarette out the crack of the window.

My hands curl into fists. "What's so funny?"

"God," she crows. "Where do I start?" Wiping the smeared mascara from under her eyes, she catches her breath. "Listen, you seem like a good girl. Why don't you go back to your beakers and Bunsen burners, all right? You're way out of your league here, and I have *real* customers waiting." She goes to turn the engine.

"No!" I grab the arm of her leather jacket. "No, Jess," I repeat again, less wildly. "You don't understand. I—I can't leave without a contact. And I know it's not much, but I have forty bucks on me." I quickly dig the crumpled twenties from my pocket and hold them up. "Just give me a name. One name. *Please.*"

Her eyes dart to the hand still gripping her like a flotation device in my sea of panic. "You have three seconds to let go of me or I'll break every one of those fucking fingers, Honor Augustine."

I let go like she's poison. "You know my name." All along she knew who I was but pretended otherwise. Terror squeezes my lungs. But somehow I stay in my seat, hold my ground.

Her glassy eyes spark with interest. "I'm not an idiot. But you are for underestimating me. I have people." She nods to the large, two-story brick building. "Eyes and ears who told me all about you."

I bite my lip. I want to ask what those "people" said, but it doesn't matter. What's more relevant is that she's right. I made assumptions about her. Foolish ones. And if I'm going to pull this off without landing in prison or getting myself killed, I can't afford rookie mistakes like this in the future.

Underestimate no one. I ink the sentiment across my frontal lobe.

Jess continues sizing me up. "So you're serious. Question is, why? What's a girl with a 4.2 GPA and a bright, shiny future want with growing dope? You know you could go to juvie for that, right? Kiss those scholarships buh-bye."

I sit up a little taller, making myself as big as possible. "You ask a lot of questions for someone with Discretion for a middle name."

She scowls, but underneath it, an ember of respect glows. "Look, this isn't a game. Good girls don't stay good in this business. They go bad or end up dead. Sometimes both."

"I never said I was good."

Her lip curls. "You didn't have to."

Jess silently eyes me through the veil of smoke between us. Coming to a decision, she leans across the console, snatching the money from my hand before tearing off a piece of a McDonald's bag. She scribbles, hostilely, the black bleeding through the other side of the paper, then thrusts the paper over to me. "Go there Sunday. Three o'clock sharp. Ask for Laks."

"Sunday. Three o'clock sharp. Ask for Laks," I repeat, pronouncing the name like *hacks* with an *L*, exactly as she did. "Thank you," I breathe, clutching the paper.

She squints back out the broken windshield. "Just don't end up with your name on a fucking headstone, yeah?"

I nod.

"Christ." Her head sways. "You have no idea, do you?"

"No idea about what?"

"About how this would've ended a million other ways if you'd gotten into any other dealer's car. You dodged a bullet today, Honor Augustine, and you don't even realize it."

I swallow. Hard.

She cranks the ignition, and the engine roars to life. "Now get out. And don't ask for my help again."

Wasting no time, I shove open the door and hop to the ground. The Jimmy's muffler sputters and coughs as she speeds away. I stay upright until her taillights disappear.

Then my whole body trembles as I pitch forward, bracing my hands to my knees. That just happened.

And the proof, oil-dotted and crinkled, is in my hand.

Somehow I make it to the end of the week without having a complete breakdown. It's Friday, but the imminence of Sunday's task haunts me like a chain-rattling ghost. It consumes my every waking moment, even managing to crowd out worries over Xander's retaliation and promised smear campaign. Which hasn't happened. Yet. Though nothing stretches time at school like waiting for something unidentifiably awful to happen.

But the reality is this: whatever Xander has in store for me will still pale in comparison to the significance of Sunday.

Because I, Honor Elizabeth Augustine, will be engaging in something 100 percent illegal and punishable by law.

Colluding with a grower.

Shit, as they say, is getting very, very real.

I glance up to the churning clouds, wishing I'd grabbed a jacket. My thin long-sleeve tee isn't cutting it in these early days of May.

But Knox should've waited. I was only seven minutes late.

And Zareen can't wait. Not with her mom impatiently honking the horn like she's getting paid per toot.

Zee rolls her eyes at me. "Four months, fifteen days, and eleven hours until I get my license—not that I'm counting." She turns toward her mom and holds up a pleading index finger before returning to me. "Sorry we can't give you a ride, Honor. We have to get home for Aditi's piano lessons."

I hug my arms. "Oh? I thought those were Wednesday."

"Wednesday *and* Friday. Apparently she needs all the help she can get. For someone so desperate to break into the music biz, she's amazingly tone-deaf." Zee tucks her hands in the pockets of her yellow jacket. "Did you try Knox again?"

"I will," I assure her. "Worst case, I'll do homework till my dad gets out and can get me. You better go before Mama K reduces us to ash with her glare." I corral her toward the sleek Mercedes.

Zee's sister preens in the back seat before taking a duck-face selfie, her glossed lips pursed in an exaggerated pout. She pauses her photo shoot to throw me a dirty look. *Stare much?* she mouths from the other side of the glass.

Aditi was a lot nicer before puberty hijacked her personality. Zareen offers a morose wave as the car pulls away.

Ten minutes and two more unanswered text messages later,

I sling my messenger bag across my chest and set out on foot for downtown. Daily Grind is the nearest coffee shop, about a twenty-minute walk. Nothing fancy. Actually, the coffee rates about a step above the tar they patch the roads with, but it's better than risking a run-in with Xander.

My overworked muscles whimper from the hours I've secretly spent annihilating insects and scrubbing mildew from the ceiling, walls, and floor of the basement. But the nastiest part of the cleaning is done.

That was the one bright spot in the week: I now have my grow space.

It took some sleuthing to track down the access door hidden beneath a rubber floor mat. And judging by the rust on the hinges and the foul, dank-smelling air that burped up from the underbelly, it'd been a long time since anyone set foot down there.

My cell chirps. I expect it to be Knox, my texting thumbs poised to deliver my fury. I should be home, face planted in my pillow. Which is how I planned to spend the afternoon, since I wasn't on the schedule. But when I pull out my cell, it isn't my brother.

It's Mom.

Mom: You missed our call the other day.
Me: Sorry. Greenhouse was super busy.

One of the rules of moving here was weekly calls with Mom. Which basically consist of her offering a buffet of details about her new life, while I politely listen, then offer stale crumbs of mine.

Mom: Did you get the dress I sent?

Yes. And if I ever become the girl my mother thinks I am, I'll be incredibly outfitted. For now, the box remains stacked in the back of my closet, unopened like the others. I grudgingly tap out a cordial response.

Me: I did. Thank you

Mom: Promise you'll make time to chat this weekend. So much to tell you. Missing our girl time!

What Mom has never figured out is there was never "our" time. It was always "her" time. Superimposed on me. But I've never had the guts to tell her that. Too much fear wrapped up in the admission. Because . . . what if my mother only loves the idea of me and not the me that actually exists? I weigh the thought down with imaginary boulders, letting it sink to the tips of my toes.

Me: OK. Sounds good

I pull my gaze from my mother's string of X's and O's when a cold drop hits my scalp. Followed by a second and a third. The charcoal-colored clouds no longer churn; they roil with a vengeance.

Tucking away my cell with a curse, I take off in a run. The messenger bag punishes my hip, and muscles that previously whimpered now shriek like banshees.

The sporadic drops fall with more urgency until they turn into a downpour. As if giant, invisible hands wring the quilt of sky like sopping-wet laundry. My jeans and shirt cling, a frozen second skin against me.

And I'm not even halfway there. *God. Please don't let me catch pneumonia.*

I imagine Mom's smug expression after warning me for the better part of my childhood never to play in the rain. But puddles were my kid kryptonite, so the threat of hospitalization was hardly going to stop me.

A car approaches from behind. I move to the muddy shoulder and wait for it to pass. When it doesn't, I peer back at the vehicle. The dark gray sedan following me slows to a crawl. My uneasiness surges. Between the tinted windows, heavy rain, and frenetic flick of the wipers, it's impossible to see the driver. I pick up my pace, heart rate rushing like the rain.

The driver suddenly hits the gas, tearing by and dousing me with water and road grit.

"Hey!" I cough, wiping my face, anger replacing the angst of moments ago.

Excruciating minutes pass, and another vehicle approaches; its headlights glance off the wet pavement.

My stomach tightens as I veer closer to the guardrail. *Please tell me this asshole didn't come back!* The car slows. Except this time when I glance over my shoulder, it's into the bug-eyed headlights of a Jeep.

But with my head turned, I don't see the upcoming dip in the ground. My ankle rolls, causing me to lose balance and stumble sideways. Had this happened three feet earlier, the guardrail would've stopped me. But instead, I slip through the small gap between the sections of railing.

Screaming, I tumble down the embankment, hurtling toward the reedy wetlands below. My view toggles between grass and sky with every bounce, until I can no longer tell up from down.

Then I land. Hard. My back hits the ground with a slurping *splat* among the tall cattails, algae, and muck.

"Honor! Oh God, are you all right?" the Good Samaritan shouts.

I *know* that voice. Because it belongs to Cole Buchannon.

Aces.

10

Dazed, I pray I'm wrong and that it's some other guy standing up there on the side of the road. But the second I lift my head, those hopes are squashed.

"Shit," I mutter, trying to figure out if I injured much beyond my dignity. My messenger bag is missing. I spot it lying—strap broken—partway down the hill and breathe a sigh of relief.

Cole cups his hands to the sides of his mouth, yelling, "Don't move, I'm coming down!" He hops the guardrail with the grace of a gymnast and rushes down the embankment.

"Cole, be careful! The grass is really slip—" But before the warning's left my lips, he begins to slip. And slide. He's gained too much speed to stop, and spills forward, rolling, then bouncing the rest of the way down the hill.

"Mother—sonofa—shhh!"

He crash-lands a few feet away, among the dense cattails, with a profanity-filled splash.

Struggling against the slimy muck, I sit upright. "Cole!" I shout. "Cole, are you okay?"

He groans as he pushes himself up from the marshes. When his face appears between the cattails and reeds, it's smeared with mud. A leaf clings to the bottom of his chin like an arboreal goatee. After some labored breaths he replies, "Never better. You?"

"You look like"—my mouth twitches—"a poop emoji without the smile."

"Yeah?" he deadpans, flicking his dark hair from his eyes. "But like, in a hot way, right?"

When I try to rein in my giggle it comes out a snort, causing him to crack. Which is all it takes for our smiles to dissolve into dueling laughter. Laughter that quickly escalates into hysterics as the merciless rain beats down.

Cole tries to say something, but all he gets out is: *"Frogs!"* Which only makes me howl louder when I notice the amphibians hopping around us like they're in on the joke.

I laugh so hard I cry. I laugh so hard I think I might rupture an organ. I laugh so hard . . . I forget what it's like to feel anything else but this, this joyous, sidesplitting delirium.

Cole lumbers to his feet, intermittently laughing as he staggers over to where I sit, mired in muck. "Come on, swamp girl. Let's get you out of here." He holds out his hand.

"My hero," I reply, with a generous dose of sarcasm, sliding my hand into his muddy grip as he hoists me to my feet. We stand toe to toe, chests heaving like we've sprinted for miles. His T-shirt is suctioned to his skin like mine, our jeans more brown than blue.

His smile wanes as his stare intensifies. "Honor?" Water drips from his spiked lashes.

"What?" My heart pounds like the rain. I grip the sides of

my arms, chilled to the bone, and painfully aware I look like something caught in a drainpipe. But he looks caught in the same pipe, so it isn't like he's fared any better.

"There's something . . ." He licks the rain from his lips as he reaches out. The backs of his trembling fingers graze my skin as he lifts up the hair plastered to my neck.

And I no longer notice the cold. My breath suspends for what feels like an eternity. I don't know what's happening, or if I even want whatever it is to happen. But clearly some part of me must because I'm leaning into him.

Suddenly, Cole's eyes widen as his face contorts in . . . horror?

Then he shouts, *"LEECHES!"*

And. I. SCREAM. More accurately, we *both* scream while scrambling all the way up the slick embankment. He grabs the busted strap of my bag as he runs past it.

We near the idling Jeep. "Hey! There's one on the back of your arm!" I holler. Panicked, he starts slapping at his skin. "No, don't pull it off like that! It'll vomit bad bacteria back into your skin!"

He freezes. The parts of Cole's skin that aren't muddy turn white enough to see through.

"It's okay!" I quickly add, "I know how to get them off."

"Salt?" he asks, looking faint. "Fire?"

"It's not an exorcism." I spare him the explanation. "Do you live nearby?" I'm not exactly sure where he lives, but it's got to be closer than my house. Virtually everyone is.

"I can get us there in five minutes," he replies, yanking the passenger door open. Seconds later he tosses me a scratchy blanket he's retrieved from the back.

I swaddle the wool around me and get inside, teeth chattering together like a wind-up toy. "D-didn't realize your house was s-s-so close."

"It isn't." Cole hops in; the plastic bag that he's thrown over his seat crinkles beneath him. "I just said I can get us there in five."

Revving the engine, he jams the gearshift and we lurch forward, tires squealing as we barrel down the road.

"I think I'm going to puke." Cole braces his palms against the marbled bathroom countertop, back muscles straining beneath his skin.

I gulp, placing a hand to his warm body. He winces, not that I blame him. My hypothermic hands have been slow to thaw despite the heat blasting from the floor register. "Try to focus on something else," I say.

"You mean other than the creatures siphoning the life out of me? That should be easy."

Standing on my tiptoes, I angle the butter knife flush with his skin. Then quickly slide under the narrowest end of the bloodsucker—the mouth. And in one swift motion, I flick off the entire body so it can't reattach.

The plump leech smacks onto the floor tile beside the other one I removed. "Oh man." He gags, his head hanging forward in the sink. Grabbing the whisk broom, I quickly sweep up the disgusting parasites and flush them away.

"How are you so cool with this?" he asks.

I'm not cool with any of this. Not with the leeches. Not

with being cramped inside this tiny, nautical-themed bath-room downstairs to avoid tracking mud all over his house. And certainly not with Cole's half-nakedness or how it makes my mouth drier than the 1930s dust bowl.

"Hand me the antiseptic, would you?" I take it, dabbing the spot with gauze. "Who said I'm cool with this? There are quite literally a million other things I'd rather be doing." I fin-ish cleaning the area. "Okay, put some pressure on that. Some-times it can take a little longer to stop bleeding because of the anticoagulants in the leech—"

"Gah, okay!" Cole cuts me off, clapping a hand over the square of gauze I've placed on the back of his arm. "Please. Talk about anything else. Just . . . nothing that involves bloodsuckers or anticoagu-whatevers." He sways and grips the towel rack.

Leaning to the side, I check his ashen reflection in the mir-ror. We're still filthy as sin, but removing the leeches seemed more pressing than showers.

"You don't look so good. Do you want to sit down?" I ask him.

He quickly shakes his head. "How many more?" he asks with a voice as tight as his muscles.

While I was fortunate and only had the one on my neck, Cole landed in more standing water. Plus his short sleeves left more of him exposed. Surveying his body, I fight against my own sudden wooziness. "Um, just two left. We're almost done."

He exhales with a nod. "You're kind of badass, you know that?"

I stifle a laugh. No one in their right mind has ever called me that. *Cautious, wary, controlling*—absolutely, these are all adjectives that have defined me. But *badass*? *Never.*

"The only reason I have experience is because Knox got a

bunch of them after swimming in a gravel pit. Dad wasn't home at the time, and when Mom saw she turned about as white as your walls."

"Great. So we have something in common," he jokes, cringing as another plops to the floor. "Probably good my parents are off at some police fundraising gig."

My movements falter at the reminder that his dad's a cop. I mean, it's not that I forgot. It's more like the information got filed way back in my brain, behind the image of the blood-suckers sucking.

"I doubt my neat-freak mom would be down with this scene, either," Cole adds as I dispose of the last leech.

What little of the house I saw in our furious dash downstairs was like a page out of a Pottery Barn catalog—subtle hues, antiqued bronze, and lots of new things manufactured to look old. It's the sort of cultivated coziness that's supposed to be inviting but just winds up making you afraid to touch anything.

I continue working to clean the area as efficiently as possible. "I'm sure you've seen way worse on the lacrosse field. From what I saw, looks like it can be a pretty brutal sport."

"Marcus got a compound fracture last year and I didn't find it *half* as disgusting as this."

My hands go still. "I'm sorry, Cole."

"Oh, Marcus is fine. It was over a year ago, so—"

"No. I mean *this*." I gesture to his patchwork of gauze. "And this whole messed-up situation."

He peers over his bare shoulder. "Why? You have nothing to be sorry for. If anyone should be apologizing, it's me."

"Come on," I say in disbelief. "You wouldn't be covered in leeches if you hadn't stopped to help."

"Yeah, and you wouldn't have taken all that shit at the beginning of school if we hadn't gone into that closet."

The comment catches me off guard, and I drop the surgical tape. It's nothing I haven't thought countless times. I'm just surprised to hear him say it. "Maybe," I reply slowly, bending to retrieve the roll. "And maybe someone would've found another reason."

He gives his head a brief shake before fixing his gaze back on the dish of decorative soaps shaped like seashells and clams. "Honor, it wasn't right what happened. Somehow I thought telling everyone the truth would set the record straight, you know?"

And that's the difference between us—I was jaded enough to know it wouldn't. A concept he still seems to be trying to reconcile almost a year later.

"People believe what they want to see, Cole. It has nothing to do with the truth." I finish attaching the last bandage and step back as he turns around.

Cole lifts his eyes to mine. "I'm sorry. I'm sorry all this happened because of a kiss."

It was a lot of kissing, but he's right. That was as far as it went, contrary to popular rumor. My mouth twists into a rueful grin. "Yeah. And then I threw up on your shoes."

There are gaps in my memory of the night, but that part I recall. Along with how my hair had gotten tangled and caught around the top button of his pants during the process of my beer's mass exodus. Then seconds before I was freed, the door burst open. And everyone at the party made assumptions about why I was on my knees. About why his hand was on my head.

And that was it. The defining moment that would be my beginning and end.

Cole sniffs. "Well, that was pretty memorable, too. Although I'd like to think one didn't lead to the other."

Warmth floods my cheeks. I avert my eyes to the starfish on the shower curtain. "Did you know when a starfish eats, its stomach extends from its mouth and then retracts once it's done eating?"

"I talked to Xander," he blurts in unison with my weirdo starfish trivia.

My lips part. *So he* did *talk to Xander.* Here I dismissed Xander's comment as BS, like everything else that comes out of his mouth.

A tornado of questions rips through my mind, so many it's hard to catch hold of a single one. "When?"

"After I saw you at the lacrosse game last week."

The day before he cornered me in the library. I gnaw my lower lip. Sure, it could've been a coincidence that Xander found me there, but the timing doesn't exactly feel coincidental.

"He denies it, Honor. That he had anything to do with the rumors from last fall, or any of it."

My spine stiffens. That's basically the same line Xander fed me. Right before he tipped his hand by propositioning me for sex under the thinly veiled guise of a date.

I fold my arms. "And you believe him because he's your best friend and you have history."

Cole leans back against the counter, the crease between his brows deepening. "I know what you're thinking, and it's not like that. Our 'history' isn't all campfires and dirt-bike races. Xander, he's . . . had it rough," he finishes quietly, redirecting his gaze to the floor. "Some things are bigger than friendship."

It would be smarter to let Cole take the easy way out. Let him be Switzerland. But I don't do the smart thing. Instead, I push. "So you believe him," I repeat, squeezing my arms. *Say the words, Cole. Just say them. Then I can be done with you. Erase you from my life, my thoughts, my—*

"I . . . no. I don't know." His shoulders sag. "I just don't get why he would. It doesn't add up. He always swore your brother pinned the blame on the wrong person."

If he's looking for me to make this existential bro crisis easier on him, that's not happening. Not in a thousand lifetimes.

"You're mad," Cole observes, eyeing my rigid stance. "You want a black-and-white answer. And I'm sorry, but I can't give you one. Because it's not the kind of situation that's black-and-white."

God. How does he manage to invoke the one idiom that speaks loudest to my heart? The one I've been grappling with for weeks? Because there was a time I could categorize my life in absolutes. Black and white. Right or wrong.

But not anymore. My life has become convoluted shades of gray.

I scratch at the dried mud on my arm, bits of my initial anger crumbling away with the dirt. "So then"—I shrug in frustration—"what is it you want? Why are you telling me this?"

"Because. I want you to understand something." Cole pauses, itching at his own mud. "I'm all Xander has. And I know he's far from perfect, but I need to give him the benefit of the doubt. There's *good* in there, Honor. I've seen it."

But have you seen the bad? I grit my teeth to keep the

question from leaping out. Too tired to stand, I sink down to the edge of the tub, my fingers curling around the porcelain lip.

"Wait. Please just"—Cole crouches so we're level—"let me finish." He cracks his knuckles. "I asked around, thinking maybe I could get some answers and get to the bottom of who did what."

"And?"

"Nothing," he replies with another joint pop. "But I made it clear that *nobody* messes with you in the future. And that includes Xander." His eyes hold the same ferocity as his tone.

I find my breath and tuck a crusted clump of hair behind my ear. "You said that?"

His brows pull together like I've asked an absurd question. "Yeah. Of course."

My eyes return to the starfish as my mind races with the implications. So Cole drew a line in the sand, and the very next day, Xander stepped over it. Except, telling Cole that would put me even more squarely in the crosshairs of Xander's wrath. Which seems dangerous given I still don't know what he's capable of.

No. For now the best strategy is to keep my mouth shut and focus on what matters most. *Stay the course,* Dad would say. And also pray Xander abandons this warped mission to expose a false truth about me.

Cole clears his throat, anchoring me back in the bathroom. "Anyway," he says as he stands, "if you do run into any trouble, you'll tell me, right?"

If there's one thing I can't stand, it's liars. That's what Cole told me moments after seeing his girlfriend cheating on him.

"Oh, no need." I force my frozen lips into a grin. "I avoid trouble like the plague."

"Right," he says doubtfully. "So then today was—"

"Gravity," I interject. "I can't avoid gravity, Cole."

He chuckles, glancing down at his dirty jeans. "Guess that makes two of us. Hang tight, okay? I'll grab you a change of clothes." When Cole returns, he hands me a pair of yoga pants he swears his mom won't miss, and one of his lacrosse sweatshirts (with regular lacrosse sticks and not wiener ones like my brother's).

I thank him again, promising to wash and return them on Monday.

"Oh . . . and, Honor?" He pushes back open the door. "There's something else. Something Xander said that's been bugging me. I wanted to ask you earlier this week, but—" Cole finishes with a shrug.

But clearly it made you too uncomfortable to ask.

I keep my face as neutral as possible despite the eruption of sirens. "What is it?"

He twists the doorknob. "Is it true you were in Jess Rennert's car the other day?"

The edges of the room go fuzzy as I grip harder to the tub. "Who?" I lie through all thirty-two of my teeth.

Cole breaks into a relieved grin. "I *knew* it. I told Xander it couldn't have been you."

I release a jittery laugh as my stomach plummets to the center of the earth. "Yeah. That would be crazy."

"Completely." Cole's still chuckling as he shuts the door.

People believe what they want to see.

Whether it takes place in a closet or a drug dealer's car.

This just happens to be the one time it works in my favor.

11

I can't find my way to sleep. A listlessness that has little to do with yesterday afternoon at Cole's. No. For this I blame the moon, fat and round, as it glares from the sky. Silver light pours through the round attic window, splashing across the bottom of my bed. I roll onto my back, gazing up at the glowing sphere, the source of my insomnia.

This has always been the way for me, when the moon is at its fullest. My insomnia used to drive Mom bananas, especially when I was little. No amount of warm milk, bedtime stories, or lavender spray would tempt me to sleep.

In the end it was always Dad, whose patience could wrap around the globe several times over. He would sit, me curled up with my favorite bear and blanket on his lap, and rock and rock and rock as I listened to his heart thump in time with the chair.

Then eventually sleep would come.

But I've outgrown my father's lap. And there's no solace to be found lying wide-eyed with these thoughts, dripping like a leaky faucet.

Drip. *What if tomorrow goes horribly wrong?*

Drip. *What if it's a setup? A DEA sting?*

Drip. *What if . . . God, what if I fail? What if I risk every-thing for nothing?*

The dripping thoughts transform into a rushing river of doubts. *What if I'm not smart enough? Careful enough? Strong enough? Brave enough?*

My heart pumps faster, blood rushing, as fear gobbles the breath from my lungs. I sit up. Press a hand to the organ that's on the brink of punching its way out of me. Then I lean forward, hooking my elbows around my knees, and force myself to inhale.

"Astilbe. Coreopsis. Rhododendron," I murmur, rattling off landscaping plants while holding their pictures in my mind. I watch them grow and reach for the sun. Watch the tightly sealed buds burst open. I add more flowers, more blooms.

And gradually, my anxiety begins to lessen.

When the worst of the panic has subsided, I wipe the sweat from my forehead and toss back the covers. The floor-boards creak, announcing my journey to the window on the other side of the attic. After a few pounds with the heel of my hand, the window releases, and fresh air rushes in. I gulp it down.

From my aerial viewpoint I can see the barn. The outbuild-ing is mostly obscured on the lower levels by the Jurassic-sized maple out back. Which is why I'm probably the only one to notice the light that glows inside.

Pulling on a sweatshirt, I slip on my canvas shoes and pad downstairs. Knox is accounted for, but as suspected, Dad's bed is empty. His blankets as twisted and disheveled as my own.

Quietly moving through the stillness of the house, I step out the back door. The night is cool and damp, alive with the deafening, high-pitched chirp of spring peepers. I quickly cross the backyard, bright with moon, slowing as I near the barn.

The back-and-forth hissing of Dad's sanding block over-powers the night noises. He's woodworking, of course. It's what he always does when he's unsettled. Like his hands have an obsessive need to create.

So my father, solely focused on the wood in his hands, doesn't hear the slide of the barn door when I open it. His back faces me, bowed over Grandma and Granddad Augustine's old dining room table. The sanding grows faster, aggressive, setting me more on edge.

As I open my mouth to speak, he stops. His shoulders suddenly buckle inward, shaking in silent sobs.

My heart splits at the seams. The sight is hard enough to endure during one of his episodes—which he rarely remembers. So it's even worse when he's conscious, knowing that he can't forget.

Tears that I'm usually good at denying fill my eyes. "Dad?"

He sniffs, dragging his arm over his face. Careful to keep his back to me, he begins to sand again. "What is it, Honor?" he asks hoarsely between the hissing scratches of wood.

I weigh my next words. Push too hard, or in the wrong direction, and he might shut down completely. So I don't ask why he's upset. Not when the possibilities are enough to out-number the stars.

"Full moon," I answer.

My father pauses. "There's another sanding block. On the workbench." He gestures with his block across the barn.

He's never invited me to join him. Woodworking's always been a solitary practice. I mop my face with my sleeve before weaving around the tractor mower and other farm equipment.

When I reach the bench, I seize the extra block. My fingers trail down the fine grit of the paper. Funny how something so insubstantial, flimsy even, with enough patience and time can wear down something as strong as hardwood.

"That part hasn't been done," Dad says, pointing to a patch of darker wood.

"Okay." I start sanding, discovering after a few minutes that my movements sync with his. Why I find this consoling, I don't know. But after a while, my arm begins burning from the repetition, so I switch the block to my left. Inevitably, that arm gets tired, too.

"It's always the restorations," I say in sudden realization. "Whenever something's bothering you. How come?" I resume sanding at a much slower pace as I wait for his answer. *If* he'll answer.

"I guess . . ." He trails off as he pushes a hand through his cropped hair, displacing the sawdust. "It's knowing you can salvage something, no matter how old or useless. It can be made new again. It can still have purpose."

I stop, mid-scratch. "But you don't believe that. That you're old and useless." I look up at him across the table. "Do you?"

My father takes a deep breath and releases it, blowing away the accumulation of dust. He rubs his hand along the smooth surface. The surface he's made new. "I believe people are a lot harder to salvage than wood."

Later that night I wake up back in my bed with little recollection of how I got there. I remember sitting down to rest. Yawning repeatedly. And the lulling, infallible tempo of my father's sanding block. Then . . . nothing. Dad must've carried me to bed.

Rolling over, the fierce pull of sleep's tide drags me back under. The grit of sawdust lingers on my skin and in my hair.

It smells like home.

My closet is in shambles as I peel off a shirt, tossing it onto the growing pile. I tug on another long-sleeve shirt that's almost identical to the others, although this one has a tiny, useless pocket on the arm.

Great, I realize, taking in my entirely black outfit. I'm dressed like a big, dark secret. But since I didn't get an insider's manual on the Etiquette and Dress for Fraternizing with Known Criminals Who Grow Weed, this is what I'm stuck with. That, and I don't have time to change. Again.

Normally I don't give much thought to what I wear. Clothes are simply a necessary barrier between nudity and me. Except, nothing about this day is normal.

Because it's Sunday.

Anticipation and anxiety cling to me like woodland burrs.

The first thing I load in my cargo pocket is a small canister of pepper spray. The second, my Swiss Army knife. And the third, the stone that carries my promise.

God help me if I have reason to use the first two or abandon the third.

I check my reflection in the floor-length mirror on the back of my door, hardly recognizing the girl who looks back.

Her cheeks are too pink, like they're hoarding the blood from the rest of her face, and her eyes have a wild look about them. I step back. Pull the girl's auburn hair into a ponytail. Decide it makes her look too childish, and yank out the rubber band, letting the long hair fall loose and heavy over her shoulders.

"*Me*. I'm still *me*," I tell the reflection. "This doesn't change anything." But the sentiment's barbed and catches in my throat.

Because I have been changing. Subtly. Like the incremental shift in tectonic plates.

Half-truths and lies roll easier off my tongue. Secrets that used to feel slippery are now becoming such a part of me, I barely have to hold them at all. They're in my skin. In my breath. In every molecule.

But all this deception, this is how it has to be. At least for a few months. Which in the scope of a person's life isn't so terribly long, is it? As soon as this is over, I can go back to my predictable existence, with its rules and reliable outcomes.

This is all temporary.

Turning my back on myself, I hoist the bag stuffed with books I have no intention of cracking to my shoulder. Then I grab the paper with the address. Or more accurately, a vague set of directions.

That I hope won't lead me to an early grave.

12

Traffic along the rural highway is nonexistent. A Sunday afternoon anomaly that ends the second tourist season begins. In a few short weeks, vehicles will be spilling off the main vein of highway with their boat trailers, WaveRunners, and campers in tow.

A sapphire slice of Lake Michigan glitters in the distance. Driving up the steep incline, I crest the top, where unspoiled green rolls out for miles. My stomach rises and falls like the glacially carved landscape.

Squinting ahead where the highway flattens, I spot the dirt road that lies past the abandoned gas station. Just like the directions said I would. A peeling, faded sign marks the entrance of the drive.

This is it. The point of no return.

My heart skips faster, doubt weakening the resolve of my right foot over the gas pedal. *What am I doing? I can't go through with this! I can't*—Then the image of Dad from last night flashes in my mind, his shoulders caving with sorrow. Needing so badly to prove that wood can be saved. To prove that *he* can be saved, salvaged, even if he tries to say otherwise.

My hands strangulate the wheel. "Don't think. Just do." Sucking in a breath, I ease up on the accelerator and take a hard right onto the private drive. The vehicle slows to a crawl as I shift to a lower gear.

I glance at the directions, but Jess's messy scratches don't give any sense of how long the stretch of road will be, only that the place I'm going will be at the end of it. Pine trees crowd the snaking road on either side, making it impossible to see anything beyond them.

My cell rings and I let out a semi-hysterical yelp. I suppose I should be comforted there's enough reception for a call to come through. But any feelings of comfort evaporate as I remember *why* my phone's ringing.

"Damn." I hug the side of the road, grabbing my cell from the console. Sure enough, *Mom calling* illuminates the screen.

If I don't answer, it'll arouse more suspicion, and I already missed last week's call. The last thing I need is Mom reigniting Dad's concerns over my "well-being." Chewing what's left of my thumbnail, I stare at my phone. Not a phone, more like a grenade. I check the time—2:51 p.m.

Gritting my teeth, I hit Accept, effectively pulling the pin.

"Hi, Mom," I answer brightly. *Wait. Do I sound too happy?*

"Honor!" she chirps, beating my happy tenfold. "Oh, it's *so* good to hear your voice. Is it a good time to talk?"

"Uh . . ." I honestly can't think of a *worse* time to chat. Not with my mind fully occupied by the magnitude of what awaits me. My knee anxiously hammers up and down in response. But I committed to this call the moment I answered. So.

"Yes, but"—I pause, then feed her the same excuse I gave Dad when I asked to borrow his truck—"I'm meeting a friend to study, so I'm a little pressed for time. Maybe I should call you later?"

"Oh, honey, I can't. Scott and I are going to an event this evening at the Renaissance Center to raise money for a bird sanctuary."

"Did you say *bird* sanctuary?"

Mom hates things that fly—bugs, birds, bats . . . basically anything winged.

Her laugh tinkles like wind chimes. "I know, right? Who'd have thought I'd be a card-carrying member of the Michigan Audubon Society?"

"Not me," I reply distractedly, keeping a vigilant watch on the woods and the sections of road ahead of and behind me.

"So," she says, the smile still in her voice, "this friend you're meeting. Is it a *boy*?"

I imagine her leaning in closer for my answer and fight the innate gravitational pull of my eyes to the roof. "No, Mom. It's my friend Zareen. We have a final coming up." Okay, 50 percent of that is true.

"Oh." Her disappointment crackles through the connection. Forget the academic achievements. I'm a failure with a capital *F* when it comes to dating.

My knee resumes its frantic bounce as the minutes click by on the clock. Fortunately, I'm spared the boy talk and she whisks on to the next topic. "Did I tell you I found the most spectacular wedding dress? The top and sleeves are this gorgeous lace—*very* Grace Kelly. I'll text you a picture."

"Great."

"And oh my goodness, I almost forgot to tell you the most important part! We have a date, Honor! December seventh," she finishes dreamily.

I slide deeper in my seat. "That's um . . . wow. That's soon. Congratulations."

This news would be difficult to digest on a regular day, but impossible given my current circumstances. Regardless, her jubilance geysers, bubbling through the phone and into my ear. Mom joyously embracing her new future, while I sit terrified over whether I'll have one.

The contrast between us is, as always, as massive as the Continental Divide.

My mother continues her oratorical assault on all things wedding, covering everything from cake flavors to the twins' silk georgette empire-waist flower girl dresses. I think I insert the appropriate amount of *uh-huh*s and *that's great*s, but I'm losing focus. Fast. And—Oh hell. *It's been seven minutes!*

"Mom?" I interrupt, working to keep my voice even. "Mom, I'm so sorry but Zee's waiting. I *really* have to go now."

"Oh. Sure," she replies, slightly deflated. "Guess we'll just pick this up next week?"

"Sounds good." Cradling the phone between my head and shoulder, I jam the truck into gear. Another minute slips by on the clock.

"Love you, baby."

"Have fun at your event. Loveyoubye." The words come out in a rush, rear-ending each other as I quickly hang up and lurch ahead.

The road curves to the left before opening up to a small clearing. Plunked within the center sits a long commercial building the earth seems determined to swallow whole. Grape-vines cast nets of dark green along areas of the aluminum-sided structure, while moss grows on the sections of roof the trees shade.

A dilapidated padlock-shaped sign outside it reads:

LOCK
AND
KEY
STORAGE

Angling the truck, I park outside the building. There are no other vehicles in sight. It's three o'clock on the dot, so Laks should be here any second. Nausea sloshes around the ham and swiss I had for lunch.

Ten minutes pass, and my nerves are beyond frayed. *"Where are you?"* I hiss under my breath, checking my mirrors.

I study the directions again, this time turning the paper so it's oriented with the building. Huh. What I initially took for a random scribble is actually a small *X* Jess has marked at the rear of the facility. It's possible Laks parked somewhere else and is waiting at one of the back storage units. Only one way to know for sure.

Eyeing the collection of weeds, brambles, and saplings that consume the access road, I decide I'll have to go on foot. My pulse kicks up again. The creep factor of this place is undeniable, and my Swiss Army knife suddenly feels like I've brought a toothpick to a sword fight.

"Don't be a coward," I mutter, gripping the wheel. "You didn't spend forty dollars to come out here just to stare at the damn building."

With my recent cash withdrawals, my savings balance now sits at a meager $3,927.63. I'm not sure it's enough for the equipment and start-up costs. But it's the accumulation of every paycheck and birthday and holiday gift since Grandma Augustine insisted Dad open individual savings accounts for my brother and me. She then placed a stiff-as-a-board hundred-dollar bill in my open hand and one in Knox's.

My brother fisted his money, held it high as he danced around the kitchen singing made-up songs. Silly odes to all the sugary sweets and toys an eight-year-old would buy. Granddad's wiry brows drifted skyward as he watched him over the top of his newspaper. He was forever telling Knox his impulsivity would be his greatest blessing and greatest curse. "Let's hope fate favors the blessings," Granddad always said.

As for me, I recall how smooth and slippery the money felt between my fingers. How something so light could be so heavy with importance. I didn't dare crumple it with abandon as my brother did. Not even as I stood on my tiptoes to slide the bill under the glass partition, over to the bank teller on the other side. She smiled and promised she'd take good care of my money. Keep it safe until I needed it.

Turns out, I need it now. Just not for reasons I ever thought I would.

I hop down from the truck and follow the subtle path along the side of the structure where the brush is less wild. Most of the doors to the storage units are defaced and rusting—marred with spray paint and pitted from BBs. I cover my nose, gagging at the noxious smell of ammonia. Urine. Broken bottles and the occasional hypodermic needle litter the ground, glinting like gypsum in the sunlight.

Kee-eeeeee-arr! A hawk shrilly screams, circling in on its prey.

The fear I managed to suppress begins to uncoil, inch by inch, moving up my spine. My breath grows increasingly shallow as I approach the back end of the building, where the trees turn daylight to dusk. The air is colder and wetter here.

Coming to a halt, heart thumping in my neck, I count down: *Three, two, one!* Then I pivot around the corner in one fluid motion.

Nothing. I release a jagged exhale, and my shoulders collapse. There's nothing and no one here. Just panels of weather-ravaged siding without any storage units. Oh, and more garbage.

I prop my hands at my hips, surveying the vacant area. And then it hits me with a jolt. *Jess played me.* Took my money and sent me on a wild-goose chase after someone named Laks who probably doesn't even exist. *What did you expect trusting a drug dealer?* I shake my head, disgusted at how easily she duped me.

Well, lesson learned, Jessica Rennert. For the bargain price of forty bucks. Forty bucks that I really couldn't afford to pointlessly flush down the toilet.

With a dejected sigh, I turn and tromp back toward the truck. As I veer around the shards of glass and sundry trash, I wonder how I'll ever find a grow-room expert now. I'm so immersed in my thoughts that the faraway sound doesn't register. Until the hum grows closer.

I freeze, my head snapping in the direction of the noise. Another vehicle is coming. And I am alone. A young girl alone, in a remote area—I check my phone—without a cell signal.

Fuck.

Adrenaline surges through my system as I tear through the

weeds, praying I reach the truck before the other vehicle does. The forest passes in a blur, my breath tripping like my feet over vines.

Nobody knows where I am.

Not a single soul.

I could disappear so easily. Buried in a shallow, unmarked grave, somewhere in the acres of woods that surround this desolate place . . .

I picture my mason jar. How it sits on the table beside my bed, almost but not quite full. The stones inside suddenly seem too few.

I burst from the side of the building then, trampling to a stop as a sedan pulls up. *Oh my God. Oh no. Nononono.* As I pant, my vision freckles with black dots. I watch the police cruiser slide in beside Dad's work truck.

A male officer opens the door and steps out then, hand poised at his weapon. My heart rate has officially broken the sound barrier. Sweat trickles down the back of my neck as I work to get my breathing under control.

"Afternoon," the officer says, his tall, muscular frame striding toward me. He pauses to murmur into the radio at his shoulder, the visor of his police hat blocking his face. Then he looks up.

And I no longer worry about controlling my breath, because my lungs have stopped moving entirely. My lips part in horrified recognition.

"I'm Officer Buchannon. We received a call about some suspicious activity out here."

Now my heart's stopped. Fear is petrifying all my organs, turning them to stony lumps. My gaze drops to a patch of dandelions as his pale eyes move over me, cataloging every detail in a sweeping glance.

"Are you aware you're trespassing on private property?" He gestures to the No Trespassing sign, crookedly hanging beneath the Lock and Key Storage padlock one.

"I—I . . . no, sir," I stammer, looking at the business sign as I struggle to contain the earthquake inside me. I suddenly notice the way the first letters stack atop one another. More importantly, what it spells. *How did I not see it before?* I briefly close my eyes. Jess never gave me the name of a person. She gave me the name of a *place*! LAKS. And I bet she's also the reason Officer Buchannon was called here.

By some miracle of physiology, I shuffle closer. "I'm sorry. I must've taken a wrong turn." My voice wobbles as I frantically spin a cover story. "I was supposed to meet a friend to study."

His head cocks to the side in disbelief. "I'm going to need to see some identification. Driver's license, please."

Blood whooshes in my ears as I pull out my license and pass it to him. He squints at it, then back to me.

I swallow and continue talking. "By the time I got all the way back here and realized I took the wrong road, I, um"—my eyes return to the scraggy patch of dandelions—"I had to go to the bathroom. *Bad*." I risk a glance at him, knowing my face has got to be a million shades of red.

Please let my terror pass for embarrassment. Please!

"Sir, am I in trouble?" I ask, not even having to fake the slight tremble in my voice.

Officer Buchannon's hardened expression softens a touch. "No," he says, relaxing his stance. "But going forward, I expect you'll pay better attention to the signage around you. Understood, Miss Augustine?"

I emphatically nod. "Yes, sir. I will."

He goes to hand back my license, then stops short, glancing at it again. "Augustine," he repeats softly. "Why do I know that name?"

I offer a helpless shrug as his eyes relentlessly search my face.

"I know," he says with a snap of his fingers. "Your family owns the old greenhouse and farmhouse out on Hickory, right?"

"Yes, sir."

He grins, running a hand along his square jaw. "Then you must go to school with my son, Cole. He's one of the lacrosse cocaptains," he adds with unmistakable pride. "Do you know him?"

I gulp. "Yes, sir. I do."

Not for long, though. Because after today's encounter with his dad, I'll do everything humanly possible to *un*know Cole. To avoid him. Which means starting tomorrow, I will become a ghost.

He will not see me.

Hear me.

And eventually, Cole will forget me altogether.

13

Two days have passed since my brush with the law, so what I'm about to do feels risky. But I'm running out of time and options. Also, this was the best/only idea I could come up with.

Peering through a gap in the leaves of the boxwood hedge, I watch the group of stoners. A hazy cloud halos above where they sit in the grass, hidden from the eyes of the school. They gather here, not far from my willow—occasionally between classes, but mostly during lunch.

And it's my second day watching them as they laugh, cough, and have deeply meaningful conversations about . . . absolutely nothing.

"Dude," a tall, lanky guy named Abe snorts, pulling the joint from his mouth with a sour look. "Abe" happens to bear a striking resemblance to a young Lincoln, so he's easy to remember. "Where'd you get this ditch weed, anyway?"

Ronan, who I've pegged as the ringleader of the bunch, snatches the joint away from him. His lips quirk into the lazy grin that seems to be his trademark. "Yo mama's panty drawer," he replies before taking a long drag. The others chuckle, while one of them echoes the word *panties* between hacking coughs.

"Yo mama jokes are *so* nineties," Chloe muses, tucking a pink lock of hair behind her ear. The joint is passed to her, and she takes a hit, immediately wrinkling her nose. "Ew. This *tastes* like it's from the nineties." Smoke escapes with her words. "You get the Rennert special or something?"

Ronan clutches his heart, tipping back his head. The multi-colored beanie falls off, revealing a spray of staticky blond hair. "You wound me, woman! As if I'd ever buy weed from her," he says, tugging his hat back on. "Everyone knows her stuff's for shit. Besides, I don't do interloafers. Straight to the source or not at all, I always say."

Max, the raven-haired, musically inclined member of the group, pauses from plucking the strings of his guitar. "What the hell's an interloafer? Some kind of shoe?"

"He means *interloper*," Chloe says, tossing a handful of grass at him like confetti. Max and Abe are still openmouthed and confused. She rolls her eyes. "Ronan doesn't buy from dealers, ding-a-lings."

My heart skips a beat or three, the conversation music to my ears. Because not only do they *not* do business with Jess, but Ronan prefers to go *straight to the source*. Meaning my chances of scoring the name of a grower just skyrocketed.

Time to make my move. Drawing an anxious breath, I shake out my hands and round the bushes. *Just be cool.* I relax my stiff posture, slowing my pace to a third of its normal speed as I approach them. Nobody notices me. They'd be so screwed if I were faculty.

"H-hi." My voice cracks in a decidedly uncool way. I clear

my throat and try again. "Hey," I say louder, causing heads to swing toward me.

Abe starts choking, quickly hiding what's left of the joint behind his back. Four pairs of red eyes squint at me with suspicion.

"Who're you?" Ronan asks, his blond brows cinching together as if trying to place me.

Using my real name suddenly feels dangerous. And since I don't recognize any of them, I'm betting their vacant stares mean they don't know me, either. "I'm . . . Lily," I blurt, dragging my gaze from a patch of lily of the valley growing nearby. "I'm sort of new here."

Chloe stops plucking at the frayed denim strings around the holes in her jeans and angles her head. "Well, this is a private club, Lily, so move along." She makes a dismissive shooing motion with her hand.

Abrasive. Distrustful. Sharp-tongued. It was already clear from my surveillance that Chloe would be the toughest nut of the group to crack.

"Easy, Chlo," Ronan murmurs, turning his sleepy gaze back on me. "No harm in hearing what sort-of-new girl has to say."

"Lily," I repeat, hugging the bag at my shoulder. *God, I hope this works.*

"Right." Ronan's lazy grin returns as he slow-motion blinks at me. "So, Lily, what brings you to our sharing circle?"

"Sharing circle?" Abe balks, taking a break from twisting his goatee into mini horns. "Dude, no. Don't ever say that again."

"Um, I actually brought you guys something." I pat the messenger bag. Intrigued, Ronan motions to the others to make room for me. I take a seat between Abe and Max, feeling my face flush under the group's scrutiny. I dig into the bag, all of them leaning in curiously as I pull out my vending machine haul. "For sharing," I explain. "In the circle."

Ronan gives Abe a pointed look. *See,* his expression suggests.

"Well, it's cute when *she* says it," Abe mutters defensively. "And I call dibs on the mini Oreos!"

Hands begin snapping out around me. But Chloe's arms remain tightly crossed at her chest. I can tell she wants the can of sour cream and onion Pringles in a bad way. They're her favorite. In fact, I made sure to bring everyone's favorite.

"What's the catch?" she asks.

"No catch," I reply, holding out the chips. "I was told never to come to a party empty-handed. So." I jiggle the can.

Chloe's near drooling, her glassy eyes locked on the chips while the boys dig into their treats. She finally breaks, snatching the Pringles and popping open the top, quickly cramming one into her mouth. Her watery stare fixes on me as she chews. "You want something. I can tell."

Well, I can't exactly argue that. Even high, the girl's perceptive as hell.

"Don't mind her," Ronan says, tearing open a bag of licorice rope with his teeth. "She always gets paranoid after a smoke sesh. Don't you, Chloe?"

She scowls.

"Hey"—he nods to me—"thanks for the provisions. I'm Ronan, by the way." He introduces the others, who raise their hands in half waves.

Max has already inhaled his candy bar. Wiping a chocolate-smudged hand over his Flaming Lips T-shirt, he hoists the guitar back to his lap. "You guys wanna hear my latest? It just came to me."

I guess the question is rhetorical, because Max immediately launches into a series of lively chords, accompanied by lyrics he seems to be making up as he goes. He sings of a girl with hair the color of old pennies, with lips puffed like pillows and limbs like a willow. *"Oh, Lily—"* he croons. *"Sweet, sweet, Lily—"*

Okay . . . wow. Max made up a song about me. And now my alias is being rhymed with words like *silly, dilly,* and *frilly.* At this rate, I'll be here till next Tuesday.

"You're not special, you know," Chloe informs me, sucking the flavored powder off her fingers. "Max has a song for everyone. Even his ferret."

Max slaps a hand to the strings, cutting the final notes short. "Uh, profoundly untrue, Chlo. Only those who are worthy get a musical tribute."

Ronan makes to flick what's left of the joint (now a charred nub) into the shrubbery.

"Wait, don't throw that!" I call out, reaching to catch his sleeve.

He does another slow blink, lowering his hand. "Why? No one's gonna find it."

Everyone's looking at me weird. Good. Because that means they don't already know the weed wisdom I'm about to drop.

"It's not that," I say to Ronan, sinking back to my spot. "You should save it. Save all your roaches. That way you can make a super blunt."

"Super blunt," Max whispers in wonder, his dark eyes

peering through me as he contemplates. "Lily, you just gave me another song idea!" Pulling a spiral notepad from his pocket, he begins scribbling.

"I don't get it," Chloe says. "What makes it 'super'?"

I grin, realizing this is my secret weapon to win her over. "Because the little bit of leftover bud in the roach is 'super' potent. Has to do with the constant flow of smoke running through it, so it usually has a higher THC content."

They are absolutely rapt.

I continue. "Just make sure to store your roaches in an air-tight glass jar to cut down on the smell. Then, once you have enough, break them open and make a newly rolled blunt out of the remains. A super blunt. Or"—I lift a shoulder—"some call it a grandfather blunt."

There's a collective wave of *aww yeah*s and *right on*s that fill the circle. I smile a little as they excitedly chatter.

Chloe fist-bumps me. "Not bad, new girl."

Already my hours of research are paying off.

But the clock is ticking, and lunch is nearly over.

"So, uh, I gotta run. Need to swing by the office to try and talk my way out of detention," I lie, gathering up my things.

"I feel you, girl," Abe says. "That was me last week. Didn't work out so well, but maybe you'll have better luck."

"Thanks." I start to leave and pivot back. "Hey, uh, you guys wouldn't happen to have a source for some decent home-grown around here, would you? I got some stuff from this dealer." I pretend to rack my brain for her name. "Janie? Jenny?" I shake my head. "Anyway, it was crap, mostly seeds and stems."

"You mean Jess," Ronan says with a snort, resting back on

his elbows. "Yeah, you don't wanna deal with her. She's bad news." Then he stares up at the sky.

And I wait for him to say more. *Willing* him to say more. Ready to crawl over there and shake the more out of him if I have to. Meanwhile, Abe and Chloe bicker over whether red M&M's cause cancer, while Max strums softly in the background.

"Ronan?" I prompt, my patience running out.

He points a piece of licorice skyward. "That cloud looks like a *T. rex,* doesn't it? And right next to it, that one there looks like a drumstick. *Mmm,* I could go for a bucket of extra-crispy about now." He chomps the end of the licorice, not breaking his gaze from the clouds.

"Ronan!"

He looks at me in a daze.

"Homegrown? Know of anyone?" I repeat.

"Huh? Oh yeah," he says with a dopey grin. "Try Ash. Asher Ford."

My skin tingles with excitement. *Finally* I'm getting somewhere. After Ronan gives me the number, I wave goodbye as Max sends me off with another rousing rendition of "Lily."

Sauntering across the school grounds, I clutch the precious number in my hand. My smile blossoms big and bright. *Asher Ford, I'm going to learn so much from you. You just don't know it yet.*

I nail a pothole with my front tire, the impact traveling all the way back in my molars. The bike wobbles, and I almost wipe out in our driveway. Which would've been tough to explain given the ungodly hour on a school night. But Tuesday's warmer temperatures have delivered a sudden fog that drapes like curtains over the low-lying areas, making it difficult to navigate the bumpy stretch home.

The warm mist clings to my skin and eyelashes. I squeeze the brakes and hop off my bike to walk the rest of the way.

Sounds of bullfrogs snap the air like rubber bands, alongside the high-pitched chitter of insects. The creatures of the night are electric, buzzing with energy. Meanwhile, I barely have the energy to step one foot in front of the other.

At least my hard work's paying off. Not only is the basement *spotless,* but I've also gathered a good amount of grow equipment—like bulbs, ballasts, and hoods. Now all I need is some guidance on how it all comes together. Which is exactly what I intend to learn from the meeting I've set up with Asher Ford on Saturday night.

Rounding to the back, I nestle my bike beside Knox's, when a loud *clunk* comes from behind me. I crane my neck toward the sound. *Tick-tick-tick-tick.* The barn door slides open along the track.

Panicked, I dive for cover behind the chicken coop. The birds stir in their roosts. It's got to be Dad. *But is he coming or going?*

A minute or more passes without sound. Sucking in a breath, I tiptoe to the rear of the coop and peek around the corner. Dad's broad-shouldered silhouette appears as he steps out from the barn, heaving the large door shut.

I plaster myself to the structure, becoming one with the wood siding. The chickens cluck and ruffle their feathers as my father approaches. His boots tromp over the naked stretch of ground where the grass has been worn away.

As long as he doesn't look back, he won't see me flattened against the coop. Blood pushes faster through my veins. Maple leaves rustle. And my breath stays bottled in my lungs . . . until he passes on the other side.

I exhale. *Keep walking, Dad. Go straight inside and up to bed.*

He stops at the bottom of the porch steps, head tipping up like he's heard something. I clamp my lips together. And just as my father starts to turn, a bark from inside the house stops him. *Geronimo.* I'm giving that dog *all* the treats tomorrow. Dad hustles up the stairs and inside.

My head drops back against the coop. I stare up at the clouds that churn like a cauldron of witch's brew. That was close. I need to do a better job of scouting the barn before—

"Well, well. Look who's out past curfew," my brother murmurs.

"Knox!" I gasp. "What are—" A light at the other end of the house clicks on. We hold our positions and conversation for the time it takes for Dad to draw his shade and the bedroom to eventually go dark. With the coast clear, I dash across the yard to the shadowy lump.

"Never thought I'd see the day I bust you for breaking curfew." Knox clucks his tongue. "Oh, how the mighty do fall." He makes a whistling noise followed by a *splat.*

"Bust me?" I repeat, winded as I slide down next to him beside the lattice. "You're not going to tell Dad, are you?"

"Depends." A lopsided grin lifts the corner of his mouth.

He wants to see me squirm, and a month ago, he probably would've succeeded.

"Don't jerk me around," I hiss. "Do you know how many times I've covered for you? *Countless*. Like seriously, I have lost count."

"Oh, relax. Besides, why would I rat you out when I'm bursting with pride?" He chuckles to himself. "Always knew you had it in you."

Knowing I've made my brother proud isn't exactly a high point. "So what are you doing out here?"

"Met up with a friend." A lighter sparks. The flash of yellow illuminates his face as he takes a drag. "Now I'm just waiting to sneak back in." Knox relays the entire sentence on his inhale. Then he snorts and coughs, a white cloud billowing from his mouth like a chimney.

"*Shh!* You want Dad to hear you?" I whisper.

He clears his throat. "Ideally, no. But a cough has to go somewhere, doesn't it? Hey, wait . . ." The soft glow coming from the cherry on the end of his joint shows his eyebrows have magnetically pulled together. My brother turns his head toward me.

I brace for him to ask the obvious question: Why am *I* out so late?

"Have you ever wondered where all the uncoughed coughs go? Or how about all the sneezes that didn't get sneezed? Man, that's some serious existential bee-in-the-forest shit."

Relieved, I sag back against the house, hooking my arms around my knees. "It really isn't. You're just high, so you think everything you say is profound." It's like Ronan and his crew all over again. "And for the record, it's *tree* in the forest. Falling bees isn't a thing."

"Wait." He scratches his head, mouth quirking. "Then

what's the bee one? A bee in hand . . . is worth two in the . . . tush?" Knox blinks. "Hell, that doesn't sound right at all."

I stifle a laugh. "Good God, everything about that idiom gumbo is wrong."

"Who you calling idiot gumbo?"

A gentle warmth seeps through me as we quietly giggle. I honestly can't remember the last time Knox and I sat together like this.

Our chuckles fade as I absently trace the edge of a morning glory bud folded up like an umbrella. The sky-blue flower lying in wait will open before dawn and die by sunset. A fleeting beauty. But come tomorrow, dozens more blossoms will pop to life, continuing the cycle until the bitter frost arrives.

"You're lucky," he muses, watching me. "You've always known what you wanted to do. Hey, remember that time I gave you a bag of dirt for your birthday?"

I smile. "Yeah. It was good dirt."

"Only you would say that." He turns his head back out toward the rippling wheat field and takes another toke. His expression grows serious. "Just think, in a few weeks, I'll be a high school graduate. And I have no idea what I'm gonna do with my life."

"You'll figure it out," I assure him.

He squints. "How do you know?"

"Because. I know you. You always figure it out. Eventually."

We sit in silence, staring at the undulating wheat.

"I asked Mom not to come," he says.

"You mean to graduation?"

He nods. This shocks me. Of the two of us, Knox has always been closer to Mom.

"How did she take it?"

My brother shrugs. "Better than Dad would take seeing her with her new insta-fam. Anyway, I told her I'd come back later this summer so she can throw me a big graduation open house party. Party planning's always been Mom's jam, so she's all good."

Rather than dwelling on the subject, I snatch the joint from his fingers to inspect it. "Talk about shoddy workmanship. Did you roll this in the dark? And what is this paper, wood pulp?"

"Hey, don't bogart my wizard stick," he mutters, grabbing it back. "And I didn't roll it, so I take no responsibility for the junk packaging."

"Where'd you get it from?" I dangle the question as nonchalantly as possible, like I don't have a vested interest.

Another white plume puffs from his mouth. "Nunya."

"Nunya?" I frown, not recognizing the name. "Who's that?"

My brother snorts. "It *means* nunya business."

The warmth of minutes ago drains from my body as a new thought enters my mind. "Knox." I pause to level my voice. "Did you get that from Jess?"

He tamps down a flash of surprise before swinging his bleary, unfocused gaze to me. "Maybe I did, maybe I didn't," he says cryptically. "Like I said, it's not your business."

Cagey, evasive—this is not the brother I know. The brother I know is an open book, practiced in the art of oversharing. He's hiding something. And judging by his reaction, I have a sinking feeling Jess might be behind it.

"Well, can you at least tell me if it came from Jess? Because, Knox, I swear that girl is trouble. And if you get mixed up in—"

"Stop, just stop. *Jeez, Hon!* I already told you to back the hell off. What don't you get about that?" Annoyed, he puts out the joint on the bottom of his Converse.

"I'm warning you to stay away from Jess for your own good! She lies and screws people out of money." I quickly amend, "From what I've heard. And besides, do you really want to jeopardize graduating by getting involved with . . ." I trail off as he listlessly flicks his lighter, watching as the amber sparks fly. "Why won't you just listen to me?"

He sniffs and shakes his head. "I'm an idiot. I thought you could be cool with this, but of *course* you're gonna lecture me. You live for that shit!"

"*Knox.*" I grab his arm when he starts to rise. "You're taking this the wrong way. Listen, I know how I can be sometimes. But honestly, I'm only trying to protect you by warn—"

He shrugs me off and rises, face screwed up in anger. "That's such a load. You do it so you get to keep playing the role of the perfect, good one, and I get to be the fuckup you're always trying to fix. Same story. Different day. I'm out," he mutters.

"Knox, don't go," I call after him.

"And I don't need protecting!" He stomps off around the other side of the house.

I rub my face. Upset. Frustrated. But most of all, I'm afraid. Afraid of the countless ways Jess could outwit and manipulate my impulsive brother. And I would know.

Because she easily outwitted and manipulated me.

14

"This day is an absolute dumpster fire," Zareen says, ferociously mixing the fruit at the bottom of her yogurt cup.

I should have dibs on the sentiment, but Zee's gone and hijacked it.

"Do you *know* who I got partnered with for my chem project?" she squawks.

I offer a half-hearted shrug and pick at my food. My stomach feels like a cement mixer.

"Mason Ayers." She jabs at the blueberries like they're responsible. "Which means I'll have to do *all* the heavy lifting because he has the work ethic of a narcoleptic sloth."

Her rant continues as my thoughts spiral out like pea shoots. I can't stop obsessing over my blowup with Knox the night before last. How he shut down and stormed off when pressed about the source of his sloppy joint. My brother is *clearly* hiding something and still won't come clean. The key question is whether it involves that conniving snake-in-the-grass Jess. One way or another, I'm going to find out.

My eyes dart to the cafeteria door as it opens. *Not Cole.* I relax a little. That's another thing: being on constant guard from Cole is *exhausting.* But four incident-free days down, and another twenty—

"Hellooo? Earth to Honor." Zee snaps her fingers, startling me from my trance. "What's with you? All week you've been a space case." Her gaze drops to the sandwich I've torn to shreds. "And, what, is this prison? You looking for a shiv in there?"

I force a chuckle and shake my head. Cement gut aside, it's hard to get jazzed about eating a peanut butter sandwich for the fourth day in a row. But after catching Dad empty the change from the coffee tin to fill his gas tank, I wasn't about to ask for lunch money.

"Sorry I'm so out of it." I cram a chunk of déjà vu sandwich in my mouth, slowly chewing. "Guess I've just been stressed about finals. Too many late nights studying the Doppler effect on light waves."

At least my excuse is a semi-honest one. What I omit is the hours I've spent scouring the internet for grow tips, so most of the time I don't even begin studying until after ten.

Her mouth flattens into a hyphen. "Okay, what is it you're not telling me? Because honestly, it's more than this week. For the last month you've been super . . . I don't know, distant." Reaching across the table, she rests a hand on my arm. "We're friends, right?"

"Yeah. Of course we're friends," I reply with a defensive edge.

"Then *talk* to me. Tell me what's—"

The lacrosse players sitting at the table adjacent to ours burst into laughter—the obnoxiously loud, roaring, table-pounding kind. Zee twists around to glare at the source of our disruption. One of the guys stands up, and I spot Cole. *When did he walk in?!* Before I can slip from his view, Cole catches sight of me. Irritation tightens his face and narrows his eyes.

"Shit," I murmur softly and duck my head under the lunch table.

"Honor? If this is an effort to convince me you're fine, it's a hard fail."

"No. I'm, uh . . ." *Gross, there's so much gum under here.* "Tying my shoe."

"Doubtful. Flip-flops don't have laces," she says without missing a beat. "Why are you hiding under the table?"

"Because of me," a male voice says. I cringe, squeezing my eyes closed in defeat. There's a knock on the tabletop. "Come on up, Honor. We need to talk."

I grudgingly poke my head up. My organs stall at the sight of Cole glowering above, his square jaw forged of steel. "I thought I dropped something under there."

Zee gives me a mutinous, disbelieving look.

"So have I done something to royally piss you off?" Cole asks. He's dressed in his game-day attire of khakis and a light blue button-down that matches his eyes. And he looks, well, royally pissed.

My friend kicks my foot to respond. *"Ow!"* Whose side is she on? "Not that I . . ." But my response fades out when I notice the entire lacrosse team staring like fancily dressed lemmings. "Not that I'm aware of."

"Interesting." Cole folds his arms and cocks his head to the side. "Then why did you have someone else deliver the clothes you borrowed instead of just giving them to me yourself? I've been trying to talk to you the entire *week,* but you keep avoiding me."

My gaze anxiously sweeps the cafeteria—elbows nudge and heads turn in our direction. Worse, Xander's taken notice. And his glare burns, hot as embers. It's been over two weeks since his library threat, and the *last* thing I need is to stoke that fire.

"Well?" Cole impatiently prompts.

I blink. "What? I haven't tried to avoid—"

"Uh-uh. I'm calling BS, Augustine. You dove behind the *trash bins* the second you saw me, *and* you've sprinted in and out of lit every day. Have you considered joining the track team? Because, no joke, you're insanely fast."

Zee's eyes ping-pong between Cole and me as she bites into an apple.

This is spiraling, and I have to put an end to it. "*Please* lower your voice. You're creating a scene."

"Fine." He swings his leg over the bench and plunks down next to my friend. "But you owe me an explanation. So how about you start with why you're ghosting me."

I was hoping he hadn't noticed. My face grows hotter than magma as I fidget. What do I say that won't dig my hole deeper?

Zee sets down her apple and clears her throat. "If I could interject here. I think the greater question is: Why do you care so much, Cole?" Her dark brow arches in that cool way I'll never master.

I love Zee. One day she's going to make a kick-ass lawyer. But today I want to stuff the apple back in her mouth like one of those cartoon pigs.

Something flickers in Cole's eyes, but I'm too preoccupied searching the cafeteria's speckled floor for an escape hatch to analyze it.

"Sorry, but how is this your business?" he pointedly counters.

Her posture stiffens as she folds her hands, placing them on the table. *Oh, holy hell. She's going full Harvard on him.* "Well, first of all," she begins her opening statement, "you made it everyone's business when you aired your grievance in front of the whole cafeteria. And second, Honor's my friend. So her business *is* my business, unless she says otherwise."

Cole inhales, and I can almost hear his mental count to ten. "Look, Zareen"—he locks eyes with her—"if I make a mistake, I'll be the first to own it." Then his gaze swings to me. "But I'm not cool with being punished when I've done nothing wrong."

Intrigued, Zee turns to me. "Is that true, Honor? *Have* you been punishing him?"

What is she, a marriage counselor? And when did she jump sides? "No!" I huff, tossing up my hands. "I'm not punishing anyone. It's just . . ." I need the guy to avoid me like patient zero. Is that really so much to ask?

"Take your time," Cole says, propping his arms on the table. "I've got all day."

No. We have all of twenty-one minutes before lunch is over. And he's high as a kite if he thinks I'm getting a tardy.

I clench my teeth, *royally pissed* he's forcing this issue now. And I know it isn't fair. Because how can he know the innumerable ways my life's going straight to hell in a handbasket? Regardless, this problem ends. Today.

"Not here," I tell him as I stuff the remains of my lunch in the bag and stand. "Let's talk outside."

Zee looks at me like I've lost my mind. *Are you sure?* she mouths.

I nod.

"Great," Cole says coolly as he rises, then gestures to the double doors. "Lead the way."

We pass the table of lacrosse players. Xander's menacing gaze doesn't waver from me. Not once. But if I succeed in what I'm about to do, Xander won't have reason to continue his crusade to ruin me in Cole's eyes.

Because I'll do it for him.

Acid's eaten holes in my stomach lining by the time we arrive at my weeping willow. *Pick a fight, a believable one,* I tell myself. *Make him hate you.* While the objective is clear, my brain still fails to supply the almighty how.

And Cole hasn't spoken a word. I think he's holding them hostage until I share mine. So he bides his time, watching me with a gaze as penetrating as an X-ray, piercing through tissue and muscle, all the way to the bone.

I nervously tuck an errant hair that's sprung free from my messy bun and lean against the willow. My hands hide behind my back as my fingers find their home in the grooves of the bark. "Why do I get the impression you're trying to solve me like a calculus equation?"

Cole looks away and tugs at a drooping branch. He lets go,

watching as the limb springs upward and bounces. "Please," he mutters. "You're harder than calc."

"But easier than quantum physics?" The joke is DOA. If I'm going to stall until I have a solid plan of attack, I've got to do better than this.

He braces his shoulder to the tree, his frown carving itself deeper. "Usually I'm pretty good at figuring people out."

I stifle the urge to add, *With the huge exception of the blind spot that is your best friend.*

Cole continues, "I learned to pick up on all the subtle, unspoken stuff—body language, facial expressions, that kind of thing. Perks of having a dad who's a cop." He doesn't say it like a perk, though.

Fear of discovery causes my fingers to dig into the bark. I keep my face placid. Unfazed. "Then I'm not sure why you're so adamant to talk. Sounds like you already have me pegged."

He shakes his head, frustration knitting his brows. "That's just it. With you I don't. I can't get a read. Maybe because it seems like there are a thousand things you're thinking but not saying. Like, every single second."

I sniff. "You make me sound a lot more mysterious than I am." But inside, his perceptions cause pure chaos.

His eyes cloud. "I thought I made it clear how I felt about liars."

A chunk of bark breaks off in my hand and drops to the ground. I swallow, struggling to hold up my calm exterior. *This is more than me avoiding him. Where is he going with this?*

Cole pushes from the willow, squaring off in front of me. "Do you know *why* I've been so 'adamant to talk' this week?"

The earth tips ever so slightly beneath my feet. "Haven't the foggiest."

"Last Friday when you were at my house, I asked you about Jessica Rennert, and you acted like you didn't know her."

Now the earth doesn't tip, it flips. And I spill up into the sky, tumbling through atmosphere and ether with no ground to break the fall.

When I say nothing, he reaches into his pocket and pulls out his phone. "So how do you explain *this*?" On the screen is a picture of me behind Jess's cracked windshield. He swipes to the next image: me holding out cash. And finally: me as I get out of her car.

There's no denying it. No way to explain it. Yes, I intended to pick a fight, but never one that could compromise the secrecy of my plan. "Who sent this to you?" I ask as the last of the blood drains from my face.

"Why does it matter?"

I cross my arms, holding myself together. "It *matters* if someone is trying to sabotage me."

"Just say it, Honor—*Xander*. You think it's *Xander*." But again, I say nothing. The line of questioning is riddled with too many land mines that have the potential to blow up in my face. "Well, it didn't come from him."

Right. He probably commissioned one of his minions to do his dirty work like before.

Cole steps closer, holding his phone up again. "This"—he zooms in on the image of me wild-eyed and clutching Jess's arm—"is not a game. This is serious, Honor. And I can't understand what this is. I can't . . . *help,* if you won't level with me."

As I step forward, the inches between us crackle with electricity. I'm close enough to see the navy band that wraps his pale irises. "Funny, but I don't remember asking for your help." I gesture with disgust to the picture. "And *you* of all people should know things aren't always what they seem."

"Then explain it to me," he pleads. "I *want* to believe you."

I want to believe you. He gives me back my words from our talk at the Hole. But they come at a price I can't afford to pay. Honesty.

"I don't owe you an explanation. I don't owe you anything, Cole." The statements aren't strong enough to drive him away for good, but I'm too rattled to come up with something better.

He catches my elbow before I part the green curtain. "Honor, please. Stop."

I clench my eyes shut but don't turn around. Not with my resolve beginning to topple like a line of dominoes. *Why?* Why does he have this way of making me want to confess every secret I've ever clung to?

"What?" I snap, spinning around and pushing away his hand. I miss it instantly. "What do you want from me?"

"You were in the car of someone who is a known dealer. So *forgive* me if I'm concerned and ask questions. That's what friends do," he replies fiercely.

Then it all crystallizes. And I know with gut-wrenching certainty how to divert his attention from the photo and end this.

"Oh? I wasn't aware we were friends."

He rocks back on his heels, blinking. "Excuse me?"

"Well, it isn't like we talk or hang out. And the few times we have, we usually pretend it didn't happen. So if this is your warped notion of friendship, then believe me, I'm better off without you." Saying this about kills me. But better to have Cole hating me than caring about whose car I'm in.

His lips part. The temperature between us drops a good twenty degrees. "That's what you really think?"

"No. It's what I know."

"That's not fair. You can't have it both ways," he says, hostility simmering in his tone. "Not when *you're* the one who's been icing me out all year and pretending like nothing happened last summer."

I sniff. "See, that's where you're wrong, Cole. It *was* nothing. Less than nothing. Which is . . . exactly what I feel for you."

The light goes out of his eyes.

And I want to take it back. Take it all back. To tell him that I really do want to be friends. And if I search my heart, more than friends. About how sometimes, when I'm wrapped up in the dark of night, I think of him. Remember flashes of how his mouth moved over mine. The way his hands held the sides of my face, like I was something precious. Something to be cherished. And how much it terrified and excited me to lose control like that. To want someone so badly the ache feels like it could dismantle you at an atomic level.

All this races through my head in the span of a few seconds. My heart pools with regret. But whatever this is with him, it's dangerous. And I cannot assume that kind of risk on top of the others.

Cole finally speaks, breaking our arctic silence. "Why do you always do that?" The wound in his voice is like a thousand paper cuts on my skin.

"Do what?" My eyes, possessing more courage than the rest of me, venture to his.

"Make me your enemy when I'm on your side. Honor, I've always been on your side."

His words are like lemon juice squeezed in my cuts. The sting of them forces me to look away.

"I gotta go," Cole says. "And don't worry, I won't tell anyone about the pictures. Good luck with your life." He swats at the branches as he storms off. They sway, lonely as I feel in his absence.

My heart collapses, folding in on itself over and over, until it's the size of the very smallest stone in my jar. Mission accomplished. I hurt him. Permanently forced him away.

And I have never felt worse.

Sliding down to the base of the tree, I cup a hand over my mouth. Otherwise the three words imprisoned in my throat will escape like these tears.

Come back.

Please.

15

The bell rings. I blink as everyone around me flies from their seats like a flock of startled gulls. I must've zoned out the entire second half of last period. Which I'm sure has nothing to do with the soul-rotting guilt I've had since saying all those despicable things to Cole yesterday. But it worked. Because neither Cole nor Xander so much as *breathed* in my direction today.

So the end justifies the means. Even if my insides are disintegrating.

Frantically jotting down the notes I missed, I pause to text Knox I'll be a couple of minutes late, then brace myself. He's heading out on a camping trip this weekend and chomping at the bit to get on the road. But my brother's weirdly cool with it, saying he has to grab some supplies and will swing by to get me when he's done.

Good. I'd rather he be in an easygoing mood when I jujitsu his mind on the ride home. To find out once and for all if he's tangled up with Jess Rennert.

The halls have already cleared, with only a handful of

stragglers left. I check the time, quickening my pace. Several lockers down from mine, a senior named Ben crams a bunch of books into his locker. The guy is tall and wiry and reminds me of pipe cleaners twisted together in the shape of a human.

I speed-dial my combination and lift up the handle.

"What the—"

I jump back as dozens and dozens of papers spill out, floating to the floor. Picking up one of the flyers, I instantly recognize the image. These are not the photos from yesterday. It's a grainy black-and-white picture of . . . *Cole and me.*

The blood crashes in my ears louder than Lake Michigan waves pound the surf. This picture was taken when the closet door was opened. I'm on my knees.

Distracted by the identical fluttering papers, it takes me a moment to notice what dangles inside my locker. *Kneepads.* Fucking kneepads.

Bastard! I tear them down from the hook and crumple the paper in my hand. My body rattles with rage. I've never seen this photo before, but someone really dug into the archives. Someone who was at the party last summer.

Someone who has a vendetta against me.

Xander. My nostrils flare. Who else would do something so disgustingly low? It was a mistake to think alienating Cole would be enough to stop him. This isn't over. In fact, I have a nagging sense . . .

It's just beginning.

Crouching down, I scoop up the flyers, angrily stuffing them in my bag so I can take them home to burn. But my actions slow as my thoughts cyclone. Why would Xander have kept this picture a secret all this time? He could've easily used it against me earlier. Why share its existence now? Was he simply biding his time? Or have I underestimated—

"Is this *you*?" Ben asks, wide-eyed. He holds up one of the papers, looking from me to the grainy image and back to me again.

I stand, snatching the flyer from his hands and shoving it in my bag with the rest.

Revelation lights his eyes. "No way." A leering smirk spreads across mouth. "You're Honor, right? The one who got down and dirty with Buchannon at that party. Heard you rocked his world. What'd they call you again? Oh yeah! Hum—"

"Shut up!" I roar.

My hand curls into a fist as I fight the all-consuming urge to punch every freckle from his face. My skull aches, throbbing at the cranial seams. I don't need this. Not now on top of the shit with Cole.

"Aww, hell!" Ben points to the floor. "Are those"—he blinks—"are those *kneepads*?" With that, he erupts in laughter.

And the world bleeds red with my fury.

Slowly his freckles disappear, replaced with an even tan. His face widens, his nose shortens, and his eyes kaleidoscope from brown to blue.

Suddenly, I'm staring at someone else. Suddenly, it's *Xander* laughing in my face. Taunting me. Relishing in my humiliation and promising more. And all that I've bottled builds and builds until there's nowhere left for it to go. But out.

WHAM!

Ben lets out a primal shriek, doubling over to cup his face. *"AHHH!"* The sound of his high-pitched yowl ricochets down the hall. "You bish! You himme!" he cries.

My eyes round. Oh. My. God. I just *punched* someone. Exactly the way Dad taught me to deliver a throw, too—fist tight, thumb untucked and securely wrapped over my second and third knuckles. Perfect form.

But *ow, my knuckles!* They're already throbbing and turning cherry red. I wince, shaking out my hand and back to reality. "Sorry! Oh God, I'm *so* sorry! I swear I'm not a violent person! I've never even hit someone bef—" I barely touch his hunched back when Ben shrinks away.

A trail of blood paints a wiggly crimson line from his nose to his upper lip. "Don toush me, you psychabath!" He stumbles backward before regaining his footing. Then races down the hall while cupping his face, bursting through a group of slacked-jawed students.

Turning away, I kick my locker shut, gnashing my teeth to keep from screaming at my own impulsive idiocy.

If the desired outcome was to maintain a low profile at school, I have failed. Spectacularly. Sure, the guy was being a colossal jerk, but he didn't deserve to be *assaulted*. I stare down at my rapidly swelling knuckles, wondering who they belong to.

A few minutes pass and my cell chirps.

Knox: YOU OK??? HEARD YOU COLDCOCKED THAT D-BAG BEN WILLARD?!

How do I answer such a complicated question? Because, uh, *no*. Nothing about me is okay. And I'm starting to doubt it ever will be.

Me: yes

I'm too shaky to type much more as the gravity of my situation sinks in.

Knox: mother ducker! for real???
Me: yes

Knox follows with a mind-blown emoji, a series of fists, and a GIF from his favorite *Rocky* movie where Rocky's punching the Russian.

Rather than responding to the images or pleas to tell him everything, I fall back against my locker to await my doom. There's no rational excuse for my behavior. None that I can fess up to, anyway. My cell goes off again. But this time it's not Knox. Or even Zee.

The text is from an unknown number.

Back off

The texting bubbles bounce as a second message appears. . . .

Or next time they go in EVERY locker

My stomach descends. And my phone might not know the sender, but I do. Looking up from the screen, I scan the hall for Xander. No way he'd miss watching this mortifying game play out. He's nowhere in sight. But when I shut my eyes he's everywhere.

The announcement speaker chimes. "Honor Augustine, report to the principal's office. Honor Augustine, report to the principal's office. *Immediately.*"

It's dark. But a total eclipse still wouldn't hold enough darkness to hide my shame.

I rap softly on the doorframe with my good hand, my heart poised to bungee from my chest. I'd do anything to avoid this conversation. Avoid feeling the excruciating pain of my father's disappointment. Avoid knowing how I've added to his worries when everything I do is meant to lessen them.

Chains rattle as Aunt Maeve rises from the porch swing, leaving my father alone. Dad and I haven't spoken. Since he was stuck on a construction site, Aunt Maeve was sent to collect his delinquent daughter from school.

So I sat in the principal's office, an ice pack on my knuckles, as the school counselor and principal explained to my aunt their theory behind this "terrible and out-of-character incident." They reasoned my displaced aggression was probably a result of unresolved anger over my parents' divorce. It's irrelevant that I'd said fewer than seven words. Adults are all-knowing.

The clichéd analysis was, of course, untrue. But their explanation was better than any justification I could come up with. So I nodded and confessed to bottling things up.

Still, it wasn't enough to spare me an automatic suspension until next Thursday. Apparently the school has a zero-tolerance policy on bullying and violence. The irony blows every one of my brain cells.

When I go to swallow, my throat feels prickly, like a cacti-filled desert aching for rain. I move aside as Aunt Maeve opens the screen door.

Her somber expression does little to lessen my fears. "I know opening up doesn't always come easy for you. So much like your father that way," Aunt Maeve adds, with a consoling pat to my cheek. "But just tell him the truth, Honor. Okay?"

I bob my head. Yes, I will give my father truths, even if they aren't the ones he seeks.

"Good girl," Aunt Maeve murmurs, dropping her hand. "Now, I'll put on the kettle and brew the pair of you my calming tea before I go. Valerian, ashwagandha, and passionflower oughta cure what ails you." She disappears into the kitchen.

As I open the screen door, Geronimo lumbers inside, head lowered. He pauses to nose my hand with his wet snout. A gesture of solidarity. "Thanks, Momo."

Despite my dire circumstances, the night exudes warmth. I ease down next to my father, still in his work clothes. At first he doesn't acknowledge my presence. Doesn't utter a sound. These are the times I wish he would scream and yell. Get it all out in the open so I'd have a window to his thoughts.

But he doesn't. Instead, he begins to rock. And again, I'm reminded of so many nights as a child spent on his lap that delivered the comfort the world couldn't.

"I didn't mean to hurt him, Dad. It wasn't even about that boy. It was about—"

But a sob fractures my carefully prepared speech. I planned to tell him I'd atone. To assure him that my *repressed anger* just caused a temporary short circuit in my brain. That I understood the severity, the wrongness of what I'd done, and would accept whatever punishment he felt was deserving of my crime.

"I'm sorry," I croak, wiping my cheek. The remainder of my vocabulary evaporates. Sorrys are all that's left.

So I repeat them.

His rocking stops, leaving my feet to dangle above the porch with its peeling paint that strains to touch my toes. My father looks to me, his eyes troubled yet soft, and holds open his arm.

I immediately fold myself into the nook, simultaneously feeling too young and too old. "I let you down." God, saying this feels worse than any suspension. Worse than any subpar grade.

"You let me down?" he echoes. "Honor, I think you're missing the point here. What concerns me most is why you punched that kid in the first place. That just"—I feel the sway of his head above mine—"isn't like you. What's going on?"

My breath stutters on the exhale as I lean back to look at him. "It's not about the divorce, Dad." I swallow, dropping my gaze back to my swollen hand. "Does it ever feel like too much? Life, I mean. Like there's all this pressure, squeezing from all sides, until you just . . . *burst*?"

He rubs my arm with a sigh. "Yeah, kiddo. I get that. But you *have* to find a better way to channel it. Preferably on a real punching bag and not a human substitute."

"I feel really awful about that." I sniff as the crickets compete loudly in song. "And I'll do whatever it takes to make it right."

"I know you will, sweetheart. We'll figure it out, okay?"

Nodding, I'm struck by another unpleasant thought. "Mom doesn't know yet. I should probably call her after dinner," I say, feeling dread compound my weight threefold.

"You should." He begins to rock again; the chains clink softly as we sway. "But you're gonna be all right, Honor," Dad says, kissing the top of my head. "You'll see."

The bleakness festering inside makes that hard to believe. "How are you so sure?"

He points out to the front yard, obscured by the heavy curtain of night. "Look out there." I do. Nothing but black emptiness as far as the eye can see. My father tips his head down, smooths the hair from my forehead, and nods. "Tomorrow there will be sun. No matter what, the sun always comes. It always comes, daughter."

My bones ache with exhaustion. Especially the ones in my right hand. But I hope he's right. Because I'm still waiting on my sun.

In fact, we both are.

16

Making a slow U-turn, I pedal back down the road. Charcoal and charred meat from Saturday barbecues scent the balmy air. A flash of light flickers in the night sky, silent and absent of thunder. *Heat lightning.* I look up, half expecting to see God etching my name on the next lightning bolt.

Because sneaking out on the heels of a suspension *and* grounding seems like a pretty good way to earn a smiting.

Please let this meeting with Asher Ford be worth it!

Suppressing the guilt, I scan the dark and crumbling streets of Birch Tree Mobile Park, but Lot #146 continues to elude me. Double-wide trailers glide by my peripherals, barely a breath of space between them. The proportionately small yards range from overly ornate (*hello, flock of plastic flamingos*) to severely neglected patches of hardscrabble earth.

I study the numbers on the fronts of the trailers and silently count. *138, 140, 142, 144 . . . Did I miss it again?* My brakes squawk softly as I stop and swing down from my bike. *Where is 146? It should be right here.* But instead of a mobile home, I'm staring at a row of industrial dumpsters in the back corner of the park.

Asher is not Jess, I think, trying to shake the awful sense of history repeating. *Do not jump to conclusions.* Except my brain has gotten rather efficient at leapfrogging to worst-case scenarios.

Before completely dissolving in a puddle of panic, I take out my cell to text Asher. A secondary wave of guilt hits as I flick past the messages and missed calls from Zee, wanting to know what happened at school and if I'm all right. But it's impossible to explain the cornucopia of wrongness in my world. Especially now, tucked in the shadows while waiting for Asher's reply with my heart fluttering like the insect wings that tick against the dingy streetlight. I fidget, pulling at my too-snug T-shirt.

Tonight I've gone whole hog with the Lily alter ego. It took me thirty minutes and about eight Q-tips just to get my eye makeup right. But by the time I finished, Honor had all but disappeared. Looking in the mirror, I only saw Lily. The kind of girl who had no qualms about biking to a sketchy trailer park in the middle of the night. The kind of girl capable of all manner of badassery. Let's hope, anyway.

My cell chirps, revving my pulse.

Asher: My bad. Meant #164

Initial relief is quickly swept away by a current of annoyance. Based on our previous texts, I shouldn't be surprised by this. The guy is not keen on details. Or short-term memory for that matter. (I had to remind him *twice* our meeting was today.) I'm starting to suspect Asher might be his own best customer.

Pushing my bike ahead, I follow the curving road beyond the trash bins where the house numbers climb. A dog barks from inside one of the trailers, yapping as I pass. Most of the mobile homes are dark. I catch glimpses of my image reflecting in their eerie glass eyes.

The trailer that occupies Lot #164 isn't the nicest on the street. But it isn't the worst, either. With some minor cosmetic repairs to the vinyl siding and a little landscaping, the place wouldn't be too shabby. Plus it's on prime real estate, backing up to a group of silvery-barked trees the park is named after.

I park my bike in front of an old Ford Pinto that's the color of butter and I climb the rickety steps. My knees go from cartilage and bone to pure jelly.

You're Lily! And Lily isn't afraid of anything.

Inhaling, I stretch myself high and knock.

The trippy music pulsing from the other side of the door lowers, followed by a muffled shout. *"Coming!"*

When the door swings open, a fog of smoke blasts me in the face. I cough, fanning at the thick cloud. This is definitely the right place.

"Aloha! You must be Lily," the guy says in a slow, unhurried speech. Like the words couldn't care less when they reach ears. "Sorry about the addy mix-up."

I blink as the vapor dissipates, revealing a cute, sandy-haired guy with large puppy-dog eyes. Dressed in board shorts and a faded *I HEART KAUAI* T-shirt, he looks like a surfer who washed up on the wrong shore. "I'm Asher. Friends call me Ash. For, uh, obvious reasons," he adds with a squinty-eyed smile.

"Lily," I repeat for some reason.

Ash pauses a beat, tilting his head as he studies me. "You look crazy familiar. Have we met before? At a party or—"

"Oh, I doubt it." My stomach flips like a coin. No. No way he could know me. I've done my homework. Asher Ford graduated a year ago, before we even moved to Ravenswood.

"Huh. Well, come on in. And welcome to the palace," he drawls, gesturing grandly as if Buckingham lies beyond the threshold.

"Thanks," I murmur, distracted first by the fanny pack around his waist and then by his feet. "Is that . . . a broom and dustpan on the end of your slippers?"

Ash turns, his grin big enough to be spotted from space. "Yup. I call 'em my Slip and Sweeps. Check it." Lifting up the slipper with the mini broom attached, he demonstrates by sweeping a Cheez-It from the kitchen floor into the pan on the other foot. "Invented these myself. Aren't they rad?"

"Very rad," I agree. Tucking my hands in my pockets, my eyes wander the hazy space. Stray Cheez-It aside, his place is surprisingly tidy.

The compact kitchen sits at the front of the trailer, with a bar-style countertop separating it from the carpeted living room. A tan couch—where the imprint of Ash's body appears to keep a permanent residence—takes up most of the living area. But he's managed to squeeze in a couple mismatched end tables, along with a beanbag chair patched together with X's of silver duct tape.

Ash notices me staring at the massive framed picture above the TV. He unzips his fanny pack and pulls out a bottle of eyedrops. "That's where I get my inventing gene," he says, squirting the drops almost in the vicinity of his eyes.

I lift my brows. "You're related to Henry Ford? As in, *the* Henry Ford, inventor of the Model T and assembly line?"

He props his hands at his hips, puffing his chest like a superhero in weird shoes. "One and only. I mean, it's a pretty distant relation, but still."

"Wow." I don't know what I was expecting of Ash, but somehow it wasn't this.

"Senior year," he continues, "I created this wake-and-bake mug in pottery. Hollowed out the handle so it's like a pipe, then I added this sweet double-hitter on the outside of the mug." He dreamily sighs, staring off at nothing in particular. "Helluva masterpiece. Till it got busted."

I'm getting the distinct impression most of his inventions revolve around reefer.

Ash clip-clops in his Slip and Sweeps back to the kitchen, ducking into the fridge to grab a can of pop. "You want?" he offers.

"I'm good, thanks." I lean against the counter, oddly at ease for someone who battled an army of nerves not ten minutes ago. Maybe that's just the magical effect Asher has on people. Or maybe I have a minor contact buzz. "So how do you know Ronan?" I ask as he pops the can.

His Adam's apple enthusiastically bobs, gulping down half the beverage before stifling a burp. "Used to be tight with his older brother, Luke. I've known Ronan since he was still afraid of the dark and pissing his pants," he says with an amused snort. "Anyway, I don't typically deal. My ganj is mostly for personal enjoyment. But Ronan said you were super cool, so"—he stretches his lanky arms wide—"here we find ourselves. Ready to check out the back garden? I just finished curing some sweet bamba. Like smoking a lemon cream pie." He kisses his fingers like a French chef.

"Uh, sure." I wonder how he'll react when I tell him I have no interest in buying his sweet bamba.

Ash leads me down the narrow, wood-paneled hallway. "My stuff's mostly indica," he explains, referring to one of the major types of cannabis. "Gives a majorly relaxed body buzz. Serious couch lock." The statement checks out given the perma-dent in his sofa.

"Sativa-dominant strains tend to wig me out too much," he continues. "Last time I had it, I was *totally* convinced a fly was gonna buzz in my ear and hear all my thoughts. Plus there was this warty troll under my bed plotting to murder me in my sleep. Dark times, man."

We slow, nearing the end of the hall, where the marijuana smell intensifies. The air's almost tangibly sticky with resin. My stomach flips and flops like his shoes.

"Ash, I have a confession," I say as he comes to a stop.

He turns, puppy eyes widening. "You had a troll under your bed, too?"

"No. No, it's . . ." I press my lips together. "Look, I'm not really here to buy."

Ash blinks. "Oh?" Then his face morphs into panicky horror. "Oh!" Doubling over, he clutches his head. "Oh no! No, no, no!" He pops back up and whispers, "You're DEA, aren't you? Please, Lily, I can't go to jail. I'm too delicate. I'll get passed around like a bong in there!"

"No. Ash, I'm not—"

But he's already dropped to his knees, hands smushed together in prayer as his eyes pinch shut. "Hail Mary, full of grace, uh . . . something . . . sinners and death."

"Ash, come on, get up," I say, pulling at his elbow while he Frankensteins a bunch of Catholic prayers together.

His eyes clench harder. "And deliver us from evil!" he fervently moans. "With thy daily bread."

"Would you stop freaking out? I'm not DEA!"

He peeps open one eye. "You're not?"

"*No,*" I reply with a small laugh. "I was just hoping you could show me your grow room. Maybe answer some setup questions." Digging in my pocket, I pull out a fifty. "I'd pay you."

Ash blinks and rises. "For real? So, all you want is the low-down on my grow-down?"

I nod.

With a gusting exhale, he sags against the wall and claps a hand to his chest. Then starts to breathlessly giggle. "Dude, you scared the hell outta me. My heart's beating out the back of my neck!"

"So, is that a yes?"

"Lily, today's your lucky day." His lips stretch into another full-toothed smile. "Because I happen to *slay* at grow-room set-ups. Behold!" Ash dramatically thrusts open the door.

My pupils contract to pinholes as the blinding light spills into the hallway, further amplified by the silvery wall-to-wall Mylar covering.

"*Whoa,*" I breathe in wonder. The room is NASA meets mad scientist.

I step inside, mouth gaping, and look up where repurposed

IV lines dangle from the ceiling. Ash has turned the medical equipment into a hanging system for precision watering. My eyes wander to the wall, where a glowing instrument panel allows you to adjust everything from temperature and humidity to the timers on the light source.

And at the room's epicenter are the fruits of his labor. A lush collection of three- and two-foot-tall marijuana plants, basking beneath their artificial sun. "You did all this yourself?" I ask.

"Yuh," he says with a snort. "I'm a Ford, remember? Now hold on to your noggin, 'cause I'ma 'bout to blow your gray matter, girl."

After close to an hour of having my gray matter (repeatedly) blown, I have determined three things about Asher Ford:

1. He is a grow-room mechanical *genius*. (Seriously. He even added a special device to his ventilation system so that all the outgoing air smells fresh as a spring meadow.)
2. He is a fanny pack–wearing germaphobe who wears surgical gloves anytime he comes in contact with dirt.
3. He knows jack about growing. Which I suspect has to do with #2.

When I pointed out the beginnings of leaf Septoria on a few of Ash's plants, I was met with an alarmingly vacant expression. I then explained how nitrogen deficiencies are often a catalyst for the fungal disease and, left untreated, could decimate a crop. Which is really . . . I mean, this is Gardening 101.

Yet somehow, against the odds, Asher has stoner-savanted his way through each and every stage of the cannabis life cycle—from seedling to harvest. It boggles the mind.

Ash is currently explaining the electrical requirements for growing. My knowledge of electricity consists of inserting a plug in the wall and basking in the miracle that follows. So, yeah. I have loads to learn.

"You gotta check your service panel first," he instructs, kicking his feet up in the folding-chair lounger. "Make sure it can handle the juice you'll have flowing through it. Most houses have about . . . eh"—lacing his hands behind his head, he squints to the ceiling—"one hundred and fifty amps."

I write in my notepad 150 amps, just as a knock sounds at the door. My eyes flit to his. "Were you expecting someone?"

"That'd be the pizza," Asher replies. My posture relaxes. Right. I forgot he placed an order. After a highly entertaining struggle to free himself from the folding chair *without* flipping over, he shuffles into the hall.

Puffing out a breath, I reread my previous page of notes. Man, I am out of my depth. If only I could wave a magic wand and have the setup complete. That's the part giving me the most angst. And for good reason. One mistake and—*KABOOM!* The whole greenhouse could explode.

Setting the notepad aside, I stand up to inspect his crop, instantly feeling calmer in my botanical element. The leaves of the mature group of plants have taken on a frosted appearance and look almost harvest ready, while the shorter crop still has another week or so to go.

I crouch to get a closer look. The swollen buds would've been twice as plentiful under my care. If the plants had been properly "topped" by shearing off the tip of the main stem earlier, Ash could've had two colas instead of one. And colas, being the flowering site of the marijuana, are where you get that primo densely packed bud.

Hmm. Studying the plants, I note a number of ways to improve their care. Adjustments in fertilizing, pruning, and definitely some larger pots so the roots can better spread . . .

"Lily! Come get your grub on!" Ash calls from the other end of the trailer.

But his voice fades, drowned out by my thoughts and rushing pulse. *With Asher's aptitude for mechanics and electrical, and my horticultural expertise, we'd be . . . a damn weed-growing wonder team!*

I begin to reimagine the room. The twelve plants double to twenty-four. Or hell, even more with the available space I have at the greenhouse. The idea of a partnership continues percolating until my veins are bubbling over with it.

I provide a large, secure grow space. We share the crops. Share the profits. And I . . . will guarantee Ash that I'll double his typical yield. Yes! This is a total win for both of us.

That is, *if* I can convince him to partner with me. Of course, there's also the hiccup of not knowing who's going to buy all this weed. School is a nonstarter. I've considered the pain clinic down in Forest Hills, but really, I'm getting ahead of myself.

First things first.

"Hey, Ash!" I bounce down the hall, fizzing with excitement. "I have a proposal for you. A brilliant way we can take your hobby to the next lev—"

My feet suddenly halt like my words. At the same time, my heart *gallumps,* going still in my rib cage. And I turn to stone.

"Lily!" Ash cries jovially, lifting his slice of pepperoni. Marinara sauce gruesomely collects at the corners of his mouth so he looks like the Joker. "Better grab a slice before *this* dude"— he gestures with his pizza to the guy at the table—"eats it all. I don't call him Augs the Hogs for nothing. Augs, this is the girl I told you about, Lily."

It seems I'm not the only statue in the room.

Knox has gone full granite. The pizza in his hand falls with a *thwack* to the paper plate, dropping like his jaw. *"Honor?"* he croaks.

Ash chuckles a little. "No, bruh, I said that's *Lily.* Who's Honor?" he asks before folding his slice and chomping into it.

Knox swings his narrowed gaze toward him, gritting his teeth. "The girl you told me about, with the 'bangin' brain who's hot as hell'? You were talking about Honor," he growls, flapping a hand in my direction. "My little *sister.*"

Asher's eyes go round and large as the pizza. Then he painfully gulps the half-chewed bite. "Well . . . shit."

Yeah. I couldn't agree more.

17

"Knox!" I thunder down the outside steps after him. Noticing my bike in front of the butter-colored Pinto, he grabs it, hefting it to his shoulder. "I said I can explain! Would you—" I latch onto the back tire, digging in my heels as he drags me with it. But my injured hand screams in pain, making it easy for him to wrench away the bike.

He tosses it in the back of the truck. "Uh-ho! Glory be, she can explain!" he mockingly cries. "Which part, sneaking out after curfew, the insane charcoal around your eyes, or THE FACT THAT YOU'RE STANDING HERE?"

I swallow. "All of it?"

Heaving open the passenger door, he thumbs toward the cab. "Get in, *Lily*. I'm taking you home. You shouldn't be here. And didn't you just get suspended, uh, *yesterday*?"

"Well . . ." I look to the cement for a clever comeback. *Wait a sec*. My eyes narrow. "Aren't *you* supposed to be on a senior camping trip?"

Knox briefly looks away, clenching his jaw. "This is about

you," he says, jabbing a finger at me. "Being someplace you have"—he shakes his head and sputters—"no place being!"

"Not to get all up in your holes, Augs," Ash says, joining us from the sidelines. "But you haven't really given Lil—I mean *Honor,*" he corrects, "a chance to explain."

"Stay out of it, Ash," Knox snaps, not breaking from our stare-down. Spine rigid, arms stiff, his posture stays locked like his gaze.

"Why are you so pissed?" I ask, baffled by his uncharacteristically explosive reaction. "You're the one always telling me to break rules. Buck the system and live a little!" I add in my best Knox voice. "Yet here you are, in a hypocritical hissy all because—"

Then it suddenly clicks. *Oh! That's not what this is about at all.* Gradually, the pieces begin to connect.

"The other night," I say slowly, "when I asked you where you got that joint. You *didn't* buy it from Jess, did you? Because you got it here." My eyes lift to his. "*That's* why you wouldn't tell me." Something else occurs to me, too. Something that made no sense until now. Ash didn't stoner-savant his way through the cannabis growth cycles. "Knox, are you helping him grow? Is that why you've been MIA lately?"

He breaks our eye contact with a surly grunt. Translation: *affirmative.*

While my brother might not follow rules, he's insanely strict when it comes to his own. And the first entry in the Knox Code of Ethics?

NEVER. GET. CAUGHT.

Sure, occasionally I spot him sneaking home late, but it's not like I've got insight into what he does or who he's with.

"Just get in the truck," Knox repeats, jaw muscle twitching.

I put my hands on my hips. "So is it that you got caught, or because you were caught by *me* that has you so ragey?"

"C'mon, guys," Asher peaceably implores, clapping a hand to our respective shoulders. "Let's just go inside, mellow with some ganj, and talk it out or whatever. Yeah?"

My brother doesn't appear to have much interest in any suggestion that involves me staying.

Stepping back from them both, I slam the passenger door shut. "I'm not leaving. Not until I finish talking to Ash."

His brows rise in challenge. "Oh, really?"

"Really."

Then Knox lunges for me. Narrowly ducking under his outstretched arms, I shout, "I said no!"

"Get back here!" He pivots, chasing after me. His Converse stomp in my wake as I sprint around the other side of the truck.

"This is bigger than your pride!"

Ash clumsily shuffles out of our path, palms raised. "Dudes, this domestic drama is a terminal bummer. Also the pizza's getting cold, and the cheese is gonna sweat."

"Honor, stop!" Knox hollers as I reverse direction and widen our gap.

"No!" But I'm growing more winded and tired with each lap around the pickup. "Not till you"—*wheeze*—"promise to listen!"

"Um, guys," Ash says as we streak past him for the sixth or seventh time. "The po-po just turned down my street." Our feet simultaneously trample to a stop as we look in the direction of Ash's index finger.

OH. HOLY. HELL.

My brother's eyes are wide with fear like mine. No doubt calculating the endless ways this'll go to shit if we're caught by the cops. His gaze darts to the door, and I can tell we're thinking the same thing—Ash's trailer's too far away to take cover.

"Bushes! Go!" Knox hisses.

The three of us sprint and then dive behind the scratchy, overgrown juniper at the base of the mobile home. Knees and elbows knocking with our haste.

Ash frantically slaps at his skin. "Oh God! That's probably from a black widow. It's butt string, it's all over me," he wails.

"Shh!" I grab his forearm to stop his wild flapping, freaked he'll blow our cover. His big brown eyes crumple in distress. Oh no, he's going to lose it. So besides germs and dirt, I can add spiders to his growing list of phobias. No wonder he smokes so much grass.

"Ash!" Knox whispers from the other side of me. "Just"—he pauses—"I don't know, pretend it's cotton candy. And you're at the county fair about to get on the Gravitron. Can you do that, bud?"

"I love the Gravitron," Ash replies in a quivery voice. "It's like space but not." He gulps and nods. "Okay. Yeah, I'll try." Ash squeezes his eyes shut. "I'm at the fair." Cupping his hands over his ears, he adds, "Tell me when it's over."

Peering through the gaps in the branches, Knox and I watch as the police cruiser slows. Our previously loud breaths go quiet. Quiet enough to hear garbled voices coming from the scanner. "Copy that," the officer responds.

And after a moment that lasts a lifetime, the cruiser accelerates, turning off Asher's road.

Our collective exhale nearly blows the shrubbery down. As we stand, Ash plows past us, manically mumbling something about the spider's ass silk and his need to shower in bleach. The door bangs behind him.

Which leaves my brother and me alone, a sea of secrets between us.

His lips puff with a sigh of resignation. Then he walks over to the steps and plunks down, resting his elbows to his knees. Since Knox is no longer trying to cram me in the truck, I figure it's safe to join him.

"So," he says as I ease down next to him. "Guess now you know what I've been doing with my spare time." Dejected, he picks up a stone, tossing it in the direction of the birch trees.

"How long have you been"—I glance behind us to the trailer—"doing this?"

Knox stares ahead. "Couple months now. Ash and I started hanging before that, though. First time I met him was at one of Stiles's parties." His mouth quirks. "He was smoking weed out of a banana, like a *literal* banana he'd turned into a pipe. Pottassium, that's what he called it. Anyway." The faint grin falls away as his anxious eyes slide to mine.

He thinks I'm going to tell. Or lecture him till his ears run scarlet with blood. But my brother has no idea that keeping secrets has become as effortless as breathing to me.

"Knox." I put a hand on his arm when he goes to throw another stone. "I won't tell. I promise you can trust me."

"Can I?"

My heart bottoms out, and I swallow. "Yeah. Always."

"What I mean is . . ." He hesitates, brushing the bangs

from his forehead. "Me being here, helping a buddy grow rec weed"—he hikes a shoulder—"not all that shocking. But *you* . . . Honor, what the hell's going on?"

The question holds no anger. No snark. No joke to take the edge off. Only genuine concern. My big brother is afraid for me.

And honestly? So am I. Afraid of what he'll think. Afraid the path I've chosen is the wrong one. But also, I'm afraid there might be more Lily in me than I ever imagined.

"Please, Hon." Knox grabs my hand. "*Talk* to me."

I do the unexpected then.

And fall apart.

Crying for all that is broken and unfixable. For all that is outside my control. And in between the hiccups and sobs, I tell Knox. Everything. About Dad's lost benefits. About how the bank is poised to seize both properties come August. About the shitty reality that we have nowhere near the amount needed to dig our way out of this chasm of debt.

"Hey, *shh, shh,*" Knox croons, his arm wrapped around my shoulders. "Why didn't you tell me about all this sooner? We promised we'd always tell each other the big stuff."

Brushing the tears from my face, my fingers come back smeared with black. "B-because"—my breath hitches—"I didn't think . . ." I guiltily peer up at him.

Knox deflates a little. "Because you didn't think I could help," he finishes dully.

I nod, feeling the tears well up again. "I'm sorry," I whisper.

"Look, I get it." He hunches forward with a heavy exhale. "But like it or not, I'm in this now. Which means you're gonna have to start having a little more faith in me, all right?"

"Yes," I croak, throat tight with emotion. "I mean, I will."

He nods firmly. "Okay, then. So lay it on me. Tell me the plan."

"The plan?" I echo.

My brother sniffs. "Honor, in all your sixteen years, I have never known you *not* to have a plan. And they're usually brilliant as fuck. So whatever it is, I'm in."

"Good. Because I'm now realizing there's no way I can do it without you, Knox." Not just my brother, though. There's another person crucial to this equation. "You think we could get Ash to help us, too?"

His eyes crinkle in amusement. "Little-known fact about Ash. Pizza was his original gateway drug. Throw in a large pepperoni on the reg"—Knox grins—"and you got a friend for life."

I let out a gurgled laugh. And just like that, I am no longer an island.

Maybe I never needed to be.

PART II

Vegetative Phase

May 19 – June 7

18

Same hallways. Same classrooms. Same faces. On the surface, nothing at school has changed in the time I've been gone. But roiling beneath the veneer of sameness, change is everywhere.

"Anyone gives you any shit, just say the word," Knox says, keeping pace at my side. He pops his knuckles like a Mafia guy who's come to crack skulls.

Close your eyes and point, I think as the serpentine hiss of whispers follow my footsteps. "There's got to be hotter gossip than me coming back to school. This'll blow over by lunch."

Knox does a Tigger-like bounce. "Ooh, that reminds me! Did you hear Cora Loredo is preggers and the baby daddy's Mr. Corvallis?"

"Mr. Corvallis," I repeat, brows lifted, picturing the nice but nerdy twentysomething who boasts more angles than a geometry book. "As in your computer teacher who you've referred to as a hipster-techno-douche who still sleeps in Star Wars feety pajamas?"

His gaze sullenly slides away. "I only said that because he

gave me a C. But bro could totally have some closeted geek game. And Cora *does* like to wear her hair in those Leia buns."

"Uh-huh," I reply flatly. "Thanks for proving my point."

Ahead the hallways and students intersect, pinging around like supercharged electrons. Voices swell and lockers bang.

My brother's eyes narrow at a girl who coughs the word *psycho* into her fist. When he opens his mouth to deliver what's sure to be a scathing comeback, I yank him aside.

"Listen, I appreciate you having my back, but you can't go around half-cocked and looking for vengeance."

"Says who?" He shoots an intimidating glare at some random guy as he passes. "That's right, keep on walking!" Knox calls after him.

I whack his arm. "Says *me*. Stunts like that put us at risk," I warn. "And now that we're in business, you have to be smarter about—"

"Hon"—his brown eyes turn oddly earnest—"this is my last week in this school. If I don't lay down the gauntlet now, people are gonna keep messing with you, and I won't be here to stop it."

His heart's in the right place. But that doesn't negate our need to keep a low profile. "Please, Knox, just . . . try to focus on *not* drawing attention to yourself, okay?"

"What, with a face like this?" he teases, pouting so his lips plump and his cheeks suck in more severely. Dropping the act, he sighs. "All right, all right. I'll try not to let my inner light shine too bright."

"Good. Oh, and I forgot to ask—" My mouth stretches in a colossal yawn.

It's been a week of backbreaking work. There was the

aboveground work, like the uptick in greenhouse traffic, my extra punishment chores, *and* struggling to keep up with my studies. While belowground, the three of us madly scrambled to finish the basement setup, relocate Asher's existing crop and equipment, *and* get the seeds in soil for the future crop that'll ensure our debts are wiped clean.

No wonder I feel split like a Horcrux.

And that's not all; we still have another monster hurdle. Finding a potential buyer for this bounty of pot. A potential buyer that fits within our qualifiers—not a kid, all cash payment, and willing to purchase . . . by the pound.

Yeah, a helluva hurdle.

"Dude." My brother points. "Your mouth's been hanging open for, like, twelve years."

Finishing the decade-plus yawn, I wave a dismissive hand. "Did we make any headway with that last lead? You know, the micro-license guy."

During my deep dive into the marijuana laws and regs I've come to know as well as the periodic table, I discovered my initial idea of trying to establish backdoor sales with the medical dispensaries was out of the question.

Regardless of the medicinal markets' desperation and thin supply, there was literally no way to inject our top-shelf, illegally grown weed into the med business. Why? Five little letters that added up to one big, insurmountable problem.

METRC.

Marijuana Enforcement Tracking Reporting and Compliance. A state regulatory system that made backdoor sales impossible because of its insanely stringent testing and accounting. Landing our crew back to square one.

That is until Ash mentioned how a friend of a friend had just gotten approved for a micro business license. Those were the newer licenses that governed the *recreational* side of the industry. And being newer, I found, meant the regulatory agencies had yet to close all the loopholes for ganjepreneurs like us.

"Yeah, killer lead." Knox looks both ways and lowers his voice. "We scored a meeting with Stan the Man at Cannabliss. Tuesday night."

I blink. "Tuesday . . . as in four days?"

My brother's smile is full and toothy. "That's right. And it's about a two-hour trip north, so start thinking of an excuse for Dad, because we'll need to crash at Ash's." He bops my messy topknot. "Catch you later," he calls before diving into the fray.

Boosted by news of our meeting, I head for my locker. A streak of Harvard crimson sails by, triggering a fresh surge of angst.

For five weeks I've somehow managed to juggle all the spheres of my life. So maybe it was inevitable I'd drop one of those balls. I just hate that the one I dropped . . .

Turned out to be Zee.

After quickly unloading the excess books from my bag into my locker, I race after her. "Zee!" I call out. "Hey, wait up!" I weave through a clot of guys, one of them doused with enough aftershave to take down a herd of wildebeests.

Her hair swings forward like a dark glossy curtain, blocking the side of her face as she spins the dial on her locker. The door sticks, lurching open with a metallic *bwong*.

"Hi, Zee." My nerves make the greeting sound shaky and unsure of itself. "I'm, um . . . back." Duh. I mean, obviously, or I wouldn't be standing here talking to the back of her head. My heart crawls higher, lodging at the base of my throat like a grapefruit when she doesn't respond. "Zee, I'm sorry. Please talk to me."

"Oh?" Her posture stiffens as she turns to face me.

Yikes. My friend looks like an ice carving of herself—cold, hard, unmoving.

"*Now* you want to talk? After I had an entire *week* of worrying? First you punched Ben, and then you wouldn't return any of my texts or calls. You know I had to track down Knox just to find out if you were even upright and breathing? Honor, what the hell is going on?" The questions pelt like angry, frozen sleet over my skin.

My eyes drop to a trampled pen cap on the floor. I feel equally crushed and small. But how *could* I respond to her stream of texts and messages when they demanded answers I had no way of giving? Zee's too smart. She'd see through my taffy-stretched truths, right down to the lies.

Guilt squeezes my neck, narrowing my windpipe. "I'm sorry," I repeat hoarsely. "I never meant to hurt you." All of this is true.

She sniffs. "And, what, that's supposed to make me feel better? That a friend decided to cut me out of her life without explanation, but hey," she adds, sarcastically lifting a shoulder, "she's *real* sorry and didn't mean to be a jerk."

"I'm *not* cutting you out," I plead, reaching for her, desperate for her to somehow understand this is all temporary.

Zee shrinks from my hand. "No, I'm done! This is it, Honor. You *owe* me an explanation. So either tell me what this is all about or . . ." She shakes her head with an air of hopelessness. No more able to bring herself to finish than I can bear to hear the words.

But the ultimatum wedges between us, tall and vast as Kilimanjaro.

My lips part, but my voice box has snapped shut like a bear trap. Spiky iron teeth grip the words I desperately wish I could say. Her fingernails blanch with bits of white as she squeezes her arms, waiting for my reply.

"It's . . . complicated," I eke out.

No sooner does the statement leave my mouth than I spot a familiar figure near the water fountain. Jess's bony fingers move so quickly, I almost miss the transaction as the guy strides past. Then, like a magician's trick, the money disappears into the sleeve of her leather jacket.

Blood drains from my face, replaced with a sense of unavoidable emptiness. *We are not the same. I'm different from Jess.*

Zee's mouth is still moving, but I can't hear what she's saying. The sound of my two worlds colliding has eclipsed everything else. I was a fool to think I could keep them separate. A fool to think I could push my friend away while still holding her tight.

Now my eyes mirror Zee's, a glossy sheen of tears and hurt and disappointment.

"I don't understand. I thought we were friends," she croaks, lower lip trembling. "I thought . . ." A tear pushes out, rolling down her cheek, and before the glistening trail reaches her jaw, I know what I must do.

"Yeah, I thought we were, too." My gaze falls back to the broken pen cap as tears pulse hot behind my eyes, my heart splintering into a million pieces. But I know now that severing our relationship is the only way to protect her.

Because I am a felon. Illegally growing and soon-to-be selling mass amounts of marijuana. I have become the very thing that Zareen despises and the very thing that could threaten her greatest dream if (God help us) this all goes sideways.

Which is why I say nothing as she slams her locker. Nothing as she declares our friendship over. Nothing as I watch her dissolve away into the crowd.

And all of this nothing?

Leaves me absolutely fucking gutted.

19

Asher hunches forward in the dark, elbows resting on the dash as he peers through the binoculars. He's dressed in head-to-toe hunting gear. Never mind we're in Knox's Chevy Silverado and not the deep woods.

On the plus side, between Ash's inherent ridiculousness and the high stakes of this meeting, my self-loathing over blowing up my friendship with Zee has taken a back seat.

"What's he saying?" Ash whispers despite the several hundred feet between us and the large, industrial warehouse.

Knox parked in the back corner of the Cannabliss lot, away from the surveillance cameras perched like birds of prey around the exterior. With my brother as the "face" of our operation, we didn't think the owner would take kindly to a couple of teenage tagalongs eavesdropping on a legally *questionable* transaction.

I adjust the volume on my headset, which is connected to Knox's Bluetooth earpiece. My stomach is a riot of winged creatures. "Mostly small talk," I report. "Knox definitely set his charisma to 'stun,' though. Stan the Man didn't question his fake ID at all."

State law requires you to be twenty-one to enter a recreational business, which left us scrambling to get a quasi-decent fake for Knox, AKA Troy Tolliver, the person who Asher's connection has vouched for.

Ash grunts in frustration. "Man, I can't see diddly. The place hardly has any windows. Wish I could get a look at their operation. Bet it's dope as hell." He snorts at his pun. "Can you believe they grow, process, and sell, all under one roof? No wonder the building's big as a—"

"*Shh-shh.*" I wave a hand at him, concentrating on the graveled voice now speaking. My heart rate kicks up a notch.

"What?" He lowers the binoculars, his eyes extra giant and glowing against the rest of his face covered in camo paint. "Does Augs need backup? Should I bust out the Tasers?"

"No, it's actually good news for us. Stan was just saying they had a small water leak that caused a spike in humidity. By the time it was discovered, his crops were already infested with mold."

"*Righteous!* One man's mold is another man's miracle."

"Hang on," I say to Ash, who's mid fist-pump. Unmuting my headset, I quickly speak into Knox's earpiece. "Ask him if the lost crops were going to be processed for edibles or used for smoking."

My brother clears his throat to indicate he's heard me. "Man, that's every grower's worst nightmare," Knox says, sounding genuinely upset for the guy. "So, Stan, the crops you lost, was it your top-shelf smoke or generic for edibles?"

A door yawns in the background. "See for yourself," Stan miserably replies.

Knox whistles. "*Daaamn*. So it's your top-shelf," he repeats for my benefit, which I then relay to Asher.

"Worst part is," Stan continues, "that's what my customers want most. I can barely keep it stocked as is. But now, I'm all demand and no supply."

Oh, Stan, I think, my excitement mounting by the second, *you've just given away all your negotiating leverage.*

"Sounds like you're in a real pot pickle, my friend," my brother muses.

"Now, Knox," I hiss into the headset. "Do it now!" Ash leans in close enough for me to get dizzy off his face paint fumes.

"A *real* pot pickle," Knox says again. "But as our mutual friend's already told you, I might be able to help. You see, I happen to have this surplus of dank. Some real primo Critical Kush." There's a rustling sound. "Here, check it out."

I hear the cap unscrewing on the little glass jar I packed, loaded with the most pristine bud I could find in Asher's collection.

A loud sniff follows. "Mm. Earthy"—another sharp sniff—"with just a touch of pine," Stan murmurs appreciatively. "Bud's well-formed, too—nice fluffy popcorn shape, minty green nugs. She's a beaut, Troy."

"What can I say, I come from a family of gifted growers," Knox adds, causing me to grin despite the circumstances. "You can keep that sample if you like. But, full disclosure, I should mention I've got some interested parties who've also fallen on hard times with their crops, so—"

"How much?" Stan cuts in. "I mean . . ." He stalls, trying to dial back his desperation. "What I mean is, how much do you have, and when would it be available?"

"Uh . . ."

I jump in when my brother falters. "Six pounds that'll be ready by the end of the week, with another six pounds dried and ready the next."

Knox recites what I've said, adding, "And I've got a much bigger crop, but that won't be harvested till . . ."

"Third week of July," I insert. In the background a lighter flicks, then a heavy inhale and a long pause. Guess Stan's doing quality assessment. Ash and I exchange anxious glances.

After what seems like hours, Stan the Man finally exhales with a cough. "Creamy," he rasps. "Real smooth finish. So how much you selling for?"

"Six—"

"Two thousand a pound," I quite possibly yell.

Ash rocks back. "Dude, the plan was to charge base whole-sale, sixteen hundred dollars. No way he's gonna cough up that kind of cash. You're gonna price us out of the market!"

"How much?" Stan asks again as Knox procrastinates with *um*s and *uh*s.

"Two thousand," I repeat, loud and firm, ignoring Asher's waving hands and thrashing head. "Knox, trust me on this. He's—" Then my headset fills with static hissing.

"Oh, come on!" I cry.

"What happened?" Ash asks.

"I don't know. It just stopped working." I yank off the device. *Of all the times for this hunk of technology to fail!*

"Lemme see." He takes the headset before I break it in frustration, sliding it on and calmly pressing a few buttons.

I squirm in my seat, gaze bouncing to the building and back again. "Well? What's wrong with it?"

"Nothing," Ash replies with a casualness disproportionate to the situation. "Augs might've turned off his earpiece." He fiddles with it for another minute or so.

"On purpose or by accident? Do you think he heard me? *Dammit!*" I pound my fist to the seat. *What if Asher's right? What if I pushed too hard and high with our price? What if I cost us the deal?*

"Door! They're coming!" Ash whisper-shouts. We immediately slide like goo down the seats and out of sight. He peers over to me, looking like a scared raccoon with reverse markings.

Footsteps approach, and the driver's door opens. Knox slides in, waving to Stan the Man, a congenial grin fixed on his face. "Well, kids," my brother says, lips barely moving, "looks like we got us a buyer." He fires up the engine. "He wants all of it."

I exhale, turning to putty, while Ash plays air guitar at my side.

"And the best part?" Knox peers down at us, ramming the truck in gear. His smile fills up the whole cab. "We got two G's a pound!" Slapping the dash, he adds, "Dude didn't even try to talk me down! You were right, sis. *Super* loud about it, but right."

So he did *shut off the earpiece on purpose.*

Asher smiles, teeth glowing as we sit upright. "My girl," he praises, holding up his fist for a bump. "Your ballsy move paid off."

"Not ballsy. That was pure ovaries, boys." I break into a grin as they chuckle.

"Yeah, yeah," Knox teases, swatting me with his flat cap. "Save your brags till this is over."

I gaze out the bug-spattered windshield, my optimism glowing like the bubbles of light before us. We have our crew, the weed, and as of tonight, a buyer.

The road home stretches out like a long charcoal-colored tongue. But somehow despite the miles ahead, the destination feels closer than ever.

Summer is on the lips and minds of every student, the collective excitement barely contained within the brick and mortar. And after last night's sealed deal at Cannabliss, I finally feel like one of them—desperately yearning for the school year to end.

Even if my desperation is rooted in very different reasons.

I'm thinking about all this, and the amount of cramming ahead of me for next week's finals, when I collide with another body. "*Oof.* Sorry." The apology reflexively tumbles out before I see who it is. My stomach plummets as I look up from the ink-smeared hand.

"Yeah," Zee mutters, quickly averting her eyes, "you always are." Clutching her Ruth Bader Ginsburg binder like a shield, she maneuvers around me as Katie Jordan, one of her debate teammates, bounds up to her side like a puppy. Zee greets her with a smile as warm as the sun. The one she used to reserve for me.

Elbows and backpacks brush me as they pass. The world rushing by while I stand motionless. I force myself to walk, the sadness pulsing through me, pooling in my chest before stretching open like a black flower.

I should be immune to the feeling after enduring Cole's cool indifference. Key word—*should*. But like my reaction to Zee, I still feel flayed every time I look at him. Haunted by the hurt in his voice as he said: *Honor, I've always been on your side.*

Nearly two weeks, and Cole's words are still rattling in my head like loose change in a pocket. The sentiment's irrelevant to what's most critical right now, and like loose change, of little value. So I should let it go. If only the phrase hadn't lodged itself inside me like a splinter.

Just seven more days of this torture.

I step inside the brightly lit main office, the door closing with a soft *shush* behind me. The air hums with electricity, smelling faintly of Febreze and something like burnt coffee.

Mrs. Newman isn't at her desk. Instead of finding the secretary, I see her computer torn open with cords and boards spread across the polka-dot desk pad. Principal Janney's voice rumbles from his adjoining office, putting me on edge with the memory of my last visit.

"Hey!" A head pops up like a jack-in-the-box from under the desk, startling me out of my skin. Mr. Corvallis cringes slightly. "Didn't mean to scare you. I was just on the hunt for a renegade screw," he explains, holding up the bit of silver before setting it down.

I unstick myself from the ceiling, loosening the hold on my bag. "Surprised is all."

Mr. Corvallis slides a tool back into the open case on the floor, pushing up his thick-rimmed glasses and griping over the task of trying to upgrade a computer older than him. "But enough about my IT troubles. What brings you in?" Rising to his feet, he brushes a hand over his shirt, which reads COM-PUTER JEDI in blocky Star Wars font.

"I'm, uh . . ." The blush pumps its way to my cheeks. Glancing away, I make the mistake of looking at a rack of brochures. The pamphlet covering sex and STDs stares back. Damn Knox for telling me that *stupid* rumor about Mr. Corvallis and Cora! "Mr. Durand said Mrs. Newman had an appointment slip for me? I'm Honor Augustine."

"Augustine? Oh yeah," he says, gesturing to me with the mini screwdriver in his hand, "I had your brother, Knox, in my computer class last semester." He shakes his head, adding, "Quite a character, that one. Anyway, Mrs. Newman just stepped into a meeting, but if you give me a sec, I can see if anything's buried under this heap of scrap metal." The teacher flashes an adorable smile and pair of dimples, softening the sharp lines of his face.

"That'd be great, thanks." I awkwardly fidget, making a concerted effort *not* to look at the brochure screaming about chlamydia and gonorrhea. My eyes safely settle on the plastic ficus in the corner while he combs through the computer guts and makes polite chitchat.

Mostly I nod and avoid direct eye contact.

"Aha!" Mr. Corvallis eventually declares, shifting aside a handful of cables. "Here we go."

I take the slip he holds out from Mrs. Rudalewski, excusing me from sixth period. The counselor's big, looping signature lines the bottom, looking like a series of interconnected balloon animals.

"Thanks again," I say.

"No problem," Mr. Corvallis replies.

Checking the room number on the note, I duck out from the office and veer left, following the hall to its end and the door marked RESTRICTED AREA. I push through and climb the stairwell to the second floor, my feet smacking out a hurried melody as I go.

With Ravenswood's dwindling population, the high school is too large for the staff and students who currently occupy it, leaving sections marked off and forbidden from entry. But with the building also being over a century old and requiring constant renovations, it isn't unusual for offices to be temporarily moved to these restricted areas.

I pass abandoned classrooms, occupied by ghostly outlines of stacked chairs and desks huddled beneath drop cloths. The sun manages to penetrate the tall, grubby windows, illuminating the air with glittery dust motes, and smelling of old, forgotten places.

I arrive at room 225B just as the late bell rings, reverberating through the deserted hallways.

Smoothing down my hair, I draw a breath. Square my shoulders. I am the epitome of composure. Of control. That's what I'll show Mrs. Rudalewski, anyway.

I knock on the door—three confident, sharp raps. When there's no response, I try knocking a bit harder. Still nothing. Shifting the messenger bag at my shoulder, I press my ear to the wood. Only the faint ticking of boiler pipes can be heard.

"Hello, Mrs. Rudalewski?" Tentatively, I crack the door. "It's Honor Augustine. I have a note you wanted to meet with me." The room is black as pitch. Pushing the door open wider, the light from the hall spills into the windowless office.

"Is anyone here?" *Maybe she had another meeting and is running late?*

Squinting inside, I see tall, hulking file cabinets lining the back wall. To the left, shelves are stuffed with globes, ancient projectors, and other antiquated classroom paraphernalia. This doesn't appear to be an office at all. Not even a temporary one.

The hair on my neck instantly stands and salutes. *What the—*

Powerful hands suddenly shove me from behind, thrusting me headlong into the abyss.

The breath rushes out of me as my bag falls from my shoulder. I throw out my hands to stop from colliding face-first with the floor. My palms smack hard, the stinging sensation buzzing up both arms.

Then the door slams shut.

"Hey!" Scrambling to my feet, I grope through the darkness toward the skinny beacon of light at the bottom of the door. My elbow bangs against something solid; it crashes loudly, scattering across the floor. Seizing the doorknob, I frantically twist it one way, then the other.

The handle doesn't budge.

"Hey, come back!" I shout at the fading slap of sneakers as the person sprints away. "Let me out of here!" I pound my fist to the door.

A sickly feeling slides down the walls of my stomach, settling heavily in the pit. *Who do you think's going to hear you? You didn't see a soul in this hallway, remember? Someone set you up.*

I frantically pat for the light switch, my thoughts pressing in like the darkness. So *this* is Xander's revenge. Locking me in some storage room in an isolated part of school, far from ears that will hear my screams. Guess the flyers were just a sadistic teaser of the glorified "closet" to come.

I admit, the timing of his strike is genius. Xander knows I'm fresh off suspension. Knows I can't risk being at the center of another student-related incident. Which means he knows . . .

My silence is virtually guaranteed.

My heart stutters with relief when I find the switch and flick it on.

Nothing. Not even a buzz or pop from a fizzled-out fluorescent tube.

Oh no. Nonono. I flip the light switch up and down countless times, but the outcome is the same. Slowly I turn, press my back to the door, and stare into the inky blackness. A black so vast and yawning it could fill galaxies.

As kids, Knox and I played endless rounds of hide-and-go-seek in the dark. One of the few games where I claimed more wins than losses. My small size and ability to pretzel myself into peculiar contortions gave me a natural advantage. And not once was I afraid of the dark.

But this isn't a game.

And you don't know what lurks in this darkness. Or how far Xander's willing to go.

I spin around and scream again, pounding and kicking until I'm winded, my vocal cords raw and frayed. My need to escape grows more primal. The air compresses; my lungs move spastically inside their cage. I grow dizzy, my balance teetering like my control.

Get a grip! Xander will be counting on me to lose it. Giving in to the terror means he wins. And I can't let him win.

Inhaling through my nose and breathing out through my

mouth, I begin flipping through my mental catalog of plants and flowers. Their whispered names spew from my lips until my pulse starts to normalize.

As the panic lifts, I retrace my steps, blindly swinging my arms in front of me. I bump against something solid. *My bag.* Crouching down, I reach out, but my fingers don't land on the canvas surface I expect.

This object is something else entirely. Smooth. Round. Hard. Swallowing, my insides clench as I graze the surface of the mystery object. It curves downward. Until my fingertips sink into two hollowed holes. And I realize what I'm touching.

Eye sockets.

I shriek. The high-pitched cry ricochets throughout the storage room, filling up every crack and crevice.

Scuttling backward from the skull, I stumble over my bag. My *real* bag and not human remains. I find my cell, quickly turning on the flashlight. The trembling beam reveals a human skeleton toppled from its stand. *That must be what I elbowed on the way to the door.* No wonder it was so loud—that was the sound of 206 bones crashing to the floor.

My chuckle of relief borders on deranged. This isn't a cold-case murder, just a skeleton hailing from an anatomy class of yesteryear. But the consolation is short-lived when I notice the display on the upper corner of my cell.

"Oh no! *No!*" Zero bars. My phone has no reception. I pan the light as I circle the room, seeing no hidden landlines or intercoms. Meaning I could be trapped here . . . indefinitely.

"All right, Honor, keep it together. Just see if there's a spot you can get a signal."

I do a thorough sweep of the room, checking near the door,

the shelving wall, and then the opposite wall with the scattered pile of bones. Not even a flicker of a signal. It isn't until I move toward the back wall with the filing cabinets that there's suddenly a bar! One precious bar! And then it's gone again.

"NOOO!" I shake my phone, willing the reception back into it, but the screen remains barless. And to make matters worse, my battery's now in the red.

Returning to the door, I glumly slide down to the concrete. Then I tap off the light to conserve what's left of my charge. Plunged back into darkness, I continue racking my brain for a means of escape and come up short.

"Don't suppose you have any ideas, Slim?" I ask the pile of bones beside me. "Yeah, me neither." My throat goes tight as the tears build. *"Shit,"* I croak, rubbing my face.

And just as I'm ready to give myself over to this black hole of despair, I hear something.

20

Sucking in a breath, I crush my ear harder to the door. *Footsteps!*

My heart flutters like a caged bird. I jump to my feet. "Help!" *Pound-pound-pound.* "Help! I'm locked inside! Please, I need help!"

The footfall outside redirects, moving toward me. "Hold on, I'm coming," the muffled voice replies. Moments later a key slides into the lock and—

The door swings open, fluorescent light washing over me.

"*Honor?* What . . . what are you doing in here?"

Freed from my supply room prison, I barrel forward, throwing grateful arms around my rescuer. "*Cole,*" I rasp.

In this suspended heartbeat of time, I forget about the wall I've built between us. And as his arms hesitantly lower around me, the imagined wall crumbles down.

"Hey, what happened?" he asks. "Are you okay? God, your heart's beating so fast."

But his voice is as sobering as smelling salts. "Er, yeah." I push from his arms, embarrassment singeing my cheeks.

"Are you?" Cole repeats doubtfully. "Because you just voluntarily hugged me."

Something I haven't done since our time in the closet. And now my traitorous body's a riot of tingles with the memory, old and new.

Breaking from his worrisome gaze, I busy myself by brushing the hoard of dust bunnies from my clothes. "If I'm being completely honest, I've had better days."

He peers inside the darkened storage room and frowns. "What is—are those *bones*?"

"Yeah. I, um, thought this was the office I was supposed to come to. See?" I show him the slip before sliding past to collect my bag and its scattered contents. Kneeling down, I continue my edited account. "Anyway, by the time I realized I was in the wrong place, the door had already swung shut and locked me inside. Then I couldn't get a cell signal, so . . ."

I fade out somewhere between stuffing away my review notes on the War of 1812 and discovering the baggie that fell from the outer pocket of my bag.

I hold up the small white pills. My eyes widen in horror. *These aren't mine!* The thought hardly comes as a comfort since they're the exact words uttered during surprise locker checks. And how many of those students were believed? *None.* Sweat springs, coating my skin in a clammy sheen, as bile swirls at the base of my esophagus.

"Need a hand?" Cole asks, nudging the door all the way open so light fills the room.

"*No!* Uh . . . I—I'm fine," I stutter, having nowhere to hide the drugs but back in my bag.

We return to the hall, where it's so bright it hurts. My heart punches beneath my T-shirt, straining the cotton and flesh. Again, Cole asks if I'm all right, but his voice sounds distorted and stretched to my ears.

"Yeah," I reply absently, while my mind sprays thoughts like greenhouse sprinklers. Flashing back to when I was pushed, I try to recall if there could've been time in the seconds before I was shoved to plant the drugs on me. *Maybe*. But it also could've happened earlier when I was distracted by Zee in the hall.

Have I miscalculated just how much Xander hates me? Because it's clear now: This isn't some juvenile prank aimed at scaring me. It's bigger. The objective is mass destruction. *Trap me in a choreographed location with drugs I didn't know I had. While I wait to be found . . .*

By his best friend.

I take a guarded step from Cole, eyeing him warily. "You never said what *you're* doing up here."

He sniffs, doing a double take when he realizes I'm serious. *"Me?"* His jaw clenches and unclenches as he gnashes his gum. "You're kidding, right? Because ten seconds ago you were *thrilled* to see me, and now you throw shade? *Unbelievable*," he mutters. "Coach sent me up to find an extra replacement net for the goal. That's the *only* reason I'm here."

"Okay," I reply evenly, "say I believe you."

He huffs, clearly offended.

But I don't have time for diplomacy. I need to know if what he says is true. "Where's your hall pass?"

"You're really something, Augustine. The way I see it, I have a lot more reason not to trust you than you have not to trust me."

I fold my arms. "And yet I still don't see a pass."

"You want proof? *Fine*." Cole shoves his hand in the pocket of his warm-up pants. Then his other pocket.

I raise my brows.

"Stop giving me that look. I swear it's here somewhere." He freezes mid-search. "What was that?"

I listen, hearing nothing but the hum of the lights and rattle of the air vent. "I don't hear anything." Until . . . I do. The distant, steady plod of footsteps as they ascend the stairs.

Which means if Cole was never really sent to find me, there's an excellent chance the person now coming up the stairs was.

The pills in my bag tick like a time bomb.

"We have to hide!"

He rolls his eyes. "Said no innocent person ever."

"I am innocent!" I insist. "Look, it doesn't matter that I ended up here by accident. I'm in a *restricted* area. How's it going to look days after getting off suspension? Please, Cole, I know you're mad at me, but . . . I can't get caught."

A heartbeat of indecision passes; his chin lifts in defiance. "Tell you what. I'll help you, *if* you offer me one truth." Cole holds up a finger. "Just one."

Terrified, I pry my eyes from the entrance and back to him. "All right! But can we do this later because—"

"No, now. Answer yes or no," he presses on. "When we were under that tree, did you mean what you said about feeling 'less than nothing'?"

Of all the damning questions. I clench my eyes shut, fear boiling in my veins. Then I blurt the truth. "No, okay? *No!* Now can we please get out of here?"

Cole's eyes come alive, lips twitching into a shadow of a grin. "Okay, then, follow me. And try to keep up," he adds.

Oh, I intend to.

Bounding after him, I skitter around the corner, nearly plowing into a sheet of plastic. Half the tarp hangs, limp and sagging from where the tape gave up holding it to the ceiling. Cole rushes to the first door we reach. The muted overhead light flickers like a strobe.

"Locked," he whispers. Quickly digging a key from his pocket, he jams it in the keyhole.

I nervously glance back in the direction we came, keeping lookout. The tarp flutters, crinkling as it catches air from an overhead vent. But try as I might, I can't hear anything over the rustling plastic. *"Hurry!"*

"I am," he says through gritted teeth, jiggling and twisting the key. Suddenly the temperamental lock springs open. "Got it!"

I pile in behind him, closing the door. Like the others, this classroom is an ode to emptiness and dust. We scurry across the open space, diving beneath a desk covered by a paint-spattered sheet.

Cole folds himself as small as possible, but being constrained by the laws of physics as we are, I'm forced to squash up against him. My back mashes to his chest, not an atom of space between us.

Tugging the sheet back into place, our breaths pant in unison. The smell of his cinnamon gum fills the air, setting fire to the back of my neck.

His exhale tickles my ear. "This is cozy."

When I turn my head to shush him, his mouth is literally *right there*. Lips all pink and full and . . . I gulp, hating how easily I remember their softness. *"Shh,"* I pathetically manage, snapping my gaze toward the rippling sheet.

Cole's heart slams a zigzagging beat into my spine until I'm dizzy with its rhythm. But even if he can be trusted, his dad is still a cop. *His dad is a cop. His dad is a cop.* The phrase cannot be repeated enough.

"Can you hear anything?"

Closing my eyes, I try to tune out Cole's presence and how he wraps me like cinnamon-infused cellophane. "There's footsteps," I reply, voice unsteady. "I think they're coming this way."

"Hello?" a deep male voice calls out from the hall, causing me to jump. "Somebody up here?" Keys jingle.

"Must be the janitor," Cole whispers. "Probably saw the mess in the storage room."

Anxiety vibrates in my every molecule as I clutch the bag to my chest. "Or it's one of the security guards." Either way, I'm monumentally screwed if someone tipped them off about the drugs in my possession.

His boots tromp over to the door, thudding heavy as my heart. *Oh my God, this is it! It's all over!* I mash my lips to keep from screaming as the handle twists and the door creaks open.

"Anyone in here?" he asks gruffly.

My face is a portrait of sheer panic as I look up at Cole. *Easy,* he mouths, cupping his hand around mine.

Nodding, I gaze back to the sheet. And I shouldn't be thinking how good it feels, having my hand swallowed up in his. Or how the union of our palms sparks a heat, reawakening the dull ache I want to wish out of existence.

The man plods closer, his shadow becoming less fuzzy and

more hard-edged as he nears. His hand reaches out, the outline spreading across the thin fabric. I bite my lip, turning my face to Cole's chest, where his heart hammers hard enough to chip ribs. And then . . .

A pulsing rhythm erupts in the air followed by the nasally rap of Eminem. The guy's phone is ringing.

"Yeah," he answers impatiently, stepping back and standing upright. A few beats of silence pass. "No, not yet." Another pause. "I already checked there." He sighs. "Yes, with my eyes open," he replies, scuffing a boot over the floor. "Fine, I'll meet you back in storage." Hanging up, the man abandons his search and exits, keys jangling like a cat bell as he moves swiftly down the hall.

My exhalation flutters the sheet.

"That was close," Cole murmurs. His hand slides away, leaving mine an empty shell.

We wait until the footsteps fade before crawling out from under the desk. Cole's cheeks are as flushed as mine feel.

I quickly cross the room and crack the door. "Looks clear," I say, adjusting the bag at my hip. We slip into the hall. "Do you know if there's another way out of here?" If these guys are going to be in the storage room, that seals off the only exit I know.

Cole squeezes the back of his neck. "There's an exit at the opposite end of this hall, but—" He abruptly falls silent following a loud *clunk*.

A new voice, low and scratchy, filters down the other hallway. *"Cole?"* I prompt, with a *hurry up* gesture of my hand.

He blinks, pale eyes going from faraway and dreamy to sharp with purpose. "I have an idea. Come on."

Together we creep down the corridor, past the drifting tarp. I hang behind as he peers around the corner, quickly ducking his head back. "Okay, here's the plan," he whispers with his intoxicating breath. "We wait until they're both in the storage room. And when I say 'go' "—he points at the distant, glowing sign—"you run like hell for that exit. Once you're through the door, take the stairs all the way down to the lower-level exit. Not the first floor, but the lower level so nobody sees you. Got it? Lower level," he repeats.

My head rapidly bobs.

"All right." Cole resumes his watch, absently cracking his knuckles. With each pop, my muscles wind up to run. "Not yet," he whispers. "Not yet . . ." The seconds tick until he suddenly turns. *"Go!"*

I take off like a shot, firing across the intersection of the two halls, eyes solely fixed on my target. Closing in on the bouncing exit, Cole brings up the rear. His stride steady as a metronome. Just as the door is within reach, I make a startling discovery. My shoes squeak as I trample to a halt.

"There's . . . an alarm," I pant. "We can't go this way. Cole, they'll hear us."

He gulps, catching his breath to reply, "I know. That's why . . . you're the only one going through."

"But they'll catch you."

"So? I'm just the idiot lacrosse player who couldn't find a net and accidentally triggered an alarm." He glances over his shoulder, then jerks his chin toward the exit. "You better go."

Bewildered, I stare up at him. "You'd do that? For me?" After everything I've done, how terribly I've treated him, distrusted him. *He would still cover for me?*

By way of answer, his palm smacks the door, pushing it open. Instantly the alarm clangs. "I said *go*!" he shouts over the din.

Thank you, I mouth, and dart past him.

"Honor!" he calls out as I clear the first flight of stairs.

Careening to a halt on the landing, I look up.

"For what it's worth," Cole says, "the kiss, it meant something to me, too."

Then the door slams shut.

21

The plan is simple. Straightforward. Knox will deliver the six pounds of marijuana to Cannabliss, collect the $12,000 in cash, and *immediately* return to the greenhouse.

"You remembered your burner phone?" I ask, trailing my brother like a night shadow. The black duffel bag bounces with my stride as we approach his truck, hidden behind one of the greenhouse outbuildings beside Asher's Pinto beater.

"Yes," Knox replies. Twisting the handle, he lifts the cover to the truck bed.

The breeze kicks up, filling the dark with the whispers of field grasses. "And your charger and fake ID?" I add, the wind ruffling my grown-out bangs.

Knox grunts an affirmative, adjusting his flat cap and looking every bit the part of an old-timey bootlegger.

"Here, lemme get it," Ash says to me, removing the bag from my shoulder. The duffel is puffed and swollen like the cured buds we've packed inside it. "False bottom I added to the tool bin can be a little touchy," he explains.

While Ash conceals the cannabis inside the hidden compartment of the large metal container, I continue running the checklist with Knox. "What about the app? Did you sign in so we can track your location? Otherwise we won't be able to tell when you—"

"*Yes,*" Knox says, no longer bothering to hide his annoyance. He slams down the cover once Asher is finished. "Relax."

"You want a hit off my onesy, Hon?" Ash offers. He unzips his ever-present fanny pack, holding out a skinny one-hitter pipe. "Guaranteed to make you feel all sweet and gooey like a melted Fudgsicle."

"Uh, no. Thanks," I reply distractedly. His head droops a little. Like a golden retriever you've just refused to play fetch with. "That just means more for you, Ash," I add, then go after my brother. "Hey, Knox, don't forget if you—"

"For the love of God, Honor," he gripes, opening the driver's door. "If the goal's to smother me like some big-bosomed grandma, mission accomplished."

"Sorry," I mumble. "First-drop nerves, I guess." Leaning against the side of the truck, I massage my temples.

Knox's face softens when he turns. "It's gonna be *fine,*" he says, oozing confidence. "What did Gran always tell us— believing is half the battle?"

My arms drop, hanging like limp noodles at my sides. "Yes, but I'm pretty sure she was talking about your baseball tryouts and not felony drug trafficking."

Knox puts his hands on my shoulders and squeezes. "Cripes, you're like a bag of ropes." He gives me a gentle shake. "Hey, you sure it's just about the drop?"

I look away, afraid he'll use some scientifically undocumented sibling osmosis to absorb my thoughts. But I have to warn him. "Promise you'll be careful. I'm just . . . I'm worried you're not taking this seriously enough."

The moon bobs and weaves among the clouds, showing his exasperated expression. "This is the part where you have to trust me, remember?"

"Knox, I *do*."

Shaking his head, he turns back to the truck.

"I mean it, that's not what this is about! Something happened at school," I confess.

Slowly, he turns around. "What kind of something?"

"I didn't want to tell you so close to graduation because . . . I didn't want anything to jeopardize that." It's jarring enough to see my brother go from diploma to drug mule in the span of thirty-two hours.

Just yesterday I was clapping proudly, sandwiched between Dad and Aunt Maeve as my brother tossed his tasseled cap high. Then, after the ceremony, the four of us piled into our favorite booth at Kringle's, a quirky place frozen in Christmas 365 days a year. We sat beneath Bud the Santa-hat-wearing moose, bumping elbows and passing ketchup. Our voices overlapped, eager to outdo one another with our best Knox stories (there were many). And for one precious evening, it seemed everyone had forgotten their worries. The laughs came quicker, the smiles more easily.

It was a portal to the simpler times I longed for. And another stark reminder of why this plan has to succeed.

Which is why Knox has to know what happened—from the

bogus appointment slip to getting locked in the storage room and the drugs I had to flush down the toilet.

"So *that's* why I'm telling you to be extra careful tonight," I conclude. "Because I still don't know who targeted me or why." True, Xander's a prime suspect, but I don't have proof, and there's already bad blood between them.

To my brother's credit, he's taking this way more in stride than I expected. "Well," he says, puffing out a breath, "we know it's not another dealer, right? I mean, that's one of the big reasons we wanted to sell to a legit business. Avoid poaching black market customers. Stay totally off their radar."

I nod. It's true. Our crew had taken painstaking steps to ensure our sales had zero overlap with local dealers. We might as well be invisible to them.

"Maybe this was a one-off," my brother continues. "Someone who thought they were being funny by sticking some aspirin in your bag and making you sweat getting busted? You know how ruthless end-of-year pranks can get."

"I guess it's possible," I reply uncertainly.

Knox crushes me to his side in a half hug. "Look, I'll stay sharp. Promise." He lets go and slides behind the wheel. "We'll talk more later."

Asher hacks in the background, pounding his chest.

My brother glances over to him. "For tonight, you and Ash just focus on harvesting the Kush, and I'll make the drop to Stan. Easy-peasy." The truck's engine rolls like my belly. "I got this, Hon," he says, the cocky smile reclaiming his mouth. "Back by midnight!" With that, he salutes and rumbles off into the night.

"Do it to it, Augs!" Asher cheers, launching himself into another coughing fit.

I watch until Knox's red taillights dissolve into blackness. My guts carry on with their twisting and turning. There's nothing more I can do now. The rest is up to Knox.

So I look to escape this powerless, angsty feeling the only way I know how.

In the dirt.

"Come on, Ash. Let's go reap some Kush."

The plan was simple. Straightforward.

So why hasn't Knox returned?

"Prolly hit a bad pocket of reception," Ash drawls, watching as I check the tracking app for the tenth time in as many minutes. "You know how it can be up there. He'll be back soon. No-ho-hoooo worries."

Easy for him to say. He's higher than a Boeing 747. Ash resumes doing a preharvest trim by plucking off the large fan leaves so I can access the cola-bearing stalks.

I inhale, the air plump with earth, and try to refocus. Picking up the shears, I begin cutting off the stems where the buds are now exposed. Hoping to shed my worries in the methodical steps of the harvest.

Pluck. Cut. Trim. Hang. Repeat.

We work in companionable silence as the once stagnant basement air swirls anew, thanks to Asher's fans and "Ford-ified" exhaust ventilators. Cobwebs that used to dangle from the ceiling have been replaced with pulleys attached to large rounded metal hoods. Beneath the hoods, 1,000-watt HPS bulbs work eighteen-hour shifts to shower light on the already five-inch seedlings I've planted below.

I might've gone a bit overboard with my crop. Once I started tucking the seeds knuckle-deep in soil, something came over me. And I just couldn't stop.

It started as ten seeds. Ten plants to rid us of our debts. But they didn't look like much for the space Ash had created for the new crop, so I added a few more. Thinking the extras would mean Dad wouldn't have to keep coming home with new calluses and worry lines. Maybe he could even replace some of his old woodworking tools.

As I continued planting, I considered my college tuition and all the expenses scholarships might not cover. Then I thought about Knox's dream of snowcapped mountains, and Aunt Maeve getting the retirement nest egg she deserves. I don't really know Asher's wishes beyond his next bowl, but I imagine it's bigger than his gig at the electronics store and double-wide trailer. So he got a few extra plants, too.

And by the time my frenzy was complete, our collective dreams had amounted to forty seedlings. When Knox saw what I'd done, his eyelashes flapped hard enough to harness wind power.

Speaking of . . .

Tugging off my powder-free gloves, now sticky with resinous THC, I check my burner again. It's 12:45 a.m. My brother is still off the grid. No calls. No updates.

"I'm gonna try calling him again," I announce to Ash, who

remains blissed out and deep in harvest mode. "He had an hour and forty-five minutes *max* of drive time. The sale couldn't have taken forty minutes on top of that."

The phone rings and rings, my ropey muscles knotting themselves tighter. Suddenly, a loud crash comes from above, followed by the tinkle of glass.

Our eyes instantly rove to the ceiling in alarm. "What was that?" Ash whispers as the fan leaf he was holding drifts to the floor.

"I don't know." Goose bumps pucker my flesh. "But it doesn't sound good."

Together we edge closer to the stairs, listening for signs of an intruder. *But then what?* If this is a break-in, what exactly are our options? We can't very well call the cops. *Hey, Officers, don't mind us and our weed. Just focus on those other criminals.* Asher's fretful expression tells me he's grappling with the same thought.

Peeling off the cumbersome baggy coveralls, I climb part-way up the stairs. Ash snaps his fingers, shaking his head so hard his eyeballs rattle.

"I'm just listening," I whisper. Knowing the hatch door is locked and concealed by the grooved rubber mat is the only thing giving me courage to venture this close. Closing my eyes, I strain to hear beyond the door.

"Anything?" he asks after a few beats.

"They're not inside. But I hear voices. And . . . hissing." Craning my neck, I listen harder to place the sound.

"Hissing?" Ash repeats, confused. "Like cats? Is it a cat fight?"

"No, more like a *shh*—" Another pane of glass breaks.

"What the hell kind of aim was that?" a male voice

reprimands. "Is your wrist as limp as your dick?" Someone laughs. There's a clanking sound, like pellets against metal, followed up by more hissing.

My anger intensifies as I grit my teeth. "The hissing isn't cats. It's a spray can. Someone's vandalizing the greenhouse."

This is more than just graffiti. It's personal. And nobody desecrates my greenhouse. *Nobody.*

"Stay here," I tell Ash as he snaps off his gloves. I pull the pepper spray from my pocket. "I'm going up before they do any more damage." When I go to push through the door my ankle is caught. "Hey!" I yelp.

"Where you go, *I* go," he says with a surprising amount of determination for someone so stoned. "Consider me the ham to your cheese, girl."

"Fine," I mutter. Ash untethers his hand from my ankle. "But it's going to be a lot easier to explain my presence at the greenhouse than yours."

"Who says anyone will see me? I can be super stealth when I wanna be."

Holding my breath, I slowly push open the floor hatch. Shards of glass glitter on the cement several feet away. Adjacent to the glass lies a can of spray paint, accounting for one of the broken windows.

"I'll sneak into the hall and turn on the exterior lights," I whisper.

Crouching low, I skirt through the greenhouse, swerving around another area of glass. Asher quietly lumbers behind me. I reach the light panel, flipping up the two switches on the end. The exterior lights blaze to life.

One of the vandals yells, "Someone's in the building!"

Now that it's brighter outside, I can make out the stocky shapes of several guys clad in black, wearing knit ski masks.

"Three dudes," Ash reports, peering out the bottom of one of the windows.

"Four," I correct. "There's another farther back toward the fence. See?" I gesture in the direction my father would describe as three o'clock.

The fourth person—no bigger than a raisin from this distance—speeds toward them.

"Don't be such a pussy!"

I know that voice. *Xander.* My blood burns with fury. "Those are probably motion lights," Xander continues. "It's the middle of the night, nobody's in there."

"What about that car out back?" a squeakier voice asks.

"That shitty banana beater?" Xander snorts.

Asher huffs beside me. "It's a classic, you flaming pee hole," he grumbles.

"Car looks like it's been parked there since the time of god-damn dinosaurs," Xander carries on with a shake of his can. "Now shut your trap and let's finish this." *Shhht-shhht-sht.* Their painting resumes.

Ash scowls, his eyebrows drawn in an angry, united front. "I know how to stop these swinging bags of dicks. Pardon my French," he adds. Then stalks over to the fire alarm.

But if he pulls the handle, then—"Ash, the cops!"

Instead of yanking down on the alarm, he punches the test button. And the air instantly erupts in piercing screeches. *Bweee! Bweee! Bweee!*

Cringing, I cover my ears and turn my attention back outside. The group scrambles away from the building in startled

212

surprise. One of them yells, "Let's get outta here!" While another screams, "Run!"

Except, scaring them off no longer feels like enough. I want Xander to *know* I saw them. That I know who they are. What they did.

I turn to Ash and shout, "This is probably a good time for you to disappear!"

Adrenaline hijacks my body as I charge outside. If Ash has hollered for me to stop, it's lost in the chaos.

"I see you, you cowards!" I scream. Two of the vandals sprint off into the darkness. As I turn to face the other two, I get a glimpse of the damage they've done.

Three broken windows, and an entire side of the greenhouse covered in pornographic drawings of dicks. They sprout like disgusting mushrooms from around my nickname.

Fuming, I whirl around, pepper spray at the ready.

Two intruders remain. The slightly taller guy grabs the other one by the collar and shakes him. I can't hear what he shouts because my ears have grown numb with noise. The other guy stumbles backward after being released and starts to run away.

"You're going to pay for this!" I yell after him. Then I swivel to the lone intruder, prepared to tear him apart with my bare hands. *"You,"* I hiss. "Don't. Move."

His eyes widen, glittering behind the mask. He raises his hands in surrender, takes several steps back, and then . . . he bolts.

Bastard! Letting him go is the sensible thing to do, and precisely what the old Honor would've done. But I'm not the old Honor anymore.

I break into a run. Past the outbuildings. Past the crab apple tree with the iron bench and kidney-shaped pond. Sprinting beyond the area that is groomed and into the tall grasses that lash at my shins. And it doesn't matter that they're hopelessly out of reach. I'm tired of standing still. Tired of holding back the storm.

Tonight, I rage. Consequences be damned.

The wailing alarm fuels my urgency even as the sound grows more distant. But in between the high-pitched beeps, there's another noise. . . . *Barking?*

Turning my head, a flash of black and white bounds past me. And Geronimo barks more ferociously than I've ever heard him bark before. The two vandals have already scaled the fence at the back of the property, with the third now mid-scramble. They race for the woods.

But the fourth is within our reach. "Get him, Geronimo! Get him!" I shout.

He growls, slicing the night with his lean, muscular body. When the intruder's within striking distance, Geronimo does what he does best. He leaps. Soaring through the air, his front paws slam into the guy's back, thrusting him face-first to the ground.

"Ger—Geronimo," I cry, gasping for air. Worried he won't hear between my winded state and his deaf ear. "Geronimo, *heel*!"

He releases the hem of the guy's jeans but continues barking at the curled-up figure.

"Move a muscle . . ." I pant. "And I swear to God, I'll unload this entire can of pepper spray."

He doesn't move. Not beyond the spastic rise and fall of his back as he tries to catch his breath.

I slip my finger under the safety guard of the spray. "Roll on your back!"

He doesn't move.

"Now!"

Geronimo bares his teeth and growls.

"Easy, boy." I take hold of his collar.

The figure releases a stifled groan as he rolls over. Then helplessly lays there, arms splayed at his sides.

"Not so tough without the rest of them, are you? Well, come on, show your face!"

We end this tonight, Xander. Once and for all. I have no intention of calling the cops, but Xander doesn't know that. So I'll put the fear of God into his cold black heart, to make sure he *never* messes with me again.

He slowly sits up, broad shoulders slumping in defeat as his fingers curl around the knitted material of the mask. Finally, I get to look Xander in the eyes. The moment of reckoning. My justice. My—

He peels off the mask.

And everything inside me freezes. My heart stops midbeat. The blood halts within my veins. My breath gets stuck in my lungs. It can't be. . . .

"Cole?"

22

Go straight home. Avoid GH, I covertly text, my ears still ringing despite the silenced alarm. *I'll handle it.* Hitting Send, I slide back on the bench, breathing a massive sigh of relief.

Knox is currently a stone's throw from Ravenswood—safe and sound, with money in hand. Or, money in box, more accurately. He wound up getting lost on the return trip because of a construction detour, then had no cell signal. Next drop I'll equip him with so many maps his glove box won't close.

Peering behind the shed, I see Asher's super-stealthy skills worked. Because he's gone. I don't know when or how his car disappeared, only that it did before Dad and an off-duty Officer Buchannon arrived.

So for now, our grow room remains safe.

Cole refuses to look at me. His dad gave him strict instructions not to speak when we were sent to opposite ends of the bench, like children forced into a playground time-out. Which is fine. I'm not interested in anything he has to say anyway.

I watch my father fume at Mr. Buchannon. Jabbing a finger

toward the vandalized wall while delivering a blistering speech that I'm too far away to hear.

To think I believed I could ever trust Cole. Not only did he nearly expose our underground business, but he also revealed his motives. His "sacrifice" at school wasn't intended to help me. It was obviously just a ruse. An orchestrated effort to build my trust and throw me off his true plan. *Helping Xander. Again.*

I glower at Cole, at the stubborn set of his shoulders, at his unblinking eyes. "So this is you always being on my side, huh?"

He doesn't even flinch when I hurl the question at him like a bucket of acid. But I know he hears me. I know because his mouth twitches downward.

Just a flicker of emotion.

But I want more than a flicker. I want to twist the knife—have Cole Buchannon feel the slicing pain of his betrayal the way I do. "I was right not to trust you. You're actually worse than Xander. At least he never pretended to be something better than he is."

He maintains his stillness, but tiny cracks beneath the surface are forming.

"Look at me." When he doesn't, I raise my voice a little louder. "I said, *look at me.*"

Grudgingly he does. But his eyes are flat, two-dimensional coins. Like a dead fish washed up on the shore, staring lifeless at a world it no longer sees.

"I wish I never met you, Cole Buchannon." My words bite like frost.

A muscle ticks in his jaw. His chest fills and lips part like he's finally going to say something.

Bring it, Buchannon. I've already sharpened my machete, prepared to shred whatever escapes his mouth.

"Cole!" his dad booms from the parking lot. "Come over here." He impatiently waves his hand for his son to join him.

My dad gestures, too. I stand and follow Cole's reluctant stride.

Mr. Buchannon runs a hand through his disheveled dark hair. Not the slicked-back, every-cowlick-tamed presentation of Officer Buchannon. Tonight he wears humanizing Clark Kent glasses, the tag of his shirt sticking out the back like a mini cape. And thank God. I would've fainted on the spot if he had rolled up in his squad car with his bulletproof vest and weapon holstered.

Dad folds his arms over his faded gray army T-shirt and nods stiffly to Mr. Buchannon.

"First, the good news," Mr. Buchannon says to his son. "Mr. Augustine has agreed not to press formal charges."

Cole's forehead relaxes a fraction as I silently exhale. My father clears his throat then.

Mr. Buchannon glances warily in Dad's direction. "In exchange for an apology and full restitution for damages." He elbows his son to speak.

"I'm very sorry," Cole rasps, eyes fixed on the gravel.

"You disrespected my daughter, my family, and our property," Dad says angrily. His fists clench beneath his arms. "That's not something I take lightly."

Cole gulps, neck muscles straining with the effort of his swallow. "There's no excuse for what I did, sir. This was"—his head pitifully sways—"*beyond* wrong. I know I deserve consequences, Mr. Augustine. And whatever they are, I accept them." His eyes lift from the ground to meet my father's.

Dad's momentarily at a loss for words. I don't think that's the response he was expecting. But once his eyebrows have descended, he juts his chin in my direction. "Go on, then."

What? Oh no. Just when I thought the night couldn't get more disastrous, now I'm subjected to a *forced* apology?

Cole turns toward me, drawing in a shaky breath. "I am so sorry, Honor." Then quieter, as if speaking to himself, he adds, "You have no idea how sorry."

God, how can he sound so sincere? So contrite? The words settle over me, transforming bitter anger into something less thorny. I nod but don't speak. Too afraid my voice will come out weak and splintered.

"I'll have someone out first thing tomorrow to begin the painting and repairs," Mr. Buchannon says to my dad. "And I sincerely appreciate your discretion in this matter, John. Cole will be further punished for this"—he glares at his son—"inexcusable behavior." Then Mr. Buchannon grips Cole's shoulder, the pair turning to leave.

"Not so fast," Dad booms like a drill sergeant, stopping them in their tracks. They turn. "You seem to have conveniently forgotten the *other* part of our agreement."

Mr. Buchannon's mask slips for the briefest of seconds, offering a glimpse of the irritation that roils beneath his calmer peacekeeping-officer facade. "Ah, right. You mentioned something about some volunteer work?"

"Good memory," Dad mutters wryly before addressing Cole. "We could use some help at the greenhouse. Summer's our busiest time and we're short-staffed."

My eyes widen as I crane my neck in my father's direction. *What the hell are you doing?*

Where Cole is slow to react, his dad sputters like a popped tire. "Hold on. Are you suggesting that Cole work for you for free the *entire* summer?" Mr. Buchannon shakes his head. "No. No, that won't work. He has lacrosse commitments and training to prepare for the fall. There's a scholarship at stake."

My father looks like he could give negative shits over this news. "Then he should've thought of that before breaking the law, *Officer* Buchannon."

Cole's dad looks like he's been gut punched. I feel a spark of pride.

"Now, your son has already stated there should be consequences for his actions. And Cole strikes me as a young man who'd sooner handle his own debts than have his dad bail him out."

Mr. Buchannon unpinches his mouth. "Can we agree," he begins slowly, trying to keep his temper in check, "that the volunteering begins after lacrosse season's over?"

"Being a"—my father flashes a tight grin—"to borrow your words from earlier, *reasonable man,* he can report in two weeks." Dad steps closer to Cole's father, gesturing again to the defaced greenhouse. "And I could give a damn about your son's lacrosse schedule."

Mr. Buchannon opens his mouth.

"Dad," Cole says firmly, putting a hand on his father's arm. "I'll do it. This is my wrong to right, okay?"

Recognizing defeat, Mr. Buchannon clacks his jaw shut and gives a curt nod.

Meanwhile, my brain unspools a thousand ways I can make every shift Cole works one of complete and utter misery. But I have time to figure that out.

Xander is my more immediate target. When I told Knox I would handle it, I didn't just mean the situation at the greenhouse. I also meant Xander.

And come next week, I will gain the upper hand.

Somehow.

Someway.

Bzzt-bzzt-bzzt. The phone vibrates, rattling on the passenger seat of the work truck. I lower my binoculars from the back window of Lucky's Bar, a local watering hole and pool hall, and check the message. Dad's wondering how much longer I'll be out. It's not even nine o'clock.

He's been on edge ever since Sunday's vandalism. Thank God for Geronimo, or our cover could've totally been blown. Not only did he catch Cole, but he also gave me a credible excuse for being at the scene of the crime. Because what responsible pet owner *wouldn't* chase after their beloved pooch who'd gotten out in the night?

I text Dad that my study session's going to run a bit later, buying myself another hour of surveillance time. Then I take a swig of tepid coffee, washing the taste of lies from my mouth. Lying to my father is giving me soul rot. I'm sure of it.

For three days I've tried to confront Xander at school. But after failing to get him alone, I decided I'd have to corner him off school grounds.

Because that's the caveat. Blackmail is only effective as long as nobody else knows.

And the moment I discovered the key chain near the fence,

glinting in the sun, I knew I finally had my leverage. Tangible proof that Xander was there the night of the greenhouse vandalism. His initials damningly engraved on the back of the key chain. *XS marks the spot.*

So Xander has a choice: either he swears a blood oath to leave me and my family alone, or I take my proof to the cops. He doesn't know my threat is an empty one.

Peering through the binoculars, I spot my target flanked by Miller and Wheeze, two thick-necked, beefy guys from the lacrosse team. Probably the other two goons who assisted Xander.

The trio spike their Cokes, passing around a silver flask when the bartender's not watching. Which is most of the time. Looks like they're celebrating the last day of school a day early. Cole's notably absent, but then I guess he has little to celebrate, since he was the one caught.

Cole. His name fills me with a fiery anger. An anger I wear like a callus, protecting the soft, tender parts beneath. The parts his betrayal wounded most. Packing down the hurt, I refocus on my current targets.

Miller flips his hat around, squinting as he lines up his next shot at the table. The pool stick crookedly slides between his sausage fingers.

I'm getting twitchy, worried this was a huge waste of time, when Xander pulls his phone from his pocket. I adjust my binoculars, and his profile zooms into sharp focus. Gone is the carefree expression. His mouth tightens as he listens to the person on the other end of the line. He pivots to face the window, the neon Budweiser sign painting a haunting red hue over his skin.

Xander's lip curls into a snarl, his eyes bouncing around the lot. But I'm safe from his view, parked back by the trees where the circle of light doesn't touch.

The call is brief. Xander says something to the guys, then slaps cash on the edge of the pool table before disappearing from view. My binoculars sweep left and right, scanning the bar. I don't see him anywhere. *Where did you go?* He must've slipped into the restroom.

Well, the douche squad doesn't appear to be in any hurry to leave. They continue pounding their drinks while sloppily banging balls. Which means this might be my only shot at catching Xander alone. I zero in on the back door and then over to his red truck with the missing tailgate.

It's now or never.

Tossing the binoculars to the seat, I drop down from the truck and tug the ball cap lower over my eyes. Anticipation crackles over my skin. The zapping intensifies as I shift from shadow to light. I glance over my shoulder.

I've been watching long enough to know the other twenty-plus vehicles are empty. And aside from a fat possum nosing through some trash, there's been little activity in the past hour. With any luck, it'll stay that way.

Xander exits, the sound of barroom chatter and classic rock erupting in the night, quieting when the door closes. The phone is pressed again to his ear. "I told you I'm on my way," he snaps. "No. Just stay where you are. I'll deal with that son of a bitch." He hangs up, and his flip-flops smack a vicious path toward his truck. Xander's gnashing his teeth, like he's hell-bent on grinding off the enamel.

My pulse flutters faster. I flex and unflex my hands. The

circumstances are less than ideal—clearly he's in a Mood. But guess what? I'm in a fucking Mood, too. My heart now pounds with every cruel blow he's delivered. Every malicious word. Every hiss from his can of paint that almost led to our downfall.

"Hey!" Rage takes charge of my mouth, crowding out commonsense caution.

Xander turns from his vehicle, surprise momentarily washing away the anger. He blinks, and the darkness fills him up again. "What the fuck do you want? You stalking me or something?"

I halt, nostrils flaring. "I should be asking you the same thing."

He sniffs, eyes narrowing to slivers of arctic blue that drag up and down me. "Now, why would I stalk a lowlife piece of country trash like you?"

His insult glances off me. "Cut the shit, Xander. You know *exactly* why I'm here."

After a quick scan of the area, he steps closer, towering above me. "Because of that dump you call a greenhouse?" he hisses, breath smelling faintly of whiskey. "I got news for you—*nobody cares*." Turning away, he hops into his truck.

I grab the handle of the door as he goes to close it, prying it back open. "*I* care," I snarl. "So let me be crystal clear. You mess with me or step foot on my property again, and I go to the police with my evidence. Understood, asshole?"

"Evidence?" Xander studies me a second, mouth twisting into a warped grin. "You're bluffing. You don't have jack. Let go of my door, or I'll smash your fingers in it."

I grip the frame harder. Attempt to level my breath so he

doesn't know the effort it's taking to keep him from closing it. "Notice something missing on those?" I ask. He follows my gaze to the assortment of bronze and silver keys dangling from the ignition. His hold on the door weakens.

"Yeah," I continue icily, "I made sure to handle your key chain with gloves to preserve the fingerprints. The cops would probably love to hear all about your vandalism. Not to mention the flyers you put in my locker, and the drugs you planted on me before shoving me in that storage room."

"What?" His brows knit, tick marks forging between them. He looks genuinely thrown. "I didn't put shit in your locker— that's your dick brother's signature move. And I didn't shove you in some room with drugs. But I'm pretty tempted to do some shoving now."

I blink. "But at the library, you said you'd make me pay. That you'd show Cole—"

"My best fucking friend took your word over mine," Xander fumes. "Yours!" His hand curls around the steering wheel, choking it like a tiny neck. "So yeah, I made sure he saw the pictures of you and Jess. To prove what a trifling, lying bitch you really are." His smile is potent with venom. "Guess I finally got Cole on board, didn't I? Better late than never."

The words cut, but not enough to make me bleed. Because I expected him to gloat. What I don't get is why he'd gloat over some but not all of his vindictive deeds.

His phone rings again. The veins at his neck pop up from his skin, ready to explode like the rest of him. "I don't have fucking time for this! Just stay the hell away from me, and I'll do the same," he barks. Then he wrenches the door shut, my fingers within millimeters of being crushed between metal.

Revving the engine, Xander hits the gas. The tires kick up dust and rocks, pelting me with both as I stumble back from the vehicle while he speeds from the lot.

Coughing, I step out of the cloud. The dirt slowly settles back to the earth like a shaken snow globe. But my thoughts are far from settled. Those continue whirling.

Because if Xander's telling the truth, that means someone else has been actively working against me. Someone with enough connections at school to forge office notes. To break into lockers and plant drugs. But if it's not him, then *who*?

Twigs snap like brittle bones within the thicket of trees, sending a shiver up my spine. I slowly turn, feeling the weight of an unseen gaze. I swallow, searching the shadows for the presence that makes my flesh prickle.

But it's only me. Standing in a pool of empty vehicles. With an ocean of unanswered questions crashing between my ears.

PART III

Flowering Phase

June 10 – July 18

23

I begin with a deep curtsy, a coquettish flutter of my lashes as I eye my dance partner. Which in this case happens to be a broom. Back straight, shoulders parallel to the floor, I move my feet in time with the make-believe orchestra. *Step-slide-step. Step-slide-step.* Exactly as Granddad taught me when I was small enough to perch on the toes of boots. Rising and falling, I spin across the elegant ballroom. Which in this case happens to be the greenhouse.

There are no customers to speak of Monday morning. No one but the plants to witness this giddiness that's sprouted wings on my feet, allowing me to float above the floor.

Dad remarked on my unusually chipper mood over breakfast. I told him it's because school's out, although that's only half the story.

Don't get me wrong. It's a huge relief to have made it through my last day unscathed and with my GPA relatively intact. But the true source of my joy?

Those thick envelopes of cash accumulating behind the air vent cover in our grow room.

Last night Knox made the second drop without a hitch. So with the remainder of Asher's crop sold, we're sitting on a cool $23,000. And then in another six weeks, the *big* harvest happens. The big one that'll make all our dreams a reality. I've planted us a better future, and that future is currently *thriving* under the concrete at my feet.

I smile with jack-o'-lantern bigness as I whirl, box-stepping my way past the rainbow of snapdragons. The room spins and spins, a spiral of colors. And then, a face twirls by.

"AHHH!" I shriek, dropping my partner. The broom handle lands with a *thwack* on the floor.

Standing beneath the nearby hanging baskets is Cole.

"*Hey,*" he says, sounding out the word before mashing his lips together. Now his eyes do the laughing his mouth cannot. "I, uh, didn't mean to interrupt your . . . dance?"

I scowl. "Do you always go around sneaking up on people?" I bend to snatch the broom as blood converges in my face.

"I wasn't sneaking." He thumbs toward the back office. "Your aunt was on a call and told me to ask you about getting a few T-shirts for work." The T-shirt he currently wears is plain gray, paired with equally plain cargo shorts. But even clothed in plainness, he manages to be memorable.

"Why? You don't even start for another week." Turning on one of the hoses, I begin watering a table of flats so he doesn't see that my complexion's turned the color of slaughtered beets. "And anyway, as far as I'm concerned, your *uniform* should be a damn trash bag."

"*Honor Elizabeth!*" Aunt Maeve's voice rips through the greenhouse.

Water dribbles over my shoes. I'm not sure when she

walked in, but obviously she's been here long enough to be of-fended on Cole's behalf. I shut off the hose.

Aunt Maeve turns to Cole. "Please excuse Honor. That's not the way we welcome new employees." She pauses to shoot me a stony look. "*Especially* on their first day."

"S'okay," he replies, looking abashed as he stuffs his hands in his pockets. "I kind of took her by surprise."

"First day?" I echo, feeling the room spin all over again.

"I offered to start early. We didn't make it to regionals this year, so," Cole finishes with a shrug.

Aunt Maeve's face softens. Even the bees on her scarf man-age to look mildly sympathetic to his plight. Two points for Cole, and I am in the negative. I've never been in the negative. Turns out, I hate it.

She continues talking to him, but I don't hear much due to this ongoing existential crisis. *When did I become the bad one?* My aunt glares at me as the words *office* and *now* escape her pinched lips.

I drop the hose and storm soggy-footed after her, knocking Cole's elbow when I pass. He says nothing, being the embodi-ment of contrition. *Jerk.*

Aunt Maeve paces the cluttered office. With its neat stacks of papers, catalogs, and boxes covering the desk and rising up from the floor like stalagmites, the room is a tidy disaster. She motions for me to close the door, which I do. Enthusiastically.

The grooves in her forehead deepen. "What was *that*? You were not raised to treat others that way. What has gotten into you, young lady?"

"*Me?*" I balk at the injustice. "How can you be defending *him* after what he did?"

She frowns. "Pip, I'm not defending—"

"Did you not *see* how he defaced the greenhouse? Or what they did to my *name*?" I've never raised my voice to her like this. But between Cole's ambush and her siding with him, I can't seem to stop.

"'They'?" Aunt Maeve repeats in confusion, resting back against the edge of the desk. A tower of papers topples over. "What do you mean 'they'?"

Shit. She doesn't know there was more than one perpetrator. The less scrutiny on the situation the better, I figured.

"I meant *him*," I say as I backpedal, sinking to the chair in front of her. "You're dressed up." Suddenly I note the dress that's replaced her usual work attire. "Do you have a morning book club meeting?"

"Don't change the subject." She folds her arms when she catches me staring at her peach nail polish. Aunt Maeve doesn't wear polish. It's either dirt or au naturel. "Honor," she says more gently, "I'm not defending what that young man did or trying to minimize the hurt his actions caused you. Believe me, I understand."

"Do you?" The pressure behind my eyes is sudden and swift. I turn my gaze to the smooth, plump-leaved jade on the windowsill.

"Course," she chirps. "What, you think I exited the womb at the ripe age of seventy-two? I was young once."

My eyes unintentionally drift to the photo of her and my grandparents on the wall. Back when her hair was the color of autumn on fire, instead of the gray-and-silver blend it is now. "And I can tell you that unconventional women weren't exactly revered back then the way they are nowadays. I've been called a lot of things not worth the breath to repeat."

I'm sure she has. It's impossible to shatter glass ceilings without getting cut.

"But then I learned," she continues, "words only have the power we give them."

"Look, I'm sorry for how you were treated then, Aunt Maeve. But I am"—my fingers twitch and curl inward—"I am *not* ready to forgive Cole."

"Sweetheart." The aroma of her gardenia soap moves with her as she leans forward, placing a hand to my cheek. "I'm not asking you to forgive him. I'm asking you to give him the chance to *earn* forgiveness. Let him make amends for what he's done."

God, she makes it sound so noble. Easy, even.

I move over to the whiteboard. "I understand what you're saying, but—" Breaking off, I stop studying the whimsical curl of Aunt Maeve's lettering and actually read what the schedule says. Cole's name lumped with mine. *For the entire month of June.*

"What's this?" I point to the glossy surface. "Are you . . . you can't be serious. You have us scheduled together *every* shift!" I can tell by the way she tugs her scarf that I'm trying her patience, but this is about twelve bridges too far. "Why can't Knox work with him?"

Aunt Maeve exhales. "You *know* why. I need Knox running deliveries. Plus he always sells out when he works the booth at the farmer's market."

Oh, I am *well aware* of my brother's ability to hustle.

"Honestly, I'm a little disappointed, Honor. I would've thought you of all people would support doing whatever it takes to keep things going around here."

"*I do.*"

She has no idea how much this is true. No idea what she stands over at this very moment.

"Aunt Maeve, I do."

"Okay, then." She distractedly sifts through the papers on her desk until she finds the one she's looking for. "So you'll give me your word you'll give him a fair shake? That you'll be *civil* to him? Because like it or not, we need his help."

She's right, I don't like it. In fact, I downright hate the idea of forced niceties with Cole. But unbeknownst to her, I also know the gravity and scope of our predicament. "Yes. I'll be civil." The phrase is thumbtacks in my mouth.

"Thank you." Aunt Maeve glances to the wall clock. "Now, I know the timing's not great, but I have some business out of town, so I'll be gone most of the day. Can I trust you to get Cole acquainted with the ins and outs of this place, *without* murdering him?"

I stop punishing my lip with my teeth long enough to answer. "Yes."

"Wonderful. Then I'll get him a few T-shirts and have him fill out some paperwork. Why don't you take a few minutes to regroup, all right?" She grasps the sides of my arms. "You can do this, Honor. Be the bigger person." Aunt Maeve's lips collide with the top of my head, and she's out the door, a trail of gardenia in her wake.

Be the bigger person.

Mostly I just want to smash the mug on her desk espousing

the virtues of forgiveness. But I've already pissed her off enough for one day.

Over the next several days, our underground operation runs like a well-oiled machine. Knox and I transfer the plants into five-gallon buckets in preparation for the final, most unforgiving stage of growth—the flowering phase. Asher, in the aftermath of the vandalism, focuses on beefing up our nonexistent security by installing motion sensors around the building and parking lot. Sensors connecting to an alarm in the basement that'll ping if anyone comes near, along with an app that sends alerts to our burners.

And while things belowground have found a peaceful, symbiotic rhythm, things aboveground are far less harmonious.

On Thursday, Cole got familiarized with the sensitive nature of the building's plumbing when I thrust a plunger into his hands. He muttered under his breath while tugging his T-shirt over his nose.

"What was that?" I asked so sweetly, I gave myself a cavity.

"Nothing," Cole replied, before ramming the plunger into the toilet a customer blocked up.

Friday delivered a heat snap, so I introduced him to the foul-smelling wonders of turning piping-hot compost. "You're a natural," I praised as he fought back a gag while shoveling the organic sludge and shooing flies.

By Saturday he was hunched in the sun, weeding the areas of landscaping that have long been ignored.

And come Sunday . . . Cole has a wicked case of poison ivy.

Knox bursts through the back door late that afternoon, a sheen of sweat covering his face. "Ugh. AC's busted in the truck."

"Maybe it caught it from the house," I say, referring to our broken central air.

"I dunno, but it's hotter than Satan's ass crack out there," he grumbles, dragging an arm along his forehead.

"That's grossly accurate." I lug another bag of fertilizer to the cart.

He pulls a wad of delivery receipts from his pocket, tossing them to the counter. "You want a water?"

"Sure." My brother disappears to raid the small fridge in the office. After wiping my face, I stuff the rag in the back pocket of my cutoffs, then boot up the computer to input the mound of receipts.

Knox returns, plunking three waters on the counter and his butt on the stool.

"Do I look that dehydrated?" I ask, unscrewing the cap and taking an exquisite gulp. The cold slides an icy path on its way down.

"The extra's for him," Knox says, nodding to where Cole works in the blistering sun. "Aunt Maeve said you were supposed to be nice to him."

"Her exact word was *civil*." I take another drink. "And I said *please* when I told him to clean the pond." While Cole's eyes might've possessed a flicker of contempt, he said nothing. Just as he's done this entire week. I keep waiting for him to break. To give me a reason to drop the pretenses and unleash hell.

"Right," my brother says, rolling the cold bottle along the

back of his neck. "So basically you've swapped the word *bitch* for *please*. Don't think it's going unnoticed you're giving him all the junk jobs around here."

The computer revs to life and I begin typing. "So? What's it to you?"

Setting down the half-chugged water, he replies, "Do I need to spell it out? You're drawing attention to yourself. The opposite of what we should be doing right now with"—he eyes the mat covering the basement access door in the most obvious way imaginable. *"You know."*

"Subtle," I say wryly.

Knox wipes his mouth on his shirt. "Honestly, I don't even think Cole did it."

My fingers freeze, hovering above the grubby keyboard. "Why do you say that?"

"Because there's some stuff that doesn't add up from that night," he says, and takes another gulp.

"Like what?" My tone is bored, contrary to the bumbling rhythm of my heart.

"Like the fact that his handwriting looks nothing like the graffiti."

I move on to the next receipt, typing faster. "He was in a hurry. Handwriting's bound to be sloppier."

"That's the thing," Knox says thoughtfully. "It was *neater.* I saw the paperwork he filled out on Aunt Maeve's desk." He shakes his head. "His handwriting looks like a failed lie detector test. Made mine look like friggin' calligraphy by comparison."

Why does my brother have to choose now to be insightful and clever? I smooth out the last of the receipts. "And I should care about this because?"

237

Knox drops his shoulders, exasperated. "Because he obviously didn't do it, Hon! Which means someone else *had* to have been there. Do you remember seeing anyone else that night?"

It's the first time he's asked me point-blank. I've been waiting for the other shoe to fall, assuming Ash would mention the multiple vandals. "Yeah," I reply hesitantly, fingering the keys, "but I didn't get a look at their faces. They were already gone."

His eyes bulge. "And you didn't think to tell me? I mean, Ash's short-term memory's for shit, but how could *you* flake on such a big—" Dawning illuminates his features. "You didn't flake. You didn't want me to know there were others. Why?" he demands.

"Because, Knox. The last thing we need is for you to go double-oh-seven–ing around Ravenswood stirring up trouble, okay?" And mentioning Xander's involvement would have done exactly that. "Just"—a frustrated breath puffs my lips— "let it go. Cole is still complicit, whether he actually sprayed the can or not. He was there."

Knox's dark eyes narrow as he taps the bottle to the counter. "Ah, I get it. So you're on a mission to punish him."

I strike the keys harder, hoping to drown him out.

"Does it even have to do with the vandalism, or was that just a convenient excuse?"

I finish the pile and plant my hands at my hips. "What are you insinuating, Knox?"

His thick brow arches. "I've never seen *anyone* get under your skin the way Cole does."

"So, what, you think I like him or something?" I let out a melodramatic peal of laughter. "You're hysterical."

"Am I? Then prove me wrong. Prove that him being here

isn't going to be a problem for you. Because for someone who's *sooo* concerned about me stirring up trouble, you sure seem hell-bent on mixing up your own."

When I don't speak, Knox slides over the unopened bottle.

"If it's really no big deal, take him the water, Hon." His tone is a dare.

I narrow my eyes. "That proves nothing other than my ability to carry light objects. But fine." I swipe the water from the counter.

"Careful," he warns as I stomp over to the automatic doors.

"I'm always careful!"

Knox hollers back, "Yeah, I used to believe that!"

Determined to prove my brother wrong, to prove I am not a liability, I head for the pond, bottle swinging with my adamant stride. But my steps falter with my approach.

Cole is shirtless. The straps of the waders dig into his broad shoulders as he lowers a rock back to the pond's clear bottom. Sun glances off his skin, highlighting his muscles as they coil and release. My eyes glue to his form like I'm cramming for an anatomy quiz.

"Water!" I shout, holding the bottle from my body like a venomous copperhead snake.

Startled, Cole fumbles with the sizable rock in his hands. It drops with a monstrous splash through the surface. "Gah! Son of—" he yelps, hopping one-footed to the edge of the knee-deep water. "My foot!"

"Oh God, I didn't mean to do that!" Mortified, I rush over to where he's hauled himself out.

He squints over at me, teeth clenched in pain. "Then why did you yell like that?"

"I—I brought you water," I say, like that's evidence I wasn't ogling him and Knox is wholly mistaken.

"Is it poisoned?" he asks, shrugging off the straps and wincing as he frees himself from the waders. When I don't answer right away, Cole repeats, "The water, did you poison it?"

"No," I retort. "Anyway, do you think I'd tell you if I did?"

A crooked grin appears on Cole's face, making the sun feel hotter. "No. Probably not."

Keeping a careful distance, I crouch down, examining the red mark blooming over the top of his right foot. "Is it okay?"

He wiggles his toes. "Yeah. Just bruised, I think. Which in some way, shape, or form, seems to be a frequent side effect of being around you."

"Ha," I deadpan. Although I genuinely feel bad about that. Make that doubly bad when I see the blistery poison ivy on his calf. "Need a cold pack? We usually have some in the freezer."

Cole's brows lift in shock. "Are you being nice to me, Augustine?"

"Lord no." I pluck the clump of clover encroaching on the Japanese irises at the water's edge. "I just don't want you tattling to Officer Buchannon and having him unleash his municipal wrath on us."

He sniffs. "Well, that would require me talking to him. Not something we've done a whole lot of lately. Pass me the poisoned water, would you?"

I start to hand it to him, then pull it shy of his reach. "Why, Cole? Why were you there?" The question tumbles out. I hadn't planned to ask him, to give him the satisfaction of seeing my pain, which I'm sure I wear as plainly as these cutoffs and sweat.

His arm lowers, the humor evaporating from his face. Gazing out at the surface of the glittering water, he answers, "When I showed you those pictures, the ones of you and Jess, you told me things aren't always how they look, remember?"

I stare at this enigma of a boy who makes me feel things I shouldn't. Who has the power to wound me more than any man-made weapon could.

Cole takes my silence for the affirmation it is. "Well, it isn't what you think. And if it takes me the entire summer, I'm going to prove it. No matter how many rocks I have to move, or how much shit I have to plunge. I'm going to make it up to you, Honor."

He's trying to compare our situations, but they're not the same. My actions didn't hurt anyone.

"Don't hold your breath." I drop the water to the grass, where it rolls from his reach. Then walk away.

24

Asher's lips twist side to side as he studies the items I've placed on the table. "This does not compute." He scrubs a hand through his hair, leaving it to stand on end. Then tracks me with his squinty gaze. Watching as I helicopter the bushy plants like an enormous bumblebee. "No offense, but you got a real cat-in-a-bathtub vibe going tonight."

For good reason. "I'll explain when Knox gets here," I say, busying myself with adjusting the plant yo-yos Ash's tied to some of the stems.

A few of the plants are getting top-heavy. The stalks will need support as the tiny "budlets" (baby buds) continue to develop. They're already producing white wispy hairs called pistils, sprouting out wherever a fan leaf meets the main stem. Then in another two weeks, the conical buds will grow bulbous and pudgy, before ripening as the hairlike pistils change from white to brown.

But the problem is, none of that will come to pass if our grow room is compromised.

Ping-ping!

Asher's sensor. The sound doesn't cause my heart to crash

like a wrecking ball against my ribs the way it did last night. But an involuntary shiver rattles my bones, despite the warm web of air that spins around me.

As my brother ambles down the stairs, Ash's fretful gaze lifts from the table.

"So what's the dealio?" Knox asks, collapsing in the chair like he's part rubber. He's been nursing a hangover all day, and it's the first I've seen him upright since his greenhouse shift. "You said this was urgent," he says to me.

"It is," I reply, pointing to the plastic bags on the table.

Knox's face scrunches as he leans in. "A cigarette butt and a bag of broken glass? I don't get it. How is trash urgent?"

"Yeah, is this like an environmental thing? Because I already recycle," Ash adds, punctuating the declaration with a yawn.

"This is evidence," I clip, joining them at the folding table. "Last night someone came to the greenhouse. When I was here alone."

Knox perks up. Even Ash looks startlingly sober. "What? Why didn't you call us?"

"*I did*." Exasperation wraps my tone like kudzu vines. I tried both their burners. And my brother clearly has no recollection of our conversation. How I whispered in terror, "Knox, there's someone at the greenhouse."

To which he shouted over the swelling music, "WHAT? THERE'S A STEER IN THE BEAN MOUSE?" So I repeated myself, sounding out each word with excruciating clarity. He then hollered, "RIGHT, *MOUSE*! JUST PUT MORE PEANUT BUTTER IN THE TRAPS."

Knox rubs his face as I finish the recap, peering sheepishly through his fingers. "That . . . sounds like it could be true."

He drops his hands with a groan. "Sorry, Hon. I didn't mean to get so carried away. Believe me," he says, massaging his temple, "my head feels beat like a piñata."

Meanwhile, Asher's giant puppy-dog eyes look ready to spout tears. "I'm sorry, too. That was super uncool of us."

Now I'm feeling bad. "Look, I'm the one who said it was fine for you guys to have a night off. I know you really wanted to go to that beach party. And when the sensors went off, I assumed it'd be a deer, like usual." My chest tightens at the memory. "It wasn't."

"What happened?" Knox and Ash ask, voices overlapping. Their twinning brows slung low and serious.

I take a breath. "A car pulled into the lot. They cut the headlights, but nobody got out. At first I thought maybe they were lost, but I would've seen the glow from their screen if they were looking up directions."

"So what was the driver doing?" Knox asks.

I shrug. "Couldn't tell. The motion light in back never came on, so I couldn't get a look at the person. They didn't stick around long, though. Five minutes tops."

Technically it wasn't long, but the minutes felt like hours of heart-pounding indecision.

My brother frowns. "Wait, why didn't the light come on? The bulb couldn't be burned out already. Dad just installed those lights two weeks ago." This was our father's solution since we couldn't afford a security system—scare the bad guys with bright lights. Although Dad had no way of knowing the higher-tech safety upgrades Asher put into place around the same time.

"No," I say, "it definitely wasn't burned out. It was broken. I found this"—I hold up the bag of glass—"when I came to work early this morning. And the cigarette was in the spot where the car was parked."

"At least we know it wasn't the cops," Knox remarks, glass perpetually half full.

Ash pops a couple Corn Nuts in his mouth. They crunch like rocks as he picks up the plastic bag with the cigarette nub to study it. "So we know whoever was here likes Camels and drives a car."

"Camels?" I repeat. "How do you know what kind they are?"

"The humped animal on the filter. Right there, see?" Ash says as I take the cigarette again to inspect it more closely, realizing what I mistook for a smudge of dirt is indeed a humped animal.

"Great," Knox mumbles morosely. "So that narrows it down to, like, a million and twelve possible suspects." He plants his face on the table with a sigh. "We'll have this case cracked in no time. *Ow.*" My brother rubs his head where Ash bounced a Corn Nut off it.

As I stare at the filter, something tugs at the back of my brain. Some connection I should be making. Some—then it hits me like the Corn Nut that pings off my shoulder. I snatch the bag of weaponized snacks. "Guys, it could've been Jess! The cigarette, it's the same brand Jess Rennert smokes! I *saw* the pack when I was in her car!"

Neither of them look impressed with my Veronica Mars flex. "Yeah," Knox says slowly, "and you know that's the brand something like one out of three smokers prefers, right? Besides, wouldn't her emo lipstick be all over the filter?"

I slump forward under my brother's annoyingly sound logic. "Well, fudge."

"So, who else do we have?" Ash asks, lacing his hands behind his head. "Who else would—Ooh!" His eyes round like an owl's. "What about one of those graffiti dicks from the other night?"

I wanted to avoid this, but with my brother already mid-speech, itemizing all the reasons it couldn't possibly be Cole, I know it's time to lay all my cards on the table. "Xander was there, too."

"Huh?" Knox swivels his head toward me, confusion giving way to anger. "Sorry, but I could've *sworn* you just said Xander was there, when I distinctly remember you saying you *didn't* see their faces."

"I didn't. Technically," I tack on in a small voice. "I *heard* Xander, when he was yelling at the others."

My brother's itching to respond, so I plow ahead before he has a chance.

I speak quickly, staring at the bag of broken glass and not looking up until I've exposed the last of my secrets like an open diary. I give them the full, uncut backstory of Xander, going into all the gory details. The kinds of details that make my skin heat with humiliation. But I have to. So they understand that my flawed thinking made sense at the time. Why—given our history—it was easy to assume Xander was responsible for all the things that happened to me at school. The flyers, threatening texts, the planted drugs . . .

At which point, Knox loses it. His hands curl into fists, knuckles ready to split clear through the flesh. "I'll kill that motherfucker!" he roars, springing to his feet. His chair falls backward, banging to the floor.

Ash winces at the noise, then squints up at him. "Bruh,

I think you just proved her point. *That's* why she didn't tell you," he says, gesturing to my brother's apish, chest-beating posture. Then Asher puts his hand over mine as my fingers knit themselves together. "Hon, it's not your fault."

I look at him and feel my face crumple, averting my eyes to the pile of hands and fingers on the table in front of me. "I—I know, Ash."

"Do you?" he presses. "Because dudes like that, they got straight-up moldy souls. Seriously. Something's eating at 'em from the inside. But this isn't yours to own, okay? That's his shit. So you hold that head high, because you got nothing to be ashamed of."

A tear rolls down my cheek. I quickly swipe it with my free hand and nod.

Knox then plants his hand atop ours, completing the hand sandwich. "Seconded. But that doesn't mean I don't wanna kick the shit out of him. I hate that he hurt you." His skin is still bright with anger, but at least it's controlled anger. Our hands separate.

"So you think it was Xander? The person who came last night?" my brother asks me.

"Actually I don't. Not with Cole already taking the heat for them."

Ash blows out a forlorn breath. "So we're back to having a nameless, faceless enemy? Buzzkill."

"You said you couldn't see the person," Knox begins, "but what about the car? Anything you can remember about it? Like, could you tell the color or make?"

My face scrunches as I strain to remember. "I'm not sure about the make. A four-door of some kind? The car was a darker color, though, a navy or maybe gray. And the windshield looked almost black. Like the glass was tinted or—"

"What is it?" Knox asks as my eyes widen.

"A gray car followed me from school a while back," I tell them. "It had tinted windows."

Ash whistles. "Helluva coinkydink if you ask me. What do you think it means?"

I glance between them uneasily. "That someone may have been watching me since I decided to grow." I swallow. "Which means the police aren't our only threat."

Suddenly Knox sits up straighter, brown eyes tracking the table. "Okay, look, we've *got* to operate as one if we're going to pull this off. That means no more secrets." His gaze lands meaningfully on me. "About anything. We all agree?"

Ash and I murmur our agreement. "We should probably discuss upping our security, right?" I offer.

"Mind meld," Ash says to me with a tap of his skull. "Here's what I'm thinking: we install hidden cameras, motion triggered like the lights and sensors."

Knox grabs the notebook, flipping to a blank page. "Something with a live feed so we can keep tabs remotely."

The boys gush over gadgetry and make a shopping list for Ash.

But wriggling in the back of my mind, I can't shake the memory of Jess telling me how I dodged a bullet.

Except now I'm left to wonder, did I trade a bullet for something worse?

"Honor?" Cole says my name like it's the second or third time he's spoken it.

I blink from my daze. My head a jumble of anxiety between spying, unknown adversaries, and Dad's latest setback. "Huh?"

He points to the planter in front of me. "I said I think you've watered that enough."

Looking down, I see the water has pooled in the container and is now creating muddy slug trails down the sides. *"Shoot,"* I mutter, and shut off the hose.

"You seem distracted today."

That's an understatement.

Cole peels off his work gloves. "Um, so there's a guy outside who's here for Maeve."

"She's not here," I tell him, wiping my hands on my shorts. "She'll be gone the rest of the afternoon."

"I know. But he says he had an appointment and drove all the way up from Port Waushuk. I can take care of this"— he nods to the mess I've made—"if you need to deal with Suit Guy."

Suit Guy? Aunt Maeve didn't say anything about an appointment, but I can see where it could slip her mind given Dad's state. I absently thank Cole and head outside.

A round man in a snug navy suit runs a hand along the edge of a window, oblivious to my presence.

I frown. "Can I help you?"

The man, now squinting up at the rain gutters, turns to offer an overzealous smile. His teeth are the size of our shutters. "Afternoon, I'm Richard Whirley. You must be Maeve

Hannigan?" He thrusts out a damp meatball of a hand and we briefly shake.

"I'm Honor, actually. Maeve's great-niece."

"Ah yes." The smile grows, enamel from sea to shining sea. "Explains why you look so young, then." Richard Whirley chuckles like he's said something supremely clever. "Say, could I impose upon you to give me a tour while we wait for her to arrive? I know I'm a bit early."

"A tour?"

He blinks. "Well, yes. Can't very well consider buying a property without getting a gander first, now, can I?"

My stomach capsizes. "Um, unfortunately my aunt won't be able to make it. We've had a family emergency." My tone makes clear this is a private matter.

"Oh," Mr. Whirley says, slightly crestfallen. "I'm sorry to hear that." He digs into his pocket and pulls out a business card. "Well, if you could pass that along to her, I'd be much obliged."

"Sure." I take the card, silently promising to throw it in a fiery chasm.

He eyes the side of the building that's in need of repainting. "Place looks like it could use a little work. Still, it's promising." Mr. Whirley raps his knuckles against the exterior. "Good bones." Then he flashes a final toothy grin, tipping an imaginary hat before he leaves.

I stare at his card, and the words *business developer* leap from the cardstock, along with the name of the town he's from— Port Waushuk. Why does the town sound so familiar? Then I remember, that's where Aunt Maeve went with her peach-colored manicure the day Cole started.

Thinking fast, I holler, "Wait! Mr. Whirley?" I jog up be-hind him as he turns. "Seems a shame to have you drive all this way for nothing. I could still show you around, if you like?" I hold up the false grin for the seconds it takes him to agree.

To begin the tour, I start with the roof at the entrance of the building—all original, circa 1969. "They don't make 'em like this anymore," I tell him, adding, "and it only leaks when it rains *really* hard." I go on to point out some wood rot where the planks have gone to mush. "But I'm sure it's a cosmetic issue and not structural. Probably."

Once inside, I disclose the occasional hiccups with the plumbing, the widening cracks in the concrete where the ground has settled, the hairline fractures in multiple windows.

And by the time I conclude the tour, Mr. Whirley no longer smiles. I wait as he scribbles down some notes, then nervously eyes the roof above the checkout area like it might collapse. "Uh, one more thing. Although I'm almost afraid to ask," he adds under his breath. "What about the foundation? Can I see what kind of condition the basement's in?" He raises his note-pad. "My associates will want to know."

"The basement?" I croak, stepping onto the mat, prepared to throw my body over it if necessary. "Oh, it's . . ." But fear has paralyzed my tongue, while my thoughts have gone all static and fuzz.

"Typical Michigan basement," Cole answers for me, the stack of terra-cotta pots clanking loudly as he sets them on the shelf behind us. "You know, dirt floor, cinder-block walls, musty. Hey, Honor, were they ever able to clear out that black mold?"

My eyes widen. I quickly rein in the surprise. "Er, most of

it. They did suggest we wear special respirators, though. Just until we get it checked again."

"Black mold?" Mr. Whirley repeats, looking faint and distressed. Cole and I glance at each other, then innocently nod. "Okay, well, you've given me a lot to consider here. Yes, indeed." He tucks the notepad away in his jacket. "I should probably be hitting the dusty trail. Got a few more properties to check out. But, uh, I'll be in touch if I have any more questions. My regards to your family." Mr. Whirley gives a half-hearted wave as he leaves. The automatic door shushes closed behind him.

"Could he have moved any faster?" Cole asks, mildly amused.

Exhaling, I drop to the stepstool, my body still in a freefall. I fold forward, my head sagging between my knees as I try to remember how to breathe. Blood is whooshing in my ears and it feels like I'm viewing everything from a curvy fishbowl.

"Whoa, are you okay?" Then he mutters to himself, "*Of course* you're not okay." Cole goes on to ask if I need water, a paper bag, or the clementine he didn't eat from his lunch. I shake my head and continue trying to push air in and out. He rests a warm hand to my shoulder. "What *do* you need, Honor?"

My head throbs with too many thoughts and unsolved problems. I'm going to crack. Or scream. Or both. "I need to get out of here. *Now.*"

He nods, pale eyes steady. "We can do that. Where do you want to go?"

"I want to"—my face crumples as I struggle to answer—"I

want to get lost. Just go into the woods and lose myself." I drag my eyes from the floor. "Does that sound crazy?"

"No." Cole reaches out to tuck back some hair that's fallen in my eyes, his fingers grazing the shell of my ear. "That's the sanest thing I've heard in a while," he says gently. "Let's go get lost."

25

The forest swallows us whole, and I dissolve into the kaleido-scope of green. Cole falls in step behind me as we tread along the narrow path where herds of deer have worn a trail. My thumbs go to hook into the straps of my backpack, forgetting Cole's insistence on carrying it.

Twigs crackle as we move, the sounds amplified in the ab-sence of conversation. But I needed the quiet to decompress, to escape the noise inside my head. And without having to ask, Cole has given it to me.

"Thanks for your help earlier with Mr. Whirley." Another thing he gave me that I didn't ask for. "The black mold touch was genius."

"Well, Dick Whirley was pretty easy to manipulate by the time you were done with him. And what's up with that name? Sounds like a seventies porn star or something."

I laugh, shocked by the sound.

"Anyway," Cole continues, "I know the greenhouse means a lot to you."

The path widens so we're back to walking side by side.

"That freak-out earlier, it was more than the greenhouse," I find myself explaining. "I'm not usually so . . . emotional. Or, I don't know, maybe I am, and I'm usually better at hiding it."

His elbow grazes my arm as he shifts the pack. "I wouldn't call you emotional."

I sniff. "Yeah? Then what would you call me?"

"Passionate," he says with a nod to himself. "I'd call you passionate." Then he smiles, and it's seven kinds of sunshine.

"And I'd call you way too nice." I wonder if my own smile illuminates the forest like his.

We delve deeper into the woods. Cole doesn't press me about why I was so upset. Instead, he points out things he doesn't want me to miss—a large ring of beigey white mushrooms, baby squirrels giving chase as they spiral up a tree, the fading blooms of the trillium flowers (although he doesn't know that's what they are).

Which is maybe why I find myself telling him what's weighing most heavily in my head and heart. Simply because he doesn't ask.

Dad is having what Knox and I call a Dark Day, I explain, as we wade through thigh-high ferns that ripple like an emerald sea. It happens a few times a year, cyclical as the seasons. The shade to my father's window will stay drawn; the door will stay shut. When I enter the tomb to leave food that I know will go uneaten, his back is always to me. He stares at the wall for hours, hardly acknowledging my voice.

So we take turns leaving offerings, reminders of the world that awaits him when the Dark Day passes, or things to help the darkness pass quicker. Aunt Maeve, of course, brews her special teas, pouring herbs and one-sided conversation into the space. Knox delivers the latest issue of *Fine Woodworking Magazine,* reading aloud the articles he thinks Dad would like most. And I bring a special arrangement of flowers and greenery, with beauty even the inkiest shadows can't hide.

And then, like Geronimo, who listlessly mopes outside Dad's door, we wait. For dawn to bring in a new day. For Dad to come back.

Cole hops up behind me on a fallen tree trunk, using it as a bridge over a large, muddy section. Our arms outstretched at our sides for balance, we look ready to take flight. My heart flutters like it already has, feeling freer than the birds that swoop branch to branch.

When the trunk no longer jiggles with both our steps, I find he's stopped midway. "What's wrong?"

His arms are still partially levitating. "Mind if we take a break?"

"Oh, sure." Grabbing a nearby limb to steady myself, I turn around on the log and totter back to the center.

Cole offers a hand as I take a seat beside him.

"Thanks," I murmur. My feet dangle above the forest floor, almost three feet to his two.

"Hey, I'm sorry about your dad," he says quietly, unshouldering the pack to pass me a water.

"I didn't tell you so you'd feel sorry for me. I told you because . . ." The forest fills the prolonged silence—creatures rustling, woodpeckers banging, a chipmunk chittering. I shake my head. "I don't really know why I told you." I chug my water.

"You don't have to give me a reason, Honor." Cole takes a drink. "And I don't feel sorry for you."

"Good." I grab the backpack and dig out a couple granola

bars, holding one out for him. "No promises. I swiped these from Aunt Maeve's stash, so you might be better off gnawing on some pine cones. To be honest, they probably have the same amount of fiber."

He takes it but doesn't immediately dig in the way I do. Instead, he squints up to the canopy of trees, the sun dancing over his tan face between the leafy gaps. "My dad's been cheating on my mom for the last five years," he says, and then shrugs. "That I know of, anyway."

I lower my granola bar. "God, Cole, I'm sorry." And as the words tumble out, I realize the world of difference between feeling sorry for a person and feeling sorry for a person's circumstances.

Cole looks over to me. "So I know how much it sucks, to see someone you love hurting and not be able to do anything about it." Turning his attention to the granola bar, he fumbles with the wrapper.

"Here," I say, taking the bar before he pulverizes it. With a flick of my stubby nail, I open it and hand it back. "Does your mom know?"

"She pretends not to, but sometimes I hear her crying. Usually when he picks up a night shift or has some kind of weekend 'training.'" He air-quotes the word and bites into the granola bar.

"That's terrible." My throat's gone bone-dry, so I take another sip of water. "Do you think she'd ever leave him?"

Cole swallows. "Doubt it. Probably for the same reason I keep playing lacrosse."

"Because you love it?"

A dark laugh spills out. "No. I fucking hate lacrosse." Cole falters, seemingly as shocked by his spontaneous confession as I am. His eyes quickly drop to the muddy earth below. "Wow. I've . . . never said that out loud before. It's true, though; I hate lacrosse. When we lost our last game, I was actually relieved we weren't going to regionals."

"Then why do you play?"

"I guess because"—he takes another bite, chewing in contemplation—"I'm really good at it. Just like my dad was. And whenever you excel at something, there's always these expectations, you know? About not squandering talent. Fulfilling potential. So I play. Just like my mom. Except instead of lacrosse, Isabelle Buchannon plays a perfect wife—chairing sports fundraisers, organizing holiday cookie bakes, smiling for the camera. She's really good at what she does, too."

"But"—I pause, turning the empty bottle over in my hands—"it isn't real."

He stares into the dense mass of trees. "I know. But what is? I mean, really?"

Swallowing, I rest my hand beside his. Close enough to feel the tickle of his arm hair. My blood thrums faster as my pinkie finger edges closer. *I shouldn't.* But feelings are illogical beasts. You can't reason with them. You can't ignore them. Not indefinitely.

And my twisting heart wants him to know he's not alone. That I understand *exactly* what it's like to play along. To be the person who fulfills expectations. To be the one who always comes through. So I gather a breath and hook my pinkie over his, praying he doesn't push it away. Then I close my eyes.

Cole's finger twitches, and I start to fear the worst. I'm

about to pull away when he draws the rest of my hand into his, like a lost thing found. And I can finally breathe again.

"I take it back," he says softly. "This is real."

I don't know if Cole means the green globe around us, or the way our palms pulse together in a wordless rhythm. But either way, I agree.

The next day, I find a scrap of paper curled in one of my work gloves. I unfurl the note, tucked inside like a fortune in a cookie.

I have an irrational fear of seaweed. #onetruth

The handwriting is horrible. If I wrote left-handed with a broken arm, my penmanship would still be better. I immediately smile. *Cole.* He's playing a game. Okay, I'll bite. Tearing off the bottom of a receipt, I neatly reply:

I can't whistle. #onetruth

Then I roll the bit of paper like a teeny joint and tuck it into the finger of his gloves.

Later that afternoon, he writes: I have a weirdly good memory that borders on photographic. #onetruth

So I respond: I kind of believe in fairies. Okay. OKAY. I believe in fairies. DON'T JUDGE. #onetruth

I hate judgy people. #onetruth

I genuinely think the fact that no two snowflakes are alike is irrefutable proof of miracles. #onetruth

And so it goes, our relentlessly addictive tit for tat, truth for truth. Cole has an extra bone in his foot. I have double-jointed wrists. He likes his eggs sunny-side up. I won't eat eggs that actively bleed.

After that, I stop wearing my gloves for fear I'll miss a single #onetruth delivery. Finding I'd rather suffer the scrapes, the calluses and splinters, for just one more fix. One more piece of Cole.

My hands fumble, greedy and eager, as I unroll Sunday's message.

This is my favorite part of the day. #onetruth

I hold his words close, mashing them to my skin. Feeling the urge to burst into tears and laugh at the same time. Because secretly, it's my favorite part, too.

Knox passes the butter after slathering his toast. "Scale of one to ten, how mad was she?" he asks in a low voice. Being stuck manning the booth at the farmer's market meant he'd missed yesterday's fireworks with Aunt Maeve.

The water pipes whine as Dad turns on the shower, having returned from his morning run. He's doing better over the past few days, but I still worry. Worry about what he doesn't tell us, and about the amount of time he spends privately sifting through his old footlocker since the Dark Day.

"Seven," I reply, smearing raspberry jam over my buttered slice. Then I picture Aunt Maeve's flushed face and twitchy eye as she demanded to know exactly what I'd done that made Mr. Whirley refuse her calls. "No, eight. Definitely an eight."

He sucks air through his teeth, making a *yikes* expression. "So how do you know she won't go out looking for another buyer?"

"You know the picture on the office wall from Augustine Greens's grand opening?"

My brother nods between chomps of toast. The photo, now over fifty years old, shows Grandma Augustine wielding a comically large pair of scissors while wearing an even larger smile as she prepares to cut the yellow ribbon. Granddad's arm loops her waist, him looking down at her like she's the reason the stars twinkle. And Aunt Maeve is forever captured beaming at them both, frozen mid-clap.

I go on to tell my brother how I'd taken the frame down, pressed it into Aunt Maeve's hands, and reminded her of the promise she made. Then I begged, pleaded for her to wait until August before we *explore all our options,* as she insisted we call it.

"So you guilted her," Knox says succinctly, a constellation of crumbs forming on his work shirt. His eyebrows bounce. "Solid move."

The orange juice feels like hydrochloric acid as it burns a path down my throat. "No, I told her the *truth*. That the greenhouse is my everything, and I can't imagine life without it." My words had an immediate effect, too. Her gray eyes turned misty as she twisted the antique ring on her finger and finally agreed.

"Well, whatever you call it, I'm glad it worked," my brother says, making a half-hearted attempt to tame the cowlick at the crown of his head. "And at least now we've got twenty-four/ seven eyes on the place." He's referring to the cameras he and Ash just installed around the building. "So we'll know if *anyone* sketchy, including douchey developers, come sniffing."

I grin faintly at the memory of the pudgy, navy-suited man torpedoing out the door. "Poor Mr. Whirley, though. Cole and I *really* did a number on him."

Knox's spark of optimism dulls out. "Yeah. About that."

The squeak of the faucet carries through the floorboards. My eyes fall from the plaster ceiling back to my brother. "About what?" I take another bite of toast.

Knox twists his lips, swishing the words around in his mouth before deciding which ones to spit out. "I was gonna save this convo for later, but what's up with you and Cole?"

"Me and Cole?" I snort. "Nothing." Grabbing my juice glass, I watch him from the bottom as I drain it.

His eyes skitter over me, like a detective hunting for clues. "Are you guys hooking up?"

"What?" My glass hits the table a little too hard. "Is that supposed to be a joke?"

Knox closes his eyes, tipping his head to the ceiling. "Christ, you are." He rubs a hand over his face. "So, lemme get this straight. You're hooking up with someone at the greenhouse, when we're within *weeks* of reaping the hell outta that Kush forest in the basement. And oh, his dad just happens to be a cop! Sound about right? Or did I miss something."

"I told you, we're not *hooking up.*"

He frowns, folding his arms. "Then that's even worse, because it means you really like him."

"You don't know what you're talking about," I huff.

"Don't I?" My brother rocks back on the legs of his chair in a way that would make Dad cringe. "So I'm hallucinating the makeup on your face and the muffins he's brought you the last few mornings?"

"A: I don't have to justify mascara to you. And B: He lives near The Sweet Shoppe." Then I add, "And he got one for you, too."

He sniffs before dismissively rolling his eyes. "Any idiot can see he does it for you. The muffins, they're all for you."

And I melted like the chocolate inside the pastry bag, but I'll be damned if I confess that to him. "Stop editorializing. Being nice isn't a crime."

"Trust me," Knox says, the legs of his chair banging like a gavel to the floor, "no guy is going to get up extra early to buy muffins for a girl unless he's *seriously* into her."

"Okay, is there an actual point to this muffin lecture?"

He sets his jaw. "I see the way you two watch each other when you think no one's looking. Don't start this thing with him, Hon. Not now. Not when we're so close to the finish line. You're losing focus, and you can't see it. Even Ash noticed. *Ash!* This is the guy who once asked me to confirm whether or not he remembered to put on pants."

"I'm not losing focus," I snap. Hell, I practically invented the word and could outfocus him any day of the week.

"You are, *too*," he retorts, mimicking my irritated tone. "Who were you on the phone with the other night?"

It's my turn to fold my arms. "That's irrelevant."

"Uh, it's super relevant when you're late to the grow room. It was Cole, wasn't it?" he asks pointedly.

"Big deal. He had a question about the schedule and then—"

Knox bulldozes on, uninterested in my explanation. "You almost screwed up the fertilizer ratio, which could've destroyed the crop."

"Because of the measuring cup! The number was scratched—"

"*Plus,* you texted my personal cell from your burner."

I close my mouth because I honestly have no good excuse for that one.

"And the fact that *I'm* the voice of reason here," he says, thumbing his chest, "should worry the shit out of you. So tighten up! And get your priorities in check."

"Get my priorities in—" I break off, fuming so hard smoke's got to be billowing from my ears. "That's rich coming from the guy who was too wasted to help me when I needed it."

His face clouds as he opens his mouth to respond.

"Morning," Dad says, heading for the coffeepot as Geronimo pads into the kitchen behind him.

"Morning," we parrot, not breaking eye contact with each other.

Dad turns around, gesturing between us with his mug. "What's this? Tension's thicker than the humidity outside."

We quickly look away from each other. "Nothing," I say to my plate at the same time Knox grumbles, "Brotherly advice."

My brother aggressively clears his dishes. "By the way, I'm gonna need some extra muscle for today's deliveries. Think you can manage without Cole for one day?"

Passive-aggressive, Knox, really? "No problem," I reply serenely, taking a page from his playbook.

Grabbing his flat cap, he tugs it on. "Later, Dad."

"Bye, son." Dad sits down at the head of the table, taking

a cold slice of toast from the stack. "So how are things going with the Buchannon boy?"

I know he's only asking because Knox mentioned him, but it feels like a pile-on. "Fine," I reply evenly, cramming the last bit of toast in my mouth. It tastes like sawdust.

"Aunt Maeve says he's quite a hard worker," he continues. "Punctual, too." Praises of the highest order in my father's estimation.

"Mm."

"Your brother seems to think Cole wasn't responsible for the vandalism," Dad casually injects while reaching for the paper. He waits a few beats. But I know my father won't push when it's something I clearly don't want to discuss. He's not usually one for hypocrisy.

"Well," Dad continues, "whatever that was with Knox, I'm sure you'll sort it out. You always do the right thing, Honor."

There was a time I thought that was true. Now I'm not so sure. I offer him a fleeting, false grin. But Knox's troubling accusations continue spinning like a pinwheel in my mind.

I clear my plate and distractedly say goodbye. Then halt in the doorway and turn. My father opens the *Ravenswood Chronicle,* giving it a brisk shake to straighten the pages. Sensing my hovering, Dad glances over his shoulder. "Everything else all right?"

"It will be," I tell him. In three and a half more weeks. It will be.

26

Over the next few shifts, I distance myself from Cole. If Cole is the sun, then I am Pluto, orbiting five billion miles away. This way I don't have to witness the disappointment when he checks his gloves for more truths. Turning them upside down and shaking them out, only to find sad remnants of mulch and dirt. But this doesn't stop him from leaving notes in mine.

Instead of quitting the game, he finds a way to reverse engineer it.

Your favorite flower is sweet alyssum. #onetruth

I don't know how he knows this. Or whether he knows it's because they remind me of Grandma Augustine and really, they are such happy, unpretentious little flowers. But he's correct.

Which is why I have to be Pluto. Why I require the billions of miles of space between us. Because the gravitational pull of his heart is too strong.

"Is that enough distance?" I ask Ash from the stepladder late Wednesday night. "I can't tell from this angle." The hood hanging over our cannabis jungle rocks back and forth. I hold tighter to the rope connected to the pulley.

Ash makes an exaggerated series of squints. His tongue pokes out as he eyes the distance between the tops of the plants and the 1,000-watt bulbs. Too close, and we risk light bleaching, or burning the leaves. Too far, and the stalks can become stretched and weak. Both extremes would wreak havoc on the yield.

"Mm, bring it up another three inches," he mumbles around a slice of pepperoni. Together, my brother and I hoist the lights up higher.

"You're making it crooked," Knox complains, gripping the rope at the other end.

"I am not," I argue. "You moved your side, so I had to level mine."

"*No,*" he replies testily. "It was straight until you messed with it."

"Was not."

"Was not," he copies in a nasally tone.

"Stop repeating everything I say." Knox's falsetto voice overlaps with mine, driving me over the edge. I shout, "I said stop—"

"Enough!" Asher hollers over us, slam-dunking what's left of his pizza back to the box. "Happy? You dinguses made me lose my appetite." He rubs his temples. "Plus, you're giving my melon a major ache. What'd I say when I agreed to join Team HAK?" That's what Ash calls us, an acronym of our names.

I lower my arms. "That you wanted a thirty percent cut of all the sales."

He exhales. "Besides that."

"Pepperoni pizza twice a week?" Knox tries.

Ash's teeth clench. *"Besides that."*

Wow. I've never seen him this worked up. I can actually see the full wheel of his irises with his eyes open this wide.

"Oh!" I say at the same time my brother snaps his fingers. "No domestic drama," we say in unison.

"Finally!" he cries. "And you know why?"

I side-eye Knox, who shrugs.

"Because Asher Ford requires a *zen* environment!" His arms flail about the basement in a most un-zen manner. "And for two days now, you two have been fighting like cats and rats!"

"I think it's dogs, dude," Knox corrects with a snort. His smile falls away when he meets Ash's granite expression. "Sorry." My brother mimes zipping his lips and tossing the key over his shoulder.

Ash starts to pace. "You think I'm in this for the money?" He sniffs. "Well, I'm not."

We exchange a confused look as we climb down from our ladders, because *of course* that's what we thought. Why else would someone take such a massive risk?

"When I was sixteen," Ash continues, "I left home because my parents never talked—they screamed. One volume." He raises a finger. "All the time. I got sick of being their ref, so when my uncle moved south, he let me crash at his old trailer. Been living in that tin box ever since.

"Then I met you." He stops pacing and looks to my brother. "Finally felt like I had a wingman." His gaze flits over to me. "And you, with your mad grow skills and fake name." I open my mouth to apologize, but Ash lifts a hand. "Point is, I said yes because you guys *needed* me." He fiddles with the tab of

268

his zipper, staring at the forgotten pizza. "Felt good to be needed for something other than breaking up fights. Felt good to be, like, a part of something, you know? *God*"—he hisses in frustration—"it's like you can't even see how lucky you are."

"I'm sorry, bruh." Knox's voice brims with the same guilt I feel.

Ash turns away as he unzips his coveralls, his trademark board shorts and graphic tee underneath. The heavy coveralls collapse in a soft thump at his ankles. He steps out of them. "Wanna hear something totally pathetic?" His eyes glisten as he slowly faces us. "You guys are kinda the only family I've got." I watch the roll of his throat as he swallows, the fan lifting his floppy hair. "Which is why I need you to be better than the one I was born into." Strapping on his fanny pack, he abruptly bolts for the stairs.

"Ash, we're sorry," I say, trailing after him, shame filling me from the top of my head to the tips of my toes.

Knox joins me at the bottom of the stairs. "We'll do better, man. Come on, don't leave. How am I supposed to fly with only one wing? I'll just go in circles," he calls after him. *"Ash!"*

Asher mumbles something about seeing us tomorrow. Then the door thuds shut behind him.

We walk home, the air sweet with the phlox that grows pink and wild along the roadside. Our heads are hung low like our spirits.

"Well, we're officially assholes," I say, half-heartedly swatting a bug.

"Raging ones," Knox grunts, and kicks a stone. The shadow of it bounces down the road. "I seriously had no idea. He's always so happy and easygoing." My brother turns quiet a moment, then glances over to me. "I don't want to fight with you, Hon."

"I don't want to fight with you, either." I sigh. "Why do we always do that?"

My brother shrugs. "Hell if I know. Old habits, I guess. Hey, remember the Patsy's Party Store blowout?"

I laugh. "The great mud fight." Knox was nine and I was seven. He planned to bike with one of the local kids up to the convenience store to buy a bounty of candy and water balloons. He said I wasn't allowed to come because I was too slow. So I used a stick to let the air out of his tires before hollering, *"Who's the slow one now?!"*

A chuckle rolls out of him. "God, Mom was so grossed out. We were totally caked."

"I know." I grin. "The human equivalent of mud flaps. And then Dad hosed us off while the grandparents tried not to laugh. Then he made us do laps around the yard until we had at least five good things to say about each other." Dad later revealed that we shared one thing in common about our answers.

"You always have my back," Knox says, plucking the thought straight from my mind garden. He shakes his head. "About the other morning," he begins, "I didn't mean to come down on you so hard. It was overkill having Cole help with deliveries when I know you were slammed at the greenhouse."

There's always a surge of business in the week or two leading up to the Fourth of July. But the extra work isn't what bothered me. It was his total lack of faith in me. *God, is this how he feels all the times I've doubted him?*

Raccoons chitter from the tree line. "Actually, I was going to say you might've had a point," I concede. "Maybe I have been distracted lately. But nothing happened with Cole," I add. Technically this is true. We've only held hands once, twice if I count under the desk, and both times were under extreme duress.

Despite the darkness, the *yeah right* cock of my brother's head is unmistakable. "Listen, Hon, just promise you'll keep your something a nothing until this is over, okay?" When I don't immediately respond he repeats, *"Okay?"*

"Okay," I parrot. We shuffle along the dirt road in silence. The silver mailbox at the end of our drive shines like a beacon ahead. "Hey, Knox?"

"Yeah?"

"I'm sorry for throwing that party in your face. I know you felt really bad about not being there when that car came."

"You wanna hear something weird? Lately, I feel like I'm turning into *you*. Worrying all the time, about all these things that are totally out of my control. Like spying creepers, and the cops, and if something happens to the big crop. It's"—he tosses up his hands—"*exhausting*. The night of the beach party was the first decent night of sleep I've had in weeks, and that's only because I was loaded. But you, you've been doing this double-life thing since April. How the hell do you deal?"

"Sometimes I scream into pillows."

"Does that work?"

"I picked a fight with my only friend, my guts feel like a rusty tub of nails, and I have semi-regular panic attacks, so you tell me," I answer glumly.

He chuckles and knocks my elbow. "You're kind of a cool mess, though."

A reluctant grin pulls at my lips. I don't know if Knox is

simply being nice, but his comment makes me glow like the fireflies that dance over the darkened fields.

The next morning, Aunt Maeve and Knox load up the truck with tin buckets of assorted cut flowers and pots of herbs and take off for the farmer's market. It's the first time Cole and I have been left alone in days. If my brother has any misgivings, he doesn't verbalize them.

I, on the other hand, have a multitude. Which is why I planned out our entire day, sequestering myself indoors to handle the register and Cole outdoors with a lengthy list of tasks to keep him occupied and out of sight.

After ringing up a customer and sending the last bags of cypress mulch out the door, I return to the table of petunias and continue pinching off the spent flowers. Only an hour to go. One hour and I won't have to think about—

The door opens as Cole pushes a line of greenhouse carts back inside. "Finished the watering and weeding," he reports, between the crash bang of metal. "And everything else on the list."

"Already?" I hear the panic in my voice. According to my timeline, it should've taken him at least another forty-five minutes. What is he, an octopus?

Cole removes his gloves, tossing them in the cubby behind the counter. I experience another stab of guilt for leaving them so empty. Then he stands there watching me. Flustered, I pluck two perfectly formed blossoms. "Need some help with those?" he asks.

"Oh, it's no problem. I got it." I toss him the Goldilocks of grins, which goes unreturned. Come to think of it, he hasn't grinned once today. "If you want to cut out early, you can," I say, expecting he'll pounce on the offer. This is unscripted territory and I suck at ad-libbing.

"I don't mind staying." Cole joins me, deadheading the flats on the opposite side of the table. We occasionally bump hands as our fingers forage the leaves. My heart gallops like a knock-kneed pony. "So"—*pluck-pluck-pluck*—"you didn't respond to my text the other night."

Thank God. A question I'm prepared to answer. "My cell's been acting up." *Pluck-pluck.* "I think maybe it needs a new battery, because it won't hold a charge lately," I fib smoothly.

He nods, eyes downcast. I can't tell if he believes me, but there's a sad sort of heaviness about him. "Any thoughts on the truth I left you this morning?"

"Oh." I briefly hold up a hand, wiggling my bare fingers. "Sorry, didn't use my gloves today." By design, of course. I was too afraid of what his messy writing might reveal. I brace for him to ask why I've stopped trading truths, but he doesn't.

"That's what I thought." Cole wipes his hands over his shorts before reaching into his pocket. "Here," he says quietly, nudging the little scroll toward my fingers. "Please?"

Something's up. Something big enough for him to insist on my reading this in front of him. I swallow, grudgingly taking the paper and flattening it out.

You still don't trust me. #onetruth

My heart sinks. So he thinks this is why I've pulled away, because I don't trust him. "Cole—"

"No. Honor, I don't blame you," he says in a rush. "You were right about Xander."

My eyes dart to his in surprise. "And I'm so sorry I didn't believe it, or . . . I don't know, maybe I didn't *want* to. But Xander showed up at my house last night and basically told me everything—about his part with the rumors, forwarding the pictures of you and Jess, harassing you in the library. All of it." His hand clenches in a tight ball as he murmurs under his breath, "Took everything I had not to throttle him."

"H-he told you?" I sputter in shock.

"Yeah. Ironically, because he assumed you already did." He sniffs and pulls off a few more dead blossoms. "But you didn't. And why would you when you had every reason to think I wouldn't believe you?" His self-loathing creates a knot in my chest.

Cole doesn't know that under his feet grows the real reason I didn't tell him. "I didn't really have proof, though," I say, hoping to lessen both our guilt. "Not until the night of the vandalism when I found his key chain."

"But you didn't turn him in. Why?"

I lift a shoulder, unable to meet his eyes.

"The only reason I was there that night was because I found out their plan and came to stop it," Cole quietly confesses. "Then I took the blame because"—he pauses, rolling a dead blossom between his fingers—"I was afraid of what might happen to Xander if I didn't."

I don't say anything. This is a truth I already knew. That Cole is inherently, to his core, *good*.

"After that night," he continues, "I realized I can't take him at his word. And I definitely can't bail him out anymore.

Because nothing ever changes. And how are you supposed to save someone from themselves?"

"You can't," I reply. A lesson I keep learning.

"Honor, I *get* why you don't trust me. Everything's been so twisted and messed up between us, but"—he takes a deep breath—"I like you." The three words form an exquisite echo in my ears. I want to cup my hands to the sides of my head to trap them forever. "I've liked you for, well, a while. And I think you . . . you might like me, too."

When I look into his eyes my world catches fire, crackling and burning around me. I should refute what he says, but for once, I can't bring myself to lie. Not about this.

Cole interprets my silence as lingering doubt. "Twenty minutes," he pleads. "Give me twenty minutes, and if you're still not convinced you can trust me"—he lifts his hands in surrender—"then I promise to back off. No more notes, or muffins, or . . . anything." A flicker of hope burns in his expression.

This is excruciating. But if all I have to do is give him twenty minutes of closure, I can endure that. There is nothing he can say that will make me abandon my promise to Knox. For better or worse, my path forward has already been chosen.

Ten minutes later Whittaker Cherry Farm comes into view. Families pour from their SUVs and minivans, buckets in hand, on the hunt for the first ripe cherries of the season. Children wear ghoulish rings of red around their mouths, the flesh of the fruit also staining their clothes and fingers.

"We're not going cherry picking," Cole says, answering my

unspoken question. We pass the farm as the landscape stretches into a patchwork quilt of fields. After a few minutes, Cole pulls off to the shoulder, cutting the engine.

The destination is even more perplexing than Whittaker Cherry Farm. "Ravenswood Pet Cemetery?" I read the sign aloud, slowly unfastening my belt. "How will this—"

"You'll see. Come on." He hops down from the seat and slams the door.

Bewildered and curious, I follow him through the iron gates. Spindly juniper trees dot the main path that leads through the small hillside graveyard. We stroll by rows of simple stone plaques and ornate marbled headstones. I read the names of the animals who rest there—Max, Cheeto, Madame Beauregard. Scores of beloved pets cover the land.

Then we stop at one grave in particular. Cole kneels down before the plaque engraved with fanciful letters. He carefully sweeps aside a cloudy blue mass of forget-me-nots that have taken over. "Do you remember now?" His hopeful eyes lift to mine.

I sink beside him, brows furrowed. "Patches?" I glance to him. "Should I know Patches?"

The flowers fluff back into place as he lets go. "Patches was my dog. He died when I was seven." He pauses, pulling at some weeds that have invaded the forget-me-nots. I wonder if this is a habit borne of working at the greenhouse, or if this is what he always does when he comes.

"I was pretty devastated," Cole continues, bracing his palms to the grass behind him. "I'd never lost anyone before. So I went down to this creek, my pocket loaded up with so many pennies, I don't know how my pants stayed on," he says with a chuckle. "Then I threw them, one after another, into the stream, and wished for Patches to come back. It wasn't a well, but it seemed like the next best thing."

There's a pull of the familiar to his story. I find myself leaning closer.

"Then this little girl came along." He smiles wistfully, gazing up to the passing clouds, as if her likeness resides within them. "She wore these"—he gestures up and down—"overalls. Her hair was in braids with dandelions stuck in the ends, and she was missing a front tooth. I remember she had this lonely freckle." He taps near his upper lip. "Right here."

My heart knocks harder and harder, chipping away at my resolve. I stare at him with new eyes.

His smile grows as he watches the girl made of clouds, so close and so far. "And it sounds crazy, but I swear she sparkled. Like nothing I'd ever seen." Cole looks at me then. "She was my very first crush."

The lump rises in my throat. "It was *you*," I whisper. "The boy with the scraped knees and pretty blue eyes. The one I gave forget-me-nots."

The memory hits me in a rush as I recall the gurgle of the stream and rustle of leaves. The sounds of summer. There was a boy perched on a big rock, chucking coins into the water, face wet with tears. He swore he wasn't crying. I remember telling him that sometimes my dad cried, but he was still stronger than Paul Bunyan and his ox put together. Some hurts can only get out through our eyes.

Then the boy—*Cole*—told me his dog died. I told him we had a cat named Colonel Whiskers that went to heaven, too. He was grumpy and sometimes peed in our shoes. Cole said his dog was never grumpy, and he started crying again. The really hard cry that turns your breath bumpy. I didn't know what to do. But then I found a patch of blue forget-me-nots. Pulled them out of the ground roots and all, and told him how they help you remember everything good about someone. Plus forget-me-nots come back every year and you don't even have to replant them. So it's kind of like they live forever. Which means you never really have to say goodbye.

Just goodbye for now.

Cole sniffs as I return to the present. "Guess you could say the flowers worked. Because I never forgot Patches." He swallows and licks his lips. "Or you."

And I feel it. That pinpoint in time when my heart breaks wide open. When no amount of metal, wood, or brick can contain it. And like a blossom straining for the sun, I lift my chin as he moves closer, his warmth soaking into my skin. Our lips briefly touch, and the breath leaves my body. I feel the puff of his exhale, too. We shiver. His hand curves around the back of my neck as our mouths reunite.

And what begins as a tender, exploratory kiss spirals into something more desperate. Every truth I've withheld. Every feeling I've guarded. Every want I've denied. I pour it all into the kiss. Because I need him to know, even if I can't speak the words. We are tongues and teeth. Skin and hands and want.

After some time, Cole pulls back, panting, hands tangled up in my hair. "That should've been our first kiss."

My fingers skim the contours of his face, needing proof the moment is real. "All this time, why didn't you just tell me?"

"Because." Cole presses his mouth to my throat, my cheeks, the small freckle near my lip. "I wanted you to remember."

27

Kissing Cole has opened Pandora's box. And now, God help me, I can't stop. I tell myself over and over this is the last time I'm breaking my promise to Knox. I'll be good. I'll come up with a solid excuse to postpone things.

But then Cole shows up at work with a pastry bag. Smiling like we are the only two people on the planet. And the sky turns bluer, the grass grows greener, and I can't fathom waiting another second to be with him when we've already wasted so many.

So we steal our moments, the time thieves that we are.

"Aunt Maeve left for the day, and Knox won't be back for half an hour," I whisper huskily.

Cole drops the sack he carries with a wolfish grin. Then he lifts me up, my legs squeezing around his middle, as we stumble back against the shelves of terra-cotta pots (we break two). And he kisses me until I forget my name.

The next day Cole finds me doing inventory in the back shed. He doesn't say a word. Doesn't have to. Just locks the door and rushes toward me like I'm the last drop of water in a desert. But our dueling thirsts have grown unquenchable. One drop is never enough. It only makes us crave more.

"I hate all this sneaking around," Cole says one afternoon between kisses. We're sticky with sweat and want on the ground behind one of the outbuildings. He studies me, his mouth curving down in a pout. "How much longer do we have to keep this on the down-low? It'd be nice to actually *do* things with my girlfriend."

A thrill runs through me at the two-syllable word. I've never been anyone's girlfriend but find I love the cadence of it coming from his lips. My fingers smooth over his hair as he nuzzles my neck. "I'd like to point out we *are* doing things."

His sigh paints a brushstroke of heat across my skin. "You know what I mean. Upright, public things, like going out to dinner, or the movies, or . . . we could hike to the Hole and you could help me conquer my fear of seaweed."

I smile and continue stroking his hair. "And you could teach me to whistle."

"I could. Also, origami. I read a book on it once as a kid," he adds. "I'm a fount of knowledge."

"Mm, humble, too," I joke. "Just a couple more weeks, okay? It's complicated, with my dad."

"I know." Cole pushes up on his elbow; the clouds gather ominously behind his head like empty thought bubbles. "But you're sure there isn't something else?" His eyes search mine.

My face remains placid, a lake with no ripples. "What else could there be?"

"I dunno"—his thumb drifts along the plane of my collarbone—"some deep, dark secret you're afraid to tell me?" The question is teasing.

But I find it hard to smile when the air has turned gritty and impossible to breathe. My lungs feel like two sacks of sand. "Do I really strike you as being the deep, dark secret type?"

Cole eyes me suspiciously before cracking a grin. "Nah. But maybe that's why you'd make a perfect deep, dark secret keeper. You're the person no one would ever expect."

My eyes roll with my stomach. "Ugh. So cliché."

He lies on his back, lacing his hands behind his head. "Can I ask you something?"

"Define *something,*" I manage with the lightness of cottonwood fluff.

"Does anyone know about us?"

I swallow, hearing the hope that's nestled between his consonants and vowels. "Not yet."

He deflates at my side. I'm a fanged monster. Rolling to my hip, I hook my arm around him, resting my head to his chest. His heart pounds at my ear. *Lub-dub, lub-dub, lub-dub.* "Cole?" I say between the beats. "You know I hate this sneaking around as much as you, right?"

"Yeah," he replies with little conviction.

Lifting my head, I look into his eyes. The color could be chiseled from the sky. "I love being with you. Every minute."

Cole grins softly, pulling me down to brush his lips over mine. "I love being with you, too," he whispers. "I just want more minutes."

"Soon, I promise." I settle back against his chest and close my eyes, the *lub-dub* melody repeating. And as I memorize the lilting rhythm, I pray that this time, I have made a promise I can keep.

I find myself humming—wearing the dopiest of smiles—as I shake the fresh cedar shavings into the nesting boxes of the chicken coop, my thoughts circling around Cole. Although he's not the only inspiration for this goofy grin.

Today marks the first of July. Eighteen days till the final harvest, and our grow room has returned to a zen-like environment. With Knox and I staunchly observing the No Domestic Drama rule, Ash is back to his smiley, toking self. And there's been no other skulking night visitors, so even those fears have begun to fade.

Geronimo barks and growls outside. Quickly finishing the last nesting box, I step out of the stuffy coop in my muck boots to see what animal's got him all worked up. Except, it isn't an animal. Not the four-legged kind. My blood instantly frosts.

Geronimo continues growling, baring his canines.

Xander holds up his hands. He's a mess—unshaven, clothes rumpled, blond hair collapsed and slightly frizzed without the layers of gel. "I'm . . . I'm not here to cause any trouble." He quickly removes his sunglasses so I can see his eyes, one of them black and swollen halfway shut. "I swear. When there weren't any cars, I wasn't even sure anyone was home."

I'm the only one here at the moment, a realization that twists my insides. I grab Geronimo's collar when he inches forward. "Why are you here?"

"Cole still won't talk to me," he says with a heavy exhale. "It's been a week. We've never gone this long without talking."

"That sounds like a you problem."

Geronimo growls again, low and rumbly.

"Um . . ." Xander nervously eyes my protector. "Think we could talk without the attack dog?"

"No."

He swallows, nodding to the ground. "Fair enough." Xander cautiously backs up a step, leaning against a section of split rail fencing. "You know, Cole and I used to do this annual swim race as kids every spring. Ever been in Lake Michigan in May? Man"—he sucks air through his teeth—"colder than a witch's tit."

I'm neither amused by nor interested in this trip down memory lane. "You still haven't said why you came or what any of this has to do with me."

"Please, Honor . . . I know you have every reason to hate me. But I'm asking you to hear me out anyway."

Maybe it's the black eye, or the oddly genuine nature of his tone, but against my better judgment, I nod.

Xander appears relieved. "So we were seven," he continues, "and the water that May was even colder than usual. Didn't matter, though. We were hell-bent on having our swim race to the sandbar." A faint grin pulls at his lips. "You should've seen Cole, I actually used to call him Pole because he was so skinny." He laughs. "Anyway, the wind made the current really strong that day. We'd gotten partway to the sandbar when his legs started to cramp up. Bad. Next thing I know, his head goes under. It happened so quick—one second Cole was there, and the next he was gone. Just"—his head sways—"bubbles. So I dove down after him. We were both coughing and spewing out half the lake by the time I got him back to the surface. But I promised I'd get him to shore. I *promised* not to let go."

A heroic Xander? It defies imagination.

He stuffs a hand in his pocket. "Then when we were twelve, my dad laid into me for breaking the garage window. It was an accident, but Vic didn't see it that way. Said I needed to be taught a lesson. When Cole saw the welts, he showed up at my house on his bike with a baseball bat. He was terrified of Vic, but he stood there, knobby knees just shaking. Then, he threatened to take a swing at my dad if he ever hurt me again."

My gaze lifts to Xander's black eye. A blood vessel has broken inside it, clouding the white a ghastly crimson.

He self-consciously slides his sunglasses back on. "When I asked Cole why he came back that day, why he'd risk a whooping from my old man, he said, 'Because. We promised we'd always get each other to shore.'" Xander grows quiet then, angrily brushing at his cheek.

"What happened to you, Xander, it's not okay." I hesitate, looking at him before pushing out the last of my unsteady words. "But neither is what you did to me."

Xander turns his head away. "I know. It's just . . . it was always me and Cole against the world. Then *you* came," he says bitterly, scuffing a shoe along the ground. "And everything changed. Like, I wasn't even in his world. I was just this clingy dick outsider with no way back in. You know he doesn't even wanna play lacrosse anymore?" He sniffs in disbelief.

I do know. And I also know his lacrosse loathing has nothing to do with me. But Xander won't see it that way. To him I'm the enemy. The one who stole his best friend. *This is why he hates me.* I finally understand what I represent, no matter how warped and untrue it is.

I scratch behind Geronimo's ear as he slumps against my leg, black fur hot from the sun. "Why are you telling me all this?"

"My mom and me, we're leaving town," he replies, voice still thick with emotion. "To stay with my aunt in North Carolina."

I blink. "You mean for the summer?"

"For"—he shrugs, wiping his nose—"indefinitely, I guess. Fresh start and shit. Look after Cole for me, would you? In case he ever needs help getting back to shore?"

My throat tightens. Now I get why he came to my house. Why he opened up like a reluctant clamshell. I nod. "I will."

"One more thing." He reaches into his pocket and pulls out a folded envelope. "Think you could give this to him? I don't want my last words to be the ones I said. He probably wouldn't take it from me now, but I bet he'd read it if you gave it to him."

I take the envelope he holds out, turning it over in my hands. "Okay."

"Thanks." Xander backs away slowly. "Oh, and I talked to the guys. Nobody's gonna give you any more trouble." Nodding to himself, he turns for his truck.

The engine revs to life. There's no farewell wave. No poignant goodbye. No apology for the hurt he's caused. Because this isn't a movie. And in real life, I'm finding a lot more goes unsaid.

Shading my eyes, I watch as he drives away, dust unspooling in his wake. Then I drop my arm, and Xander is gone.

28

Whenever my anxiety got the better of me, Grandma Augustine would say I was "more nervous than a cat in a room full of rocking chairs." Then I'd declare myself a tailless Manx, and we'd both get a giggle.

Today, I am no Manx. My tail has never felt longer, and the rocking chairs have never been so plentiful.

Because as it turns out, someone is *still* watching us.

The vehicle arrived in the dead of night. Our phones pinged us awake just past two. And within minutes, Knox had crept up to my room, hair wild as his eyes. "There's an SUV at the greenhouse," he whispered.

"I know." I sat, huddled on my bed, already watching the live feed. Watching the unfamiliar vehicle as it performed a slow, predatory lap around the parking lot. Once again, nobody got out. But this time, there wasn't a cigarette butt parting gift. All we had was the plate number: HGB 098. For whatever good that does us.

"You're sure you saw a car the other night," my brother murmured, "right?"

I took a break from chewing my stubby nails. "Positive. It wasn't an SUV." The implication that we had a new stalker made my skin feel crawly and bug-covered. Danger seemed to be circling closer, and we still had no idea who the enemy was.

Which is why Knox, Ash, and I have agreed our defense readiness condition must remain at DEFCON 1, until every pound of weed has been removed from the basement. We will stay on guard. Vigilant to anyone who comes within—

A hand suddenly drops to my shoulder. "Ahh!" I screech and jump all the way to the ceiling. *"Cole,"* I breathe, pushing my heart back in my chest.

"Sorry." He eyes me with concern. "What's up? You've been so jumpy today. Is it because of the stuff with Xander?"

As promised, I delivered the letter to Cole, who was none too happy to learn that Xander had come to my house. So unhappy, he crumpled up the letter and threw it in the trash without even reading it. I don't know why I felt so compelled to rescue the envelope from the garbage. To smooth the crinkled paper and brush away coffee grounds, saving it until Cole was in a better place to read it. It wasn't altruism, that's for sure. Maybe it was guilt. A deep-seated need to know if Cole could forgive Xander, then maybe there'd be absolution for me.

"No. I'm fine." I set down the stack of fives I was counting on autopilot. "I must've been so focused on balancing the till I didn't hear you. You taking off?"

Cole loops his arms around me, pressing his lips to my forehead. "If that's all right? I still have to pick up my Jeep from the shop and pack for that trip with my folks before we meet up later." He tilts his head and frowns. "You didn't forget, did you?"

"Course not," I reply, burying my face to his chest. "Who could forget an invitation to a midnight picnic?" Me. I did. I totally forgot our rendezvous because fear and paranoia have become a full-time occupation. And since Cole's heading north first thing tomorrow for the long holiday weekend, this is our last chance to be together before he leaves.

He gives me a kiss and everything inside loosens. I let go, flying and falling all at once. Circled in his arms, I become a simple girl. Who doesn't have destructive secrets and lies crawling under her skin.

Cole pulls away, ending the kiss too quickly. "Mm, I better grab my stuff from the office." He starts to walk backward, still holding my hand, tugging me along with him. His smile takes up the whole greenhouse.

"*Go,*" I laugh, nudging him away. "I have to finish this, and you're destroying my ability to count."

The door chimes. My smile drops like my hand from my lips. A warm flush erupts over my skin. "M-Mr. Buchannon," I stutter. *You mean* Officer *Buchannon*. How could I be so careless? Had Cole's dad walked in a few seconds earlier, he'd have seen something far more incriminating than the aftermath of a kiss.

"Hello, Honor." He slides his sunglasses to the top of his head, glancing toward the hall where his son disappeared. His blue eyes scan my face in that practiced-cop way. "I came to pick up Cole," he says, giving nothing away.

"He just went to grab his things from the back." I pull the twenties from the drawer and begin counting. My palms have gone instantly sweaty, causing the money to stick to my fingers.

No big deal. Just a minor drug lord hanging with her boy-friend's law-enforcement dad.

Now all I can think about is the fuckton of fragrant Kush in the basement, and whether Mr. Buchannon has the nose of a drug-sniffing police dog.

"You know"—he pauses, tucking his hands in the pockets of his khaki shorts and rattling his keys—"Cole will be starting lacrosse training next month. Schedule's going to be pretty intense. Especially after last season's disappointing end."

I glance up from the bills in my hands. *Okayyy.* I mean, I'm aware Cole isn't here indefinitely.

"Yep." Mr. Buchannon's eyes rove the greenhouse. His mouth pinches a bit like he finds it lacking. "Which means no distractions—from friends, parties . . . girls."

My counting slows as I absorb the subtext. I swallow, my pulse kicking up a notch.

"He's going to need to stay focused if he wants a shot at a good scholarship," Mr. Buchannon continues. "You understand, don't you?"

I understand Mr. Buchannon suspects there's something between us. And that he's cool with me being a seasonal fling and nothing more. I also understand this man knows nothing about his son. "Yes," I say evenly, tucking the cash into the zippered bag.

"Good. Then we're all on the same page." Gazing out at the picked-over flats, he strolls over to some geraniums. "Looks like business has been steady."

"June and July are usually good months," I manage, pretending to be absorbed in the task of bundling the receipts.

But I watch him from the corner of my eye, moving closer to the basement door. My heart thumps harder, causing my surroundings to jump with it.

Mr. Buchannon stops in front of the mat. And points. "Look at that."

My head snaps in his direction. *Look? He couldn't possibly mean*—I hear myself gasp as he bends for the floor. The receipts fall from my hand, fluttering like strips of paper snow to the floor. *NOOO!*

He pops upright like he hears my silent cry. "A lucky penny," he says cheerfully, then flips the coin for good measure. "Did you know most pennies nowadays aren't copper? They're mostly zinc with a copper coating. The composition changed in the forties when they had to ration copper for shell casings during the Second World War." Mr. Buchannon shakes his head with a chuckle. "Sorry, I'm kind of a history nut. Cole gets that same glazed-over look anytime I go there."

A nervous titter tumbles out with my exhale. But inside, I'm dying. *DYING.*

"Couldn't find my keys," Cole announces when he returns. "Oh," he says, noticing his father's arrival. "Hey, Dad."

Mr. Buchannon lifts his chin in my direction. "I was just boring Honor here with historical trivia. You ready to go?" He eyes his watch. "Dealership closes soon."

Cole sees the receipts that surround me like a chalk outline. I sink down, quickly scooping them up before he can question it. "Um, so I'll see you next week, Honor. Have a good Fourth." Cole speaks as if we are polite strangers.

"Uh-huh." I can barely make eye contact. It takes all my concentration to keep my movements smooth. "You too."

There's the dull scrape and slide of the coin across the counter as Mr. Buchannon pushes it over to me. "In case you're low on luck," he says with a mild grin.

The door chimes with their departure, and I collapse down to the stool, clutching my head in my hands. I can't keep this up much longer. I feel myself fraying. There are too many secrets to guard. Too many lies to protect. Danger lurks everywhere.

When my heart rate no longer rivals that of a humming-bird, I stand and finish gathering up the deposit. The phone rings. I debate whether to answer, since we're closed.

I sigh. "Augustine Greens, how may I help you?"

"Honor?" Aunt Maeve's voice quakes on the other end. "I . . . is Knox there?"

"He should be back any minute. What's wrong?"

"It's your d-dad. He was working and—" A sob interrupts her speech.

"What happened?" I demand. The building tips like a boat on choppy waters. She's crying. And I can count on one hand the number of times I've seen her fully break down. "Aunt Maeve?" I hold the edge of the counter through her annihilating silence.

"Some kids were goofing off since . . . it's almost the Fourth. They lit a bunch of firecrackers." Her voice possesses the same jaggedness as the black stone in my jar. "He was on the roof at one of the construction sites and—"

"Is he okay?" Maybe I scream the question. Maybe it's a whisper. I don't know. But my entire existence hangs in the balance of her answer.

"He ran off the roof, Pip. He just . . . *ran*." Her breath shudders like my heart. "The doctors have him stabilized now."

Stabilized. I cling to the word like it's a glowing health pronouncement. "Where are you?"

"Mercy General."

"I'll be there as fast as I can."

My father's eyes roll back and forth under his lids. Even sedated, he doesn't cease the battle. A chain of bruises mar his jaw, growing angrier and darker by the minute.

Knox sidles up next to him, reaching through the bed rail to take hold of his hand. "Hey, Dad." His vocal cords tighten with the same emotion that keeps me from speaking.

Unlike my brother, I hang back beside the IV pole because my feet have grown taproots. Restraints bind our father's wrists and ankles to the hospital bed. I look away before the tears can push from my eyes, focusing instead on counting the steady drips of his IV bag.

The beeping machines fill the silence in the sterile room.

Aunt Maeve returns carrying two paper cups, the scent of chemical antiseptics combining with bitter coffee. The tea pickings must've been pretty slim.

"Good news," she says, holding out a cup to me before passing the other to Knox. I notice the antique ring missing from her finger and the pale line of skin left in its absence. She takes a seat in the chair on the other side of Dad. "I cornered one of the nurses and found out the doctors reviewed the results of the CT scans and X-rays. Dr. Chang will be here shortly. The nurse said she's one of the best and brightest doctors she knows."

I wrap my clammy hands around my cup, drawing on its heat. I can't seem to get warm.

"Honor?" Aunt Maeve says, squashing herself to one side of the seat and patting the empty space. "Want to sit?"

I shake my head and resume drip counting. *Eighty-nine. Ninety. Ninety-one . . .*

A white coat suddenly breezes into the room. "Hello, I'm Dr. Chang." A gentle grin curves her lips as she extends a hand to shake each of ours. Her eyes are sharp yet warm. And she looks young for a top-notch doctor, but that hardly means anything.

"When will the restraints be taken off?" I ask.

Dr. Chang gives me a sympathetic look. "Very soon. Please understand your father was extremely agitated when he was admitted. Without knowing the extent of his injuries, there was concern he might accidentally do himself greater harm. But the sedative has helped calm him, and his vitals are stable."

Aunt Maeve inches to the edge of her chair, anxiously rubbing her rose quartz pendant. "How serious are his injuries, Dr. Chang? What did the tests show?"

"That Mr. Augustine is a very resilient and very lucky man," she replies with another soft, reassuring grin. If the kind doctor knew that the tattoo on my father's upper arm was the army's insignia for airborne infantry, she'd understand we didn't need tests to confirm that. "Honestly, we were anticipating much more extensive injuries based on the height of his fall. But beyond the bruises, the CT and X-rays have shown three cracked ribs and a sprained ankle. All in all, this is the very best-case scenario."

The breath rushes from my lips as my brother asks, "So that's good, right? We can expect a full recovery?"

"Yes," Dr. Chang says carefully, "physically speaking, he's going to be just fine." She skims over Dad's chart.

Knox pumps his fist. "Hear that, Dad? Doc says you'll be aces in no time." He squeezes his limp hand.

Wait. Why has the doctor's mouth gone into a straight line? What happened to the upward lift? I set down my coffee cup, my stomach queasy again.

Dr. Chang pulls over a stool and sits down. "My greatest concern at this stage isn't Mr. Augustine's physical recovery but his mental state. There's"—she pauses, flicking through the tablet—"no record of ongoing treatment for the post-traumatic stress disorder. Is this his first episode of this nature? Sometimes the psychological effects can take years, decades even, to become apparent."

"No," all of us answer.

"But this is the worst," Aunt Maeve adds, her eyes glistening. She dabs them with the end of her scarf. "John doesn't like to talk about what happened during the war. I've encouraged him to seek help, but . . ." She hopelessly shrugs.

"So have I," my brother chimes in.

I turn my head in surprise, although maybe I shouldn't be. Knox has always tackled things head-on, whereas I tend to cautiously circle, examining every pro and con under the sun. Making lists. Calculating odds.

"Unfortunately, PTSD symptoms can become more severe over time if left untreated." Dr. Chang studies my dad's chart again. "I understand when he was in Iraq there was a night raid that resulted in much of his platoon being lost. A trauma of that magnitude—"

"No," Knox interrupts, pushing a hand through his hair. "No, it wasn't most of the platoon. AJ Knox, his battle buddy, he was the one who died in the raid."

I nod.

The doctor's forehead creases as her eyes travel uncomfortably to Aunt Maeve.

What does she know that we don't?

Aunt Maeve twists the scarf in her hands. "That's . . . not entirely true, Knox. He just didn't want you to know how bad it was. His way of protecting you, I guess. But he"—she falters, wiping her eyes before loudly gulping—"he was one of only three soldiers who survived the attack."

All this time. All this time I believed like my brother that Dad survived a tragedy. Not a massacre. No wonder he paces at night. No wonder he works so hard to fix things that are beyond repair.

When I close my eyes I see the picture of the men in uniform, standing proud. Virtually every single one of them dead. Gone. Instead of their loved one returning, their families received a knock at the door. A meticulously folded flag. A handful of medals. And a promise the soldier's sacrifice would not be forgotten.

But none of it brings them home.

None of it.

It isn't until Dr. Chang holds out a box of tissues that I realize I'm crying.

29

I wake the next morning to roaring applause. My skull literally pounds with the clapping. Not clapping . . . Rain tramples the roof. With a whimper, I lift my thousand-pound eyelids.

The attic is a carnival ride, and I can't get off the spinning teacup. *God, what happened?* My foot bumps against something when I swing my leg over the side of the bed. The wine bottle rolls slowly across the floor, leaving a dotted trail of ruby on my rug. My belly turns with the bottle's revolutions. Cupping a hand to my mouth, I drag the trash can closer.

When the swell of nausea is mostly gone, I sink back into bed, balling up like a gray pill bug. *What the hell did I do?* Everything is so hazy.

Rain streaks the windowpanes, the blurry tracks about as clear as my recollections of last night. Too bad they don't make brain squeegees. Rubbing my head, I try to piece together the murky events.

Dad is in the hospital. That part I vividly recall. Aunt Maeve insisted on staying with Dad overnight, promising she'd call with any updates. I flop a hand to the table, patting around until my fingers land on my phone. No messages. Visiting hours don't start for another two and a half hours, sparing me enough time (I hope) to feel relatively human.

Ugh. My head continues throbbing like a second heart has grown inside it, making it impossible to think. *Start at the beginning,* I tell myself. *Start with what you remember first.*

Knox and I rode back from the hospital in silence, him chewing his lower lip like rawhide. He holed himself up in his room once we were home. Loud, frenzied music pulsed through his door. Between the songs, I heard the smack of his fists against his punching bag.

But punching through heartache isn't my way. Instead, I wound up drifting from room to room like a housekeeping specter. Straightening couch pillows, shuffling the mail into a neat pile, organizing the contents of the fridge—creating order in chaos.

I open my eyes briefly because of the dizziness, placing a hand to the unmoving table before pinching them shut again.

Then what? Oh, Knox left. Around the time the sun had slid most of the way down the sky, stealing its light from the walls. The house turned gray. "I'm going out," my brother said as I sat in front of the TV, not really seeing anything. "I'll be back in time to visit Dad in the morning."

Pulling myself from the vision, I rise on quivery legs from my mattress. Knox isn't home. A puddle gathers where his truck would normally be parked. I sink back down, clawing through the mangled memories for the next clue.

I went to bed. Then something woke me up. Not something. It was someone. Cole.

My stomach churns. A foil wrapper from Cole's gum sits on

my dresser. I pull my pillow to my chest and inhale, smelling his minty shampoo. The events begin to flicker more rapidly now. Pressing the heels of my hands to my eyes, I try and slow the typhoon of images.

Cole knocking at the front door, worried when I didn't show or reply to his texts. Me telling him my dad ran off a roof and how I didn't know he had survived a massacre. Him gathering me in his arms to console me. But his arms weren't enough, so I kissed him. Hard. Twining myself like ivy around his body. "I just"—my chest heaved—"I just want to feel something good. Please," I begged him.

We went to my bedroom then. Collapsed on the tiny twin mattress, disproportionate to his size. The words "I need, I need, I need" streamed uncontrollably from my lips.

"I know," Cole said hoarsely between hungry kisses.

Primal kisses. Even more intense than the others. Our clothed bodies pressed together, interwoven in such a way no space could exist between us.

I bunch the pillow to my nose again, the night revealing itself in more flashes and feelings.

Cole was only trying to give me what I asked for. How could he know my physical release would trigger an emotional one? I certainly didn't.

"I n-never wanted to hurt you. That's why I tried so hard, so hard to push you away," I wept. "You're going to hate me."

He held me, kissed at my tears. "Honor, why would you say that? I could never hate you. Shh, it's okay. I'm not going anywhere," Cole said.

But he didn't know this was temporary. It was all temporary.

"You will," I whispered as his fingers moved through my hair. "You'll hate me just like you hate Xander."

Confusion formed creases in his forehead. "I don't hate . . . This isn't about Xander. Hey"—he crooked a finger under my chin—"just tell me what it is."

My damp eyes lifted to his, knowing he would never look at me the same. Knowing these words that burned like acid and caught like thorns in my throat . . . would break us.

Then I took a small piece of paper, tore it in half, and wrote down two truths. Just in case my vocal cords stayed frozen.

Handing him the first, I watched his gaze dance across the slip of paper. The corners of his mouth dipped lower. "But . . . I don't understand. How are you a criminal?"

I finally found my voice and told him what was growing in the basement, and about the weed I'd already sold. Purging all my secrets like the poison they were until the air was polluted and thick. Toxic with my deceit. Maybe that was why Cole said nothing—there was no oxygen left to breathe.

He then moved quickly through the house, his footsteps pounding out the betrayal, anger, and hurt he felt.

"Please!" I begged, catching him at the front door as I pushed the second truth I'd written into his hands. "Please just read it," I choked on salty tears.

Cole skimmed the six words I'd written. Then wadded up the paper like he had with Xander's envelope. "This isn't a truth," he said dully, dropping the ball of paper at my feet and slamming the door behind him.

I lower the pillow from my face, no longer having to wonder how Cole will react when he learns of the lies I've been weaving. Because I have my answer looking around this dim and foggy space.

Cole will leave.

Leaning over the side of the bed, I grab the trash can. In the bottom are the two scraps of discarded paper. The second truth, which bore the brunt of his hostility, lays wrinkled and battered, but still legible.

I am in love with you.

My handwriting is small, insignificant even. But it might be the truest thing I've ever written.

Then I heave, vomiting on them both. And the wine I pilfered from the liquor cabinet to forget exits my body with the speed of Cole's Jeep down the driveway.

"Need another pillow?" I ask Dad, who winces as he repositions himself in bed.

Stifling a groan, he replies, "The six you brought me outta suffice."

Since Dad's homecoming three days ago, we've spent the weekend flapping like mother hens around him. Making sure he has water for his pills. Enough pillows to keep him comfortably propped. We offer cold compresses, warm compresses, and strong, foul-smelling teas that Aunt Maeve swears on Mother Earth will create miraculous healings.

"It's stuffy in here. I'll open your window," I announce, crossing the room. My reflection in the glass shows a girl made of ash. She is no longer hungover, stinking of sour, fermented grapes. But her lies have burned through her, leaving a human-shaped pile of calcium carbonate and potash. One stiff breeze and she will scatter.

I burn for Cole. Who has not responded to my texts. To my apologies. To my pleas for understanding. I burn for Knox and for Asher. Unaware of the secrets I revealed five nights ago.

But that changes tomorrow with the greenhouse reopening Monday and the grow team reuniting. So I guess I'll have my reckoning with them all.

The wind pushes past me, carrying the smell of the grass Knox cut earlier. *How haven't I blown away?*

"Honor?"

Before turning, I force my mouth upright. "Yeah?"

"Come here." He pats the empty side of the brick mattress.

After moving some pillows, I settle in beside him. Geronimo whines because he did not get an invitation to bed, which is the doggy equivalent of *Moby Dick*'s white whale. But Geronimo doesn't understand it's for his own good—Dad often kicks and thrashes in his sleep.

My father's eyes have gone tender, like the bruises on his face. "What are you doing?"

"Taking care of you," I reply, which I thought was fairly obvious.

His grin is rueful. "Arguably too well, all of you. You know Aunt Maeve knitted me a sweater?" Dad gestures toward the chair where the navy garment is draped. "Never mind it's July, and the sleeves are long enough for an orangutan. And your brother? He was up here doing some bizarre comedy routine. Telling a joke about a guy who walked into a bar with . . ."

"A hamster and a pound of ring bologna," we say at the same time.

I grin for real. Then add, "Yeah, he really needs to shape that one more." Knox, the natural-born entertainer. I swear his blood beats with carnie magic.

Dad's face turns more serious as he continues, "Honey, taking care of me isn't your job. Or your brother's or aunt's. It's mine. So you can stop worrying about me, all right?"

"How?" I blurt. "I mean, what happens next time?"

His brow furrows. "Who says there'll be a next time?"

"History. Maybe it won't be a roof, but something will happen. And keep happening until . . ." I fade out, grasping for the right words. "The situation changes. The doctor mentioned there were some programs that could help with—"

"Honor," Dad says firmly, "what part of 'it's not your job to take care of me' was unclear? I'm going to be *fine*." He squeezes my hand.

But the sentiment rings hollow in my ears. Because how can he be fine if he keeps refusing the help he needs? Once again, we are at an impasse.

"I take it back," Dad says abruptly, scrunching his nose. "I will not be fine if Aunt Maeve brings another one of those *disgusting* teas. They smell like hot, steamy garbage."

The aroma hits me then, too, and I retch, pulling my T-shirt over my nose. "Actually, I think that's Geronimo. He got into the trash earlier."

My cell rings. *Cole calling* illuminates the screen. My chest, which for days has been an empty drum, suddenly pounds to life. "Dad, um, do you mind if I—"

"*God yes!* Do something normal. Go!" he hollers, fanning his face. "Save yourself!"

We exchange *good night*s and *I love you*s as I scurry from the room and up the attic steps, two at a time.

"H-hello?" I gulp and catch my breath. "Cole?" I hang there, wrung out by the beats of silence. "I'm so sorry," I gush into the dead space. "I didn't know what to do. How to tell you without . . . *telling* you why everything's so messed up. And I know you probably think I'm as bad as Chelsea and Xander and your dad, and basically . . . everyone who's ever lied to you, but—"

"Honor, stop," Cole says gently. "This is different." The line goes quiet a moment, and I fall headlong into the silence, gripping the phone like a life preserver. "Hell, I've had days to think, and I still can't wrap my head around all of it."

My eyes well with tears at the sound of his voice. I grab his gum wrapper, sinking to the floor in front of the dresser. "What would you have done? If our roles were reversed?" I ask, voice cracking. "What would you have done, if someone you loved was in trouble?"

He sighs. I can't tell if it's a good sigh or bad sigh. "I don't know. I *didn't* know." Then he adds, "Until now."

Sniffing, I wipe my cheek. "Until now?"

"I love you," he says in one rushing breath.

The sob I work to contain breaks free.

"I wanted to say that even before I read your truths. And the only reason I crumpled it up was because I was upset, not because I didn't believe you. I love you, Honor Augustine. So I do know what I'd do for someone I love. I would do anything."

There I sit, a soupy puddle of emotion on my bedroom floor. But I have enough wherewithal to see what he's implying. "Cole, no." I wipe my nose. "That's not what I wanted. I won't let you get involved. I only told you because—"

"Okay, then answer me this," he quickly cuts in. "Would you do it for me? Would you get involved if *our* roles were reversed?" He's turning my question from earlier around on me.

And I cannot lie, not anymore. Catching my hiccupping breath, I reply, "In a heartbeat."

"Then meet me tomorrow night," Cole says. "I have an idea."

30

For last two days, Cole's idea has been rolling in my thoughts like a rock in my tumbler. Ash will be easy to convince. It's Knox I'm worried about.

One could argue that the point's a bit moot, since I've already revealed our secret lair to Cole. Already acquainted him with the forty plants we plan to harvest in ten days' time. So like it or not, there isn't much Knox can do about Cole knowing. Which is what will piss him off most of all. And a pissed-off Knox also doesn't bode well for keeping the peace around Ash.

Cole places a hand to my hammering knee. I glance up from the cluster of tiny tornados I've doodled on the back of my notebook that twirl like my insides. "Sorry." The table—and by extension his laptop—wobbles with aftershocks.

"Honor, it's gonna be all right," Cole says calmly. Eerily calm for someone sitting with a forest of bushy, four-foot-tall marijuana at his back while hacking into a police database. Technically, not hacking. He ran across his dad's passcodes and memorized them. Just like he's already researched and memorized the steps for harvesting cannabis. I'm starting to believe his memory is a lot more than *borderline* photographic.

"Easy for you to say." I shrug out of my coveralls, tying the arms at my waist. "You don't know Knox like I do. If there's one thing we Augustines universally hate, it's being boxed in. Which is exactly what I've done to him by telling you."

Cole glances up from the computer screen between clicks of the keyboard. "He'll understand."

"But I promised him, Cole. I *promised* I wouldn't start anything with you until every gram of weed was out of this basement." Sighing, I slump back in my seat. "So besides betraying his trust, I've also broken my promise to him."

He stops typing to hook his foot in the leg of my chair, then drags me closer in one swift motion. He cups his hands on either side of my face. "Your brother will understand *and* forgive you. I've spent enough time around all of you to know that's just what your family does. No matter what."

My brows furrow as I rest my hand to his. "I hope you're right."

"I am. And let's not forget"—he leans in, brushing his lips over mine—"I can be pretty persuasive when I need to be. You used to hate my guts, and now you're my girlfriend."

"C'mon, I didn't *hate* your guts." A small grin emerges. "I just . . . passionately loathed them."

"Oh, is that all?" He chuckles, hands sliding away as he returns to the computer.

Then I quickly add, "But that was before I knew the *real* Cole Buchannon. And learned how selfless, amazing, and brilliant you are."

"Well"—he hits Return, a triumphant grin on his face—

"your selfless, amazing, and brilliant boyfriend just got into the police database. Got that plate number? We can run it through the system before they get here."

"Ooh, great idea." Opening my notebook, I flip to the page with the scribbled license plate of the mystery SUV and read it aloud.

Cole types it in, and the screen blips to reveal the owner's identity.

"Zachary Ryan Mellner. Goes by the alias Thumper." Cole quickly does the math based on his birth date. "Age twenty-two. Six foot one, one hundred and eighty-five pounds. Prior record includes a DUI and two misdemeanor assaults. Does he look familiar?" He glances to me.

I study the broad face and sorta soul patch under his lower lip. The deep-set brown eyes and wide neck leading down to wider shoulders.

"No." Inching back from the screen, I swallow. "I've never seen him before."

"Yeah, me neither." Cole's mouth is tight as he gazes at Zachary. "I don't like that he was here."

That makes two of us. "On the bright side, at least we can rule out police surveillance. So that's one less threat."

He frowns. "Was that a concern?"

I shrug. "It could've been an unmarked car. I had to consider every angle."

"No wonder you were so jumpy when my dad came around." Cole says *dad* like the word leaves a bad aftertaste in his mouth. He was pretty salty when I told him how his father made it clear I'd be kicked to the curb come lacrosse season.

My burner rings. The angst I suppressed rears its ugly

head. "It's Knox," I say before taking a deep breath and answering. "Hey, I'm here. Where are you guys?"

"On our way." My brother sounds winded. "Listen, something's come up—"

"Yeah, I actually have something to tell you, too." My eyes slide to Cole, whose forehead is tensed in concentration as he taps the trackpad. "It's about Co—"

"No time," Knox barks. "Grab the first aid kit and bring it down to the basement!"

The cement floor turns spongy.

"Why? What's—"

Asher moans in the background, and my pulse ratchets higher.

"Knox, what happened? What's going on?"

Cole stops, glancing up in alarm.

"Is Ash okay? Knox? Talk to me!"

"He's . . . two guys . . . when I found . . . smashed his . . ."

"What? Knox, I don't know what you're saying! You're breaking up!" Cole's at my side now, head pressed to mine as we work to decipher the fragmented message. But the reception continues cutting in and out, so we only get a few of his chopped-up words: *Hurt. Ice. Minutes.*

Then the line goes dead.

I curse. "They've got to be close," I say, already moving for the stairs. "My calls always drop around Lakeview Drive."

Cole's hot on my heels as we pound up the stairs. Racing into the office, he immediately empties all the ice trays into plastic bags, while I collect the first aid kit and some clean rags. I have no idea what to prepare for, but everyone seems to need clean rags in a crisis on TV.

The motion sensor pings. My body stiffens, dread prickling my skin. I swivel to Cole. "Can you take everything downstairs?"

"Already on it," he replies, gathering up the supplies with fast and measured movements. I shouldn't be surprised he does so well under pressure. He's his father's son, the by-product of a man who demands perfection on and off the field.

As I race to the back door, Knox's truck comes to a crunching halt on the gravel. He hops out, quickly hefting a large duffel bag to his shoulder. "Hold the door open for us!"

I nod, my nerves arcing like downed power lines. Jogging around to the passenger side, he eases Ash out.

When they round the vehicle so there's enough moon to light their faces, I see Ash has a gash along his cheekbone. Blood spatters his *It's Gotta Be 4:20 Somewhere* T-shirt.

"What happened?" Propping the door with my foot, I grasp Asher's other side to give him more support.

"Ahh!" Ash instantly cries and recoils, eyes clenched like his teeth.

"His arm's hurt," Knox explains.

Which is when I notice the unnatural way it hangs lower.

"It's okay, bud," he says soothingly to Ash. "We're gonna get you all fixed up. Then we'll keep you safe. Nothing safer in the world than Fort Knox."

"Fort Snox," he pathetically echoes, head lolling to my brother's shoulder like it's too heavy to hold up.

I push aside boxes and anything that might slow their path to the grow room.

"He got out of work early," Knox continues while wrangling Ash, whose legs seem to keep wandering away from him.

"Surprised the two guys who were there trashing his place. They tore apart everything. Destroyed all his stuff except what's in the duffel bag."

Ash winces as we navigate the first step down to the basement. "They were looking"—his breath hitches and he draws air through his teeth—"for my stash."

The stash we sold over six weeks ago. I study the weeping wound on his face. How does a small-time grower suddenly gain the interest of big-time players? This can't be a coincidence. Whoever did this must know there's a connection between us and Ash.

Which makes my guilt all the more crushing.

"What the living fuck, Honor?!" Knox suddenly roars.

Yanked from my mental mea culpa, I realize he's looking at Cole.

"Knox, I'm here to help," Cole says quickly, hands raised.

My brother looks to me, horror and betrayal sketched over his face. "You didn't." His nostrils flare. "Tell me you didn't!"

Somehow I'm able to keep my voice firm and steady. "Ash needs us right now. You can yell at me later."

Cole's gaze drops to Asher's arm as he approaches us. "Looks like a dislocated shoulder. Seen a number of those on the field. Hurts like a bitch, doesn't it?" he says to Ash.

"Like a mofo," Ash slurs, an odd, dopey grin creeping over his face. He blinks in slow motion. "A *mooofoo000o.*"

Exchanging concerned glances, we lay him down on the blanket Cole's spread over the floor, then crouch like gargoyles around him.

"I assume the ER's out of the question," Cole says, to which Asher thrashes his head side to side.

"Can you fix it?" Knox asks Cole, momentarily boxing up his anger.

"Well, I'm not a doctor," Cole says, eyes fixed on the injured shoulder. "But yeah, I can get it back in place. Won't feel good, though. He'll probably need something for the pain."

"He ate a pot brownie on the way over," Knox says. "Should be kicking in any time."

"Try three," Ash adds with googly eyes and a slow-growing smile. "Ate two before you got there, Augs. Figured I'd need some medicals." He squints up at Cole. "Hold on, I know you. You're the one who plays stick 'n' ball . . . *Bole Cuchannon!*"

Cole's lips twitch. "Close enough, man. Let's fix your arm now, okay?"

Then, for no particular reason, Ash bursts into a rousing rendition of "Eye of the Tiger." *"Risin' up, back on concre-heeete! Did my time, toke my chances!"*

Knox lifts his brows. "Oh, he's rolling, all right."

"Just a man, and his will to get hiiiiigh!" Ash continues, singing deliriously in the background.

"What do you need us to do?" I ask Cole.

"We'll need a makeshift sling for after. Like a pillowcase, or a long rag." He turns to my brother. "Knox, can you keep him distracted?"

"Baby, I was born to distract. You ready for a duet, bruh?" my brother says to Ash, moving over to his good shoulder. Asher gives him a toothy smile. And the pair launch into the bastardized song—singing loud and off-key—as they gaze ridiculously into each other's eyes.

I rejoin Cole, the fabric for the sling in hand. "All right," he says with a gulp, "here we go." Cole lifts Asher's injured arm, gently moving it away from his body to a forty-five-degree angle. Knox must be doing an amazing job distracting him, because Ash doesn't seem to notice.

Yet.

"This part's gonna be a little more intense," Cole says, bracing his foot at the side of Asher's chest near his armpit. "On my count—three . . . two . . . *one*." He then pulls Ash's hand, firm and steady toward him.

Ash cries, *"Son of a—ahhh!"* And just as he gathers another breath to scream, we hear it. The nauseating *POP!* And the bone slips back in the socket.

Knox takes a slug of whiskey he's pulled from the duffel bag of essentials. Then another. "He's like the gentlest dude I know. Probably didn't even fight back when those sons-a-bitches were beating on him. He's too good for this world." My brother rubs his eyes.

After Cole took care of Asher's shoulder, we cleaned the cut on his cheek and applied a butterfly bandage. He's now resting peacefully on an old cot we found in storage that we padded with mismatched lawn-chair cushions.

"So"—he swings the neck of the bottle between Cole and me—"how long's this been going on?"

I steel myself for the explosion. For Knox to turn red-faced and holler with self-righteousness. After all, I've earned it.

Cole's eyes flit to mine in deference. He wants me to answer, decide what I'm willing to share. But I'm still waiting for my brother to burst. His oddly calm demeanor is somehow worse than if he just lost it. I realize then why it's so unsettling. Because he reminds me of Dad right now.

"Aren't you going to yell at me?" I ask.

Knox hunches forward, running his fingers through his hair. "I'm too tired to yell," he answers dully. Asher's snore crescendos in the background. "And I don't wanna wake him up." He thumbs over his shoulder. "Poor guy's been through enough."

"I didn't tell Cole until a few days ago," I say to Knox, framing my answer to the more relevant part of the question. "After Dad's accident." My brother pulls a face, tipping the bottle back to his lips. "Knox, I'm sorry. I tried to wait, *I did*. But then—"

"Enough." The bottle thunks back to the table. "Let's cut to the chase." He narrows his eyes on Cole. "Your dad's a cop, right? So how do I know I can trust you?"

Cole swallows, then looks to me. "Because." Taking my hand in his, he stares back at my brother. "I love her." My heart swells so large it hurts.

Knox sniffs, his lip curling. "So I *was* right. I was right all along about you two."

"You were." I scoot forward. "But, Knox, think about it, we're going to need more hands for the harvest. Especially with Ash being hurt. Plus, Cole has a great idea for how to get Dad and Aunt Maeve out of town next weekend so we can work uninterrupted."

My brother contemplates this as he taps the bottle. "I'm listening."

"So my parents go to all these police fundraisers," Cole explains, unzipping the outer pouch of his backpack. "They're always bidding on silent-auction stuff, so they won't even notice this is gone." He holds out the envelope he's removed. "You can tell them you won it or something."

Knox takes the envelope, removing the folded paper inside and reading aloud, "A four-day, all-expense-paid trip to Beaver Island for two." My brother blinks and looks up. "The dates are already set for next weekend."

"Honor told me the dates you needed them gone," Cole replies.

More blinking, then my brother's lips stretch wide. "Man, this is *perfect*!" He says to me, "Dad'll still be on medical leave."

"I know," I say excitedly. "There's no way they'll turn down a free trip."

"And another bonus of having a dad in law enforcement," Cole continues, turning his laptop so Knox can see. "You can do things like run license plates and keep tabs on incoming calls to dispatch. Which means I can watch your backs in ways nobody else can."

"Damn," Knox murmurs. I can tell he's reluctantly impressed. He leans closer to the photo. "Hey, wait a sec, I've seen that guy before." He points. "Is this the owner of the SUV we saw the other night?"

"Yeah," I breathe. "How do you know him?"

"I don't," Knox says. "Not really. Saw him a few times at the farmer's market when I was working. Kept coming around our stall. Never bought anything, though."

"Did you talk to him?" Cole asks.

"No. But I'm sure it's the same guy because, well"—he gestures to the screen—"look at him. He's jacked. Dude stuck out like a sore thumb at a finger party."

I sit up straighter, struck with a sudden thought. "Do you

think this could've been one of the guys who jumped Ash and trashed his place?"

"Could be," my brother muses, absently rubbing his chin. "They were gone by the time I got there and found Ash. We'll have to ask him when he wakes up. He definitely can't go back home, though. Not until we're sure they won't come back for him."

"He can hide out here until we know it's safe," I say.

Cole nods. "We've got one of those fancy inflatable beds at home. I can bring it in tomorrow. Might make him more comfortable."

Knox stares at the whiskey bottle in contemplation. Then he slides it over to Cole like an olive branch. "You *sure* you wanna do this, Buchannon? This is a lot bigger than getting up twenty minutes early to buy my sister her favorite muffins. This is serious-felony shit. Oh, I should also mention if you hurt Honor, I'll kick the testicles clean off you. Clean. Off. You'll be a goddamn Ken doll down there."

"Oh, for heaven's sakes!" I whack my brother's arm with my notebook. "What is *wrong* with you? This isn't Elizabethan England and I'm not some damsel in distress."

He gives me a side-eye. "Yeah, I *know*," he hisses under his breath, "but this is a guy thing." Turning his attention back to Cole he adds, "And I don't care how many trophies you're packing, Captain Lacrosse. I fight dirty, and I fight to win."

By way of answer, Cole lifts the bottle to his mouth and takes a drink. Then sets it down, gazing intensely at my brother. "I'm doing this, Augustine. I'm all in."

I stand up, grab the bottle, and take three hearty gulps. Then slam the whiskey to the table. "Okay, that was disgusting." I cough, wiping my mouth. "But now that I have your attention, we've got ten days to harvest, and another five for the bud to dry. And Zachary 'Thumper' Mellner, or whoever he works for, is closing in. So I think our time would be better spent strategizing. Starting by running a full search on Thumper to see if we can find anyone he might be associated with."

PART IV

The Reaping

July 19 – 27

31

Eighty-one days.

Fourteen hours.

And . . . I check my watch. Twenty-six seconds.

For eighty-one days, fourteen hours, and twenty-six seconds, I have lived an idea. Sustained myself by it, really. I breathed it, drank it, let it swim in my veins and in my thoughts. I watched as the idea grew, inch by inch, feeling its phantom roots latch onto something inside me. And now the time has finally come to cut the idea free.

It is time for harvest.

I know this because over half the hairlike pistils, once fuzzy and white and reaching in all directions from the bud, have turned rusty brown and curl inward. The buds themselves are swollen, coating the air with potent, sticky resins.

But the biggest tell of all is in the trichomes—those microscopic, mushroom-shaped protrusions on the bud and surrounding leaves where the THC is housed. The trichomes are why our plants now have the illusion of being dipped in frost.

Holding the jeweler's loupe to my eye, I confirm that the

crystalline trichomes have indeed turned cloudy. Maturation is complete. Our plants are officially ready.

I take a moment to whisper my thanks. To the new life the plants will bring us all. A life gained for a life lost. I promise them their sacrifice will not be in vain.

"Twenty-three thousand, two hundred dollars," Asher announces. I'm so thick in my thoughts, I'd almost forgotten I wasn't alone. Turning, I see the neat stacks of hundred-dollar bills that cover the table. "That's minus the cabbage I gave Augs for the hardware-store run and this month's electric bill."

Knox is currently shopping for the dehumidifier needed to dry our large crop. My brother tried to get Ash to join him, but he's been reluctant to leave the greenhouse since the attack. So for the last ten days, Ash has been keeping vampire hours—rising around four in the afternoon and crashing at sunrise.

After scrubbing his hands in the utility sink, Ash digs into the hearty serving of Aunt Maeve's breakfast casserole I brought him.

Aunt Maeve stocked our fridge to cubic capacity before she left with Dad and Geronimo for their Beaver Island adventure. Afraid that with Knox and me left to our own devices, they might return from the long weekend only to discover two bags of bones riddled with scurvy. There's currently enough food to feed a village.

Ash gestures to the money with his fork, mumbling around a mouthful of egg, cheese, and sausage. "You wanna recount it?"

"No. I'm sure you're right." While he finishes breakfast, I gather the stacks of hundreds and place them back in the cashbox. After sliding the box back into the hole in the wall, I screw the air vent cover back into place.

"You do that every time," Ash observes as he pours the coffee from the thermos. "Did you know that? Almost like a ritual or something."

I stop grazing the bumpy letters inside the heart drawn in the concrete and sit back on my heels. "Habit, I guess."

He snaps the lid back on the empty container. "So what does LA + HA stand for?"

"Lizzie and Henry Augustine, our grandparents. It was always Gran's dream to own a greenhouse. Granddad had to sell his favorite car, a cherry-red 1960 Chevy Impala, just to pay for this cement." I tap the heart. "He never regretted it, though. Said he got all the joy he could ask for just by beholding Gran's."

Ash whistles. "Now *that's* big love."

"Yeah. And if you think that's big, you should hear the story of my great-grandma Bleu Gerard and how she—" My burner rings. Dusting off my hands, I pull the phone from my cargo pocket. "Hey, everything okay?"

"Dad called," Knox says over the hardware store's grainy loudspeaker. "They made it to Beaver Island *and* he got on the list for that woodworking seminar. You should have heard him, Hon. Sounded like a little kid Christmas morning. Haven't heard him that happy in forever."

"That's great," I reply with a relieved grin. Dad's not keen on overnighters in unfamiliar places. But I assured him they'd have a great time and that we'd hold down the fort and stay out of trouble. Which triggered Knox to cough on the irony.

Meanwhile, Geronimo made up for all the enthusiasm Dad lacked—smiling and barking from the back seat, tail swishing like a high-speed windshield wiper.

"Anyway," my brother continues, "got the dehumidifier and should be back in ten or fifteen. Is Cole there yet?"

"He had to grab some stuff from home, then he was going to do another security check before we start. He'll probably be here in another twenty minutes—give or take," I reply.

To be safe, we've been doing regular sweeps of the area. And so far, like our fruitless database search, there's been nothing to report. I wish I could say this put me at ease, but until our forty pounds of weed is gone, breathing won't be easy.

"Roger that," Knox says. "Over and out."

The crew arrives just as Ash and I finish hanging the dry lines across the basement. Knox and Ash immediately unbox the dehumidifier, while Cole reports the area's all clear. Dumping his backpack to the floor, he moves toward me.

I wonder if my heart will ever stop tripping over its own beat when he enters a room. Clumsy organ.

"Hey." Cole kisses my cheek and murmurs, "You good? Ready for tonight?"

Blowing out a breath, I snap on a pair of gloves. "Ready as I'll ever be."

"Okay," Ash says to my brother, "plug her in." Knox does and the unit hums to life. "Right on, Augs." He flashes a thumbs-up. "We're ready to rock and roll."

The atmosphere buzzes with collective energy as Knox turns up the bass-heavy music. His head bobs to the beat. "All right, Team HACK, let's get our last reap on!"

Ash organizes us into an assembly line that would make Henry Ford proud. Truly, I've never seen Asher Ford so articulate and focused. With the fan leaves removed, he makes the first cut, snipping the large cola-bearing sections of stalks from the plant.

Knox takes the stalk, carefully trimming away the larger leaves before passing it off to me. From there, I perform a detailed trim, snipping away the smaller stems and leaves, so only the large, conical buds remain. Then Cole hangs the colas upside down on the dry lines that stretch across the basement. While Cole waits for the finished stalks, he collects the buckets of clippings, piling them on the tarp for disposal.

We work like this for six hot, hand-cramping hours, occasionally switching out jobs. And like lumberjacks, we fell the cannabis forest, one tree at a time. I lose track of the number of times we trudge up and down the stairs, carrying tarps bulging with trimmings, along with bucket after bucket of heavy dirt and dense root balls.

But eventually, the harvest is done.

I return downstairs, where the grow lights have gone dark and the pallets are empty. Nothing but leafy fragments and crumbs of dirt remain. The dehumidifier continues to hum, sucking moisture from the air.

"You coming?" I ask Ash. "The trailer's all loaded up." We agreed in the interest of time and limited dry space to simply bury the leftover trimmings.

Asher finishes repositioning one of the colas on the line, then pulls off his disposable gloves with a snap. "Think I'll hang back and finish up the cleaning. You guys go ahead without me."

"Okay." I frown, noticing his duffel is packed. Which is weird because he said he wasn't going to stay at the house, even though Dad's gone. "Are you going somewhere?"

When his gaze locks with mine, I find his brown eyes are absent of that hazy, liquid quality I've come to know. *Asher*

Ford is . . . sober. I must've been so distracted with the harvest, I didn't notice till now. No wonder he was so clear and focused.

Ash looks away and scrubs a hand through his hair. "Yeah," he answers reluctantly. "I was actually gonna take off after you guys left. Just for a while, though. I'd be back in time to package all this up." He gestures to the dry lines.

"So where will you go?" I ask pensively.

Ash picks up the broom and begins sweeping. "Buddy of mine has a place a few hours north on this chill little lake. Said I can crash at his cabin. And yeah . . ." He sniffs, tossing me a lopsided grin. "I've already prepared myself for the possibility of spiders, but"—he shrugs—"guess we all have to face our fears eventually, right? Eight-leggers or otherwise."

"Or you could just stay with us," I offer, with a hopeful grin. "Plenty of spiders for you to slay down in the cellar."

"Thanks"—he pauses, leaning on the broom handle—"but I think this is something I gotta do solo, you know? Need to clear my head, decide my next move, and figure some shit out. Been foggy for too long."

My brows lift. "Asher Ford, are you making a *plan*?"

"Ha, yeah." He sways the handle back and forth. "Guess maybe I am. Getting jumped by those goons definitely has me questioning some life choices." Then he points an accusatory finger at me. "But you're partly to blame. All your systems and plans musta woke my latent adulting gene."

I laugh.

Ash smiles in that sweet, easy way of his. "Okay, bring it in," he says with a sigh, stretching his arms wide.

I hug him then, his T-shirt ripe with the strong, woodsy odor of the crop. "We'll miss you."

Ash squeezes me back, resting his chin to my head. "C'mon, I'll be back in a week or two. You won't even have *time* to miss me."

After separating, I move for the stairs, then stop. "Ash?" I say, turning around. "Thank you . . . for everything. We couldn't have done this without you."

"Anytime." He winks. *"Lily."*

The full moon watches us curiously from above the thicket of trees as we dig and dig and dig. Nobody questions Asher's absence. I think they figure it wouldn't be good for his shoulder, so it makes sense he'd hang back and do the final clean.

Our lanterns glow around the pit while we heap shovelfuls of soil, roots, and rock to the ground. We are filthy, dirt speckling our faces, smudged over our arms, and caked to the coveralls tied at our waists. And we are exhausted. Knox, too tired to even crack a joke.

But by sometime around midnight, we toss the final mound of soil atop our cannabis gravesite. Then we trample the spongy ground, stomping until the area is leveled, tossing pine cones and leaves to camouflage the earth we've disturbed.

Knox exhales, propping his hands on his hips as he gazes down at the burial pit. "I feel like we should play taps or something."

"Do we need to worry about it growing?" Cole asks, dragging a grubby arm across his forehead.

Dumping the folded tarps in the trailer, I explain, "No. The soil's too acidic because of the pines, and there isn't enough light in this part of the woods, anyway."

Knox salutes the mass grave and grabs the lanterns.

With the equipment loaded up, Cole and I climb into the trailer, collapsing on the pile of tarps. The forest brightens again as Knox fires up the tractor and the headlights blaze.

"Westward ho, kids! Westward ho!" my brother calls from the driver's seat. We lurch forward as Knox weaves his way across the uneven terrain, the pair of us bouncing on the crinkly plastic.

Once we break from the forest the ground levels. The outline of pines and deciduous trees slowly shrinks in our wake. Cole tips his gaze back to the swaths of deep navy that paint the sky, glittering with pinpricks of light.

Finding his hand, I take it in mine and release the words I've held back all night. *"I love you."* At first I worry he hasn't heard me over the loud chug of the motor.

But then a gentle smile curves his mouth, luminous as the stars.

I wake with a start in bed, jerked to consciousness by invisible hands. My heart stutters uneasily.

Cole stirs at my side. "Mm, what is it?" he slurs, tongue heavy with sleep.

"Nothing. Full moon," I murmur, lowering myself to the mattress with a jittery exhale. He mumbles incoherently and drapes his arm across my middle. The weight of it comforts and grounds me.

But for some reason, I can't shake the nagging sense of offness.

So I focus on Cole's breath, the effortless rhythm that rolls and recedes like the tide. When I try to match my breathing with his, it doesn't sync. I'm wound too tight. *You're fine. Just relax.*

I fixate on the symbols of normalcy around me. The jar of stones at my bedside. The curly shadows cast by my lucky bamboo. The tidy corner desk topped with the paper flowers Cole made me. Everything around me is *exactly* as it should be.

And yet, my veins crackle like live wires.

The air in the room suddenly feels stifling. The blades of the oscillating fan at the foot of the bed are unmoving. *Did I turn it off, or forget to turn it on?* I can't remember anything after we tumbled into bed, free of grime and smelling of soap and skin.

Careful not to disturb Cole, I check both my phones—no messages. It's two thirty in the morning, and the paunchy moon has no intention of giving up its spot in the sky. I sigh, blinking up at the ceiling. Listening to the darkness. The house moans and groans like a chatty old man, always prepared to tell you of its bunions and backaches. So I should not feel unsettled by the farmhouse's settling.

And yet . . .

Grabbing my burner, I slide out from beneath his arm and tiptoe down the narrow staircase, sticking close to the wall to avoid the creaky center. My veins continue to spark and pop.

The door to my brother's room hangs open. But he is not

inside it. There are only glossy wall posters, a shadowed mound of clothes on a papasan chair, and a statue-still punching bag. *Where is Knox?* He was out cold—mouth open and snoring—by the time I got out of the shower.

I peer down the gloomy hallway. The shadows take the shape of monsters.

My breath catches at the loud squawk of hinges—the back door. I stand, frozen. Someone enters the kitchen, moving with heavy, cautious footsteps. Someone who is not my brother.

My heart pounds the drum of war.

As quietly as I can, I race back up to the attic, easing my door shut and locking it.

"Cole," I frantically whisper and shake him. "Cole, I think someone's in the house."

"Hmm, what?" His eyes gradually flutter open.

"I think someone's in the house!" I repeat more urgently. The boom of my heart now seismic.

He sits up then, blinking and rubbing his face. "You're sure it's not Knox?"

I shake my head. "Knox is gone. I just checked his room, and he wasn't in it."

Cole tries to mute his reaction, but I can tell from the nervous darting of his gaze, he's worried. "We should get out of here," he says, flicking off the sheet. He quickly tugs on his T-shirt and shorts, car keys jingling in the pocket, then jams on his shoes.

I grab my lightweight hoodie. The phone barely fits in the side pocket, but I cram it in and zip it. "We'll have to go out the window," I say. "There's an emergency ladder under my bed." My limbs shake like my breath as I pull on my shoes.

Cole darts across the attic and feeds the rope ladder out the window as I watch the door. We clamber down onto the porch roof. Then crouch, listening to the night. The insects are loud. So loud, it would be easy to mask the sound of footsteps, the rustle of grasses. Not to mention the countless hiding spots in the shadows.

A screech owl shrieks, sounding more human than animal. Drawing an unsteady breath, I look to Cole, hunched at my side.

"We can't stay here," he says in a low voice, peering up to the attic window. "I say we make a run for the Jeep."

I nod. "Okay."

Together, we bolt across the roof, ducking beneath windows before scrambling down the trellis. My feet hit the grass, dew licking at my ankles as Cole drops down seconds after me. We race across the front and over to his Jeep, parked behind Knox's truck.

"Shit!" Cole breathes. "They got my tires." My spirits sink like the deflated rubber. All four rims lie flat to the ground. The wind gusts, carrying with it an ominous sound as the screen door creaks open. Whoever was inside must be slipping back out through the mudroom.

We dive into the tall grasses, crouching low and scanning the darkness. "What do you think? Make a run for it?" he whispers, voice tight.

My pulse, my breath, my thoughts—all of it speeds too fast. I nod. "Let's stick to the fields so there's less chance of being spotted. Once we're in the clear we can try to reach Knox," I say quickly. "Come on!"

We race the moon. Our feet pound like our hearts as we tear through the wheat that whips at our legs. Suddenly, my phone chimes. "Cole, stop!" I pant and trample to a halt, pulling out my cell. "It's Knox!" As I open the message, Cole leans in, the glow of the screen turning our faces a ghostly hue.

Knox: Problem at greenhouse. Come ASAP

My eyes flick uneasily to his. "This text"—I shake my head—"it isn't right. He never spells out the word *greenhouse*. We always use *GH*." Then my world narrows to a terrifying pinpoint. *Someone is impersonating Knox. Possibly the same someone who took him from the house and slashed Cole's tires.*

"Wait, Honor!" He grabs my arm as I pivot to run. "It's a trap."

"I know." Terror clogs my throat, forming a thick, thorny ball. I choke it down. "But it's my *brother*, Cole. You saw what they did to Ash. What am I supposed to do?"

"Listen to me," he pleads, sliding his hands along either side of my face. "We'll find Knox. We *will*. But let's take a second to think, okay?"

I nod, sucking in a breath. He's right. Whoever it is will be expecting emotion to drive my actions. Muddy my thoughts. *Think, Honor.* "Security cameras!" I quickly launch the app. "The video might be able to show us who's . . ." Grainy pixel patterns cloud the screen. "*Dammit!* It's just static."

Cole's face is grim as he frantically taps out a text.

"W-what are you doing?" I sputter in alarm. "You can't call the cops yet with—"

"I didn't. I'm texting my cousin. Told him if I don't check in by a certain time to call for help," Cole replies, hitting Send and pocketing his phone. "Now we take the bait."

32

As I sprint down the barren road, my mind reels with images of Knox, tangled in a web of horror set to the sound of night birds screaming. The greenhouse bounces into view, its glass glinting with moonlight. My nerves stretch and quiver, like rubber bands ready to snap.

We trample to a stop at the rear entrance, chests heaving.

Cole blocks my hand when I grab for the handle. "Let me go first, okay?"

I don't argue. My head is too stuffed with worry over Knox to give any consideration to the danger on the other side. I just want my brother back.

Cole slowly cracks the door, both of us working to muffle the loud huff of our breaths. The hall is dark, electric with stillness. A tang of sweat and fear spikes the air. We tentatively step inside, moving cautiously into the hall, our eyes roving the grainy darkness.

We don't make it far.

A massive shadow lunges from behind, wrapping strong

arms around me. At the same time, Cole lets out a strangled grunt as his attacker strikes. The large men with large arms wrestle us into chokeholds. Squeezing as we struggle, kick, and claw. My teeth find flesh to bite—deep enough to elicit a cry and loosen his grip. And I almost escape.

But almosts are meaningless when everything around you fades to black.

A dull ache in my skull flares to life as I slowly come to, inhaling the residual scent of the harvest mixed with another strong odor. *Cigarettes.* Air moves like daggers scraping down my throat. When I go to swallow, my mouth is gluey and tastes of blood.

Everything feels heavy. Even my eyelids refuse to crack open.

"Wake up," the gruff voice commands from the end of a long tunnel. The voice has a strange familiarity, but my brain is too sluggish and fog-filled to place why. "I *said,* wake up!"

Cold water hits me in the face, stinging my skin and shocking me back to full consciousness. I choke, thrashing under the forceful stream, unable to block it. My arms won't move, my wrists painfully bound at my back. The water stops as suddenly as it began.

Sagging forward, I cough out liquid and drag in air. My bindings catch on something poking from the wall, briefly straining my arms in their sockets before the rope unsnags. As my choking subsides, I sit up, blinking rapidly. The atmosphere is murky, with only the light from the moon filtering through the glass ceiling.

My blurry gaze fixes on the utility boots and the tree trunk legs covered in dark pants growing out of them, and finally on the nozzle gripped in his meaty hand. The elaborate snake tattoo wraps his arm like it did my neck. An angry half circle dimples the serpent's back where I bit him.

Zachary "Thumper" Mellner's sunken eyes stare down. Fear prickles my scalp, raising an army of goose bumps as he lifts the nozzle again.

"No," I rasp. Recoiling, I pinch shut my eyes and hold my breath at the sound of the high-powered spray. But the freezing water I expect doesn't come.

Because, I discover, it's directed at the motionless body propped along the wall a few feet down. Thumper zigzags the stream over him, moving up to his face, where dark blood seeps from a gash at his hairline.

"Cole!" I cry hoarsely as he jerks awake with a gurgled shout. My heart rolls in its cage.

Thumper chuckles darkly, cutting the water to tug and reposition the hose. Cole lets out a series of rattling coughs, before swinging his disoriented gaze my way. Our eyes lock, a flood of desperate, unspoken questions passing between them.

Are you okay? How do we get out of here? What will they do to us?

The hissing spray resumes; this time the blast is directed at my brother, slumped on the other side of Cole. Knox quickly comes to, and a string of waterlogged curses geyser from his mouth.

"Enough!" I scream, the word punishing my bruised throat. The brute drops the nozzle to the floor while Knox wheezes and hacks. But he hasn't stopped because of anything I've said.

It's the pulsing ringtone that blares from his pocket. The

same ringtone we heard while hiding at school. *That's why Thumper's voice was familiar. He was the one searching for me.* Cole's grim expression confirms he remembers too.

"Mickey, whatcha got?" Thumper answers. "Anything in those back buildings?" He must be talking to the other guy outside.

I lean forward to check on Knox. His breath is labored as he flicks the wet hair from his eyes, a bump swelling high on his cheek. He offers me a weak nod before collapsing back to the wall.

The wall.

During my coughing jag, my rope had gotten caught on something. I scoot back a couple inches, clumsily exploring the wall with numb and wooden fingers. *Ouch!* I wince, scraping a knuckle on the sharp-edged side of an old metal bracket. The display shelves were moved forever ago, but there's still remnants of leftover hardware.

"He's en route now. And his dick's in a real twist tonight," Thumper continues, turning his mountainous form away from us. "I dunno. But something's off because he's extra edgy."

Seizing the opportunity, I shift slightly to the side, angling the rope so it's positioned along the sharpest part of the metal. I test it then, applying pressure as I drag the fibers back and forth over what amounts to a dull steak knife.

But . . . *it's working.* I can feel the gradual give of the fibers, causing my heart to spasm with hope.

"No, stay on lookout until we get the orders," our captor says in the background. "Yeah, they're awake." He shoots a glance over his shoulder and I stop.

I don't know what *the orders* are, but if it has to do with us, it can't be good. Keeping my eyes trained on Thumper as he looks away, I increase the speed of my sawing. "Cole," I whisper.

He stops writhing in his restraints to see what I'm doing.

"There used to be shelving here," I quickly whisper. "Look for brackets or screws. Tell Knox."

With a nod, he leans to relay this to my brother, the two of them now covertly searching the wall.

A sudden flash of headlights pans across the greenhouse. Dread squeezes my chest. This must be the puppet master. The reason we're bruised and bloodied, lining the wall like a trio of sad marionettes with cut strings.

Thumper squints into the light, ending his call and turning toward us. We go instantly still. "Talk and I'll break your goddamn jaws, understood?" Our wet heads bob. He stalks toward the front as the headlights wink out, plunging us back into gloom.

The second we're alone Knox rasps, "We gotta get the hell out of here." His long legs struggle for purchase against the floor.

"How? They're blocking both the entrances," I point out. "And even if we tried to run, how would we defend ourselves?"

"She's right," Cole says through gritted teeth, tilted to the side as he frantically hacks at the restraints. "Focus on getting out of the ropes. At least it'll give us the element of surprise. Otherwise we won't have a fighting chance."

"Well, there's nothing down here with enough of an edge to—*shit!*" My brother yelps. "Never mind, I just found something. Also, I'm gonna need a tetanus shot once we're out of this mess," he finishes wryly.

The snort pains me, but hearing Knox say something so Knoxian is a balm like no other. Flicking back the hair stuck to my face, I keep sawing, my restraints loosening. Another hard tug and—*Yes!* My arms roll forward, achy but free.

I turn to help Cole just as he grunts, snapping apart the remainder of his bindings. Then the automatic doors whoosh open. Fear shudders through me. I quickly hide the frayed rope behind my back and work to control my shaking.

Thumper lumbers in behind the slim shadow that strides toward us, cutting the darkness like a knife. The gaunt man halts in front of us, tension crackling in a cloud around him. The sharp planes of his face illuminated by the night sky.

"M-Mr. Corvallis?" Knox sputters, mouth agape. Shock has siphoned the air from my lungs, leaving me as speechless as Cole. "But . . . you were my computer teacher."

His lip twitches. "I'm a lot of things, Knox. You only know what I show you." The friendly teacher facade has disappeared with his glasses. His dark eyes skip like a stone over us. My stomach turns at the sight of the pistol that hangs in his hand.

"Thump," Mr. Corvallis calls to his muscle, who's now lighting a cigarette I'd stake my life is a Camel. "There should be four. Where's Ford?"

"Skipped town after Mick and I paid him a visit," he replies through pinched lips. "Don't think he'll be back anytime soon."

"I don't recall you being paid to think," Mr. Corvallis says icily. Thumper grumbles an apology. "And then there were three," Corvallis murmurs, turning his attention back on us.

The gun taps slowly against his leg with the rhythm of his steps. "One of you is going to tell me where you hid the dope and the cash." Reaching the end of the line, he performs a sharp pivot. "Now, I'd prefer to have all of you walk out of here. But that's all it is, a preference. Either way"—he pauses, lifting the pistol in case we'd forgotten its presence—"I *will* get what I came for."

While his tone holds a cool control, it's the dark and restless thing crawling underneath it that makes me doubt he intends to let any of us walk out of here.

Stall, I think desperately, wishing I knew if my brother has worked his way free.

"You knew what I was doing because of Jess." My voice wobbles, but I push through the fear and continue. "She reported to you after I met with her, didn't she? And then you had the cop sent to find me trespassing." The picture comes into sudden clarity. "The storage room, the photos . . . it was you all along." Jess might've had eyes and ears at school, but Mr. Corvallis was the one commanding them all.

The dimples I once thought gave him softness now look like sinkholes in his cheeks. "Extra fucking credit for this one," he sneers. The false grin vanishes. "Couldn't have you cutting into my profits, now, could I? And I thought for sure I'd nail you with those drugs."

My eyes flick to Cole and the blood-and-water mix that tracks his face. *I know he's free, but what about Knox?* "Then you let us finish the job," I say, keeping Mr. Corvallis focused on me. "Why?"

"My circumstances changed," Mr. Corvallis replies cryptically, gripping his pistol tighter. "Which can have deadly consequences in this line of work. And what do I always tell my crew, Thump?" he asks, not taking his eyes off us.

The brute smiles, smoke crawling out from around his teeth as he flicks his cigarette aside. "Always have a backup plan."

Mr. Corvallis crouches so our eyes are level. His pupils have devoured his irises, and a veil of sweat appears on his unnaturally pale skin, giving him a waxy appearance. "Guess that makes you my backup plan," he hisses, jaw muscle twitching. His cell chimes. Glancing at the screen, he draws in a sharp breath.

Our time is slipping like his control. I can't stall any longer. *God, Knox, please be ready!*

Mr. Corvallis rises swiftly to his feet, aiming the pistol at us. "Now, for the last fucking time," he growls, wild-eyed, "where did you stash the weed and cash from your sales?" When we don't reply fast enough, he cocks the gun and shouts, *"Tell me!"*

I swallow; my adrenaline-glutted blood pulses faster. And just as I start to speak, the back door crashes open.

A panicky voice carries down the hall, "Corv, something's up. I just heard on the scan—"

Distracted, Mr. Corvallis momentarily lowers the pistol. *"Now!"* Knox shouts as Cole rolls to his side, delivering a scissor kick that sweeps Mr. Corvallis's legs right out from under him. With a yelp, he tumbles backward, the weapon falling from his hand, skittering over the concrete and into the darkness.

At the same time, Knox rockets to his feet, charging Mickey, while Cole redirects to take on Thumper. Shadows collide as the sound of punches surrounds me.

The gun. I scramble in the direction of the pistol. My palms madly slap beneath the potting station. *Pleasepleaseplease.*

"Ahh!" A hand wraps my ankle, just as my grip closes around a spongey handle. My fingers slide into the dips formed

by years of use. Then I'm dragged backward with a fierce tug, the cement scraping my skin.

"You little bitch!" Mr. Corvallis spits, yanking my hair to lift my face from the floor. "Where is it?" he demands.

When I don't answer, he punches me. I howl. The pain is blinding, causing my eyes to water as fire erupts along my cheekbone. A sudden burning smell fills the air.

Fight. You have to fight! The chant is pounded out in the beats of my heart.

When he flips me over, hands reaching for my neck, I let out a guttural cry.

And with all my might, I swing the hand rake toward him. The three metal claws sink deep in his thigh. He shrieks in pain as I scramble out from under him.

The chaos and shouts around me swell to deafening levels. Ceramic pots smash to the floor. More crashes and yells. The air grows thicker, harder to breathe. I cough. Disoriented, I stagger to my feet, eyes tearing so much that everything's gone shapeless and blurry.

Then I hear a sudden crackle and . . . *WHOOSH.*

I scream, staggering back from the bags of peat moss that burst into violent flames. Embers pop and shoot in all directions. I crouch, throwing my arms over my head.

The alarm clangs, but the sprinklers haven't kicked on. Choking, I pull my shirt over my nose and mouth, shouting for Knox and Cole. There's a hazy outline of Mr. Corvallis staggering away alongside one of his men.

My name is yelled. I stumble through the white fog in the direction of the sound. "I'm coming!" I cry.

The fire spreads fast, too fast to contain it. The blaze has already swallowed the pallet of peat moss where it started and reaches the shelves of fertilizer. *Fertilizer.* Ammonium nitrate.

Which is stable, unless it comes into contact with open—

"Oh my God," I rasp. Swinging my head, I spot the shape of my brother through the smoke veil. Cole's silhouette stumbles up beside him. *"RUN!"*

Ducking down where the air's less thick, we race for the nearest exit. The alarm continues wailing as the heat of the flames licks at our backs.

The automatic doors shush open, and we burst into the night, coughing and gagging.

"Woods!" Knox wheezes, pointing to the distant trees for cover as we sprint.

I struggle to keep up. Cole grabs my arm to propel me forward and—

BOOM!

An explosion hits, rocking the ground beneath us.

My legs give out, and I fall. Greedy flames engulf the building. *"NOOO!"* I cry. Crawling back to my feet, I lunge toward the inferno.

"Stop! Honor, no!" Cole hooks his arm at my waist, catching me as the windows shatter. They burst like balloons, spewing shards into the night. Roiling fire replaces what was once glass. He shouts, "You have to let it go!"

I cry out again, fighting against his grip, my hand reaching, straining for the greenhouse. "Please!" My brother grabs on to me, adding to Cole's force, as they drag me into the forest, our lungs and limbs burning.

When a second blast strikes, I'm pushed flat to the earth. Bodies shield me, hearts punching, muscles trembling. Rubble and glass rain over us. Tapping the canopy of leaves with their descent.

"It's gonna be okay. It's gonna be okay," my brother's voice repeats until the phrase turns to a single mumbled word.

But how can it be okay when there's so much screaming? The screaming won't stop.

I realize it comes from me. From my own mouth, salted with tears and peppered with ash. Then a high-pitched ring washes over the world. And I hear nothing.

I don't know how long I lie pinned to the forest floor. Long enough for my hearing to return with a cataclysmic boom. I blink. Sparks shoot out through billows of smoke that stretch like mushrooms.

I sit up then. Staring at the stars and wondering how they haven't shook loose from the sky. "Nothing." My voice breaks like my heart. "It was all for nothing."

Knox rises unsteadily to his feet. Staggering a few steps, he braces his hand to a tree and doubles over, retching.

There are sirens in the distance.

They are too late.

Cole holds me while I watch the fiery structure strain and bow inward. Hungry flames devour the vines that cling to what remains of the greenhouse. I watch as their leaves shriek and recoil, absorbing their pain like it's my own. Watch as the flowers wilt before withering into blackness.

They are too late.

33

Sunlight cheerfully streams inside the attic, the golden glow hot across my swollen lids. Outside the birds are singing, happiness infused in each warbling note. The sun and birds have teamed up to flaunt their joy, while I lie here telling myself to do something as basic as breathe.

Slowly, I open my eyes. I see Despair has already reported for duty. The charcoal swirling mass hovers inches above my body, invisible to all but me. *"How can I make your day as hellish as possible, Honor?"* Despair asks. Because Despair is a dick that way.

For two days I've been swimming in a fog. Watching the world through clouded eyes. Stumbling around in someone else's skin, like I'm a visitor in another body. I often feel numb, my head a detached dark balloon.

Until night comes and the numbness clears, triggering my senses into overload and tangling dream with reality. I smell smoke that isn't there. Feel the squeeze of phantom hands. Even the screams in my ears turn out to be just an echo, like the sound of the sea trapped inside a shell.

It isn't real, I tell myself in the aftermath, as I sweat and shake and gasp for air. Except . . . it *was* real.

A reality I'm now bombarded with by the slew of news notifications that light up the screen of the loaner phone Cole's given me. It's stupid, reading the articles. Like a scab I can't stop picking. GREENHOUSE EXPLOSION ROCKS SLEEPY TOWN OF RAVENSWOOD, reads one headline.

I scroll down to the next. HIGH SCHOOL TEACHER DIES FOLLOWING HIGH-SPEED POLICE CHASE. I click on it, skimming the story. But there's nothing I don't already know. How Adam Corvallis and Zachary "Thumper" Mellner both died in a fatal bid to evade the cops that night. And that the third alleged assailant, Michael Rancine, remains in critical condition with a less-than-rosy prognosis.

I push upright with a groan, my legs dangling over the edge of the bed. Like my brother and Cole, my skin is a tapestry of scratches, cuts, and bruises. And while doctors and nurses have bandaged and stitched our collective wounds, they could not touch where my damage is greatest.

Knox says we should be counting our lucky stars things turned out the way they did and that losing the greenhouse, the cash, and the crop was a small price to pay for what could've been. I know that's true. But right now, I'm still stuck on the loss. It feels like a part of me burned away with the greenhouse that night.

I can't help but wonder if we will ever be able to rebuild all that's been destroyed, or whether I can forgive myself for being the reason for its destruction in the first place.

Feeling more steady, I rise and turn off the fan. In the absence of the white noise, I make out the murmur of voices below.

There's a burgundy car parked out front. *Great.* Probably another follow-up visit from one of the police investigators. They still come with their questions. Their notepads. Their pens that click just a bit too loud.

But I've already confessed everything in my statement, about what I did and why. How it was all my idea and that I recruited Knox and Cole. I didn't tell them about Asher's involvement. None of us did. Ash doesn't deserve any of this fallout when his only fault was having a heart that's too big and good for this world.

Making my way from the attic, I see Knox sitting partway down the stairs leading to the first floor. His shorts and T-shirt rumpled from sleep, cowlick standing at attention.

"Hey, sis," he whispers as I sink down beside him. The swelling on his cheek has gone down some. Enough so the skin doesn't look so pissed off and ready to split. He gestures with his broken, splinted finger down the stairwell. "Dad's talking to Detective Devereaux."

Detective Devereaux. It takes my muddled brain a moment to picture him—average height, salt-and-pepper hair, cutting green eyes. He also happens to be the lead detective on the case.

I wrap my arms around my middle, the scent of coffee sharp and strong, like my sudden urge to vomit.

"You mentioned there's been a new development?" Dad says, followed by the *tink* of a spoon against ceramic.

"Yes, involving Corvallis," Detective Devereaux replies crisply. "We now have a clearer understanding of his motives."

My circumstances changed. Corvallis's ghostly voice resurrects from the grave, burrowing into my ears like worms through dirt.

He's dead, I remind myself. *He can't hurt you.* I pin my trembling hands under my arms so my brother doesn't notice.

When I can focus again, I hear the detective continuing. "It seems Corvallis intended to skip town that night because his boss, a reputed leader of a statewide drug ring by the name of Frank Palmer, discovered he'd been skimming off the profits. We had a strong hunch this was the case, but what we *didn't* know until the last twenty-four hours is that Corvallis had set up an insurance policy of sorts."

"Insurance policy?" Dad echoes. "How so?"

Knox and I exchange questioning glances.

A coffee mug taps down on the table. "Corvallis arranged for a series of time-released computer files to be automatically forwarded to authorities, in the event that anything happened to him. Files that appear to offer a substantial blueprint of Frank Palmer's entire operation. We've had Palmer in our sights for some time now, but this finally gives us enough to open a grand-scale investigation against him."

I remember Corvallis saying to always have a backup plan. Guess it shouldn't come as a surprise he'd have one to use as leverage in case things went south. But his backup plan couldn't protect him from a car crash.

I'm so deep in my thoughts, I miss whatever Dad's just said. "What did he ask?"

Knox swallows. "He . . . he wants to know if they're planning to prosecute us."

My misery compounds. Which seemed impossible given how bad I already feel. The clock in the living room ticks too loud, echoing in my skull.

"They've fully cooperated," Dad says. "Detective Devereaux, they're *good* kids. The only reason they did what they did was because of me and—" Emotion chokes off his words.

I press the heels of my hands to my eyes, pushing back in the sorrow.

"Mr. Augustine"—the detective's rigid voice takes on a gentler tone—"understand that we are still very early in the investigation. *However*," he adds with a weighted pause, "given the unique circumstances of this case, coupled with the kids' ages, motives, and state laws, I'm strongly recommending leniency."

Knox lets out a gust of air, tipping his head to the ceiling before looking at me. "Did you hear what he just said? *Leniency*," he whisper-squeals. "He's strongly recommending leniency!"

And I wait for it. The surge of elation. The gush of relief that should find me as I sit, my brother's arms joyously circled around me, telling me it's going to be all right.

But the feeling never comes.

Instead, there is just a void. A hole, immense and gaping, where all my good feelings used to be.

I can't account for the hours that pass, only that they slide like water through my fingers. Night is coming. So I try to soak up the moment of peace in twilight. Before shadows that shouldn't move awaken and stir.

A trail of violets, peaches, and golds blaze at the horizon

where the sun loses its grip on the earth. But the colors feel false, like a flimsy curtain tacked up to hide an ugly gray backdrop.

Cole lies beside me on my bed, our hands clasped together as we stare out the window. He came yesterday evening, too. We barely spoke. But somehow just his presence calms me, keeps the fog and fear more at bay.

"When I was little," I say, voice creaky from underuse, "I used to wish I could tear open the sky, just to see what was on the other side. I even convinced myself there were rows of special stars that might be zippers, and all I had to do was get close enough to pull."

"A zipper through the universe," Cole muses.

I roll to my hip. The bruises that mottle his face and sutures puckering his hairline are still jarring, even though I know to expect them. "Would you want to see, Cole? If you could?"

He searches the waning sunset for an answer before curling toward me. Our faces inches apart on the pillow. "I don't know," he replies. "I think I'd be too worried it would ruin the—" He breaks off with a grimace. "It'll sound too cheesy."

"I'm not opposed to cheese right now."

"I was going to say I'd hate to ruin the magic. The wonder or, I don't know, mystery of whatever's beyond it. Maybe there are some things we're better off not knowing."

"I want to feel that way." My eyes water. I wish so badly to believe as Cole does. That the unknown could be a source of wonder rather than terror. "I'm just so tired of being afraid. Tired of all the not knowing."

He's quiet a moment. Then his fingertips move a tender

path along my face to wipe away the tear. "Would it help to hear some things I know?"

"Can't hurt."

"I know I love you."

My battered heart swells. "I love you, too."

Cole kisses my forehead. "And I know no matter how fucked-up things are right now, today is not forever."

"Tell me more knowns," I whisper. "Please?"

"All right." His gaze briefly wanders the wood knots on the ceiling before returning to me. "Glacier buttercups."

I blink, brow creasing. "I don't know glacier buttercups."

"Yet," he corrects. Once I've rearranged myself, the little spoon to his big spoon, Cole goes on to tell me about a paper he wrote on Finland in the ninth grade. "And they've got these endangered plants," he continues, words fluttering soft at my ear, "that only grow in arctic areas or frozen mountaintops. Brutal climate, depleted soil, high elevation—virtually nothing up there survives. Except, somehow these little plants do. And against all the odds, every July and August, they still manage to bloom." I feel him shrug a little behind me. "Guess I always thought there was something cool about that. Like if the buttercups can do it, then maybe we can, too."

I want to be the glacier buttercup. I want to be the little plant that endures despite harsh conditions, coming back year after year. I ask him to describe them, so I can hold the picture in my mind.

Cole obliges, painting floral images as my eyelids grow heavier and heavier.

And that night I dream of buttercups.

There's a small scrap of paper rolled like a tiny joint on my nightstand when I wake alone.

As I smooth out the paper, his sloppy writing reveals itself, letter by letter. And for the first time in days, I'm reminded not of what I lost. But what I have gained.

There are 1,440 minutes in a single day, and I think of you for all of them.
#onetruth

34

"Still no word from Ash," Knox says in a low voice. We stand side by side at the kitchen sink, a large colander of sugar snap peas between us. "It's been a week since—" He catches himself when I reflexively stiffen. "You know," he finishes vaguely.

I do, unfortunately. The memories of that night are never far from my mind's reach, even though I've stuffed them all in titanium boxes, reinforced with locks and chains. They keep breaking free.

"Anyway," Knox carries on, "I tried his burner, his cell—everything just keeps going to voice mail." He stares thoughtfully out the back window, snapping off the end of the pea pod with his uninjured hand. "Bet he's got no clue the shit that's gone down."

I remove the strip from the center of the hull, popping it open. "You know cell towers are practically nonexistent up there." With a sweep of my finger, the plump peas rain down into the bowl. "Besides, he'll be back any day now. He promised he'd only be gone a week or two." I hear the forced hope in my tone.

His brows furrow as he grabs another pea pod. "What if

they sent someone after him?" he asks, with uncharacteristic pessimism.

"Knox, don't say that. He—"

"But what if he was followed?" The faint circles under his eyes suddenly cast a darker shadow.

"No. Ash is fine," I repeat firmly, popping another pod. "He was long gone before . . . everything." I nod. "Ash is totally fine."

Knox looks skeptical. "Which is why you keep repeating it?"

The back door bangs, and I jump out of my skin. Every muscle contracts. Clutching the edge of the counter, I will my heartbeat to normalize.

When I open my eyes Knox is watching me, mouth in a grim line.

"I'm all right," I whisper. "Seriously, stop looking at me like that."

Dad's on the phone talking to Mom, who's been calling—often multiple times a day—for progress checks. Scott had surprised Mom with a trip to Croatia, so she was midflight when everything happened. It took *a lot* of reassurance from everyone to convince her not to hop the next ten-hour flight back.

"Uh-huh," Dad murmurs. There's the thud of his work boots as he kicks them off in the mudroom, then steps into the kitchen. "I'll pass that along. Okay, Viv, you too. Bye." He hangs up.

"Your mom sends her love." Then he says to Knox, "She also said she understands if you want to cancel or postpone your graduation party for next month. Just let her know what you want to do."

"Oh." Judging by my brother's expression, this wasn't even a blip on his radar. "Right, thanks."

Dad nods to the unfinished sugar snaps while rolling up

his sleeves. "How about I take over with those, Knox. Aunt Maeve'll be here around six, and we could use some more charcoal for the grill."

My brother does a double take. "You kidding? Shelling peas is about half a step above watching paint dry." He quickly brushes his hands on his cargo shorts. "Go nuts."

"Go peas," Dad counters dryly.

Knox snorts and grabs his keys. "Anyone need anything else while I'm out?"

My sanity. But I doubt they sell that at Patsy's Party Store. We both say we're fine, and this time when the door slams, I'm ready for it.

My father joins me at the sink. His elbow gently bumps mine as he scrubs his hands like he's preparing to do an appendectomy. Shaking off the excess water, he asks, "Cole joining us for dinner? We'll have plenty."

"He can't tonight. Has to take care of some stuff at home."

Dad nods, grabbing a sugar snap and liberating the peas in an eyeblink. Seeing my raised brows, he grins crookedly. "Muscle memory. Your gran had me helping her shell ever since I could hold a pea without squashing it." The grin suspiciously evaporates with his next breath.

My eyes slide from his, uneasiness growing in the pit of my stomach. This two-of-us-alone scenario suddenly feels orchestrated. Wait a sec. *We didn't need more charcoal,* I think, recalling the half bag in the mudroom.

I focus on keeping my movements seamless and smooth. But the atmospheric pressure of the room rises with the strain of his unsaid words. They fill the entire kitchen, pressing against plaster, causing microscopic cracks in glass.

We continue working in this pressurized silence for several minutes. Veggie flesh snapping then tapping down into the bowl.

"Noticed the stack of boxes with return labels by the front door," he remarks.

My shoulders lower. Okay, maybe I'm being paranoid.

"Are those the dresses from your mom?"

"Yeah," I say, my hands moving more effortlessly. During one of our calls this week, I finally worked up the courage to tell my mother the truth—that she's been shopping for a daughter who doesn't exist. "They're just not me," I add.

Dad nods. "She means well."

"I know." We've actually had some decent talks. She said we'd find our way forward without dresses. Mom's trying to do better getting to know the real me, and I'm trying to do better at showing her. We're kind of a work in progress, I guess. Like much of my life at the moment.

The conversation hits a lull again, setting me on edge.

"I'm worried about you, Hon," Dad blurts in a single breath. "About how you're . . . processing all this."

I scoop the mound of hulls into the compost bucket with only a minor hiccup. "I'm handling it, Dad. I told you."

He thinks he's been low-key, but my father's everywhere, hanging in my peripherals like a well-intentioned eye floaty. It's like living under a microscope, my words and actions constantly magnified and pored over.

"I . . . I don't think you are, though, sweetheart." His mouth pinches like my insides. "Just yesterday you—"

"Accidentally broke a mug," I cut in defensively, whipping an empty pod to the pile. "Yes, I remember."

It happened when Dad struck a match to ignite the pilot light on the stove. And the second I smelled the faint whiff of smoke and heard the soft *whoosh* of flame, an earthquake unleashed inside me.

Dad stops shelling. "You *know* it was more than an accident. And this is not something that you can continue to bury or pretend away or ignore. It's—"

"*Me?*" I squawk, wide-eyed. "How can *you,* of all people, stand there with a straight face and lecture me about burying things?"

He looks away. The late-afternoon sun catches the silver dots in his stubble as he clenches his jaw. "This is about you, Honor, not me. Tell me, how many times a day do you jump at an unexpected sound? Or . . . or find yourself paralyzed by something that used to be normal? And when was the last time you slept through the night?" My father's brown eyes cut to mine, seeing too much and not enough. "It's getting worse."

The titanium boxes in my head begin to shake as if he's summoned them. Chains rattle and strain, my breath quickens with my pulse. I close my eyes. *Not now. Don't let them come out now.*

"I'm going to shuck the corn," I say abruptly.

Dad blocks my path to the back door, wearing the same pained expression as when I was little and the doctor had to give me a shot. *Sometimes the things that help us hurt a little.*

"What do want from me, huh? Can't you *see* how hard I'm trying?" I cry, gripping the sides of my arms. "H-how much I wish I could be like Knox and carry on like a normal person?"

"Honey, I *know* you're trying." He takes a step closer. "But the doctor said you could develop acute stress disorder, remember?" His voice is gentle, soft like cotton. "It's sort of a temporary form of PTSD that—"

"Stop it, Dad!" I recoil, shuffling backward. "Stop looking at me like everyone else, like this weak and broken thing!" The kitchen is shrinking like my lungs' ability to expand.

My father's face crumples. "No, that is not what you are at all. But this is bigger than both of us. And I just can't"—he briefly holds the heels of his hands to his eyes—"I can't keep watching you relive this. That's why your mom and I made an appointment for you to see Dr. Laney next week."

The invisible bindings at my chest cinch tighter. Links in the chains that reinforce my boxes are breaking. I bite my cheek; blood tangs my otherwise dry mouth.

"No!" I shout, turning away just as the memories explode, unleashing darkness and chaos around me. Dad calls out, reaching to catch my wrist. His fingers turn to ropes while the room suddenly billows with smoke. With a strangled cry I yank away. Something metal hits the floor.

The gun! I have to find the gun!

The air's gone thick as I scream, dropping to my hands and knees. Flames reach out with spiky, hot tips. The earth rumbles. Cole and Knox shout for me while sirens shriek and blue and red lights pulse. I cover my ears to block the sound. *"Make it stop! Please make it stop!"*

And somewhere in the wall of white fog, I hear my father's desperate calls.

"Honor! Baby, please, listen to my voice. You're having a flashback. I *know* how real it feels, but I swear to God, it's not happening. You're home. You're home in the kitchen and—"

I blink as the smoke slowly begins to dissipate, burning off like morning haze. I'm under the table on all fours, weeping and gasping for air. Peas are flattened all over the floor.

"Honor?" Dad chokes, his face wet with tears like my own. He opens his arms wide. I scramble out from the table, curling into his lap and holding on for dear life.

Together we are an imperfect tangle of limbs, jagged breaths, and breaking hearts.

His body shakes. "I just," he sobs, breath hot on my scalp, "I can't watch my daughter become me. My precious, *precious* girl. I want so much more for you."

I bury my face into his chest, feeling the frantic punch under the layers of tissue, muscle, and bone. "I want more for you, too," I croak.

"I—I told you once that I didn't want to remember," Dad rasps as he cradles my head. "To have everything torn back open. But"—his chest shudders against my cheek—"if things never healed right, maybe they need to be. Maybe . . . that's what we both have to do."

I hiccup. The army tattoo peeks out from under his sleeve as I lift my watery gaze to his. "What"—I pause, my breath stuttering—"what are you saying?"

He swallows thickly. The side of his thumb brushes away one of my tears. "I'll try if you will." Fear makes his voice waver, but the determination in his eyes shows me something else.

Courage.

Not the kind of courage found in medals of valor, or in great and heroic feats. But the kind that can only be found sitting on a kitchen floor, soaked in sadness and pea guts.

While offering to do the thing you fear most.

"Okay," I whisper, gripping his hand. "I'll try."

PART V

The Yield

August 4

35

My eyes look brighter without the half-moons of blue underneath. It helps that the nights are getting better. So are the days for that matter, and Despair doesn't visit with the frequency it once did.

Instead, I have a new visitor. Hope.

My cell rings. Without looking I answer, expecting it's Cole. He planned to come early to go for a walk before Sunday brunch. I put the phone on speaker so my fingers can continue the complicated dance of braiding my hair. "Heddo?" The greeting muddled by the hair tie held in my teeth.

"Honor . . . hi." Her voice is hesitant.

I drop the hair tie, lowering my arms as my hair unravels. "Zee?" I breathe, immediately taking the phone off speaker and holding it with both hands. The iridescent swirl I've come to recognize as Hope surrounds me in a delicate bubble. "Hi."

"I got your letter," she begins, her tone unreadable. "All eight pages."

I stop biting my lip long enough to respond. "Yeah. I, um, had a lot to say."

Much like Xander did in the letter Cole finally read. And whatever was in those redemptive words moved Cole enough to crack the door of communication between them. Guess I hoped if I took the same soul-bearing plunge, I'd find my own redemption with Zee.

"And apparently a lot to knit judging by the length of the scarf you sent with it," Zee teases warmly. "I know it's been a couple months, but my neck didn't grow. It's still regular human-sized."

My tension drains. *Same old Zee.*

A watery smile touches my lips. "Aunt Maeve's been teaching me," I explain. "I find it oddly . . . calming, like it helps me get out of my head. And you know, length aside, I'm actually pretty good. I can knit anything as long as it's a rectangle. Or a square."

Zee giggles; the sound is music to my ears.

"I've really missed you," I gush into the receiver. "Missed us." These are things I already covered when I loosened the tap on my heart and let everything spill onto the blue-lined paper. Still, they bear repeating. Along with my apology.

"I've really missed you, too." A sudden wobble enters her voice. "There's so much I didn't know until I read your letter." Her silence is punctuated with a quiet sniffle before she clears her throat. "Like that your favorite color was purple or what a deep and abiding love you have for queso dip."

My laugh topples out with a partial sob. "Well, some of that might've been stream of consciousness. I just didn't want to leave anything out." I swallow and sit down at my desk. "I don't want to do that with you anymore."

"And I don't want you to feel like you have to because

you're afraid of what I'll think. Honor"—she says my name with feathery softness—"I wouldn't have judged you. Not now. Not ever. That's just not what real friends do."

Real friends. I latch onto what she's implied as happiness bursts like a dandelion puff. My fingers graze the photo of us tacked on my bulletin board next to the get well card she sent. Our smiles wide, faces pressed cheek to cheek.

"I'm going to do better," I vow to the girls in the picture. "At putting the same trust in you that you've put in me. I promise to be a better friend, Zee."

"You already are," she says.

The August sun beats warm on our backs as grasshoppers spring across the dusty road. My steps carry the same lightness as the insects. Occasionally Geronimo tries to spring with them, but being wingless makes for much clumsier landings.

Knox chuckles, removing the blade of grass from his mouth to point. "And *that's* why we didn't name him Grace."

Cole grins, our joined hands swaying with our stride. "So when's your next—" He breaks off at the rumble of an approaching vehicle.

Aunt Maeve slows the silver Blazer and lowers the window. Our trio of *good morning*s and *hello*s overlap.

"Well, hope you kids are working up your appetites," she says, bright as the morning, a heavenly smell wafting from her car. "I made an extra pan of breakfast casserole."

Knox slaps his belly like a bongo drum. "My appetite's always ready for your cooking, Aunt Maeve."

Geronimo and Cole are clearly in agreement, both near drooling.

She chuckles, shaking her head, the sun catching on her dangly beehive earrings. "Knox Augustine, I swear you were born hollow-legged." Her warm gaze moves over to me. "We still on for our knitting session later? Figured now that you've got the stocking stitch down, we'll tackle the moss stitch."

"Wouldn't miss it," I say with a grin.

Aunt Maeve blows a kiss, wiggling her fingers out the window as she rolls off toward the farmhouse.

We continue walking. "What were you saying?" I ask Cole.

"Oh, I was just going to ask when your next appointment was."

"Tuesday," I reply as a breeze surges, stirring up the golden wheat fields.

At first I was afraid to tell him about seeing Dr. Laney. It felt weird to tell my boyfriend I was seeing a therapist. But then I realized it would feel weirder if I didn't. Because when you truly love someone, I think you're supposed to love the whole, imperfect person.

"You hear Dad got approved for that one treatment?" Knox asks as Geronimo trots ahead to a sumac bush and pees for the hundredth time. How he's not pissing dust by now is a medical miracle. "What's it called? EDM?"

Cole gets a funny look, scrunching his face. "Electronic dance music?"

I laugh. "I think you mean EMDR," I say to Knox. "Yeah, Dad mentioned it the other day." I've been reading up on eye movement desensitization and reprocessing, and it sounds like a really promising treatment for his PTSD. And now that Dad's been fully evaluated at the VA medical center, he's even quali-fied for monthly disability compensation.

But until those checks come, a few of Dad's old army bud-dies, having heard about our situation, banded together to start a GoFundMe campaign on his behalf. Last I saw, donations had reached $7,200. Dad got pretty choked up over the gesture. All of us did. After seeing the dark side of humanity, it was great to be reminded of the good out there.

"Speaking of dads," Knox says, glancing to Cole, "how'd yours take the news? Had to be better than when he came to pick you up from the hospital."

"You'd think, but this is Ben Buchannon." Cole sniffs, gin-gerly itching at the area where his stitches are healing.

"So . . . he took it shitty?" Knox adjusts his flat cap.

"You don't have to answer that," I say, squeezing Cole's hand. I'm really proud of him for finally telling his dad he didn't want to play lacrosse anymore. It's never easy telling someone you can't live up to the expectations they set for you. I would know.

"It's okay," he reassures me before answering Knox. "He was pretty mad at first. I had some legit concerns the vein in his temple might burst. Then he called me an idiot for pissing away my future and launched into this tirade about how selfish I was, and after that I . . . sorta snapped."

Knox grabs Geronimo's collar when he spots him preparing to dive into a ditch. "What did you do?"

"I told him it wasn't nearly as selfish as having an affair."

My brother's eyes pop. "Look at the cojones on you!" He shakes his head. "How'd he respond to that smackdown?"

Shrugging against my arm, Cole replies, "Wasn't much he could say. Can't really argue with the truth."

Turns out, Cole's confession became something of a catalyst in the Buchannon household. Once his mom realized that Cole's known all along about the affair, she decided it was pointless to keep up the marital facade. And then *she* snapped.

I hear Mr. Buchannon is still trying to find all his clothes after Mrs. Buchannon chucked them out the bedroom window. And the winds reached fifty miles per hour that day, so . . . good luck with that.

We finally reach our destination, where the commercial dumpsters rise from the blackened soil like headstones in the Augustine Greens graveyard. I feel a familiar pang of grief at the sight of it.

This isn't the first time I've come. I cried a lot that visit. Even more when I found a charred bit of concrete that had a piece of the heart Granddad drew. I scoured the area for the other three-quarters of the heart that bore their initials. But it was gone like everything else.

The piece of heart I did salvage now sits in my mason jar.

Knox coughs, crouching down to fuss over Geronimo, but I see his eyes are glassy. I move up beside him, putting a hand to his shoulder. "Why did it have to end up like this, Hon?" He gestures out to the scorched earth. "You know Aunt Maeve even sold that old ring of hers to buy us more time on the loans?"

"I know. We all tried, Knock Knox," I say sadly. While her selfless act and the summer's profits has brought our debt down to roughly $14,000, with the greenhouse reduced to rubble and ash, I'm not sure what that means for the future. Sure, we'll see an insurance settlement someday, but will it be enough to rebuild, too?

Geronimo, who'd abandoned us to chase the chipmunks weaving in and out of the debris, suddenly stops and quirks his head. Then he takes off in a run. Barking while kicking up a dust cloud behind him.

"*Geronimo!*" my brother and I shout while Cole whistles.

But Geronimo's stride doesn't break, and he continues streaking along the roadside.

At first I worry he's spotted a rabbit, or some other critter that won't stand a chance against those iron jaws, but as I shade my eyes I discover . . . *That's no rabbit.*

The figure moves closer, bobbing along the road, a massive rucksack strapped to his back and walking stick in his hand. His floppy hiking hat bounces with his stride.

"Is that who I think . . ." Knox trails off, all traces of melancholy evaporating. Then his smile breaks wide open. He cups a hand to the side of his mouth. "*Ash!*"

"*Aloha, dudes!*" He waves as Geronimo jumps up to greet him like they're old friends.

Laughing, my brother jogs over while Cole and I follow. They embrace, Knox clapping his bulky back. "Where the hell you been?" They separate.

Asher's eyes are clear and bright as he replies, "Two roads diverged and I"—he stomps on the packed earth and rocks beneath his feet—"I took the one less graveled."

"I think it's *traveled,* bruh," Knox says with a chuckle.

"Welcome home," I say as Ash opens up his arms and bear hugs me.

"Good to be home," he murmurs before setting me down to do one of those back-slappy guy hugs with Cole.

My forehead wrinkles. "Um, what happened to your car, Ash?"

"Oh." He thumbs behind him. "She's somewhere along M-35 a few hundred miles back." He pauses, solemnly placing a hand to his chest. "God rest her yellow Pinto soul. Had to catch a ride with some long-haul trucker from Poughkeepsie who smelled like tobacky and a musty old cupboard. Anyway, what's new with you guys? Team HACK ready to pack that weed or what?" he says, giggling while he fake punches Knox in the gut. We look uncertainly to one another.

Asher's mouth twists as he takes a second look at us. "Don't take this the wrong way, but you guys look like hell. You get in a bar brawl or something?"

I touch the yellowing bruise at my cheek. I forget how we must look to the rest of the world.

"Something like that," Knox answers, and bites his lip. My brother and I do a telepathic coin toss over who has to break the news to him.

Turns out we don't need to. "What the—?" Asher's brows conjoin as he squints into the distance. He scratches the emerging beard at his chin and takes a few steps forward. Then he turns back, his face a mask of confusion. "What happened to the greenhouse? I swear it was here when I left a couple weeks ago."

The three of us launch into our explanations all at once. Asher's gaze bounces from Knox's wild, sweeping arm movements to Cole's systematic play-by-play of events to my overly detailed account.

"Whoa! Whoa!" Ash says, raising up his hands. "So, first you were kidnapped, then there was a fire, and then the fertilizer and propane tank exploded? Because . . . the computer teacher was in deep with some drug lord?"

Our heads bob. Those are the bullet points, anyway. Along with the all-important fact that we didn't implicate him in anything.

"But you guys are okay?" Ash continues. "Like, physically and *legally*?"

"Well," I add, "we do have to do some community service—highway and public garden cleanup, that kind of thing. But we got really lucky."

"Especially compared to Jess Rennert," Cole adds. "She's in juvie. Guess she already had trafficking and possession strikes on her record, so trying to lie her way out didn't help."

The air whooshes from Ash's lungs as he stares out at the mini mountains of debris. "*Damn*. I really loved that old greenhouse. And all that primo Kush gone? Just toss my heart in a blender and hit frappe," he murmurs before looking back to us. "Good thing I hid the cashbox somewhere else, huh? Man, that would've sucked even harder minus those twenty-three G's."

I blink. I'm hallucinating. My brain is so faulty I'm hearing things I desperately wish were true. Cole grabs on to my arm. Or maybe I imagined that, too.

"You . . . what?" Knox asks, slack-jawed.

Ash cocks his head. "The money. It's in the hidden compartment of your truck, Augs," he explains, like we're weirdly slow on the uptake. "Yeah." He strokes his not-beard. "Before I left I got to thinking, maybe it wasn't such a hot idea having everything in one place. You know, after the way my trailer got trashed."

We're still watching him like he's speaking in tongues.

"*Dude,* I covered all this in the note I left in the base—" Ash breaks off, glancing to the hollowed-out hole where the greenhouse used to exist. "Oh . . . right."

"*You,*" Knox breathes, eyes wild, stepping toward him.

Ash shuffles back. "You're puttin' off kind of a creepy, murdery vibe."

"*You* beautiful, brilliant son of a bitch!" My brother grabs Ash's face and plants a huge kiss on his forehead. "We still have the money!" Turning toward me, he shouts, "Hon, we still have the money! *Ha-ha-haaallelujah!*"

As badly as I want to leap and scream and dance the jig like my brother, I can't. "But, Knox"—I shake my head—"the investigators, all the scrutiny . . . we can't just drop . . ." I quickly do the mental math of our cut. "Fifteen thousand into our bank account."

Silence falls over us in a heavy blanket of disappointment. Knox sighs. "But there's gotta be a way to—"

"Dudes!" Ash cries, his walking stick dropping with a dusty puff to the road. "I got an idea!" Expanding his chest, he tugs down on his shabby shirt, then pantomimes tying a tie at his neck. He looks at us, head held high and regal, arms outstretched.

"Well?" he asks expectantly.

My brother looks to me in confusion and I shrug.

"I'm, uh . . . not sure what we're looking at, Ash," Cole vocalizes for the group.

He rolls his eyes. "I'm an *investor*! In the new, kickass Augustine Greens! Which means you don't *have* to put any money in your account, because I'll put it all in mine. And," he adds, the seismic grin growing, "I could even flex my engineering muscles to help with the whole setup. What do you guys think?"

What do I think? The idea, it's . . . so simple. So straightforward. And so damn genius! Plus, with Asher not being implicated, no one would think twice about his business venture.

My hostage breath comes rolling out, along with about a million emotions I couldn't even begin to name. I must have cried yes, because everyone is cheering and hugging, while happy tears gather at my eyes.

Cole scoops me up and twirls me around. I laugh as my legs glide through the air.

When our shouts subside, Knox smiles crookedly and says, "Guys, we're gonna be late for brunch!" He elbows Ash. "What do you say? Would some of Aunt Maeve's egg, sausage, and cheese casserole set your tummy rumbling? Least we can do for our man of the hour."

"Augs, I would friggin' marry that casserole!" Doing an about-face, he takes off at a run, hollering over his shoulder, "Last one there's a rotten leg!"

Knox cracks up, shouting to Asher and his bouncing rucksack, "It's *egg*!" My brother chases after him as Geronimo barks, darting ahead and outpacing them both.

"You wanna race?" Cole asks, a glint in his eye.

"Nah. I think I've been running long enough."

And the next thing I know, Cole's crouching down to hoist me up on his shoulders.

I giggle. When I look up, there's a chain of clouds that *almost* looks like a zipper. A zipper through the universe. To the unknown.

And for once the unknown doesn't feel like the terrifying

black pit of nothing I've always imagined it to be. It's more like . . . the endless blue of the sky. Rainbows trapped in dew. The possibilities that dwell in a single seed. It is the wind in my hair and sun on my face.

Because today, I choose wonder.

Dear Reader,

Three years ago, I had this seed of an idea—a story about a girl whose father was a war veteran with severe PTSD and found relief through the use of medical marijuana. A girl who also struggled with her own anxieties and inability to fix all that was broken, but was hell-bent on trying anyhow. A girl who was . . . a lot like me. And while *Smoke* is undoubtedly a work of fiction—because, no, I never cultivated a bonanza of basement weed as a teen!—the roots of Honor's story grew directly from my own.

As the daughter of a Vietnam veteran, and a veteran myself, I have seen firsthand the lasting effects of war. I've witnessed the unique and heart-wrenching struggles that can echo through a person's lifetime. These experiences formed the taproot, that strong central vein driving deep to the heart of the story.

My choice to incorporate the topic of marijuana into this book was also inspired by events that have touched my life. In 2008, the state of Michigan legalized medical marijuana. Shortly thereafter, I had a family member who became a licensed grower and provider, giving me insight into the agricultural process and uses of cannabis. Leaning into this knowledge became a natural extension of nature-loving Honor's narrative.

While the gradual legalization of marijuana is changing the dynamic for the present and future, it does not right the historical wrongs in the glaring disparity of incarceration rates among white offenders and Black and Latinx offenders. There is much work to do to ensure that the color of a person's skin has no influence on their punishment. Even in states where marijuana has been decriminalized, many remain imprisoned for prior cannabis offenses. However, hearing the unified demands for criminal justice reform fills me with hope. *Liberty and justice for all* must be more than empty words.

Darcy Woods

Acknowledgments

Because this story struck *so* close to home, I almost couldn't tell it. And if not for the support of an army of extraordinary folks, fear would've won out.

To my magnificent, indispensable agent, Catherine Drayton, thank you for giving me the sun and soil to grow, and for your steadfast belief that I was capable of cultivating more than dandelions. You are fierce and wise and kind, and I'm pretty sure (scratch that, *positive*) there is magic running in your veins. Thanks also to Claire Friedman for lending your lovely eyes and plotting virtuoso—next quiche is on me! And to Lyndsey Blessing and the entire InkWell team, thank you for all that you do.

Endless thanks to my brilliant editor, Emily Easton, who tended this word garden with such fervent passion, patience, and care. You always knew which blooms to foster, which to cut, and when to break out the bug spray in the form of phone calls. My gratitude and adoration for you could fill oceans. Thank you to Claire Nist, for your unbridled awesomeness and sideways smilies, and also to the many talented hands at Crown

Books for Young Readers that have touched this book and made it better. For this bold yet nuanced cover of my dreams, heaps of gratitude go to the design genius of Ray Shappell.

And to my writer friends! I'm so grateful to Pintip Dunn for the countless talks off the ledge, and when that proved impossible, joining me with bread crumbs so we could at least feed the pigeons together. You are dazzling and true blue. To Jenn Stark, for being the embodiment of emosewa and swearing on the stars it'll all work out. To Jen Malone, for writing it in stone and . . . so much more. To Sarah Tomp, my sweet nanner champion! Your fortifying peels give me super fruit strength, every day and in every way. To Laurie Elizabeth Flynn, for knowing bubbles make it better and saying "I told you so" with such love. To Kate Brauning, for sustaining me with heartfelt words and homemade treats. To Eric Smith and Nena Boling-Smith, for providing light in my darkest hours. To Brenda Drake, for wholeheartedly believing in this concept and my guacamole. And to Marisa Reichardt, who always inspires and keeps my roots strong.

Thanks to my Michigan author pals: Erica Chapman, Lori Nelson Spielman, Tracy Brogan, Alyssa Alexander, Meika Usher, Lyssa Kay Adams, and Christina Mitchell, for your strong shoulders, listening ears, and ability to turn anything into a celebration. Or a circus. The line we walk is tightrope-thin.

Thank you to Elizabeth Lyon for sending cookies when queso wouldn't ship so very well—this is why you're my forever Boo. And to Dr. Rishi Kundi, for the vital checks and laughs along the way. Also, deepest thanks to my dear Douglas J coworkers and clients—I wish I could name you all! But know that I adore you and could not have done this without your ceaseless support.

This book required a lot of research, so any mistakes are mine and mine alone. Many thanks to Tee O'Fallon, who on more than one occasion helped me (fictionally!) crime in believable ways. Thanks to Dan White for the industry insights, and to my beloved dad for all the basement grow-how.

Extra-special thanks to my entire family—the heartbeat, lifeblood, and soul of this story—who instilled in me a deep love of nature and belief in miracles. Without you, I surely would have withered and died on the vine long ago. I love you. And finally, to my heart's keeper and soul mate, David, who never fails to see the wonder. Who has built us a life of perpetual wonderment. Ah*ooga* horns and all.

Lastly, eternal gratitude to all the incredible booksellers, bloggers, librarians, and teachers who so passionately champion books. You are needed now, more than ever. And of course, thank you, dear reader. Without you, my passion would have no purpose, and my stories would be little more than really long diary entries. Thanks for giving my words a home.

About the Author

Award-winning young adult author Darcy Woods has held an eclectic mix of professions—from refueling helicopters in the US Army to recharging bodies and spirits at a spa—but her most beloved career is being an author. She lives in Michigan with her husband and two tuxedo cats (who overdress for everything). *Summer of Supernovas* is her double RITA®-nominated debut novel and has been translated into five languages. *Smoke* is her second novel. darcywoods.com